MEAN STREETS

The gang spotted me and began to approach my car. Their shirts, even the girls', were cut off at the shoulders and the sternum, revealing rolling arms and sculpted bellies. From half a block away they had seen everything about me that was relevant—I was white and I was alone and I was on their turf and I wasn't a cop.

They swarmed over the Buick, leaning on the doors and fenders, sitting on the hood and trunk. The leader snapped his fingers. I heard a whir and a click, the sound of a blade snapping out of a sheath and locking. They moved in close around me, driving me back against the car door.

The one with the knife moved to where I could see him and began waving it. I looked to see if Grinder's men were anywhere around, and when I didn't spot them, I spent some time planning what I would do when the knife made its move.

The plan wasn't worth a damn.

A JOHN MARSHALL TANNER MYSTERY

STATE'S EVIDENCE

STEPHEN GREENLEAF

CRIME LINE™

BANTAM BOOKS

NEW YORK • TORONTO • LONDON • SYDNEY • AUCKLAND

This edition contains the complete text
of the original hardcover edition.
NOT ONE WORD HAS BEEN OMITTED.

STATE'S EVIDENCE

A Bantam Crime Line Book / published by arrangement with
the author

PRINTING HISTORY

Dial Press edition published 1982
Bantam edition / January 1992

ISBN 0-553-29349-4

Published simultaneously in the United States and Canada

*Bantam Books are published by Bantam Books, a division of Bantam Doubleday Dell
Publishing Group, Inc. Its trademark, consisting of the words "Bantam Books" and
the portrayal of a rooster, is Registered in U.S. Patent and Trademark Office and in
other countries. Marca Registrada. Bantam Books, 666 Fifth Avenue, New York, New
York 10103.*

PRINTED IN THE UNITED STATES OF AMERICA

RAD   0 9 8 7 6 5 4 3 2 1

for Aaron

STATE'S
EVIDENCE

Chapter
1

The building was broad and squat and thick, designed to house a substance that was heavy and unwieldy and potentially hazardous, as dense and inert as the granite blocks that had been quarried to contain it. Form followed function, for the substance that eddied and bubbled within the building was Justice, and the steps I was climbing had been worn concave by the footfalls of the convicts and petitioners, litigants and constituents, who had marched toward that abstraction over the years. Unless I missed my guess, most had gone up the steps a lot faster than they'd come down.

The fluted columns flanking the iron doors were nicked and gouged from errant bullets fired during an attempt to assassinate a governor at the end of the previous century. Atop the columns the Corinthian capitals bore protrusions that resembled tongues more than acanthus leaves. The words "El Gordo City Hall" had been chiseled into the architrave, deep, immutable, forbidding, but splashed with pigeon droppings all the same. Like the building itself, the city of El Gordo was old and tough, without pretense or allure, decades past its prime. I felt a bit that way myself.

I buried my cigarette in the sand urn next to the door and pushed my way into the municipal gloom of the interior. A dyspeptic elevator with an operator to match raised me to the third floor. Along the way I muttered unrequited words about the weather. The only other passenger had the look of a lawyer who specialized in champerty.

The girl behind the desk behind the door marked Wilson P. Ridges, District Attorney, nodded after I told her my name and told me to go on back, second door on the right. Then she plucked a crumb of tobacco off her tongue. I followed my nose and came to an office with an open door, a ceiling fan, and two men in it.

Like the fan, the men were motionless, waiting for whatever it was I was bringing them. They were seated on either side of an oak desk piled high with manila file folders, open law books, and teeming ashtrays. The walls of the room were lined with *Pacific Reporters* and *Federal Supplements* and the floor was covered with green and white linoleum, which sagged ominously as I crossed it. The desk and its cargo were dotted, as if by the droppings from some great bird, by a score of tea bags in various stages of dampness.

When he saw me, the man on the far side of the desk stood to shake my hand. His movements were measured and precise, the acts of a man accustomed to being watched and judged. His hand was puffy but hard, and skillfully used.

He introduced himself as Ray Tolson, the Chief Trial Deputy to the El Gordo District Attorney, then released my fingers. He was short and stout, half-blond and half-bald. His face wore the open, almost addled, look of a clergyman or a politician on the top of his game. His eyes were perched directly atop his cheeks, emerging from their lairs like young and eager marsupials. Two wide red suspenders were visible between his vest and his belt, and a plaid coat embraced the back of the chair he had vacated.

Tolson thanked me for driving down from the city.

"Always happy to call on someone with the subpoena power," I said.

He laughed with a bursting bubble of sound and asked me to sit in the only empty chair in the room. On my way to it I looked at the other man. He didn't move and didn't speak, but if I'd had a facial tic he would have already noticed it. As I tried to get comfortable in the cracked and creaking leather, Tolson pressed a button and asked someone on the other end of the wire to bring three coffees. For some reason, I envisioned them arriving in tin cups.

"We've got ourselves a little problem down here, Mr. Tanner," Tolson said laconically, after the coffees arrived. "We're hoping you can help us out."

Which meant we were already on new ground. Usually when a district attorney invites me by for a chat the problem is mine, because someone has complained about the way I've gone about my business and the Bureau of Collection and Investigative Services has asked the local authorities to look into it. So far it's never gotten beyond the chatting stage, and if they keep cutting the bureau's budget that's as far as it will ever get. I settled back in the chair and asked Tolson to tell me his troubles.

"First, I'd better ask if you have any objections to working for the prosecution. I know you're usually on the other side."

"No objection," I said. "Not at this point. If it involves manufacturing evidence, though, you'll be wasting your time. And your money."

"That doesn't happen."

"The hell it doesn't. It's happening right now in a drug case over in the East Bay and you know it."

"Well, it doesn't happen in this office."

I smiled. "The way I hear it this office doesn't manufacture evidence, it just loses it."

"What do you mean by that?"

"Let's just say that the word is there are things for sale in El Gordo you can't find in the Yellow Pages."

It made Tolson angry, more angry than I thought it would. His fair complexion became flushed and piebald. He opened his mouth to defend himself or his profession or his ontology or something, but just then a young woman stuck her head through the doorway. "Bernstein says his man will cop to aggravated assault, with two years' probation," she said with a twinkle in her eye.

"I told you and I told him," Tolson growled. "No deal that doesn't include jail time. If he was in custody now, it'd be different. I don't like knives," he added by way of explanation.

The woman smiled and nodded and disappeared. Tolson ran a hand through his thinning hair and looked back at me. "You worked a case down here a few years ago, didn't you, Tanner?"

I nodded. "The Abbott case."

"Truckers being extorted by lumpers, wasn't it? Had to pay to have their rigs unloaded whether they wanted to or not? Or the cargo would be trashed?"

"That's about it."

"I heard you did a good job."

"They paid my fee."

"You were the main witness for the U.S. Attorney, right?"

"Right. Is your problem anything like that one?"

"Why?"

"Because after the trial a guy with a face like an elbow followed me around for a month."

"What happened?"

"In his spare time he beat up a guy in a bar somewhere

down here. The guy's friends looked him up a few days later and stuck a screwdriver in his eye."

Tolson smiled sadly. "I guess you learned a little about the town while you were here, huh?"

"More than enough."

"That was four years ago, right? Well, the town is changing," Tolson declared firmly. "It's not the way it was."

"Good," I said. "I guess that means if I talk to the bartender across the street he'll tell me he's stopped paying protection money to keep his windows from being broken and paying kickbacks to keep his liquor supply current and his jukebox working. I guess that means there aren't more prostitutes per square mile in El Gordo than in any other city on the Bay. And I guess that means the mayor has stopped getting thirty grand a year as a consultant to the Association of Retail Merchants."

Tolson held up a hand. "Okay, okay. I didn't say it was Disneyland; I just said it was getting better. We've got some good young cops who know how to build a case and we've got some prosecutors who are willing to take anything or anyone to trial, no matter *who* puts pressure on them."

"Namely, you," I said.

"Namely, me." Tolson's smile was almost but not quite as confident as his words.

"You're going to be the man who cleans up El Gordo, is that it?" I asked. "Is that why I'm here, to play Sancho Panza in the El Gordo Community Playhouse? Or is it Doc Holliday?"

Tolson curled his lips inward until they disappeared, then shook his head. "It's nothing like that," he said. "It's just a little case that's all too symbolic of what's been wrong down here and how it's going to be different from now on."

"What kind of case?"

"Hit and run."

"Who got hit?"

"Nobody special. Some guy who works in the county clerk's office over in Oakland. Filed papers all day or something. Had a wife at home and a kid in the Navy."

"So who hit him?"

"A man named Fluto. Tony Fluto. Ever heard of him?"

"Nope. Should I?"

"Not really. He's been around El Gordo a long time. He and his son run a big paint contracting business on the East Side. They do pretty well, drive big cars, own big houses, wear big diamonds, drop big names. Wired politically and socially as well."

"Okay, so this guy Fluto hit and ran. Where do I fit in?"

Tolson sighed heavily and leaned back in his chair and put his heels on the corner of the desk and clasped his hands behind his head. Directly behind him the royal blue spines of *Corpus Juris Secundum* rose in tiers of precise if obsolescent sovereignty. The disembodied drone of trucks floated off U.S. 101 and seeped through the stone and glass of City Hall.

Tolson was an old thirty or a young forty, most likely the latter. To have reached the level of Chief Trial Deputy he must have been good with a jury and even better with fawning publicly over his superior, the DA. If he ran to form, though, right about now he would be spending his nights talking to fat cats about financing a campaign to knock off his boss in the next election and his days listening to lawyers in private practice tell him that, despite mountains of evidence to the contrary, you really could make a good living doing criminal defense work in a place like El Gordo. In the meantime, Tolson would be doing what all DA's do, deciding who to prosecute and who not to, what charge to file, what sentence to stipulate, dispensing more justice in a day than anyone else in the county would dish out in a month.

Tolson lit a thick cigar. I glanced briefly and curiously at the other man.

He was still perched on the edge of his chair, feet on floor, palms on patellae, back as straight as a plebe's. His eyes locked on mine. They were sterile and ascetic, the eyes of an accountant or an undertaker. His black hair was trimmed short above the ears and combed straight and flat across his scalp in rigid, oiled furrows. His suit was blue and came in three pressed pieces. Chalk stripes cut through each of them, like the lines on a Big Chief tablet. A gold chain swung across the flat plane of his abdomen like a streamer at the junior prom. The bauble that dangled from it was a Phi Beta Kappa key or a coke spoon. My guess was the former, but these days you can't be sure.

"Tony Fluto is a big wheel in this town," Tolson said when his cigar was fully fired, "and the guy he ran down was a nobody. In the old days Fluto probably wouldn't have been arrested, let alone tried. That's why this case is so important. A conviction will establish that there's justice for everyone in El Gordo, that this office isn't for sale, that law enforcement is here to help people, not persecute them."

I had to wait for Tolson's words to quit bouncing off the walls. "What's that from?" I asked. "The speeches of Cicero or the opinions of Justice Douglas?"

Tolson ignored my smile. "I have to be a bit fanatical," he said simply. "Why else would I stay in this job? The pay's lousy, the facilities stink, and the public despises me. The people I was in law school with are all partners in big law firms, drawing down a hundred grand a year."

Tolson's declaration was a little too absolute and a little too righteous for my comfort. "If it's so bad, why do you stay?" I asked him.

"I just want to make a difference," he said quietly. "I grew up in El Gordo. It was a lousy place then, and it's not much better now. I want to change that. I want my son to be proud of where he lives, proud enough to want to live here, too."

I couldn't argue with the sentiment. The first thing I

remember my father saying to me was to get out of the little town where we lived, that there was nothing there for me. I took his advice. A year later he was dead.

The phone on the shelf behind Tolson rang once and Tolson picked it up. He listened, then said, "Thanks, honey," and hung up. I widened my eyes.

"My wife," Tolson explained. "I've gotten some threats. She calls to tell me my boy has made it to school. Around three she'll tell me he made it home. I hope." The expression on his face was strangely apologetic. "Another reason not to do what I'm doing," he said softly.

I shot another glance at the second man. He was still mysteriously silent.

"What's the program?" I asked Tolson. "This Fluto is a mover and shaker and he ran someone down. Are you planning to unleash me against him willy-nilly or do you have something a little more structured in mind?"

Tolson grinned briefly, then glanced at the other man. "What I want you to do with Fluto is stay the hell away from him, no matter what. Is that clear?"

"Yes," I said. "What's *not* clear is why I've been sitting here listening to all this."

Tolson looked at the other man again, and got the reaction he would have gotten from a stump. I was tempted to throw a book at the guy myself, just to make sure I wasn't an unwitting participant in a freshman psychology experiment.

"Exactly seventy-two hours ago," Tolson explained slowly, "I had Tony Fluto right where I wanted him. His ass was mine. A year in Quentin, for certain. Probably a lot more."

The smile on Tolson's face turned momentarily thin and evil, revealing for just an instant the contamination he had experienced during a decade of work in the El Gordo criminal courts. If his smile was all that had been contaminated, he was luckier than most. I lit a cigarette and

Tolson's smile again became benign, almost paternal. I asked what had happened with Fluto.

"Back in June Tony had some bad luck. He was driving his Lincoln down on Oswego late on a Sunday, coming home from a visit to his mistress up in Burlingame, is what we figure. Not much going on, fairly light traffic. We think he was alone in the car. As he approached the Ninth Street intersection, a man stepped off the curb and into his path. There was a crosswalk there, and the man was in it, but Fluto must have been going at least fifty in a twenty-five and he hit the guy head on. Killed instantly, but Fluto didn't know it. He kept driving."

"Failure to stop and render aid," I said, in the words of the statute.

"At least. Voluntary manslaughter, if I'm as good as I think I am. Maybe more. As far as we can tell, there were three witnesses to the incident. One saw the car, and got the license number, and caught a glimpse of the driver. He picked Fluto out of a lineup. The car was registered to Fluto, by the way, but we've never been able to locate it. Fluto claimed it was stolen. The problem is, this witness is a lush. A wino who was between fits at the time. Impeachable as hell."

"How about the other two?"

"One is a kid. About twelve, fourteen, somewhere in there. The lush saw him in the area just before the impact, and gave us a vague description, but we've never been able to turn him up. I got through the grand jury with only the lush, mainly because the grand jury indicts whoever I want them to. But the case was as thin as a dime, and Fluto and his lawyer knew it. They spouted off to the press that I was crusading for higher office, abusing the power of my position, all that shit. Pissed me off so much I swore not to dismiss, no matter what. And then I got lucky."

"Witness number three," I prompted.

"Right. A woman walked in and said she'd seen the

whole thing, that she hadn't wanted to get involved but when she saw what Fluto was saying in the papers, she knew she had to tell us what she'd seen. And suddenly I had a laydown. And Fluto knew it. I had it made."

"But you lost your witness," I said.

Tolson took two deep breaths, then pinched a nostril between thumb and forefinger. "Three days ago."

"You should have had her under surveillance."

"Oh, we were surveilling, all right. Bed to bed. Somehow she got out." Tolson was about to add something, but after a glance at the other man he kept quiet.

"What's the best guess?" I asked.

Tolson shrugged. "It's the obvious one, of course."

"Is Fluto the kind of guy who'd try something like that?"

"I'm not saying he killed her or anything," Tolson answered, "but he's got a lot to lose. He wouldn't be above scaring the hell out of her, and that's why we had a guy out there. Of course he could have done it with a phone call, but I think it's more likely she took off on her own."

"Why?"

"Fear. What else?"

I could think of about a hundred other reasons a woman might leave home, but it didn't seem worth mentioning until I knew more about the woman and the home. "Any idea how she left?"

"Not specifically, but there are ways. We were set up to keep people out, not keep her in."

"When was she missed?"

"Noon. Three days ago. Mr. Blair called and she didn't answer. Then he called us. We checked it out and she was gone."

"What'd you do then?"

"How do you mean?"

"I mean did you pull your men off the stakeout or leave them in place?"

Tolson snorted. "We're undermanned. We've got better things to do than watch an empty house."

"If she skipped voluntarily, I'll bet she just hid, the attic or someplace, and waited for you to leave. You didn't search the place thoroughly, did you?"

"Shit."

Tolson shook his head and reddened again, then grinned ruefully.

All this time the thin man had been staring intently at Tolson, as though he expected to hear something he had never heard before. From the expression on his face, Tolson had disappointed him.

The thin man's silence was making me nervous. In order to force Tolson to introduce me to him I kept my eyes focused on the man's mustache. After a few seconds of that nonsense the man finally squirmed and Tolson finally spoke. "Our witness's name is Teresa Blair. This is her husband. James."

Tolson gestured with his left hand and Blair and I nodded simultaneously. He remained intent and mute, an automaton fueled by a pair of blue eyes that looked fissionable. There was something decidedly scientific about the man, as though his natural passion was checked by carefully marshaled reason and prudence. He appeared competent and formidable, but detached. A device.

"So what do you want with me?" I asked Tolson.

"We're covering the Fluto angle," he said. "We're pretty certain if Fluto has her we'll know it within a few days. One complication is that Fluto himself seems to have dropped out of sight."

"Maybe he's skipped bail."

"I'm not that lucky and Fluto's not that dumb. He'll show for the trial on Monday. If he doesn't, the judge will issue a bench warrant quicker than flies find shit. Then we'll really have him where we want him."

"How about a continuance?"

"Fluto's lawyer has refused to waive time, so it's now or never. If we have to go to trial without Mrs. Blair, that leaves us with the lush and the kid, assuming we turn him up between now and Monday. And kids don't make good witnesses—I guess because jurors were all kids once themselves and remember what little liars they were. Without Mrs. Blair or the kid we've got nothing. I'll have to dismiss."

"What am I," I joked, "your star witness?"

Tolson barely stretched his lips. "I suggested to Mr. Blair here that it might help if he hired someone on the outside to assist in checking his wife's family, friends, the personal side of the thing. He agreed and asked us to recommend someone. I talked to a few people and ended up recommending you. I just want to make certain you know the ground rules before you decide whether to take the case."

"What ground rules are those?"

"Mainly, that you tell me every single thing you learn. Immediately, if not sooner. And also that you stay away from Tony Fluto and his people. Your job is Mrs. Blair, not Tony. Leave him to us."

"I will if he lets me."

"Yeah. Well, if you have any trouble, just let me know."

"I will if he lets me," I repeated. "Who's paying the freight?"

"Mr. Blair," Tolson said.

I looked at Blair. He nodded.

"Are the terms agreeable to you?" I asked him.

He nodded again.

"My rate's forty an hour."

He nodded again.

"Do you speak?"

He nodded again. I thought the blue eyes twinkled a tad, but I couldn't be sure.

Tolson glanced at the clock on the wall and then at his watch and then stood up. "Mr. Blair is an accountant," he explained. "Since this is the tax season, he has very little time to spare, or so he tells me. He had to juggle some meetings just to be here this morning, which we appreciate, but he has to leave now. I suggest you set up an appointment with him at his office to talk in greater detail about Mrs. Blair."

"I'd rather meet at his home," I said. "I'd like to look over Mrs. Blair's things, the layout of the house, all that. Let's say this evening at eight?"

Tolson and I looked inquiringly at Blair, who frowned, then shrugged, then nodded. Without apparent effort Blair stood and, with the liquid stride of a panther, moved to the door. Tolson looked at me and grinned.

"Maybe she left home to make sure her ears still worked," I said to Tolson in what I thought was a whisper.

Blair stopped and turned back. "It's more complicated than that," he said. His voice was as soft as chamois.

Tolson waited until Blair's steps had died away. "He wants his wife back but he's not crazy about having her testify. So if you find her, you tell me first. I'll put her in protective custody till after the trial. She's not going home to hubby until she's done her duty as a citizen."

From the flare of Tolson's nostrils and the set of his jaw, the duty he talked about was owed only to him.

Chapter 2

I'd left my car on the street opposite City Hall, at the juncture of an adult bookstore and a fern bar. When I got back to it, there was someone sitting on the fender and it wasn't the meter maid. He was short and wiry, his shoulders raised in a perpetual shrug, his arms long and awkward, seemingly without joints. His suit and tie were different shades of brown, his shirt a rumpled yellow. When he smiled, his lips formed an accent rather than a hyphen. The potbelly above his belt was as incongruent as a misplaced prosthesis.

"Mr. Tanner?" he asked as I approached. "My name is Grinder. Conway Grinder. Welcome to El Gordo." There was no hospitality in his tone. I took his proffered hand and got a squinting appraisal in return. "You've been talking to Ray Tolson," he went on with feigned cheer. "Maybe he mentioned my name."

"Why would he do that?"

Grinder smiled lazily. "Oh, because I'm the Chief of Detectives in this town. Because I'm the guy who's keeping

Tony Fluto's place under surveillance for any sign of the Blair woman. Because I'm the guy you should talk to when and if you come up with anything on her."

"Really?" I said. "Why should I do that?"

Grinder reached into his shirt pocket and took out a matchstick, fit it into the left corner of his mouth, and began to gnaw on the end. "I'll tell you straight, Tanner. I didn't want Tolson to bring you in on this. We can handle our own problems down here. El Gordo's a funny place," Grinder announced around the match. "We don't like outsiders much, especially not civilians from the big city who don't know the town and don't want to, and who might just screw everything up because of it. But Tolson didn't listen to me, did he?"

"Evidently not. Somehow I doubt it's the first time."

Grinder snarled, his voice suddenly full and sinister. "Don't get smart with me, Tanner. In about three minutes I can have you in the foulest jail cell you've ever seen." The match head darted and bobbed like the nipple of a grinding stripper.

I held up a hand. "What do you want from me, Grinder? I'm not going to run back home just because you like to play the Lone Ranger, if that's what you're thinking."

"I just want to make sure you got your instructions straight, Tanner, that's all."

"I report to Tolson, Grinder. You want to know what I learn, give him a call. I'm sure he'll share it with you."

"You know anything at all about El Gordo, Tanner, you know you never know for sure who you can trust down here. Now, if you call Tolson, and he happens to be in court or in the john or home banging his wife, and you leave a message for him, well, that message just might fall into the wrong hands. And then we just might lose the lovely Mrs. Blair all over again." Grinder smiled a huckster's smile.

"But that won't happen if I report directly to you, is that it?"

"That's it. Because when you call me, I'm going to get your number and then I'm going to leave the station and go to a pay phone tacked to the back wall of a poolroom I know and I'm going to call you back and then and only then are you going to tell me what you've got. Because that way only you and me know the whereabouts of the party in question. Not that I think you're going to locate the lady."

"Why not?"

"Because Mr. Fluto has her and because sooner or later I'm going to prove it. And when I do, it's going to put him up on more than a measly hit-and-run charge. It's going to mean a two-oh-seven."

"What might that be?"

"Kidnapping." Grinder gave the word a strange joy.

"You sound a bit intense on the subject of Mr. Fluto," I said. "What's behind it?"

"I got my reasons. You just remember what I said. And I don't want to see you anywhere near Fluto's place. You stick to Mrs. Blair and her friends. Leave the scumbags to me." Grinder tossed the matchstick on the ground and shoved himself off my fender and walked off toward City Hall, the bulge over his left hip advertising an accessible and functional tool of death.

There were still three hours to kill before I was due at James Blair's house, and I spent them loitering in a couple of bars and driving through the streets of El Gordo. The town gave off a dispiriting mist. Without guidance or plan it had drifted on the tide of history, pitifully victimized by time's fickle and unforgiving march. The center of town was a relic that was rapidly becoming refuse rather than icon. The halfhearted attempts at rehabilitation and restoration were limited to easy and cosmetic approaches—some flags hoisted, some bricks laid, some spindly trees planted in square stone pots, some freshly striped and metered parking lots. From the number of boarded doors and painted windows the effort had resulted only in a bleak monument to the cheap and the quick.

The rim of the town was just as bad—malls and tracts approved by officials who thought the only function of good government was to say yes. Traffic sped aimlessly through all parts of town, unchanneled and directionless. Freeways sliced neighborhoods in half and turned the sky into a looming, buzzing slab. Multiunit apartments, square and featureless, sprouted randomly, turning once private back-yards into public pits. Every second building was an abandoned bowling alley or a taco stand.

Even though I'd been ordered by Tolson to keep away from Tony Fluto, out of curiosity I dropped his name in a few bars and cigar stores, just to see what would happen. What happened most was paralytic paranoia, followed by rapid and elaborate protestations of ignorance. Tony Fluto was definitely a presence in El Gordo, sort of the way the stockyards used to be a presence in Chicago, and the reaction of a couple of bartenders when I mentioned his name made me quite willing to comply with Tolson's orders to stay out of Fluto's way. I just hoped he'd stay out of mine.

It wasn't quite eight when I pulled to a stop across from 2190 Vista Grande Terrace, the home of my client and his missing wife. And I wasn't the only new arrival in the neighborhood. Sometime during the day I'd picked up a tail, a green one with a dented fender and two men in it which was now parked fifty yards on up the hill. Grinder wasn't leaving anything to chance, but I guessed I didn't care. Not yet.

The Blair house was more than halfway up the hill that rose out of the mud flats and salt evaporators that rimmed the West Bay and, like all hills, took the socio-economic level of the community up with it. The homes ornamenting the slope all came complete with moats of semitropical flora and, if the little pickup down the block was an indication, with ethnically appropriate gardeners to tend them. Several of the houses were named. The one across from the Blairs' was the Casa Schmidt.

I got out of my car and walked to the middle of the street, then looked back toward the bay and the lights of Fremont and Milpitas, which were just flicking on beyond it. A scintillating but disturbing view, as mesmerizing as a fireplace or a waterfall. The odd thing was that James Blair couldn't see an inch of it. His house was as well guarded as his personality, entirely masked by a high fence of inter-woven slats of brown-stained pine and two heavy wooden gates painted with glossy black enamel. The gates and the fence seemed impenetrable by any means at my disposal, and the tops of the coastal redwoods growing within the enclosure swaggered in the evening breeze, mocking my ostracism. I walked to the gate and pressed the latch. It didn't move. I pressed the white button in the post beside the gate. Nothing happened. I went to the far end of the fence, where the second gate would open to admit vehicles, but that section wouldn't budge, either. I jumped up and down several times, to see what I could see, but all that registered was dusk and shadow, triumphant and belligerent seclusion. When the change in my pocket spilled out during the fourth jump, I scraped it up and went back to my car to sulk.

Dusk turned to dark. The early evening lights danced a hypnotic nocturne and within minutes I was half sleeping, half dreaming. A while later the car door opened and a woman's head joined me beneath the golden glow of the dome light.

"Are you from Wayne?" she demanded.

"What?"

"Are you from *Wayne*, I said. Did he hire you? Is that why you're sitting out here spying on me? Is it?"

"Lady, I don't even know who you are."

I brought the talking head into focus. It was a handsome

head, fortyish, waved brown hair, broad brown eyes, creased brown skin—one of those heads that probably had increased in pulchritude over the years. It was also an outraged head.

"A likely story," she charged, the words harsh, but not naturally so. I envisioned the woman observing me for the past half hour from behind lace curtains, gulping a highball, gradually working up the avalanche of indignation which had shoved her out of the door and into this confrontation.

"Believe me, ma'am," I said, "I don't know you or Duane or anything about either of you."

"Wayne. His name is Wayne. And you know it."

"No, I don't. But if you want to discuss it further, why don't you come in and sit down before you fuse a few vertebrae."

"Don't be ridiculous."

"Why not?" I said, then shrugged and thought of what I could say that would be irreverent enough to get rid of her. Then I decided I didn't want to be rid of her quite yet.

"Do you happen to know a woman named Teresa Blair?" I asked. I was as bland as bananas.

The head stayed where it was, a terra-cotta amulet suspended beneath the roof of my car, but its expression softened dramatically. "Teresa? What about Teresa? Where is she? Have you seen her?" The questions became a glissando of concern.

I put a hand up to ward off the words. "I haven't seen her, no. Have you? You seem worried about her."

"I am. I'm *very* worried. Is she all right? Can you tell me that, at least?"

"I don't know," I said truthfully. "Do you have any reason to believe she's been harmed?"

The head measured me critically, cocked to one side, aiming from behind an unseen musket. "Did Wayne Martin hire you to spy on me?"

"No."

"Are you following me? For *any* reason?"

"No."

"Are you *really* interested in finding Teresa Blair?"

"Yes."

"Then let's go inside. My back *is* killing me."

She smiled for the first time, and moved from handsome to comely, but the smile was brief and reluctant. I got out of the car and did a knee bend to loosen things up, then followed her across the street and into the house just south of the Blairs'.

It was a house without character. The mailbox was a windmill, the doormat a flag, the umbrella stand a milk can, the mirror a porthole, the lamp a cookie jar. Much of the contents looked out of place and scattered, as though the place had been hastily and thoroughly searched for something never found. The tables and shelves were occupied by scores of porcelain figurines in various positions of piety.

We came to a stop in what realtors call the family room. On the wall were a Sierra Club calendar and a decoupage version of the *Desiderata*. The furniture was Colonial, busily patterned, and shoved to the edges of the room. The TV was on: *The Brady Bunch*. At the counter separating the family room from the kitchen was a blond boy of twelve or so, eating something round and frozen to a stick. His shirt was a 49ers model, number 32. There was a scab the size of a quarter on his left elbow and a wad of something or other in his back pocket. "This is my son," the woman said. "Davy."

"Hi, Davy," I said.

Davy left the room.

His mother remained standing in the center of the wall-to-wall shag, staring at the Miss Piggy poster taped to the refrigerator. She was tall and straight-bodied, an eastern preppie more than an active westerner. The seams of her white sailcloth slacks were puckered, as though just retrieved from the dryer; the sleeves of her blouse were rolled into blue doughnuts above her elbows. I bet myself that everything she wore had come from an Eddie Bauer catalog. Her hair was a pixieish sprout of wheatish brown and, like her face, without cosmetic layers. When not in use her mouth lapsed into a pleasant, expectant smile. She would have been the last person to realize she had actually become lovely twenty years after the last time she wished for it.

"Do you want something to drink?" she asked distractedly, the request no more than filler.

"Scotch, if you have it."

She shook her head. "I'm sorry. I don't have any liquor, not since Wayne decided to . . . not since Wayne."

"Coffee?"

"Coffee. It's old, though."

"So am I."

She smiled feebly and moved into the kitchen. When she came back, she had a mug for me and a tall glass of something or other for herself. The liquid in the glass was cloudy, the color of fingernails. I asked her what it was.

"Just a little pick-me-up I mix in the blender. Celery, grapefruit rind, bean curd, and soy. Would you like some?" She thrust her glass my way.

I shook my head. "If God meant for us to drink that stuff, he would have invented a cow that dispensed it."

My joke fell flat. I took a sip of coffee and looked at the mug I had raised to my lips. The seal of Ohio State University was stamped on it, in silver and red. The woman saw me looking. "Wayne thought I'd like a set of those, can you imagine?" Her lip curled. "I hated Ohio State. Just *hated* it."

With that, we took chairs on opposite sides of the room and sat and looked at each other. The coffee wasn't hot and wasn't good and the liquid celery must have been worse but we both drank our potions heavily, thinking other things.

She spoke first, while I was struggling to get a taste out of my mouth.

"You know, you're the first prayer of mine that's been answered in more than a year. And I've prayed a lot in that time, believe me."

I hadn't been the answer to anyone's prayer in a long time and I told her so. Then I asked her name.

"Kathryn Martin. Kathryn Ellington Martin."

Obviously distracted, she mused a moment more. "It's just that on top of Wayne and all that I've been frantic for days," she said finally, "wondering what to do about Teresa. You wouldn't believe how many times I've put my hand on that telephone, ready to phone the police or someone. And now, here you are."

"Here I am."

"What *are* you, exactly?"

"Professionally or biologically?"

"Professionally, silly. A detective, or what?"

"That's close enough."

"Are you with the police?"

"Sort of."

"You don't look like a policeman."

She meant it as a compliment, so I smiled. Then she decided a compliment was more daring than she wanted to be, and her face froze. "You're looking for her, aren't you? I can tell. Actually," she went on, "I did talk to a private detective about Teresa. But she's family. She didn't feel she should tell me what to do."

"Which detective was that?"

"A woman named Ruthie Spring. She's my aunt. She lives in San Francisco."

"I know Ruthie. You come from good stock."

Her brows lifted. "Then maybe you know the man she said I should see. His name is Tanner, I think. I've got it written down somewhere."

She started to get up and I waved her back to her seat. "I know Tanner. Oddly enough, I *am* Tanner."

"You are?" Her brow furled like a flag. "Did Ruthie send you? She said she wouldn't do anything until she heard from me."

"Ruthie didn't send me. I got here by coincidence."

"I find that hard to believe, Mr. Tanner."

"Now that you mention it, so do I, Mrs. Martin. But there it is."

We left it there for a time, while we tried to strike a balance between fact and fancy, intrigue and chance. Mrs. Martin was skeptical, and I didn't blame her, but as for me, I'm a great believer in coincidence. It's helped me frequently in my work, and hurt me once or twice, but it's always around, lurking like an ex-wife or a missed opportunity. That doesn't mean I don't scrutinize things when scrutiny's called for, but so far this didn't seem that kind of case.

"Ruthie went on and on about you, Mr. Tanner," Kathryn Martin said suddenly, with an impish grin. "Is there some kind of relationship there?"

"Only symbiotic."

"I'm not sure I know what that means."

"I'm not sure I do, either. I think it means we make each other laugh."

We grinned for a second too long, deferring the future, then Kathryn Martin turned solemn. Her lips shrank like old lemons. "Ruthie said you hunted down the man who killed her husband."

I nodded. I had found Harry Spring's killer a couple of years back, but it wasn't a man who killed him, it was a woman. Ruthie didn't know that. No one knew that but me. It's one of those decisions you sometimes make in this business. The woman who killed Harry is dead. I try to believe her death made the moral issue moot. But those kinds of issues are never moot. I haven't seen Ruthie in a long time. I feel bad about it.

"Why are you worried about Mrs. Blair?" I asked, after a glance at my watch. It was ten minutes till eight. James Blair didn't seem like the type who would enjoy waiting, for me or anyone.

"I'm worried because Teresa's missing. You must know that, if you're looking for her. She's dropped completely out of sight, without a word to anyone. I'm certain something is terribly wrong. Now with you here I'm more certain than ever."

I ignored the implied question. "How long's she been gone, as far as you know?"

"Four days."

"She probably just went home to see her mother," I said, to check the reaction.

"No," Kathryn Martin objected. "You don't understand. She would have told me, if that's all it was. I *know* she would." The words were vehement.

"What's her husband say about it?"

"Nothing. He won't discuss it at all. Not with me. Of course, he's never talked to me about anything. Or to anyone else I've ever seen."

"Does he admit his wife is missing?"

"No. Not to me, at least."

"Is that peculiar? His silence?"

"Everything about James Blair is peculiar. He's got the emotions of a squid, for one thing. Sometimes I think the only things he cares about are his rock garden and his judo chop."

"What's that mean?"

Kathryn Martin swiped at a lock that had strayed across her forehead, then sighed and shook her head. She looked as forlorn as an orphan. "I don't know what it means," she said absently. "I don't know what anything means anymore.

Once I thought I knew all the rules, all the ways to play the game. Now I find I don't know any of them."

"Maybe it's a different game."

She shrugged listlessly. "Maybe you're right. I just wish someone would tell me which one it is. And who's keeping score."

"I'm not sure they keep score anymore," I said. "How does Wayne fit into all this?"

She looked at me for the first time in a long while. "What do you know about Wayne?"

I held up a hand. "Nothing. Absolutely nothing. I swear."

"Well, it was about Wayne in the beginning—my hysteria, I mean—but it's not about him anymore. It's about Teresa. I miss her. I *need* her. Are you going to find her? Is that for real?"

"That's for real."

"I can pay you to look for her. I have some money."

"It's not necessary," I told her. "I already have a client."

"Who?"

"Confidential."

"I'll bet it's James. Trying a bluff," she added after a moment.

"What kind of bluff?"

Kathryn Martin clasped her head with her hands, shutting out the world in general and me in particular. "Forget it," she said wearily, "Just don't tell James I talked to you."

"Why not?"

She didn't say anything.

"You seem afraid of him," I said, as casual as I could be.

"I guess I am afraid. Of what he might do."

"To you or to Teresa?"

"Both."

I took a deep breath and held it. I didn't want her to be right, didn't want the search for Teresa Blair to become something other than it had appeared to be that morning in Tolson's office. "What makes you think he'd do anything to either of you?" I asked.

She shook her head, her eyes shifting widely. "All I know is James Blair has no use for me and never has had. And once when he caught a neighborhood boy letting air out of his tires, he broke the boy's arm. Teresa told me he paid ten thousand dollars to keep the parents from suing him." She stood and pointed to the window. "Look over there. That house is a fortress. No one goes in there, absolutely no one. There are rooms in that house that are locked and even Teresa doesn't have a key. I've only been over there once, and Teresa was nervous the whole time. It's the only time I've ever seen her frightened. So, it may be crazy, but I don't want James Blair to know I'm involved in this, *whatever* it is."

I stood and walked to the window and looked over toward the Blair house. As far as I could tell it was unoccupied. A squirrel climbed to the top of the fence and ran along it, sure and swift. "What's the bottom line, Mrs. Martin?" I said, still facing the window. "Do you think James Blair killed his wife? Is that it?"

"I tell you I don't know." She fidgeted, making little noises behind me. "Yes."

"What?"

"YES! That's really what it amounts to and I've been afraid to admit it. I'm afraid James Blair has done something to Teresa. I'm afraid he's murdered her."

The room grew warm and shrank around the words.

Chapter
3

The indictment had been a long time coming, but its utterance left Kathryn Martin gratefully purged, suddenly blithe. To me the charge was juvenile, ridiculous, as credible as a kid's tale about the old man in the big house at the top of the hill. But I'd keep it in mind.

"Am I terrible to say such a thing?" she asked artfully, not feeling terrible at all.

"Only if you're wrong," I said. "Have you any evidence at all that Mrs. Blair has been killed?"

She thrust out her chin and shook her head. "Not legal evidence. No."

"Then what?"

She shrugged. "Nothing you'd understand."

"Have you any evidence at all that James Blair wanted his wife dead?"

"No."

"Were they having marital troubles?"

"No, nothing specific. But I wouldn't call it a happy marriage."

"What you'd call it isn't relevant, Mrs. Martin. What did Mrs. Blair call it?"

"She didn't. She didn't talk about her marriage, one way or another. But she *couldn't* have been happy with him," she added stubbornly.

"Come on, Mrs. Martin. What are we doing? Playing head games? Developing TV pilots? What? Do you plan to go to the police with the idea that James Blair killed his wife?"

"No. They'd laugh at me. Like you're doing."

"I'm not laughing. Murder dries up my sense of humor."

Whatever she saw on my face caused her to leave her chair and come to the window and stand beside me and grip my hand in both of hers. Her fingers were cold and thin, as dry as road dust. "You just don't understand," she said. "I'll admit I don't know for sure that James did anything to Teresa. I shouldn't have said what I did. But I'm absolutely certain something terrible has happened to her."

"What makes you so sure?"

She dropped my hand and began to pace. The carpet bent without sound. "I'm going through a divorce. It's been a very difficult time for me. I've been almost crazy, and I mean that literally. Teresa Blair, God bless her, has held my hand through all of it. She's come over for coffee every morning for the past six months, just to listen to my little tales of woe. I don't think I would be here without Teresa. I really don't," she mused softly. "Well, anyhow, last week I had this meeting scheduled with my lawyer. I'd discussed it all with Teresa beforehand. The lawyer wanted me to sign some sort of property settlement agreement he'd drawn up, and Teresa didn't think I should do it, not right away. So she and I were going to get together the next morning, like always, and talk over what the lawyer had to say. Teresa was worried about, what was it? Fraudulent concealment of assets, I think she called it."

Teresa Blair had passed on some useful information to her friend. I wondered where she had gotten it in the first place.

"But you see, the next morning Teresa *didn't* come over. She didn't call, didn't leave a note, nothing. I know she would have told me if something came up. I *know* it."

"People skip appointments all the time, Mrs. Martin. It doesn't mean they're the victim of a forcible felony."

Kathryn Martin made fists and planted them on her hips. "You're just like every man I've ever met. I'm sure you make decisions all the time based on nothing more than a hunch—everything from horse bets to business deals—but when a woman does the same thing all of a sudden it's a silly, *female* way to behave. It makes me sick."

She pricked me with her eyes. She was right in what she said, but I didn't stop to think about it.

"Do you do divorce work, Mr. Tanner?"

"No, I don't," I told her. "Not anymore."

"I guess to make you understand why I said that about Teresa I'm going to have to go into my marital situation," she said evenly. "I suppose you find domestic disturbances distasteful; I'm sure they bore you to death."

"Actually, I always found them pretty compelling and pretty awful. It was the clients who always seemed bored by it all."

"Well, *I* certainly don't view my divorce as boring. I've been frantic for months. I'm from the Midwest. Ohio. My father's a judge. There's never been a divorce in our family. Never. My parents were not supportive at all when I told them, I suppose because I couldn't, or at least wouldn't, talk about the sordid details. For the first time in my life I refused to let them counsel me about a major decision. They were so insulted they immediately assumed *I* was the cause of the breakup. My mother calls every Sunday, asks if I've let Wayne come back, and hangs up when I tell her I haven't."

Mrs. Martin had resolved to tell me her story, and although I didn't particularly want to hear it, at least not right then, I didn't tell her that. Instead, I leaned back against the wall and tried to look trustworthy and receptive. I'm pretty good at it, I guess; people tell me all kinds of things. Listening. It's what I do in lieu of charitable contributions. "Tell me about Wayne," I said, giving her a nudge.

"Wayne. Well, Wayne is a good man, or at least he was when I married him. He is, or was, in insurance executive, a church elder, scoutmaster, Little League coach, all those things husbands are supposed to be, or so I was taught. But all that ended a year ago. Since then he's gone completely crazy. He turned forty in September. Midlife crisis, isn't that what they're calling it nowadays? Whatever it was, Wayne's personality changed totally in a period of six months."

"How?"

"Well, to put it bluntly, Wayne was born again."

I guess I laughed.

"It's not funny," Kathryn Martin declared. "Believe me. Although it's *good* you laughed. I never could, not until it was too late. They take advantage of that, of course. They prey on your guilt, on your reluctance to call someone who quotes Bible verses and goes to church six days a week a jerk. A nut. A *devil*."

"Is that what Wayne became? A devil?"

She considered my question more seriously than I'd expected. "If a devil is someone who spends all his time judging others and finding them wanting, and condemning them for their imperfections, then that's exactly what Wayne became. It was terrible. He began with himself. No booze, no swearing, no books or movies that weren't properly 'religious.' Then he went after me. Change my hair, my clothes, my friends. Church five nights a week. *Discussions*. Prayers every ten minutes. It was inconvenient, and maddening, and utterly boring and stupid, but I suppose I could have taken it if he hadn't started in on David! He wanted our son to be Jesus, just the way he wanted me to be the Virgin Mary. And we weren't. And we didn't want to be. And the more we resisted, the more people he brought in to help us see the light." Kathryn Martin fought back a tear.

"What kind of people?"

"Fanatics. Men with eyes that never closed. Women with hands that were always clasped. People with tolerance and rectitude oozing from every pore, but of course it wasn't tolerance or rectitude at all."

"What was it?"

"Hate, more than anything. To those people God was their bully, their bodyguard. His only duty was to strike down all those who disagreed, explicitly or implicitly, with their ideas. Their prayers weren't requests for forgiveness but *instructions* to the Lord, lists of the people who did and who most definitely did not deserve His benevolence. My own friends were driven out. Whores and blasphemers, Wayne called them." Kathryn Martin sniffled, then pulled out a Kleenex from her pants pocket and blew her nose. "I have a pin in my jewel box," she went on. "A little round pin that I got in the sixth grade. You know what it's for?"

"What?"

"For going to church a hundred Sundays without a miss. And now look at me."

She closed her eyes and pressed her hand to her forehead, her memory a narcotic and addictive. I wanted to help her, but the subject was too complex.

"He sent me to see other men, you know," she said slowly, almost inaudibly. "They were supposed to counsel me, to get me on God's team. What they mostly did was pat my knee and put their arms around me and spout nonsense about the evils of *humanism*. That's the dirty word, believe it or not. One of them suggested I express my rebirth by casting off my garments, as he called them. When I refused, he slapped me and sent me home to Wayne."

She stopped talking. The sound of the slap seemed to briefly inhabit the room. "When Wayne began talking about sending Davy off to some 'Christian' school in South Carolina, I threw him out. Bag and baggage. I cried for three days, but I didn't give in. Davy still cries, and it breaks my heart, but I won't give in. And Teresa Blair was here every morning, through all of it. Up until last Friday. Then nothing. Do you understand now why I think something terrible has happened? She gave me a whole new life. Now I want to help *her*, in any way I can. Will you find her for me?"

"I'll find her," I said. What I didn't say was that I was working for James Blair and for the El Gordo District Attorney, not for her, and that finding Teresa Blair might not necessarily be in Teresa's best interest or her friend Kathryn Martin's, either. If Tony Fluto hadn't put a scare into Mrs. Blair, the thought must have crossed his mind more than once. I had one of those hunches Mrs. Martin had mentioned, and my hunch was that in finding Teresa Blair I wouldn't be doing anyone but Ray Tolson any favors.

"Tell me everything you know about Teresa Blair," I said.

Kathryn Martin's expression darkened. "That's another thing. I spent all day yesterday thinking back over our conversations, and I just now realized that we spent virtually our entire time together talking about me and *my* problems. I know almost nothing about her."

"Surely there's something."

"Well, she has a job. She works afternoons in a boutique in El Gordo called Bathsheba's. In fact, she owns part of it. She plays tennis at the El Gordo Racquet Club. That's where she goes after she holds my hand in the mornings. She reads a lot. She's absolutely wonderful with children—she has Davy in the palm of her hand. She's very independent, very intelligent, very beautiful, and totally unshockable. Wayne at his worst didn't even faze her."

"Has she always lived in El Gordo?"

"I don't know."

"Anything at all peculiar about her marriage?"

Kathryn Martin shook her head. "She almost never mentioned her husband or their life together. They seldom went out. Every time I asked Teresa if she wanted to go to a movie or something she was always free to go. Like I said, she just never talked about it. I realize now that might have been because I was so busy talking about mine."

"Do you have a picture of her?"

"Yes. Not a very good one, though."

She went into the kitchen and pulled something off the bulletin board beside the telephone and came back and handed me a square of newsprint. The picture was under the heading "New Business in El Gordo." The paper was the El Gordo *Democrat*. The date was June 1979. The man in the picture was Elliott Farnsworth, the woman Teresa Blair. The paper said they were the co-owners of Bathsheba's. The man was tall and daintily elegant, the woman darkly sensual. She seemed slightly amused by the proceedings. The picture quality was such that if I knew Teresa Blair was in a room with me I could pick her out of the crowd, but if I didn't know that for certain, then I couldn't.

"How about her friends?" I asked.

"She certainly acted as though I was the only one she had. There must have been others, of course. I'm sure the Racquet Club people would know."

"Other men?"

"No."

"Sure?"

"Virtually. She just didn't seem interested."

"Where's she from originally?"

She paused. "I don't know. I haven't the vaguest idea. That's strange, isn't it?"

"Parents?"

"Dead. At least she never mentioned them."

"Siblings?"

"No."

"Haunts?"

She shrugged.

"Enemies?"

"I can't believe there were any."

"Children?"

"No."

"College?"

"No. At least I don't think so."

"Anything else? Anything at all?"

She shook her head again. "It seems silly, but I can't think of a thing. She dressed beautifully, of course, what with the boutique. She was athletic. She was a truly liberated woman without going on about it, if you know what I mean. But she had no particular interests as far as I know. Except me, I guess is what I mean."

"Why haven't you gone to the police?"

I slipped the question in fast, hoping that while she fumbled for an answer she would tell me something useful. But she had an answer ready: "Teresa wouldn't like it."

"Why not?"

"She just wouldn't."

"Did she tell you that?"

"No, it's just something I know. She didn't trust the police. She didn't trust anyone."

I walked into the kitchen and put my empty coffee mug on the counter next to the sink. The remains of Davy's peanut butter sandwich lay on the counter, too, oozing jelly as thick as sludge. I went back to Mrs. Martin. "What happened the last time you saw Mrs. Blair?" I asked her.

"Let's see. She came over about eight thirty in the morning."

"What day?"

"Last Thursday."

"Anything at all different about her?"

She frowned and shook her head. "I don't think so. She looked like she'd just stepped out of *Vogue*, as usual. Camel slacks. White boat-neck sweater. Carrying her coffee cup and her newspaper, as usual. She always brought her own cup."

"And you talked about the meeting with the lawyer?"

"Yes. Teresa thought Wayne might have hidden some assets away. She didn't want me to sign anything until Wayne had been forced to swear under oath as to what property we owned."

"Who's your lawyer?"

"C. Dale Gibson."

"Where's his office?"

"Here in El Gordo."

"Did Mrs. Blair know him?"

"I don't think so."

"Anything else happen?"

"I'm trying to see her that morning, envision what she did. She skimmed the paper, like she always did. Somehow she could read and talk to me at the same time and absorb from both sources. Looking back, it does seem like she was worried about something. But it's probably my imagination."

"Any idea what might have worried her?"

"No. I don't think Teresa ever once complained to me about anything."

"She sounds like quite a woman."

"She *is* quite a woman."

I smiled. "Do you know anything about her being a witness in a criminal case?"

"What? Oh, that auto accident thing? Is that the one?"

"That's the one. Did she talk about that at all?"

Kathryn Martin shrugged. "Back when it occurred, I saw something in the paper so I asked her what had happened. She told me she'd seen a car run down a pedestrian and would probably be called to testify against the driver if it ever went to trial."

"Did she seemed worried about it?"

"Not at all."

"Did she mention it again?"

"No."

"Was she the kind of person to run away from having to do something like that? Appear in court, I mean?"

"Teresa Blair wasn't the type of person to run away from anything."

The testimonial was heartfelt and didactic and as a result impressive. I asked Mrs. Martin if she could think of anything else that might be helpful and she shook her head. I glanced at my watch. I was late. I stood up.

"Hey," Mrs. Martin said. "How about staying for dinner? I mean, I'm starving, and Davy hasn't eaten anything hot for days. It's easy to set an extra place." Her words trailed off into silence. The invitation was awkward, too eagerly issued, revealing a lack of practice.

"Sorry," I said. "I've got an appointment and I'm late already."

I left Kathryn Ellington Martin standing in the middle of her family room and her divorce, a dazed and slightly apprehensive look on her face, and went over to call on the man she had just accused of murder.

Chapter
4

This time when I pressed the little white button beside the gate, the gate swung open. Somewhere behind the bushes a little motor whirred. After I entered, the gate closed, silently and automatically, at my back. I felt as though I'd entered a carnival attraction, dark and cavernous, the Pirate Cave or the House of Horrors. An instant later the darkness vanished, the ground became lit like a stage by scores of invisible bulbs, the theatrical light and shadow creating shapes as vague and undefined as the new life Mrs. Martin was building for herself on the next lot.

I absorbed the scene for a few seconds, then started down a flagstone path through a rock garden of raked white pebbles, thick green moss, and bleached, twisted wood. Halfway down the path an arching footbridge took me across a small pool that was lit from below the water line and azure as a result. Gold and black carp swam listlessly in the clear, still water. The bamboo fronds and Boston ferns at the edge of the pool fondled each other in the wind. It was ethereal, a special place, a Zen place, a place reminiscent of my past, of my stay in Kyoto during the Korean War, of the Awata Palace and the Kiyomizu and the Moss Temple. I wanted badly to linger, but I followed the path instead.

A monkey puzzle tree guarded the door of the house with wispy, spindly arms. Beside it a stone lantern served both as porch light and as caution: when I crossed this threshold, it said, I would cross an ocean and a culture.

The house itself was low and broad, its dimensions subtly disguised by landscaping and perspective. Alternating panels of glass and stone were separated by redwood squares arranged geometrically, like *shoji* screens. The effect was delicate and striking. I punched the buzzer with eagerness.

James Blair opened the door, bowed slightly at the waist, and beckoned me to enter, as polite as a man with something to sell. He was formally dressed, down to the rep tie knotted snugly beneath the roll of his white collar, but over it all he wore a black silk robe, loose at the arms and wrapped at the waist with a white cloth band. The silk whispered secrets when he moved.

I followed his slippered feet across the tatami floor mats in the foyer and into the living room, which was sunken and bordered on three sides by sliding screens and glass. I obeyed his gesture and took a seat on a flat, low sedan, feeling guilty for wearing shoes.

On the teak table beside me a bonsai cypress wound out of a small thick pot of soil. On the far wall was a set of four woodblock prints—deeply colorful, precisely wrought— Hiroshige or one of his imitators. On another wall a large scroll hung, partially unrolled, between two of the door screens. From where I sat the rows of ideographs seemed to move about, a swarm of bees servicing their queen. Above the scroll a cloth carp swayed in the air at the end of a string, colorful, festive, symbolic of manhood.

Blair bowed to me again and sat cross-legged on a cushion in the middle of the floor. I wondered if I was supposed to worship him, or vice versa. For the next few seconds Blair didn't move, didn't seem to see or breathe. Then suddenly he smiled and asked if I wanted a drink. I told him I had a sudden craving for sake. He said it was available, and he would be happy to serve it, but it would be better warmed. I opted for Scotch instead. Blair rose, almost floated, from the floor, slid open a screen, and disappeared. To the left of the door a collection of kendo swords rose up the wall like rungs on a silver ladder.

The room, its woods and brasses, ceramics and lacquers, massaged me with pulses from a host of different and refreshing wavelengths. I resolved to delve into Zen once again, in light of what seemed to be a new receptivity, or perhaps a new need.

When Blair returned with my drink, I complimented him on the house. He seemed pleased, although he spoke no words that said so. When he asked if the Scotch was satisfactory, I told him it was. When I asked if he would join me in a drink, he told me he drank only tea, and nothing after sundown. In a careful but nonobvious way Blair had put me on the defensive, awakening my slumbering sense of inadequacy. Since he possessed control of the situation, I decided to see what he would do with it.

For several minutes he did nothing but watch me sip my drink. I glanced idly about, uneasy and insecure in the silence. When I found myself looking at a particularly stark scroll on the far wall, I asked Blair what it was.

"It's a koan," he said. "One of my favorites."

"What does it say?"

He smiled. "If you meet the Buddha, kill him."

I was startled and must have looked it. Blair's smile widened. "I find it particularly helpful in reminding me that the path to satori lies within, not without, that there is in my world no separation between the human and the divine." He paused for effect. "Can you imagine a Christian saying the same of Mister Christ?" he asked, his eyes flickering with mischief.

I told him I couldn't. Blair nodded. I expected him to slip me a cookie as a reward.

"What made you embrace Zen and all this?" I asked.

Blair shrugged. "When a thinking man finds himself in a madhouse, he must either become twice mad or seek to escape to another place. I have made my choice."

"But you still work on the outside, don't you?"

"Ah. One must eat. Few accommodations are perfect."

"Does your wife share your philosophy?"

"Not entirely. We are different people. In the beginning our differences bound us together. I hope they will not now destroy us."

Blair returned to the mat across from me and sank onto it and sat, erect and cross-legged, with his hands poised like blossoms on his knees. He explained that he could only give me an hour, that he had to return to the office to review the confirmations of some receivables. When I asked about his business, he told me he was an independent accountant, employed by a small number of individuals and businesses for whom he prepared tax returns and financial statements. When he glanced briefly at his watch, I assured him I would get down to business.

"Tolson seems to think this Fluto character might be responsible for your wife's disappearance." I said. "Was there any evidence at all your wife was taken by force?"

"No."

"Any sign of forced entry?"

He shook his head. "I checked very carefully. I know this house well. I believe I would know if an entry was forced."

"So there isn't any basis, other than theoretical, for you to believe that Tony Fluto has your wife."

"That is correct."

Our eyes met then, because we both knew where we

were going, and we were both uneasy. "I'm going to proceed on the assumption that your wife left on her own," I told him. "For whatever reason. If I'm wrong, someone will let me know, sooner or later. In the meantime, I'm going to have to know a lot about her. Everything you can tell me. Including how she felt about you."

Blair remained as he was for a moment, a breathing Buddha, then stood and crossed the room and stared at one of the prints on the wall. The water in the little fishing scene was a fathomless blue, and Blair seemed to probe its depths, to immerse himself in its mystery. "I want to help," he said finally, his. back still to me. "But you will be disappointed, perhaps even dismayed, at how little I know. About her."

When he turned to face me, there was the beginning of a sheepish smile on his face. "I am an accountant, as you know," he said, "and I am also, perhaps naturally, a student of Eastern philosophy and art, particularly the teachings of the Japanese Zen masters. I lived in Kyoto for a year. I briefly attended Otani University, the school of Dr. Suzuki. I considered becoming a monk, until I realized I was unworthy and would always be."

"Why?"

"It's not important. I tell you this simply to confirm what you have doubtless observed. I am a man of precision, of patience, of exactitude. In my work. In my habits. In my pleasures. In one area only have I deviated. That is the conjugal. I met and married Teresa in eleven days."

Coming from Blair that was tantamount to an admission of treason. I grinned. "Have you ever regretted the impulse?"

"Never."

"Has Mrs. Blair ever regretted it?" I asked, without quite meeting his eyes.

It was almost impossible to detect, but I thought a bit of anguish was twisting his features, creating disharmony. "I cannot speak for her," Blair began slowly. "We have never communicated a great deal, at least not as that term is normally understood. Our relationship is one of conventions, of roles. It is as we both wish it. However, I am sure Teresa has no doubts about my feelings for her. I have admitted her and no one else into my life. At times Teresa seizes me like a savior, an antidote for some mysterious poison she has somehow ingested. But at other times, well, there is a gulf, and we exist as islands. It is not unpleasant, but it is not, how shall I put it, a life of shared experience. It is not a confluence."

"Was Mrs. Blair frightened of Tony Fluto?"

"Of course. But not hysterically so. She seemed determined to testify." His tone was nonchalant, his attention unfocused for the first time that evening.

I looked at him carefully, alert for any reaction he might give to what I would say next. "You think she's running from you, don't you? Not from Fluto at all. That's why you suggested that someone like me be brought in on the case. You think the cops are on the wrong trail."

Blair met my eyes. "Basically, that's correct. I don't like to acknowledge it, but yes, that's what I believe."

"That leaves us with motivation. Why would she want to leave you?"

Blair closed his eyes momentarily, then opened them. They were orbs of flickering blue flame. "I am perfectly content here," he said, his hand sweeping the room, the house, the compound. "I built the house before I met Teresa. Except for her it contains everything that interests me. My texts, my dojo, my bonsai, my rock garden. I am at peace here, but the same cannot be said for Teresa. She is not given to contemplation. She likes people, movement, to be directed away from her center, not toward it. It was part of her charm, part of what she brought to me, but it created tensions. She may have concluded that another life would offer more. If so, it would sadden but not surprise me."

"If you two were so different, why did she marry you in the first place?"

"We each had goals, duties to perform, obligations we had to fulfill, that we could not escape. We came to realize we could do it best together."

"What kinds of obligations?"

Blair blinked. "Just those that life bestows. I didn't mean to sound so dramatic. It's a failure of those who spend much time alone—their existence tends to assume exaggerated significance. It is one of many impulses I try to suppress, but I often fail. As I said: unworthy."

Blair stopped talking, the strange rhythms of his speech leaving ripples in the room. I sensed I had all the details of his domestic intimacies I was going to get. "Thank you for your candor," I said to him. "It might help me find your wife. A woman on the run from a man like Fluto will do things differently from a woman on the run from her husband. One question is, assuming Mrs. Blair is running from you, what do I do if I find her? From experience I can tell you that it's almost impossible to force a woman to return to a man she definitely decided to leave."

Blair shook his head. "I simply want to know where she is," he answered. "So I can speak with her briefly. I would certainly not force her to come back to me, even if I had the power to. But I would like to talk with her, to make one final attempt to put it, to put *us*, together."

"That's fine," I said. "You're the client, you can do whatever you want. But just remember the information goes to Tolson, too. Those were the rules, and you agreed to them. I assume they still apply."

He nodded. "But I'll be frank with you, Mr. Tanner. If you do find Teresa and if she agrees to speak with me, I intend to advise her to refuse to testify against this Fluto. For her own good and for mine."

"Does Tolson know that?"

"No. I'd prefer you not tell him."

"I guess that's his problem, isn't it?"

"I believe it is."

I looked at Blair. His jaw was knotted in determination, and more than a little masochism. He was a man who swam, if at all, only upstream, a man perpetually at odds with the world he had been placed in, impervious to all but the charms of his wife and of his adoptive culture. I wonder if he ever laughed, and at what.

"Let's start at the beginning," I said.

"What beginning?"

"Your wife's."

He shook his head. "I don't know the beginning. Only the middle. I hope also to know the end," he added wistfully.

"I think you'd better explain."

"I simply mean that I know nothing about Teresa's past. Purposely. From the first the present was always more than enough. The past could only detract. I made no inquiries; she made no confessions. It seemed to suit us both."

I thought of Blair's description of the two islands. John Donne was wrong, apparently, "You must know something," I urged. "Where was she born? Where did she grow up? Go to school?"

Blair shook his head once again. "I simply lack that information. I know nothing of her family, of her adolescence, her education, nothing. As far as I know, none of that touches her any longer, except in the sense that we are all touched gently by our histories. She never mentions any of those subjects and, for my part, I have been content in my ignorance. She has traveled much; every place I have taken her has been already familiar to her. She had much expertise in . . . matters of the flesh, from sources I preferred not be identified. Other than that, I can tell you nothing, except the events after we met."

"Which was when?"

"Six years ago."

"Where?"

"Here. El Gordo."

"What circumstances?"

"Nothing dramatic. A client of mine gave a party. I had declined his previous invitations to so many functions I felt compelled to attend this one. I was smitten first by Teresa's beauty, then by her wit, then by my good fortune. I kept asking if I could see her again. She kept saying yes, even when I changed the question. As I said, we married two weeks later. She was, I hope you understand, like an elixir for me, a treat. A sin, if you will."

"Were you married before?"

"No."

"Was she?"

"No."

"What was Mrs. Blair's maiden name?"

"Goodrum. Teresa Goodrum."

"Who introduced you?"

"I'm not sure. It was a large party. We simply introduced ourselves, I believe."

"Who was the client?"

Blair frowned, hesitating for the first time. "Is that necessary?" he asked. "I'd prefer not to involve my business affairs in this. I don't see how it can help."

"Neither do I," I admitted, "but there's only one way to make certain it can't."

He considered. "No. There's no point in that. My business is not involved in this and I won't let it be." He gave me a look that convinced me to leave it alone for the time being.

"What was your wife doing when you met her?" I asked. "I mean for a living?"

"Working. As a salesclerk, in a boutique. Living alone. Crying a lot, so she said."

"Crying about what?"

"Emptiness. She had no center."

I let the jargon pass. "What else? Friends? Hobbies? Manias? Clubs? Groups?"

Blair rubbed his face. Although he must have been forty, the flesh was still taut, as unyielding as the cheek of a marble man. "She still works at the boutique, but now she is part owner. It's quite successful. She has her own bank account, spends only her own money. She is an instinctive businesswoman, I'm told. She has friends at the store, of course. She and a woman named Verritt play tennis every day at the Racquet Club. They are close friends. Frankly, I think it likely the Verritt woman knows where Teresa is. If so, I'm the last person she will tell."

"Why?"

"We disgust each other. Also, I believe Teresa may know the woman next door. A Mrs. Martin. I'm afraid we don't socialize as a couple—I don't enjoy it—so there really isn't anyone else I can mention."

"No men friends?"

Blair looked for my implication. I wasn't sure I had one. "The co-owner of the boutique is a man named Elliott Farnsworth," he said stiffly. "He and Teresa work closely together. All the other employees are women. I knew of no other men in her life above the level of fools and oglers."

Something in Blair's voice made me think he didn't enjoy the ogling part. I decided to press a little, to see what pressed back. "How about men who are more than friends? Past, present, or future."

"Blair's lips stiffened. "I know of none, and I resent the question."

"No, you don't. You're too smart for that. If she's as alluring as you say, someone must have made a pass at her at some time or other. I want to know if anyone made a habit of it."

"If they have, it is of no consequence. Adultery is committed by the cowardly and the self-indulgent. Teresa is neither."

"How about the guy next door?"

Blair seemed genuinely puzzled. "What about him?"

"How did he and your wife get along?"

He shrugged. "I have no idea. I can't imagine they exchanged two words a month."

"Did your wife tell you anything about the Martins' marital trouble?"

"No. I know of no trouble."

With that I let it drop. For now it was enough to know that Teresa Blair didn't tell all she knew to her husband. Perhaps she told him nothing. "What was your wife doing down on Oswego Street the day she saw Fluto run down the man?" I asked.

"I don't know."

"Didn't you ask?"

"It seems ridiculous, I suppose, but no, I didn't."

"Usually when people don't ask questions it's because they're afraid to know the answer." That platitude sounded hollow, even to me.

Blair looked at me steadily, his voice icy when he spoke. "When you've known me a bit longer, Mr. Tanner, you will discover that there's nothing at all usual about me."

Nothing I had seen so far urged me to doubt him. I eased off. "Do you have any pictures of your wife?"

"How many will you need?"

"A couple of good ones."

"You can have a couple of hundred if you wish. For a time Teresa modeled for her boutique's advertising. She has an extensive portfolio. If you'll come with me, I'll show you."

We went through another sliding door and strolled down a hall that had blue tiles on the floor and gold paper on the walls. At the end of the hall Blair opened a door and stood aside to let me enter a chamber that was as different from the rest of the house as Miami Beach is from Kyoto.

The room was vast. The sleeping area at the far end was

dominated by a canopied bed, which looked like a pillow in a clam shell, and by a dressing table with more lights around it than the marquee at Loews. The sitting room was closest to me, and the decor would have rendered Blair's favorite Zen master mute for a month. Supergraphics and chrome, Ultrasuede and shag, Breuer chairs and van der Rohe tables. The desk was glass, the chairs plastic, the prints Warhol and Lichtenstein.

"This is Teresa's room," Blair explained with a mixture of apology and wonder. He didn't enter, but peered around the door jamb like an urchin at the circus. "I rise early, for aikido training," Blair continued. "I prefer to get to the office by seven. Teresa is a night person, as she calls it. We early on decided to sleep separately. As you can see, this also serves as her office. I have not entered this room since we married. It is the sanctuary she insisted upon and I granted."

"I'd say your wife gets her philosophy from somewhere closer to Reverend Ike than Siddhartha," I said.

Blair smiled, affection showing through even in the midst of trappings that were a burlesque of everything he believed. "Do not misjudge her, Mr. Tanner," he said. "She is a free spirit, but she knows the limits I insist upon." The smile vanished. "I have tried not to get in her way," he added. "Sometimes it has been difficult."

"May I look around?" I asked.

Blair nodded. "I will be in the living room, if you need me. You understand I would not normally allow anyone in this room. However, the circumstances seem to warrant an exemption to my pledge. Her portfolio is against the wall by the desk." Blair left me to my job, his gown flapping behind him.

I did a quick once-over, pawing in simian fashion through the accessories to the life of a woman I had never seen. There were soft and frilly things in the drawers— sheer things, fragrant things, enticing things, things I had never seen before. Fashion magazines spilled off the book-shelves and onto the floor, where they reclined beside pop psychology paperbacks, soft rock records, and a horde of bite-size Tootsie Rolls. There were enough clothes in the closets to outfit the membership of NOW for a year. Her jewels lay on velvet trays and winked at me like collected eyes. Her shoes were spike-heeled and plentiful, her hats few but bombastic. There were see-through things and shiny things and shorty things and I shivered when I touched it all, though not from desire. There is nothing less noble than fumbling through a living human's clothes.

When I was through with the closets and dressers and shelves, I knew that Teresa Blair liked color and flash, liked to be noticed, liked to be hip, liked to be liked. But there was no hint of what lay beneath the veneer, and no relics of a treasured past. The woman lived entirely in the moment.

Before tackling the desk, I picked up the artist's portfolio, placed it on the bed, and unzipped it and spread it contents like a deck of playing cards. A hundred faces looked up at me, faces that pouted and preened, faces that smiled and scowled, faces that seduced and abandoned, and they were all the same face, although I had to look closely to confirm it. Teresa Blair was not a classic model, there was too much of her for that, but if she wouldn't sell any Givenchys or Balenciagas to the New York elite, she would certainly sell a hell of a lot of Anne Kleins and Halstons to the trendy young matrons of El Gordo.

The problem for me was that her hair was so variously coiffed, her lips so variously painted, her cheeks so variously rouged, her eyes so variously shadowed, I couldn't tell which of the faces was real. I picked a couple of shots that seemed more natural than the rest, then put the folder away and walked over to the desk and looked through the drawers.

Teresa Blair was obviously the buyer for the boutique. There were catalogs and price quotations and invoices stuffed helter-skelter through the drawers, without rhyme or reason. These plus the normal litter of writing materials and business correspondence were all I found until I came to a check register, old but not very. It seemed to be a mixed business and personal account. The average balance was over a thousand dollars. At times it got up to five times that.

There wasn't much of interest among the payees—grocery stores, drug stores, gas stations, credit card companies, Racquet Club, dentist. Just a few things caught my eye. Mrs. Blair made a regular payment—three hundred dollars every other week—to someone named Mary Quilk. And another—over two thousand dollars every month—to something called the Silver Season. She made a deposit of fifteen hundred dollars on the first of every month and a deposit of twelve hundred dollars on the fifteenth. Both without fail. Also, she gave to CARE and the United Way.

I replaced the register and stood in the center of the room. I was about to leave when I noticed something out of place. It was a magazine, but not a new one, an old *Vogue*, dated June of 1965. I picked it up and leafed through it. Nothing but glamour caught my eye, but as I got toward the end, something slipped from between the pages and fell to the floor. It was a picture of a man, a confident, darkly pretty one who was attempting to please whoever took the picture. There was nothing in or written on the back of the snapshot to indicate where or when it had been taken. I checked to make certain Blair hadn't returned, and slipped it in my pocket.

Blair was in the living room, as promised. I showed him the pictures of his wife I had taken from her portfolio and asked if they were good likenesses. He told me they were. I asked how old his wife was and he told me she was thirty-nine. I asked if he'd checked to see whether anything of his wife's was missing. He said he had, that she had too many clothes to be certain about them but that her favorite necklace was gone, as well as her toothbrush and her nightgown. If Tony Fluto had grabbed her, he had given her time to pack a trousseau.

I asked Blair if the names Mary Quilk or Silver Season meant anything to him. He hesitated, then said they didn't. I asked if he had any idea where his wife would have gone to hide, either from him or from Fluto or both. He said he didn't know. I asked if he knew how much his wife earned at the boutique and he didn't know that, either. The snapshot in my pocket grew warm, but I left it where it was, and called it quits.

Chapter
5

There were several places to start my search, none exactly laden with promise; I started with the friend.

The only Verritt in the book was named Tancy, and it was after ten when I called her from the first phone booth I came to after leaving James Blair and his hillside shrine. As I pulled up next to the booth, I checked to see if I was still being shadowed by Grinder's men. There was no green car, but there were a lot of stiff-necked men with lidless eyes who glanced my way as they drove past. As far as I could tell, they all kept driving.

The voice that answered my call was flat, female, and massively oppressed, the voice of taxi dispatchers and doctors' wives. I said who I was, but let the reason for my call remain vague enough for Ms. Verritt to assume I was a man on the make who had been steered her way by her friend Teresa Blair. She made the assumption quickly enough herself, anyway.

I tossed off some flattery, added a boast diluted with a dash of humility, and the mixture intoxicated her. She became quite willing to talk about whatever I had in mind, and within seconds she had decided she was perfectly happy to see me and all, but unfortunately not that night. A friend was dropping by. A late date. I understood, didn't I, love? I mean, it was *such* short notice. She was forgiven, wasn't she? Just this once?

Sure she was. I asked what time would be convenient to meet. She told me to be at the El Gordo Racquet Club at eleven the next morning. She didn't say so, but she obviously wanted to look me over in the light of day before committing her time or anything else to my cause.

I asked where the Racquet Club was and she told me. I said something semiknowledgable about Borg and McEnroe and the conversation immediately started to bore her. Then she asked me what I did for a living and I told her I found things that were lost. That perked her up. I left it to her to decide whether I was a bounty hunter or a psychoanalyst or something in between.

I drove back to the city that night still free of Grinder's minions as far as I could tell, was early to bed and early to rise, and spent some time the next morning on the phone with Peggy, my part-time secretary and full-time confidante, reviewing some old business, which mostly consisted of Peggy trying to convince me that about a third of my active cases were lost causes and my attempting to deny it. When I told her I'd probably be spending the next couple of nights in El Gordo, she told me my absence wouldn't jeopardize anything at the office. I told her I knew that already.

Before heading south I spent some time trying to get a line on Mary Quilk and the Silver Season. I started with the telephone book. There were a half-dozen Quilks, but none lived within twenty miles of El Gordo. There was no Silver Season listed. My source at the electric company was on vacation, so I called the secretary of state's office, to see if Silver Season was a registered corporate name in California. It wasn't. But something about that named poked at the underside of my consciousness. I closed my eyes and tried to become receptive to the memory that was chipping away, but I guess I didn't give it enough time or a big enough pick. After my fourth cup of coffee I locked the apartment and injected myself and my Buick into the stream of traffic heading down the Bayshore. By ten forty-five I was parked behind the ten feet of wall that surrounded the El Gordo Racquet Club, between a blue Corvette and a red Interceptor.

El Gordo is not one of your upper-crust California towns—not a La Jolla or a Pebble Beach, a Hillsborough or a San Marino—but all California towns of whatever crust have people with big money living in them, and people with big money always build playpens for themselves, to ease the burden of all that cash. The playpens come in various styles—concert halls, art museums, social clubs, golf courses, tennis ranches, health spas—but they all manage to have one thing in common. They all manage to be deductible.

The El Gordo Racquet Club was a very private playpen. Five signs nailed to five palm trees reminded me it was open to members only. I strolled to the door anyway, a cross between Joshua and a shoe shine boy.

The clubhouse was long and single-storied, with a thick limestone face and narrow, recessed windows and a tile roof the color of a three ball. There were large brass rings on the twin front doors, but before I got to the doors I got to the guardhouse, a red, peak-roofed booth with a man wearing a white pith helmet sitting inside it. When he saw me coming, he eased off his stool and came out to meet me, his limbs moving haphazardly, like an unmanned puppet. I guessed he was seventy.

"Who is your host, sir?" he said as he approached. He was too gaunt to be menacing and he knew it. Above his beaked nose his eyes shifted with embarrassment.

"How do you know I'm not a member?" I asked pleasantly.

"I know all the members," he said sternly.

"My name's Tanner. I'm here to see Miss Verritt. She's expecting me."

"I'll have to check the list."

He shuffled back to his booth and rifled through some papers, then came back. He was still more alert than he would have been if my suit were in style, but he told me I could go on in.

"Do you know Teresa Blair?" I asked as he was about to return to his stool.

"Mrs. Blair? Sure I do."

"Is she in the club now?"

"Nope."

"When's the last time she was here?"

"Let me think. Middle of last week, I'd say. She's generally here every morning. Nothing happened to Mrs. Blair, did it?"

"Why do you ask?"

"Someone else asked about her yesterday."

"Who?"

"A man."

"What man?"

"Don't know the gentleman."

"Her husband?"

"Wouldn't know her husband if he crapped in my hat. Hope he's a good man, though."

"Why?"

The old man looked away, at something beyond the wall. "Mrs. Blair, she's my favorite. Always says hello to me. Every time. It's a simple thing, even babies can manage it, but you'd be surprised at how many people around here think they got something better to do."

"No, I wouldn't," I said, then reached in my pocket and

brought out the snapshot I'd taken from Teresa Blair's room. "This the guy looking for Mrs. Blair?"

"Nope."

"Ever seen this guy before?"

"Nope."

"What did the man who was here yesterday look like?"

"Clean. Chipped tooth. Butch haircut. Like a man who wears what someone else tells him to."

I smiled at the description. "You ever see Mrs. Blair with any other members besides Miss Verritt?"

"Well, she's real friendly to all of them, but no one special."

"How about men?"

The old eyes narrowed. "I tell you, son. If I *had* seen her with someone, which I'm not saying I did, I wouldn't tell you about it. Or anyone else."

I patted the old man on a bony shoulder and tugged on one of the brass rings and went inside the club.

The tile foyer took me past a reservation desk and a sports shop and a simulated tide pool and through a glass door, which opened onto a deck full of tables and chairs and men and women in short, white clothes. Beyond the deck were the courts. Beyond the courts was a hedge. Beyond the hedge echoed the laughs and screams of youthful high jinks: a swimming pool or a Woody Allen film festival.

They were all dressed for tennis, but the only balls in sight were highballs. They sat in small groups, whispering, gasping, gaping, exclaiming. I had no idea what Tancy Verritt looked like, but if she was there on the deck, she looked like every other woman in the place.

I stood there in my brown suit, a fly in the frappé, trying to catch the eye of one of the waiters who looked blasé enough to be able to identify the members for me, when a woman rose out of a group of particularly beautiful people clustered around a white table with a yellow umbrella sprouting from it and walked toward me. She was tall and richly burnished, full-bodied and careless. The mole above the left corner of her mouth was the same color as her lips. Her nose was pert, possibly bobbed. A row of pale blue ruffles was visible beneath her tennis skirt. The visor over her eyes reminded me of crap games of my youth. Behind it, her hair fell in a single, heavy braid. Her eyes and neck looked older than the rest of her.

"Mr. Tanner?"

"Ms. Verritt?"

"Won't you join me? I'm afraid I don't have much time to give you, love." She gave me an appraisal that lacked only a loupe. "Not now, at any rate," she added.

"I don't collect time, Ms. Verritt; I don't like the container it comes in. Just information."

"Oh? Somehow I thought . . . oh, well. Come on."

She was still frowning at my obscure flippancy when she pirouetted, her skirt flaring briefly above the blue ruffled pants, and led me toward an empty table at the far end of the deck. As she walked past the group she'd come from, she wiggled three of her fingers and received smiles mirroring her own exactly calibrated indifference. I just kept looking like the sap they assumed me to be.

She sat in the shade and left me in a sun so hot it made everything but my necktie expand. We hadn't been seated more than a second when a waiter sidled up. He was young and swarthy, with thick lips and a black mustache, tight pants and short red jacket, every man's idea of what every woman likes. He stood with pen poised, silent and still and in a great position to look down the bodice of Ms. Verritt's little white dress. When I said, "Beer," his glance rolled down my face along with my sweat. Tancy Verritt ordered a gimlet and the waiter slipped away on two crepe soles.

Tancy Verritt raised her visor off her head and shook her auburn mane, then lit a cigarette. The nails on the fingers that held it were long and as red as wine. "Well, love? I have court three reserved for exactly ten minutes from now."

I glanced at the empty rectangles beyond the deck. "For what? Air races?"

The paste on her lips cracked. "You don't like the club, do you, Mr. Tanner?"

"I don't waste energy disliking *places,* Ms. Verritt."

"Oh? On what do you expend it, then?"

"People."

In a place where adverse personal comment always came from the backhand side, my forehand took Ms. Verritt aback. "Let's get to the point, shall we?" she said brusquely. "Why did Teresa sic you onto me? Are you a lonely bachelor? A misunderstood husband? Or are you something Tessa thinks I need for what ails me?"

"What ails you, Ms. Verritt?"

She looked at me squarely for the first time. "Boredom, love. Unadulterated boredom."

"Why don't you try spending your time somewhere else?"

She rolled her eyes and curled her lips, and just for a moment something other than her own image came to mind, but she wouldn't or couldn't hold the thought. When the waiter brought the drinks, Tancy Verritt sipped hers avidly, draining half the glass. From the way she slammed the glass to the table she'd already drained several others that morning. Before she spoke again I knew we weren't going to be discussing the Racquet Club any longer. Enough was apparently enough, even for the terminally bored.

"You can tell Tessa she's been neglecting me shamelessly," Tancy Verritt exclaimed suddenly. The anger was mock; the milieu was vaudeville. We were going to ham it up, pretend nothing was wrong with life the way we were living it.

"You mentioned her on the phone, didn't you, love?" she asked when I didn't respond. "Tessa Blair? I haven't mixed you up with someone else, have I? I do that sometimes."

"You're not mixed up, Ms. Verritt. At least not about me."

She let that one skip past. Ace. "Well? What is it you want? Or did you come here just to insult my friends?"

I gave her a relaxed smile, a harmless mien. "I'm here to talk to you about Teresa Blair."

"Tessa?" Her eyes grew. "Oh. Well. What am I, a character reference? Is Tessa up for an ambassadorship? The CIA? Pope?" Her laugh was strained, possibly frightened.

"When's the last time you saw Mrs. Blair?" I asked.

"Let's see. Last week. Right here. Thursday, I think. Thursday morning."

"How did she seem?"

"What do you mean?"

"Was she nervous? Frightened? Angry? Anything at all unusual?"

As her attention shifted to something other than herself, Tancy Verritt's jaunty pose gave way. "What's wrong? What's happened to Tessa?"

"Mrs. Blair is missing," I said flatly.

"No. Oh, no. What happened?"

"I don't know," I admitted. "I was hoping you could tell me."

She was surprised and off balance, and if I could have kept the pressure on, I might have learned everything she knew, but just then a man strolled up to our table, a tennis type. He was cradling three rackets in his arms, as if he was ready to burp them. He wore manufacturers' labels like battle decorations—Head, Prince, Puma, Donnay. He placed a hand on Tancy Verritt's shoulder and asked if she was ready. She shrugged the hand away absently and told the man she couldn't play just yet. She called him by name. His name was Chip. His face stiffened at the rejection and he pranced away, calling out to another woman, setting up a game. He called the woman Mimzy. I looked around for Scott Fitzgerald and John O'Hara. They must have just left.

"How long has Tessa been gone?" Tancy Verritt asked.

"Three days. Since just after you saw her."

"Do the police know?"

"Yes."

"Was it the Vegas people?"

The question was a surprise. It floated there beneath the umbrella, sheltered and safe, for quite some time. "What Vegas people are those?" I asked after a minute.

She plucked at the strap of her dress. "Forget what I said," she ordered. The words caught in her throat. "It's nothing." She didn't believe it and neither did I.

"Did Mrs. Blair live in Vegas? . . . Is someone there after her? . . . Is she running from something?"

Tancy Verritt's head shook through my questions, stamping them void. "Are you a cop?" she asked.

I shook my head. "Private. Her husband hired me."

"James?"

I nodded. "Do you know about Mrs. Blair's problem with a man named Fluto?"

Tancy Verritt nodded. "A little."

"Was Mrs. Blair frightened enough of Fluto to have run off to avoid testifying against him?"

"Are you asking me if that's what I think happened?"

"Sure."

"Well, I most definitely *don't* think that's what happened."

"Why not?"

"Because Tessa wasn't afraid of men. Any men, including that one."

"Explain."

"It's just that Tessa wasn't awed by men. She didn't

need them, didn't use them as crutches, the way a lot of us do. Sometimes I think she didn't even want them."

I took a flier. "Lesbian?"

Her smile was sour. "Don't be ridiculous. All I'm saying is Tessa challenged men. It was an adversary thing, a contest. She gave in once in a while, but it was always on her own terms."

"You sound awfully positive."

"About her not running from Fluto? I am. Tessa was the bravest person I've ever met." She glanced at something behind me. "She may have been the *only* brave person I've ever met," she added with what from her must have been reverence. "God, I hope nothing's happened to Tessa. She's really my only friend, you know? Or was until I caught on to her." Her voice lacked artfulness for the first time since I'd spoken to her on the phone the day before. It was clear she'd forgotten about her spat with Teresa Blair until just that moment.

"What happened?"

"I discovered dear Tessa was using me for a bird dog."

"What do you mean?"

"I talk about my men, love. Always have, always will. Mostly I talked to Tessa. I date a whole lot of guys, some of them even nice, some of them even single. And every time I found a nice single one, he'd drop me a couple of weeks later. Not exactly unprecedented, but I finally found out why my failure rate was zooming. Tessa took them away."

"How'd you find out?"

"One of the guys said something one night. When he was zonked on pot. And after that I started watching Tessa. And I could tell."

"Did you ask her about it?"

"No."

"Why not?"

She shrugged. "What could I say? Men preferred her to me. Any man in his right mind would."

"Did you ask the men about it?"

"One."

"What'd he say?"

"Just that Tessa called him up a few days after I'd told her about him. Arranged a rendezvous at some hideaway. Swore him to secrecy and gave him the best fuck of his life. A few months later she broke it off. Great while it lasted."

"How many guys you figure she did this with?"

"Six. Ten. Who counts?"

Tancy Verritt took a second pull at her drink and finished it off, then beckoned for the waiter to bring her another. "All this raises the possibility Mrs. Blair may have disappeared because of a domestic problem," I said. "Do you know of any reason why she'd want to leave her husband?"

Tancy Verritt chuckled. "Have you met James?"

I nodded.

"Did he tell you how he almost became a Buddhist monk?"

"Yes."

"Well, what he probably didn't tell you was that he lives like a monk anyway. No good food, no good booze, no good sex. Seaweed and sake and Saturday night, that's it for old Jimmy. I don't know what you know about monks, love, but you never hear a lot about how much their wives like it there at the monastery."

I laughed. "So Tessa felt neglected."

"She *was* neglected."

"What did she do about it?"

"The same thing sixty percent of American wives do. Like I said, she fooled around. Very quietly, but all the same."

The waiter placed a fresh gimlet in front of her. She

drained half of it while he was still looking down her dress. "And don't think I'm a snitch. I tell you this only because you say Tessa could be in trouble."

"Did her husband know?"

"No, but that's probably because he never asked."

"Who did she fool with?"

"Lots. At least one of them is sitting within ten yards of you. Another was the guy who came to the table a while back, the one I was supposed to play with this morning. The one I woke up next to about four hours ago." She added the last as though she still didn't quite believe it herself.

I resisted the temptation to look around for the men. "Any point in my talking to them?"

"None."

"Why not?"

"Old news. Tessa hasn't been with either of them in more than a year."

"Do you know the names of all her playmates?"

She shook her head. "I used to, I think. Lately, I'm not so sure."

"Something changed?"

She shrugged. "Tessa just didn't talk about her fucks. I don't know, maybe it's because I spent so much time talking about mine."

She paused a moment, deciding whether to go on. I thought about how Tancy Verritt had just used words similar to those I'd heard from Kathryn Martin the night before. I asked Ms. Verritt if she knew Kathryn Martin. "Never heard of her," she said.

"When I talked with James Blair, he didn't seem to know much about his wife's background," I said. "Where she grew up, her family, things like that. What do you know about her?"

"Nothing. Neither of us is the type to dwell on our pasts."

"Why not?"

She shrugged. "Maybe because all we have going for us is the future. Such as it is."

"I take it from what you said before that she spent some time in Vegas."

"You take it wrong."

She was lying, and she knew I knew it. "Can you tell me anything at all?" I urged. "She could be in serious trouble."

"Sorry."

I pulled out the snapshot and put it on the table next to her drink.

"Where'd you get that?" Her eyes were wide, the words blurted without thought.

"Who is it?"

She glanced quickly around the deck. "I don't know," she said softly. "I never saw him before."

The set of her jaw told me I had all I was going to get. I made one last try. "Who else might know where Mrs. Blair is?"

"If I don't know, I don't think anyone would." She paused. "Unless maybe it was Elliott."

"The owner of Bathsheba's?"

"Yes. Tessa gave it away to lots of guys, but poor Elliott couldn't get any even for a part interest in the store. And he wanted it worse than anyone. He'll probably die trying to get in Tessa's pants." Her smile turned bitter and resigned, and then wasn't a smile at all.

Chapter
6

I flipped some bills on the table and bid Ms. Verritt adieu and strolled back to my car, waving to the guard in the booth as I went by. The engine was running and my hand was on the shift lever when someone else's hand reached through the window and poked me on the shoulder. Hard.

What I saw when I turned was Mr. Tennis himself, "Chip."

"Tancy told me you were asking about Tessa," he said. His voice carried a threat. He'd used it that way before.

"Tancy talks too much," I said pleasantly, "which makes at least three things she does to excess."

"What are the other two?"

"You figure it out the next time you have some spare time." His whole life was spare, and I wanted him to know I knew it.

"I didn't come out here to talk about Tancy," he said. "I don't care about her. No one cares about her. I came to tell you not to go nosing around town asking about me and Tessa."

"Why not?"

"Because it might get back to certain people I'd rather it didn't."

I smiled at his country club puritanism, that peculiar philosophy which deems any act acceptable as long as certain people know about it and certain other people don't. "If you don't want me asking questions about you and Mrs. Blair, why don't you tell me about it? Then I won't have to ring any doorbells."

"There's nothing to tell," he said quickly. "We had some good times a few months back, and then we didn't. That's all there is to it."

"Whose idea was it to stop?"

"Mine." He looked at my skepticism. "All right. It was hers."

"No tears, no recriminations, is that it?"

"You got it," he said mildly.

"You're used to women tossing you out the door, I guess," I taunted.

"Yeah, well, Tessa tossed lots of guys out, one time or another. I was with her as long as anyone."

"How long was that?"

"A month. Just don't advertise it, get it? My wife wouldn't like it. Tessa wouldn't like it either."

"How do you know?"

"She told me she'd cut my balls off if I ever blabbed about us." It was more than he'd wanted to say.

"Okay, Chip," I said roughly. "Why don't you take your sweatlets in there and give them something to do. The first chance I get, I'll ask Mrs. Blair to let you keep your balls."

His face flushed over and above his tan. "Listen, buddy. If you want to talk to someone who had it in for Tessa, look up a guy named Martin. Wayne Martin. He hated her guts."

"How do you know Martin?"

"We used to hang out at the same club. The Buccaneers.

It's kind of a service club downtown. Martin was a member till we threw him out."

"Why'd you do that?"

"He got religion. Started passing out those damned pamphlets at all the meetings. Really a bummer, you know?"

"Why did Wayne Martin hate Mrs. Blair?"

Chip grinned. "He claimed she broke up his marriage, told his wife to throw him out of the house. Old Wayne couldn't get Tessa Blair out of his mind. He was a little crazy about her there for a while. Still is, I imagine. The damned Christer." Chip turned to go. "Just lay off me, man," he said.

I didn't make any promises.

After the Racquet Club the rest of El Gordo looked almost good. The boutique—Bathsheba's—languished behind a narrow storefront that was sandwiched between the macrobiotic diner and the Gucci luggage shop in a shopping mall known as Cash Country. The display windows on either side of the door projected toward the sidewalk in rectangular blisters of glass, subdivided by precise, leaded panes, which were lightly tinted. Behind them two headless mannequins were draped in dresses slit to the thigh from below and to the navel from above and sufficiently thin and clinging to display the mannequins' nipples, which were plastic but nevertheless erect.

I opened the bottom half of the Dutch door and wandered idly among circular clothing racks and tiny display tables and overdressed salesclerks, fingering this and that—a husband on the eve of a double-digit anniversary. Most of the clothes had names or initials on them, which might say something about the ego structure of the women who wore them, or might not. The price tags were computerized and indecipherable. Neither the word "Sale" nor the fabric denim was visible anyplace in the store.

The only person who paid any attention to me was a

young salesgirl, blond and svelte, raised four inches off the floor by heels the size of cheroots. When she noticed me notice her, she sent me a ridiculously maternal smile, but when I gave no clear sign of distress she stayed where she was, which was directly across from a full-length mirror.

If there was an office in the store, I guessed it was in the loft that extended out over the rear half. The walled portion of the loft had a window in it, but it was dark and I couldn't see anyone behind it. I stared at the window long enough for the salesgirl to come over and ask if she could be of assistance.

Her hair was braided into ropes that had bells and feathers attached to them. Her teeth were as white as clouds. I asked if Elliott was in. She said he wasn't, but that he was expected back from lunch any minute. I told her I'd wait awhile. After assuring me she would be pleased to render me aid, she hobbled away on her heels, looking both drunk and palsied and leaving me wondering what thirtieth-century anthropologists will conclude when they unearth a twentieth-century shoe store.

I toured the place for another quarter hour, periodically exchanging witless grins with the young salesgirl. The absence of customers indicated either that the store wasn't doing well—which was not true according to James Blair—or that the profit margins were high enough to dispense with volume.

When the little gold clock on the wall chimed twice I went over to the salesgirl. The brass bells on her braids clanked like a set of loose dentures.

"Slow day," I commented, looking around.

"It usually picks up after lunch."

"Your customers must like to eat," I said, looking at my watch.

"They don't eat much, but they eat long," the girl said, and laughed. "Me, I just scarf it down. I could eat Whoppers all day long."

I looked her over. "It doesn't show."

"Mama says it's my, oh, what's the word?"

"Metabolism."

"That's it. Anyway, seeing as how I've got one I sure hope I can keep it. I love to eat."

The girl was as friendly as a newly weaned puppy. If she knew anything else she would tell me, as long as I didn't get in the way of her upbringing. "This is sure a nice store," I said.

"Isn't it? Oh, I could just hang out here forever. Really. You should see the wallpaper in the women's john."

"I used to know someone who worked here, I think."

"Who?"

"Teresa Blair."

"Mrs. Blair. Sure. I know her. She's the nicest person in the world. Really." Her gloriously unlined brow knit suddenly. "That explains it."

"What?"

"Why she hasn't been in. She must have quit."

"She didn't quit," I said.

"But Elliott—Mr. Farnsworth, he's the owner—he would *never* fire Mrs. Blair. I mean . . ." She struggled for the word.

"You mean he holds her in high personal regard."

"I . . . sure. That's what I mean, I guess. Geez, you talk the same way my boyfriend did when he came home from junior college the first time."

In the silence that followed, the girl became gradually confused, her role suddenly complex, perhaps ominous. I asked where she'd seen Mrs. Blair last. She said she'd seen her Thursday, at work. I asked if she'd known her well.

"I think so. I mean, I liked her a whole lot. She was real good to me. Like a mother. Better than a mother, if you want to know the truth."

"How do you mean?"

"Oh, I had some hard times a while back."

"What kind of hard times?"

The girl was both guileless and garrulous—unless I missed my guess, not long removed from the Central Valley, where people trade life stories the way city folks trade recipes for quiche. She put a hand on a hip and told me hers.

"Ever since I was ten, I wanted to be a model," the girl said seriously. "A fashion model, you know? Cheryl Tiegs? You know her? She's my idol. Her and Cybill Shepherd, except Cybill's too stuck-up. Anyway, after I graduated from high school, Mama drove me down to Frisco and we tried all the modeling agencies, every single one. But they weren't interested, you could just tell, they didn't ask me to wear any fashions or anything, and we were about to give up and go back to Red Bluff and then someone told Mama about this man down on Oswego Street here in El Gordo. So we went down to see him. He acted real nice, and told me I had good cheekbones and calf length and everything, so we signed, Mama and me. But six months later all I had for five hundred dollars was a black-and-blue rear end from being pinched and a job standing all day in a used car lot wearing a white bikini and a red cape and handing out balloons with elephants on them. Mama thought everything was going real good, but only because I didn't tell her what a creep the guy was and some of the things he wanted me to do. I hated to let Mama down—she wanted to see my picture in a fashion magazine so much she could hardly stand it—and there was no one I could talk to about it. Then one day, right after my agent had chased me around the office for about the hundredth time, trying to feel me up, Teresa—Mrs. Blair—saw me standing there on Oswego Street, crying my eyes out in front of God and everybody. Well, she up and took me to a restaurant and bought me whatever I wanted—I had a steak sandwich and cottage fries—and after that she took care of the creep and got me this job and everything. I even got my five hundred dollars back."

"How did she manage that?"

The girl shrugged. "She just did. I think she went down to see the man and he gave it to her."

"What was your agent's name?"

"Lane Starr? Two *r*'s."

"You're kidding."

"No. It's right on the door. The Moran Building."

"What's *your* name?"

"Fawn. Fawn Jones, it was, only I changed it."

"To what?"

"Forest. I'm Fawn Forest now."

I managed to hold my tongue.

"There's nothing wrong with Mrs. Blair, is there?" Fawn asked seriously. "I mean, I'd do *anything* for Mrs. Blair. I really would."

I said something calming but noncommittal, then probed a bit. Fawn wasn't holding back, but she didn't have anything more I could use. She'd never met James Blair or Tancy Verritt, had never heard of Mary Quilk or Silver Season, didn't have any idea where Teresa Blair might be if she wasn't at home. The only place she'd ever gone with Mrs. Blair was to a bar in the shopping center called the Velvet Phone Booth. The only time they'd been there was right after work, during the period when Fawn was having her problems with Lane Starr.

I made one last pass at it. "Did Mrs. Blair say anything at all that might help me locate her?"

"I can't think what it would be. She just gave me advice, mostly."

"What kind of advice?"

"Oh, about what to do with my life. You know. Learn a trade, get a job with a future, don't believe what men say, be good to my family. Things like that."

"Did she tell you anything about her own family?"

"Not really, I guess. She just said your family is the only thing you can count on when things get bad. Not your looks, not your boyfriends, not anything or anybody, only family. I think she must have had some real hard times, too, don't you?"

I nodded. If she hadn't had them before, I had a feeling she was having a few right then.

Just then two women marched through the door like a pair of Prussians and began to paw their way through the store. Fawn excused herself and hurried toward them, a smile as big as my Buick on her face.

The man entering the store just after them was tall, white-haired though not old, as thin as twine. He wore a striped shirt, his slacks were white, his loafers were burgundy, and he wasn't wearing socks. A gold chain was snug at his throat, making it look from a distance as though someone had slit it. His movements were dainty and precise, making him one of those men who has been or has been assumed to be homosexual since the day he left home.

Fawn called out, "Hello, Mr. Farnsworth," then looked back to make sure I realized this was the man I'd been waiting to see.

I hustled along behind Farnsworth, matching him step for step as he climbed to the loft, and trailed him into his office. When he turned and saw me, he started for an instant, then asked if I was the man from Koret of California. I shook my head.

"I only see tradesmen before ten," he said politely. His eyebrows were thin, possibly plucked. When I showed no sign of leaving, they rose like twigs carried aloft by birds.

"I'm an investigator, Mr. Farnsworth," I began. "I'm here because of Teresa Blair."

"Tessa? Is anything wrong?"

"I'm not sure. I hope you can help me find out."

"I . . . who employs you?"

"I'd prefer not to say."

"I see." He curved his fingers and examined his nails as though they were mirrors. "I think perhaps I should call my lawyer."

"Should you?"

His upper lip trembled slightly. "Yes. That is, I'm not certain. I guess it depends on why you're here. I assume James Blair sent you."

"Never mind who sent me. What makes you think you might need legal advice?" I asked heavily.

Farnsworth walked around the desk and wiggled into the chair, seeking comfort but failing to find it. His cheeks were smooth and tan, his hair stylishly awry. "Although I've never met the man," Farnsworth said uncertainly, "it's understandable that Mr. Blair might harbor me ill will. Of course, he has no grounds for displeasure, no *actual* grounds. That is, nothing ever, ah, *came* of any of it. And of course Mrs. Blair has *profited,* that is, the store has been quite successful and Tessa has shared in the profits for over a year now, and I just think we should let bygones by bygones. *I'm* certainly willing to. Perhaps if Mr. Blair and I were to meet without intermediaries? What do you think?"

This babble finally came to a stop, although the guilt that prompted it was unabated. Farnsworth plucked an imported cigarette out of a pack and lit it with a trembling hand. He inhaled the smoke as though it was a mix of four parts courage and one part forgiveness.

"I'd like to know a little about your business, Mr. Farnsworth," I said after a silence that was too long for his comfort. "My name's Tanner."

Farnsworth leaned back in his chair and drummed his fingers on the desk top in bursts of staccato rhythm. "I get it," he said. "It's *me* you're after. Aren't you? Tessa must have told stories. It's an *audit,* isn't it?"

"What makes you think that?"

"IRS or Franchise Tax Board? Which is it?"

I just smiled.

"Was it the Paris trip? Was it that? I bought *several* gowns in Paris. Two Saint Laurents. I can *prove it*. One of them is still on the floor. Do you want to see it? I'll have Fawn model it. She looks stunning, in a bucolic sort of way. Shall I call her?"

Farnsworth became too nonplussed to breathe. His face bleached, and intaglio wrinkles spread across his forehead and leaked from the corners of his eyes. "I'm interested in Teresa Blair, Mr. Farnsworth," I explained, "not in your accounting methods. I'm not IRS or Franchise Tax or even Roto-Rooter."

Farnsworth stared at me for a time. "I'm going to believe you," he said. "I don't care if it *is* a lie, I'm going to believe you. What do you want to know?"

"What's Mrs. Blair's function here at the store?"

"Tessa is the chief buyer and personnel manager of Bathsheba's. I handle the books and the advertising and do some buying myself. Tessa has a one-quarter partnership interest in the business. Now, is that all you want to know? If so, I have work to do." With an exaggerated motion he scraped some papers toward him from the corners of the desk.

"Just a few more things," I said. "How much does Mrs. Blair draw a month?"

A muscle bulged along his jaw, a muscle I doubted had seen much prior use. "I can't imagine what business that could be of yours, at least if you're who you say you are."

I like it when people resist giving out information about their friends or employees. Of course, it seldom takes much to get past the initial resistance, but still. Two points for effort. "You know Mrs. Blair hasn't been at work this week," I said.

"Of course I know that."

"Do you know why?"

He shook his head, his brows angling like carets.

"She's missing," I said. "For four days. Her husband,

along with the El Gordo DA's office, has asked me to find her. You don't have any objections, do you?"

"Of *course* not. This is terrible. I just assumed she was annoyed with me again. She's stayed away before when that's happened."

"Why would she be annoyed with you?"

Farnsworth paused. He had regained some color and some backbone since the conversation had drifted away from his business affairs and into his personal ones. "What do you know about Tessa and me, Mr. Tanner?"

"Not much," I admitted. "Why don't you tell me about it?"

"There's nothing much to tell. I was smitten the first day I laid eyes on her, six years ago. Have you ever been smitten, Mr. Tanner?"

"My seventh-grade music teacher. She wore perfume and no slips. Whenever she asked me to sing, I sounded like a cross between a bullfrog and a bulldozer."

Farnsworth smiled for the first time since I'd entered his office. "Then you know what I mean. I'm helpless in Tessa's presence. I admit it freely. She has given me my sexual . . . identity, I suppose you could say. I would give *her* anything. I *have* given her a share of my store. Of my life. I would give more if asked."

"What have you gotten in return?"

His smile twisted with embarrassment. "Professionally, an excellent business partner. Personally, only her presence. Her proximity. My love is entirely unrequited, to put it bluntly, but I must confess I do become excessively ardent at times, and Tessa becomes justly exasperated. When she didn't come in on Friday, I simply assumed she needed to be away from me for a while."

"I'm afraid it may be more mysterious than that," I said. "If I knew more about her financial situation, I might be able to estimate more precisely where she might have gone."

"I see." Farnsworth gave some more thought to his position. "I suppose I must trust you, under the circumstances. I can hardly call Mr. *Blair* to vouch for you." He opened a drawer and pulled out a long, gray ledger and opened it, then nodded. "Tessa draws fifteen hundred dollars a month. On the first. Some of it is in merchandise, of course, but not always. In fact, lately she seems to have been taking strictly cash."

I thought about the additional deposit of twelve hundred dollars Mrs. Blair made on the fifteenth of every month. "Are you sure that's all she ever draws?"

He nodded. "I keep very close track of my cash flow. I *have* to," he added defensively.

"How much is her partnership interest worth?"

"Roughly fifty thousand."

"That's roughly a nice piece of change. I'm finding it hard to believe you gave it up for mere proximity."

Farnsworth shrugged. "Believe what you will. I don't pretend my gesture was rational, and I don't claim that I didn't hope that eventually more would come of it. But it didn't. It never will. Still, Tessa is here five afternoons a week. Quid pro quo."

Farnsworth asked me some questions about the police investigation of Mrs. Blair's disappearance, and about Tony Fluto and his possible involvement. I asked him about Mrs. Blair's background and friends, and neither of us got much out of the other. Teresa Blair had led Farnsworth around like an unbroken terrier, and somehow he had managed to retain some dignity and objectivity during it all. But he knew nothing of her background or her home life, had never met her husband, had rarely been alone with her. He didn't believe for a moment that she had love affairs with other men, but if she had he knew nothing about them. Because I was beginning to feel sorry for him, I said the rumors about her love affairs were most likely untrue, the stuff of jealousy and envy.

I asked Farnsworth to let me know if he heard from Mrs. Blair and he promised he would. He also promised to have the bank call him if Mrs. Blair wrote a check on the store account. He also promised to call if he remembered anything that might be helpful.

I was halfway down the steps from the loft, giving some thought to my next move, when Farnsworth called me back. "There's *one* thing," he said when I got back to his office.

"My shame is bottomless," he began apologetically. "But I suppose I must tell you this. I hope you understand." He took a deep breath. "For a period of several weeks, back when my infatuation was at its peak, I used to follow Tessa when she left work at the end of the day. Just to watch her, to see what she did with the rest of her life. To make her just a little more *mine*, I suppose. Can you *believe* it?"

"Sure. I make a living doing the same thing."

Farnsworth smiled. "Thank you for that, but it's not the same and you know it. Anyhow, a few weeks after I started my little espionage, Tessa saw me. I knew if she discovered me again she'd realize what I was doing and most likely leave the store for good, so I stopped."

"What kinds of things did she do?"

"The usual, mostly. But one time she did do something rather strange."

"What?"

"She went to a completely disgusting place down on Tenth and Oswego, off El Camino. You know where that is?"

I shook my head. It was the third time Oswego Street had been mentioned, though each time by a different person. I began to get interested in the neighborhood.

"Well, it's a rough area. Perfectly *filthy*. Warehouses, a few slums, some tacky stores."

"What did she do down there?"

"She parked outside a decrepit old warehouse and went inside and stayed for almost an hour."

"Which warehouse was it?"

"There was a sign on it, something like El Gordo Industries, I think, but I couldn't tell what kind of business it was. Frankly, it looked abandoned. *Quarantined*, even."

"Anything else happen?"

"Yes, as a matter of fact. After Tessa was inside the warehouse, this rather seedy-looking family—husband, wife, and child—drove up in a *truck* of all things, and they all piled out and went inside the same building. That is, the woman and the child did. The man stayed in the truck and smoked. Then finally Tessa came back out and left, so I did, too."

"Was she still by herself?"

"Yes."

"Did you ask her about it?"

"Of course not. She'd have known I was following her."

"When was this?"

"About a year ago. Maybe longer."

"Ever see any of the people again?"

"No."

"Did you get the license number of the truck?"

"No. Why would I?"

"Anything else you can tell me about it?"

"Not really. It just seemed strange, is all."

I thought so, too.

I thanked Farnsworth, and trotted down the loft steps. As I passed her along the way, Fawn Forest waved and smiled and tickled my ears with the sound of her bells.

Chapter
7

I reentered the acquisitive swirl of the mall and headed back to where I'd parked—aisle 6, row 13 of Tulip Lot, between Hyacinth and Gardenia lots—but when I saw a pay phone rising like a periscope out of a bed of azaleas, I sat down on the bench across from it and waited for a girl in clear plastic slacks and a crocheted bikini halter to finish her call. From the look on her face, the party on the other end was her lover or her savior or her pusher. I had a feeling that for her they each performed the same function.

For the next several minutes I watched people shop, watched them glide from store to store with movements more feline than human, acquiring merchandise that would have made their grandparents quail and consult the Bible for both an explanation and an admonition. We already have too much but we want still more. It's a disease that no one wants to cure.

Without meaning to, I began thinking over what I knew about the Blair case. A few seconds later I did something more productive—I thought about what I *didn't* know about the case. That was the surprise, of course, how little anyone knew about Teresa Blair, and what different aspects she presented to the various people who thought they knew her well. To her husband she was the perfect if somewhat distant spouse; to Tancy Verritt she was a fellow swinger who used sex like a dueling pistol; to Fawn Forest she was a motherly confidante; to Elliott Farnsworth, an irresistible siren; to Kathryn Martin, a psychological prop. It seemed possible that, like most people who try to be all things to all people, the real Teresa Blair might not in fact exist at all. Luckily, I hadn't been hired to find out what she was. Only where.

The girl in the plastic pants moved away and I put in a call to my answering service. Both Kathryn Martin and James Blair had called. I tried Mrs. Martin at home but got no answer. James Blair was in his office; his voice sounded weary and wary. He wanted to know if I'd come up with anything. I told him I hadn't.

"I've trained myself not to express emotion," Blair said slowly. "You should not assume from this that I have none, Mr. Tanner. I want Teresa back. Very badly."

"I'll do what I can," I said, then waited for him to go on. When he didn't, I replaced the receiver, looked up the Lane Starr Agency in the Yellow Pages and jotted the address in my notebook, dodged three girls on roller skates and one man on muscatel, and found the Tulip Lot. I pointed my Buick south. By the time I'd gone a mile, I'd spotted the green car that had tailed me the day before. I let it tag along.

Oswego Street east of El Camino ran along the extreme south edge of the city. The area was mostly industrial and mostly decayed, a jumble of buildings that had lost both color and utility over the years. On the north side of town were the new industries—the microcircuit plants, the software manufacturers, the solar engineers—but on the south side were the businesses that time had left bruised and orphaned—the foundries, the asphalt contractors, the steel fabricators, the rail yards. And in the middle of the warehouses and the freight depots and storage tanks and mounds of rock and sand were the people that time had left adrift as well—the old and the sick and the poor—wedged into bungalows and apartments that crumbled minute by doleful minute, from a lack of hope as much as from a lack of funds.

The intersection of Ninth and Oswego was nothing special, its chief features a pothole the size of Nebraska and an abandoned Texaco station that was sprayed with enough graffiti to fill the Egyptian Book of the Dead. The buildings were flush with the streets—no set-back zoning for this part of town—and the lines for the crosswalks had been obliterated by decades of commercial traffic. Even an alert driver would have had trouble avoiding a man who staggered from between two buildings and into his path. For someone driving as fast as Fluto had been, it would be virtually impossible.

The warehouse Elliott Farnsworth had seen Teresa Blair enter was just one block down. It was old, naturally, its shell a scaly, dusty brick. Tar had leaked over the flat roof and streaked the face of the building with black, perpetual tears. The windows high in the walls had all been targets for neighborhood sharpshooters. We did the same thing when I was young, but with rocks. I didn't even want to guess what kind of weaponry the current crop of kids had used.

I walked around the place, fear gradually becoming a tangible presence in the pit of my stomach. There was a lake of filth on the ground, as though it had recently rained garbage. Beneath the filth was dirt the color of dawn, baked bone-hard. Against the back fence was a ramshackle structure built from discarded shipping crates, oil drums, and sheets of corrugated tin. A sound came from inside it, a rustling sound. I made no effort to learn if it was a rat or a man or something worse than either.

The bay doors on the side of the building were locked, their fittings rusted, unused for years. The wooden freight dock listed above rotten pilings. A dolly with one wheel missing leaned against the wall, crippled and abandoned. An engine block lay in the middle of the freight yard, valve covers and pistons missing, its cylinders as black as mortars. I went back around to the front.

There was nothing elaborate about the main entrance. A single small door was cut into the wall at the right corner. The sign over it read "El Gordo Industrial Services— Contractors Use Rear Entrance." I tried the knob, but it was frozen. The fit between the door and jamb was loose, however, the wood soft and yielding as I scratched at it with my knife. The dead bolt was loose as well, and would almost certainly break clear if I applied enough pressure. I glanced up and down the deserted block, then walked back to my car and climbed inside and debated whether to commit a felony.

I turned the key and flipped on the radio and closed my eyes and leaned back and thought about breaking and entering for a while. The girl singing through the radio was called Blondie, but she didn't sound like anyone Dagwood ever knew. When the song ended I shook my head and opened my eyes.

There were nine of them, as young and vivid as dreams, sauntering down the street to the pulse of some rhythm and blues that spurted like blood from a tape deck the size of a tire that one of them balanced on his shoulder and pressed to his ear. They were different shapes and sizes, even different sexes, but they were a monolith all the same, a many-footed, hydra-headed juggernaut that owned the world or this part of it.

While I struggled to become fully awake the gang spotted me and began to approach my car, moving surely and silently, as though specifically assigned to nullify me. Their shirts, even the girls', were cut off at the shoulders and the sternum, revealing rolling arms and sculpted bellies and the lower arc of breasts. From half a block away they had seen everything about me that was relevant—I was white and I was alone and I was on their turf and I wasn't a cop. By the time I decided I'd be better off outside the car it was too late to get there.

They swarmed over the Buick, leaning on the doors and fenders, sitting on the hood and trunk. I was a corpse in a glass coffin. One girl and a bullet-headed boy I decided was the leader watched the action from a distance, alert for a new and thrilling variation on the theme. Words came at me like bats. Bristly spheres of hair bobbed beyond the windows, as menacing as brandished maces. I was fully awake and fully afraid, the fear was as real as it was irrational. When one of them backed away from the door for an instant, I opened it and clambered outside, fleeing my carriage to the grave.

"Hey, pops."

"What's shakin', motherfucker?"

"You lost, Jack?"

"You dealing, man?"

The leader took a step forward, his eyes ablaze with atavistic cunning. The rest of them fell silent. "Only two reasons a white man come down here, friend," he said mildly, his voice accented and slurred. "To pick up the rent or to pick up some pussy. Which *you* after?" He smiled with lethal friendliness. He had played this game before.

I didn't say anything. The leader turned toward the girl. "Hey, Wanda. I think the dude here is after some of that Rutland Avenue pussy. You figure his dick will reach that far?"

"Ain't no *white* man's dick gonna reach that far."

"You the one that knows, Wanda."

And with the girl's low laugh and the leader's false grin the gibing and strutting, the smiles and sneers and curses began again, and what it all came down to was that they weren't sure yet whether they were looking for fun or for blood, or whether there was any longer a reason to choose one over the other. For long minutes I could think of no response that wouldn't increase my risk.

"Do you live around here?" I asked, looking at the leader.

His lips were strangely soft and feminine, but the eyes above them were from the center of the earth. For a long time nothing above his neck had moved. "What's it to you, man?" he asked finally.

"I'm interested in that building over there," I said and pointed. "Any idea who owns it?"

"You gonna move in, man? Bust the block? Ruin the fucking property values?" His smile was sarcastic, almost sadly so.

"The man gonna put in a disco. Gonna bring Sister fucking Sledge down here to *sing* to the blood."

"Naw, he gonna put in one of them community *action* centers, to get the brothers thinking more about the white man's politics than about his own black self."

"I bet it be one of them condofuckingminiums. With a view of the *ghetto* for the man."

The leader held up his hand and the jesting stopped. "We interested in *you*, pops," he said softly. "You got any money to pay for learning the shit about that building?"

"A little."

"How little?"

"Twenty."

"Shit."

"Twenty-five, if it's good."

"Get it out."

"I don't think so."

"I said get the bread *out*, man."

"It's bad business to pay before receiving the merchandise. You tell me about the building; I hand you the money."

"You do your business down *here*, pops, *I* the one say what's good business and what ain't. Now get it *out*." He held out his hand, palm up. The ivory fingers seemed to accuse me of something, perhaps two hundred years of abominations.

I shook my head.

The leader snapped his fingers. I heard a whir and a click, the sound of a blade snapping out of a sheath and locking. They moved in close around me in the next few seconds, driving me back against the car door.

Time was dead. The one with the knife moved to where I could see him and began waving it with the grace of Stokowski. I looked to see if Grinder's men in their green car were anywhere around, and when I didn't spot them, I spent some time planning what I would do when the knife made its move. The plan wasn't worth a damn.

"The dude drives a Buick, Leon."

The voice came from somewhere behind me. It sounded like the girl Wanda but I couldn't be sure and couldn't afford to look. "He gotta be a pig. I say we leave him be."

"You remember what Buck say about that building, Leon. He say don't mess with it."

"Yeah, Leon. Besides. Sly's holding some China White over on Wabash. He won't wait, man. Leave the motherfucker be."

I didn't see who they were, my saviors, because I still had my eye on the kid with the knife. The only sound was the scrape of shoes on the street.

Leon thought it over. Although I did nothing but live and breathe, he finally backed off. Moving as slow as Sunday, he reached into his pocket and pulled out a black leather pouch, then dipped his little finger in and extracted some powder in the crescent of his half-inch fingernail. With a face that showed neither pleasure nor pain he snorted the powder up a nostril then turned and walked on down the street. Wanda snuggled quickly to his side. The others fell into place behind them and ambled off, as full of life as tiger cubs, as beautiful and as deadly and as branded from the day of birth.

Leon and his friends had exhausted my ration of courage. I had no desire to prowl in empty buildings, peek in dark huts, challenge hidden rooms. I got back in my car and drove two blocks and parked again.

The Moran Building was the centerpiece of an Oswego Street commercial oasis that, like its surroundings, had seen better days, though not recently. Still, the area had a cosmopolitan air to it, with an Italian market and an Irish saloon sharing the block with a taco stand and an S. S. Kresge and a soul food café. The Moran Building itself sheltered Mimi's House of Beauty and a cigar store at the street level. Directly above, the words "Notary Public" and "Income Tax" were printed on a third-story window in yellow enamel. I went inside.

There was no building directory but there were stairs and I took them. My shoes caused the grit on the steps to crackle.

On the second floor Marilyn Montegna, Public Stenographer, shared the fetid dimness with a real estate broker and a credit dentist. The two other offices had For Rent signs taped to their doors. I kept climbing.

The third floor had even fewer attractions. A used-clothing store and a rare-coin dealer faced each other at one end of the hall, and a collection agency and a tax preparer did likewise at the other. In between was the office of Lane Starr Commercial Modeling Agency. I started to laugh, and then didn't. If I'd lived in El Gordo, my office would have been on the next flight up.

The door to Starr's office was open. The office was a single room, drab and sparely furnished except for the walls, which blazed with the color of magazine photos, carefully clipped from their original bindings and covered with sheets of acetate and pinned in place with colored thumbtacks, four per picture. At one time there had been a whole row of them, circling the room like a high-fashion equator, but there were gaps in the ring now, places where the pictures had fallen or been removed, possibly by the desperate fingers of those who aspired to displace their subjects professionally.

I looked away from the decor. A man was sitting behind a battered metal desk at the back of the room, feet up, head back, mouth open: asleep. A small crater had formed in the sole of his right shoe and a brown scorch mark lay like a slug on his shirt front. He smelled like socks and wet cigars. I called his name twice, then pounded on the desk till it rattled enough to wake him.

"What the hell? Who the fuck?"

Starr righted himself and brushed the ashes off his shirt and got his feet on the floor beneath the desk. "Late night," he apologized. "Contract negotiations."

There are all kinds of contracts. Ordering a drink at a bar is a contract, and from the blue veins that crawled up the flanks of Starr's nose I guessed those were the contracts with which he was most conversant.

"Well, where is she?" Starr asked. "Down the hall? Jesus, that's a sewer, not a toilet. You should have asked, I'd have sent you to the second floor. Oh, well."

His geniality was as misplaced as his accent, which was Brooklyn. I told him there was no one in the john.

"Well, get her in here then. Let's have a look."

"There's no one with me."

"No?" His voice lost cheer. "Beat it, mac. I handle broads. This is a modeling agency, not a hiring hall. Get lost."

"Fawn Forest," I said.

"Who?"

"Fawn Forest."

His brow wrinkled, and a bit too much light came from

behind the puffy lids that shaded his eyes. "Never heard of her."

"Sure you have."

"Says who?"

"Teresa Blair."

"Who?" His eyes hopped on coals of guilt.

I put my hands on the desk and leaned toward him. "You signed Fawn Forest to one of those personal services contracts you negotiate, and copped her five hundred, then let her rot except for a stint at a used car lot and some laps around the desk. In other words, business as usual. But all of a sudden Teresa Blair came to see you, and all of a sudden Fawn had her money back. Am I helping you remember?"

A line of sweat broke out on Starr's upper lip. "So? The chickie was upset. I want my clients to be happy—a happy model means a happy layout. She wanted the money, I gave her the money. Big deal."

"Bullshit."

"Hey. What kind of talk is that? Listen, you from the state? The DA? Who? I got a legitimate business here, you know what I'm saying? I provide chickies to guys who get their jollies looking at tits and ass. And that's no crime. I treat my girls right, too. No rough stuff. Not like some guys in the business, send the chickies anywhere and half the time they come back looking like hamburger patties, you know what I'm saying? Sure, I take a little out in trade when I can, but what the hell? What's a piece of ass, anyway? The chickies expect it. I don't come on to them right away they pull out a pocket mirror and start looking for zits."

I leaned even closer to him. His breath threatened to melt my teeth. "I just want to know what Teresa Blair told you that persuaded you to give Fawn her money back."

"That's all?"

"That's all."

"Who are you?"

"It doesn't matter."

Starr nodded twice, then reached into the desk, pulled out a cigar and lit it, then puffed mightily to get it fueled, making sounds of milking machines and offset presses. Finally he looked at me again, through a milky cloud. "You live here in town?" he asked carefully.

I shook my head. "San Francisco."

"Yeah. Nice town. Compared to Frisco's skin men I'm an Eagle Scout, you know what I'm saying? Well, this Blair broad, what she does is she mentions some names to me."

"What names?"

"It don't matter," he said, throwing my words back at me. "What matters is that these were names that broads like this Blair woman don't usually know. These were names that my life wouldn't be worth fish heads in this town if I went up against them. For five yards it didn't seem worth finding out if she was trying to stiff me, you know what I'm saying?"

"What else did Mrs. Blair say?"

"Nothing. In and out in thirty seconds. What's her story, anyway?"

"That's what I'm trying to find out," I said, then left. The clatter of someone else's footsteps preceded me down the stairs.

Chapter
8

When I walked out the door of the Moran Building, the green car was double-parked beside my Buick and a pair of Grinder's men were standing on the sidewalk, hands in pockets, waiting for me. One of them was below average in all visible respects, with a hairstyle that prevails at boot camps and prisons. The other was big and bald. They both wore double-knit suits, wide ties, and Hush Puppies.

"What's the matter, men?" I asked heartily. "Grinder afraid I'll find her before he does?"

The smaller one smiled, displaying the chipped tooth that my friend in the pith helmet had seen, but the big one just stayed big. "We just want to ask you a question, Mr. Tanner. And then give you a tip."

"What's the question?"

"The question is, what does this guy Starr you've been visiting have to do with Teresa Blair's disappearance?"

"Nothing as far as I know," I said, knowing I would not be believed. "Now what's the tip?"

The small one glanced briefly at the big one. The big

one shrugged. The small one crossed his arms. "The tip is to leave town, Tanner. Right now. Forget you ever heard of Teresa Blair or Tony Fluto or El Gordo, either. Go back to San Franciso and ride a cable car or dress up in drag or whatever else turns you on. Get the picture?"

He was serious, and it meant he and his partner weren't from Conway Grinder at all. Which meant they could be from another faction of the El Gordo police, or, even more likely, from Tony Fluto himself.

I looked at the men more closely. They seemed used to giving orders and used to being obeyed. I couldn't figure it out, but the East End of El Gordo wasn't the best place to be doing the figuring. I moved toward my car. "That all you got to say?" I asked.

"If you're smart, that's enough," the small one answered.

"The last tip I got wasn't worth a damn," I said. "Horse called Fleet Foot. Flat Foot was more like it. Ever since then I've been real leery about gratuitous advice." I opened the door to the car and got inside.

The small one followed me and leaned in the window, his breath hot on my neck. "You don't want to counteract us, Tanner. Believe me, you don't."

"Who owns you, pal?" I asked. "Tony Fluto?"

He frowned. "Fuck you," he said, and backed away and slid behind the wheel of the green car. The big one clambered in beside him and they drove the green car away, leaving me alone with a cloud of hydrocarbons.

I let the engine idle and my thoughts along with it. They both needed a tune-up. Something had been strange about the case from the beginning, the waves far too big for the tiny and fortuitous pebble that supposedly had launched them. But as yet I didn't have enough boards to build a lifeboat.

On the assumption I was still being watched, I drove over to El Camino and headed north, then stopped at a Denny's just outside the El Gordo city limits. I went inside and ordered a patty melt, then squeezed into the phone booth while I waited for the sandwich. LaVerne Blanc, professional gossip and practicing alcoholic, answered after a dozen rings. I asked him how he was.

"If I was any lower, you'd have to dig a hole to kick my ass," LaVerne answered, his words sloshing like beer in a keg. "What's on your mind besides premature ejaculation?"

I laughed. "You're projecting again, LaVerne. I'm calling from El Gordo."

"My sympathies."

"You know much about the place?"

"What's to know? The world ever gets a set of the piles, it'll get them in El Gordo. And if you got something more specific in mind you better make it snappy. There's some crazy cunt in here, keeps threatening to wrap duct tape around my pecker so she can mount me again."

"A man named Fluto, LaVerne. Tony Fluto. Runs a paint contracting business down here. What else can you tell me about him?"

LaVerne was silent for a long time, and in my imagination his crazy girlfriend carried out her threat. "I can tell you some things you won't want to know, Marsh. Not if you're mixed up in his shit. Why don't you leave it be?"

"Can't do it, LaVerne. You know how it is. Got to save face."

"Hey. You worried about your face, you stay the hell away from Tony Fluto. A tough old duck. Believe me."

"What's the story, LaVerne?" I asked, suddenly not at all eager to know.

LaVerne snorted something through his nose and swallowed it. "What do you know about mob activity around the Bay, Marsh?"

"The mob?" I repeated stupidly.

"Mafia. Cosa Nostra. The syndicate. Are these terms at all familiar to you, Tanner?" LaVerne asked sarcastically.

"It just wasn't what I expected you to say. I know

Duckie Bollo calls the tune in San Franciso, and some guy named Donatelli heads the family in San Jose. There's one in Oakland, too, I think."

"Sure. But you're talking big time. Mafia. Sicilians. East Coast shit. What we're talking when we're talking Tony Fluto is the rest of the places around here, the Haywards and Fremonts and San Mateos and El Gordos. The action in those burgs is organized, too. Not by Sicilians, necessarily, but organized all the same. And even though it's small potatoes in Mafia terms, there's still big bucks involved. A little graft here, a kickback there, some extortion and loan sharking over there, it adds up to a pretty big number. The way I understand it is, a guy from each of the towns I named, plus San Leandro and Palo Alto, too, they get together twice a month for dinner. Once in Jack London Square, once at the Pruneyard. And they divvy up the action, everything from coke deals to garbage collection to linen service to massage parlors."

"And the man from El Gordo is Tony Fluto," I said.

"You got it, Marsh. Been the big man down there for a long time. Plus, Tony's got a little specialty of his own."

"What?"

"Arson. Tony's a torch."

"Shit."

Arson. The word was frightening to me, more frightening than murder. I knew the number of arson cases was climbing dramatically, in the Bay area and elsewhere, increasing twenty-five percent a year and more, to the point where fully half of all fires were believed intentionally set. A few years ago the motive usually involved revenge or vandalism, but when the prime rate hit twenty percent and the recession arrived as a result, a lot of businessmen were pushed to the edge, and arson was the best way out, or so it looked to some. If it's done right, it's virtually impossible to tell a crime has even been committed, and even if it's done wrong, there's seldom any link to the torch that hasn't been burned to a pile of ash.

But none of that was the source of my fear. When I was about nine, my family's house caught fire in the middle of the night. When I woke up, my father was carrying me through a sheet of blue and yellow flame that seemed as high as Mars, through smoke that squeezed my throat like a monster's hand. Even now I see those flames at least once a month, at some time between midnight and morning. I'm told that when I see them I scream.

"Anything else?" I asked.

"That's plenty for a sane man," LaVerne said, then cursed. "Christ. Now she's trying to put an ice cube in my drink. The woman's a sadist." LaVerne hung up.

I went back to the counter and nibbled my patty melt, thinking of fires and the kind of people who set them, and about the men who had warned me to stay away from El Gordo. When the last french fry was gone, I got in my Buick and drove north long enough to make sure I wasn't being tailed, then doubled back to El Gordo and took side streets to the rear of City Hall and parked. Ray Tolson wasn't glad to see me.

"I've got no time, Tanner," he said when he saw me come through the door.

"If you want me to stay on the Blair case, you'd better make some," I told him.

He looked at me closely, then gestured to a chair and picked up his phone and said something I couldn't hear, then put it down. "What's the problem?" he asked mildly.

"Prevarication."

"Whose?"

"Yours."

"Such as?"

"Oh, the local paint contractor who turns out to be an arsonist. The little hit-and-run case that's more like a vendetta by you and Grinder against organized crime in El Gordo. Little things like that."

Tolson grinned.

"I suppose you're throwing in the towel," he said.

"I don't know yet. If it wasn't for one thing I would."

"What thing is that?"

"I'll get to it later."

"So what do you want me to do?" Tolson asked.

"Start at the beginning. And this time try the truth."

"Okay," Tolson said. "I would have in the first place but I thought you'd refuse the job if you knew."

"If you thought that, then I wasn't the man for the job anyway."

"I suppose not," Tolson agreed. "First, Fluto. You're right, he runs things here and on top of that he's a torch. We estimate he's been responsible for at least fifty fires in the area over the past couple of years. The losses come to more than twenty million, give or take. You can imagine the pressure we're under from the insurance companies. They shell out two billion a year on arson claims and they're getting real tired of it. We've been after Tony for years, for arson and other things. Our office has a special Arson Task Force and Tony's their number one priority. But so far, nothing."

"How does he operate?"

"Tony's a bit obvious, but he's not stupid. He leaves the actual torching to his son and the scum he hangs around with. Tony's more the broker. A finder, so to speak, peddling fire for hire. He buys off clerks in fire and casualty companies in Dallas and Omaha and in financial institutions all around the Bay. From them he learns which businessmen are flirting with Chapter Eleven of the Bankruptcy Act and what their fire insurance arrangements are. When he has the poop, Tony knocks on their door and makes them an offer, right down to the penny. When he throws some crooked public adjusters into the act, men who'll jack the damage estimate by a factor of three once Tony's dropped the building, he can present a package that has enough juice in it to make everyone happy. You'd be surprised how many previously upright businessmen take old Tony up on his deal."

"No, I wouldn't."

Tolson raised his eyebrows. "Maybe you wouldn't, at that. Maybe that's why they suggested I give you a call."

"Who's 'they'?"

"Does it matter?"

"Only to my biographer, I guess. What about the dead guy, Tolson? Was this a hit?"

"I don't think so. Tony just had some bad luck."

"And what was bad for Tony was good for you."

"Right. We were a lead pipe cinch to send Tony to Quentin with a felony conviction, and once we got him there it was better than even he'd never get out. Tony's made a lot of enemies getting where he is. He cut a lot of guys out of some lucrative action along the way, for one thing, and put some of his more ambitious competitors beneath a monument, for another, so it's real likely Tony would end up with a fork in his throat at Quentin. Either that or the Board of Prison Terms would see to it he never made parole. Yep, we had it made."

"You and Grinder. Making El Gordo safe for democracy."

"Is that something I'm supposed to be ashamed of, Tanner?" Tolson asked soberly.

"I guess not," I answered, sober as well and not particularly pleased about it. "What's Fluto been up to?"

"Still no sign of him. But his people are going about their business as though nothing was wrong. How about your end?"

"Not much," I said. "Teresa Blair's descended from a long line of chameleons, from all I can tell. A different shade every hour. I've talked to several people but I don't have a line on her at all. It's not impossible, though, that she just left her husband, for reasons that don't have anything to do with Tony Fluto."

"That could make it tough."

I agreed with him.

"Anything I can do to help?" Tolson asked.

I considered his offer. Normally I like to keep the cops out of my business entirely, even on a case when we're supposed to be cooperating. But I decided to let Tolson do a little of my legwork. "There's a chance Teresa Blair spent time in Vegas some time back," I said.

"Doing what?"

"I don't know."

"When?"

"No idea."

"Where'd you get the tip?"

"Her friend, a woman named Tancy Verritt. When I told her Mrs. Blair was missing, she immediately mentioned Vegas, or more precisely, 'the Vegas people.' When I tried to follow up, she dummied up. There's something there, but I can't guarantee it'll help you find her."

"I'll call the Vegas police and let you know."

"She was probably using her maiden name back then," I said. "Goodrum. She's called Tessa by most of the people who know her."

"But not by her husband," Tolson observed.

"Very astute."

"What people have you been talking to?" Tolson asked.

I didn't see any reason not to tell him, so I ran through the list of names. I got no reaction to any of them. "What do you know about an outfit called El Gordo Industrial Services?" I asked. "Has a warehouse down on Tenth and Oswego."

"Nothing comes to mind. What should I know about it?"

"I'm not sure. Teresa Blair was seen going in there a year or so back."

"What was she doing?"

"I'm not sure of that, either. Neither was the man who saw her. The place isn't exactly her style."

"I'll ask around."

"Where exactly on Oswego did Fluto run over the guy?" I asked.

"Let me check the file."

Tolson thumbed through a stack of papers as thick as a prime filet. "Ninth and Oswego."

"A block away from the warehouse," I said.

"So?"

"Who knows? You said Fluto had some competitors from time to time. Who are the current ones?"

"I think you'd best let me worry about that," Tolson said.

"Don't worry, I'll be happy to. I just thought the names might help, in case one of them invites me in for tea."

"Well, this isn't my area of specialization," Tolson said, "but there's a guy named Moskowitz, he's into hot cars and gambling, and a guy named Wadley, owns a restaurant and controls food and liquor distribution, things like that. And a black guy named Buck, he's into drugs. But Fluto's still the king."

"How old is he?"

"Seventy, give or take."

"Somebody may think it's time for the king to abdicate."

"Maybe," Tolson agreed. "Well, you going to stay on it?"

"I guess so," I said. "But only because some guy with a haircut like a drill sergeant told me to get out of town. And because Teresa Blair sounds like a woman I'd like to meet."

"Good," Tolson said. "Fluto makes life tougher than it needs to be for about half the people in this town, one way or another. You'll be doing a real service to help us convict him."

"Service to whom?" I asked. Tolson didn't answer. "There's one last thing," I went on.

"What?"

"Is there any chance Teresa Blair's a plant?"

"What?"

"You know what I'm talking about, Tolson. Mrs. Blair came onto the scene pretty late in the day. Without her, Fluto would walk, according to you and according to the papers. What if she was sent down here by one of Fluto's competitors, so she could put him behind bars?"

"What the fuck makes you think that's even remotely possible?" Tolson asked wildly.

"I'm not sure," I said. "Mrs. Blair drops some tough names around town, according to a little man down in the Moran Building. Plus the Vegas thing. Plus a feeling I've got that something's rotten in the city of El Gordo."

"You're wrong, Tanner. You've got to be."

"Maybe."

"Okay. I'll go over her statement again. But I'm sure she's genuine. She knew too much about what went on down there to be a plant. Things she couldn't have known unless she saw it all go down. I'm sure of it." His last words were firm enough to move reality.

"I'll check in later," I said.

"Good," Tolson answered, then rubbed his face. "The trial starts Monday." He made it sound like Doomsday.

Chapter
9

You take your leads where and when you find them. I found mine on a billboard high above the Bayshore Freeway as I was driving north out of El Gordo, looking without enthusiasm for a motel to occupy for the night. The metallic gold letters on the royal blue background were lit from below, and in the gray of early evening their message seemed elegant and warm and boundlessly sincere:

SILVER SEASON

The Retirement Residence
and Custodial Facility
for the Young at Heart

Located in the San Ramon Valley,
in the Shadow of Mount Diablo
Rock Valley Road Exit off I-680
A Project of the Columbus Development Company

Teresa Blair was paying some two thousand dollars every month to the Silver Season, and she didn't need either a residence or a custodian. I abandoned my search for a motel and kept driving.

The route took me across the Bay Bridge, through Oakland and the Caldecott Tunnel and Orinda to Walnut Creek, where I turned south for about ten miles, then took the Rock Valley Road exit just south of Danville. For about ten minutes I meandered among the rail fences and flagstone driveways, carefully rustic outbuildings and adobe haciendas of Contra Costa County's horsey set. Nothing that happened anywhere in the world—whether famine or pestilence, riot or revolution—could possibly penetrate this little valley, this decorator remnant of the Wild West. That was the way they wanted it, and that was the way it was.

Some three miles east of the freeway the road began to climb toward the top of a grassy knoll that had somehow escaped the developer's blade. At the summit was an arched gateway with the words "Silver Season" etched, in silver of course, along its top. A brass plate set into the stone gatepost announced that I had arrived at a Retirement Residence, Est. 1972.

A cobbled driveway took me through a stand of live oaks and Scotch pines to a macadam parking area occupied by the kinds of cars that serve more as announcements than conveyances. I slipped in between two of them and tried to decide how to proceed in light of my rather pervasive ignorance of what was in there waiting for me.

While I thought about it, a young nurse in a powder blue pants suit walked through the lot and passed me without noticing. She was lithe and unburdened and humming a tune old enough for me to recognize. The kid who'd sung it originally was dead. The Day the Music Died. I got out and followed the nurse under a canopy and through the heavy oaken door at the end of it.

A sign on a chrome pedestal placed just inside the door welcomed me to the Silver Season, then ordered me to Proceed to the Administrator's Office Before Attempting to Visit a Resident. I decided to obey, and yellow arrows taped to the smooth green floor showed me how.

A string of offices opened onto the hallway. If I deciphered the abbreviations on the doorplates correctly they contained a medical doctor, an osteopath, a chiropractor, a dentist, two nurses, and another individual who could have been anything from a dietician to an acupuncturist. The Silver Season was not exactly the county home.

On the walls between the office doors were a series of cork bulletin boards. On one were Polaroid snapshots of the residents who had birthdays that month; on another announcements of various entertainments and other diversions: glee clubs and church choirs, magicians and polka bands, organists and tap dancers, exhibits by artists, readings by poets. One particular board caught my eye. The sign at the top read Life and Afterlife, and below it were listed a gaggle of speakers and their specialties:

Oscar Hambleton, Attorney-at-Law: The Execution of Holographic Wills and Codicils

O. Renfrew Jones, C.L.U.: Variable Annuities—Pathway to Survivor's Security

Rex Butler: Cancer Insurance—Best Buy for the Buck

Robert Alliance, Alliance & Alliance: Medicare Is Not Enough

Albert X. White, Bay Area University: The Inter Vivos Gift and the Charitable Unitrust

Conrad Jansson, Jansson Associates: Burial Insurance and the Perpetual Maintenance Contract

Major Ulysses Stanton, Salvation Army: The Gift of Hope

An entire parade lined up to profit from death or the anticipation of it. Since I still didn't know precisely why I was in the place, I was probably marching in the parade as well. By the time I got to the door marked "Administrator—Mrs. Ball" I felt outsized and bound, like Gulliver.

The administrator's secretary had a silver guest register for me to sign, and a silver pen for me to sign it with. When I asked to see the administrator herself, the secretary didn't like it much, but since she had never seen me before, and since I didn't have the preternaturally thankful expression of the relative of a resident, she let me proceed to the inner sanctum. Mrs. Ball didn't seem to mind my intrusion. She wore a smile that couldn't be dislodged by anything short of sciatica.

"How may we help you?" Mrs. Ball asked. Her silvery bouffant floated atop her head like a helium-filled advertisement for the establishment itself. A pair of silver-framed eyeglasses dangled from a silver chain around her neck and came to rest atop her ample bosom, where they half disappeared in a swirl of silver taffeta. The Hunt brothers would have loved Mrs. Ball, but not as much as Mrs. Ball loved herself.

"I'm not certain how to begin," I began, clasping my hands before me and bowing my head over them. "That is, I want to be certain my mission is not misinterpreted."

"Yes?" Her voice was still syrupy, but it had begun to crystallize.

"Mrs. Blair sent me, you see, Teresa Blair. That is, she asked me to come."

"Yes?"

"I'm a family friend, you see. A psychologist, actually. Behavioral, of course, and I believe she just wanted me to assure her that her funds are being, how shall I put it . . ."

"Don't be shy, Mr. . . . ?"

"Blaisdal. *Professor* Blaisdal, actually."

Mrs. Ball oozed pure cane sugar. "Mrs. Blair wants to

be certain she's getting her money's worth, Professor Blaisdal? Well, why on earth shouldn't she? We applaud her. Really, we do. She has every right to inspect Silver Season in any manner she chooses. Frankly, we welcome the opportunity to show off. We're very proud of our facility, Professor. Very proud."

"I can see that," I said, nodding until my neck ached. "And I must say, and I don't mean to be premature, that so far I am favorably impressed. Exceedingly so. Yes, indeed." I nodded some more.

Mrs. Ball smiled even more sweetly, a feat I would have deemed impossible before she managed it. "We're entirely at your disposal, Professor. Shall I give you the guided tour? Or would you rather begin by visiting the resident and going on from there?" The words had become musical, an aria of goodwill.

I looked at my watch. "I think the resident. Yes."

"I believe that's wise. They will be preparing to retire shortly, you know. Lights out at eight; breakfast at five thirty. No exceptions. Now, I want you to feel absolutely free to inquire in whatever manner you choose, so I'll just point you in the right direction. All right?"

"Wonderful. Yes, indeed."

"And if you have any questions, any at all, I'll be right here. Charlene—Mrs. Goodrum—is having an especially good day, by the way, although of course that could change at any moment." Mrs. Ball shook her head. "She's so young; still so lovely. She'll be thrilled to see you, I'm sure."

"What exactly is the nature of her treatment?"

"Well, of course, with a stroke victim the primary component of the program is physical therapy. She alternates heavy and light sessions in our Fitness Center."

"Is she on medication?"

"Why, I believe so. Tranquilizers, I believe. Vitamins. Perhaps a diuretic, I'm not certain. She does have a problem with incontinence from time to time. Dr. Wilton has gone for the evening, but perhaps I can reach him by phone."

I held up a hand and fluttered it. "That won't be necessary. Not at all. Just a general idea, you understand. And now perhaps you can tell me what the basic fee for the residence is."

Mrs. Ball frowned for the first time. "Didn't Mrs. Blair tell you?"

"Well, she mentioned a figure, but I wasn't clear whether it was all-encompassing, to include the medical component, you see, or not."

"Of course. Let me check."

Mrs. Ball walked briskly to a file cabinet and rummaged through some papers and returned. "The fee to Mrs. Blair is two thousand a month," she said slowly. Something in the file had disturbed her.

"It seems low," I said truthfully.

"Well, of course, the arrangement in this case is special. Our normal rate is twice that."

"I see," I said, even though I didn't.

"Yes. Perhaps, Professor, given the hour, we should do this another time." She fidgeted with her glasses chain, winding it around her fingers like a rosary. Her eyelids flapped. Mrs. Ball was nervous and not used to it.

"Mrs. Blair is very concerned about Mrs. Goodrum," I said sternly. "I have adjusted my schedule to make this visit on her behalf. I may not be able to return for many months. I would not like to tell her that I was refused admittance. But I will if I must."

"If you had called ahead . . ."

"Very well." I turned to go.

"Just a moment, Professor. Please. You are welcome to do whatever you like. Please." Her voice burbled like a clogged drain.

"Thank you," I said gravely.

"Mrs. Goodrum speaks of Mrs. Blair constantly, you know, almost as often as she speaks of her father."

"It'll be a great pleasure to see her again."

"Oh, and be sure to tell Mrs. Blair that she herself is most welcome at Silver Season at any time. Any time at all."

"I'll do that."

"Wonderful."

"Yes, indeed."

Mrs. Ball patted her hair and freed her glasses from the taffeta and clutched my arm to her bosom and pulled me toward the door. "Mrs. Goodrum is in Sunrise Wing. She has a thrilling view of the mountain from her window. Room one-twenty-four. The first corridor on the right, just off the Togetherness Room. You can't miss it. But if you do get lost, any of the staff can show you the way. We have a one-to-three staff-patient ratio, by the way. We're very proud of that. Very proud."

"Wonderful. Yes, indeed."

Mrs. Ball returned my arm to me and I backed out of her domain and took the first right turn I came to and found myself in the Togetherness Room, the hub of the four wings that radiated from it.

As I moved into the room, I was greeted from all sides, in all ways—voices, giggles, smiles, gestures. A tiny lady suddenly materialized squarely in my path. She was lovely, as immaculate and as crisp as a laundered shirt. I asked her how she was. She told me she was confused, but she would be better soon. I told her I was glad. She asked me why. I couldn't manage to tell her before she left.

There were fifty people in the Togetherness Room, at least five women for every man. Most were clustered in front of one or the other of the four televison sets that occupied the corners, strapped into wheel chairs, slumped and motionless, silver hair atop silver garments atop silver flesh. The volume knobs on the TV sets were turned as high as they would go, and from where I stood the programs blended into a single cacophony of canned laughter, gunshots, and the shrieks of prize winners.

In the center of the room one man stood alone, a giant, snapping his belt up and down and around like a bullwhip. A smile of wonder displaced his face after each pop, evidence of his pleasure that something on the earth still responded to his will. He was given a wide berth. A second man, gaunt and stooped, shuffled over to me and asked what kind of car I drove. When I told him, he seemed inordinately pleased, for both of us.

I turned to look for the Sunrise Wing, but before I found it, I felt a hand in the center of my back. When I turned back around, I saw a woman with no teeth. She was trying to shove me out of her way. After she got the job done, she continued circling the room, counterclockwise, her eyes locked on a path visible only to her. She was carrying a doll in her left arm. The doll wore lipstick and a string of pearls that looked real and had a daisy in its hair. I think the woman was singing to it.

I was suddenly conscious of my heart—of its size, its rhythm, its frailty. Sweat poured forth, released by valves activated first by fear and apprehension and then by shame and guilt. I hadn't wanted as badly to be elsewhere since the last time I was in jail. As I watched the woman with the doll, another woman came up to me and poked me with her finger. "We are all nice people here," she proclaimed, then turned and walked away. Somewhere, someone clapped.

My eyes shorted out. Nothing registered that was external to my discomfort. A magic, psychic mist descended over the room, and I was suddenly, gratefully alone. I took a deep breath and walked toward the door with "Sunrise" written above it, looking straight ahead, moving as rapidly as I could without running.

Number 124 was halfway down the wing. As I strolled

along, my sight returned and in spite of myself I glanced into the rooms, glimpsing only beds and, less frequently, shrouded bodies, cadaverous souls whose vista, if anything, included only the dappled ceiling above their heads. From somewhere behind me a voice called: "Help me. Please. Let me go. Help me." I looked at the nearest nurse. She didn't pay any attention to me or to it. No one paid any attention. I walked faster.

There were two beds in room 124, but neither was occupied. The dusk, which entered like a burglar through the narrow window on the far wall, provided the only light. For a moment I thought the room was empty, and then I saw her.

She was sitting in a wheelchair, her back to me, leaning forward at the waist in order to study the row of potted violets and succulents arrayed on the shelf just next to the window. In the few seconds I watched her she raised her hand several times as if to stroke the plants, but each time the hand dropped back to her lap without touching anything but air.

I knocked on the door but she didn't hear me. From behind the other door in the room came the sound of a flushing toilet. I made more noises, with voice and feet and everything else I could think of, and I was about to risk touching and therefore frightening her when she wheeled her chair around to face me.

Her eyes were blue and clear, her hair sparse and white, her body twisted slightly in the chair, one shoulder higher than the other. A multicolored afghan draped her lap and legs. Someone had pinned a yellow Happy Face to her pink sweater. "Is that you, Anthony?" Her voice was small and tremulous, but fortified with hope.

"No," I said. "I'm . . ."

"Papa?"

"No. My name is Tanner. I'm . . ."

"You must be the new doctor," she concluded, her

voice suddenly round and monarchical, entirely different from before. "Is it true they fired Dr. Slavin? For stealing pills? That's what they say, you know. I always liked Dr. Slavin. He reminded me of Papa. Do you know Papa?"

"No."

"He was a wonderful man. I cared for him all by myself after mother died, you know. I was his favorite. He never said so, but I could tell. And why wouldn't I be? Would any of the others take him in? They would not," she announced sharply, responding to her own rhetoric.

I wasn't even sure whom I was talking to, and as I was about to ask, the woman began looking anxiously around the room. "My Salems. Where are they? You didn't take them, did you, Doctor? The other one, Slavin, said at my age I didn't need to worry about smoking. I hope you're not going to tell me different. I won't listen if you do. I might even throw a fit," she added. It was a youthful dare.

I smiled and shook my head, spotting the Salems on the little night table. I walked over and picked them up. Next to the pack, in small silver frames, were three snapshots. One was unmistakably Teresa Blair, young, vibrant, as stunning as a blooming gardenia but without the glint of calculation that marred the photos in her modeling portfolio. In the second frame was another young girl, plain and sloe-eyed, wearing black robe and mortarboard, squinting into the sun. She seemed uncertain and confused, auditioning for a role she didn't want. The third picture was a baby; sex indeterminable, at least by me. I took the cigarettes around the bed and held them out to the woman.

"You'll have to help," she said, raising her right hand out of her lap and shoving it toward my face.

Even in the darkness I could tell it was not a human limb, rather something bent and smashed, a hand that had been twisted, grotesquely and diabolically, into a cubist fist of altered proportion, skewed perspectives, sabotaged utility. The fingers, broad and bent, were flattened against the palm as though permanently pressed there by an act of torture. The flesh over the thumb was white and bloodless. I thought of dungeons, of freaks, of madness.

"Lift my finger." The words were firm and shockingly brave. "Go on. It won't hurt. No more than usual. You act like you've never seen a case of rheumatoid arthritis before, Doctor. You *must* be new."

I mumbled that I *hadn't* seen it before, and it was true. I had no idea, no idea at all. Whenever I think I've seen cruelty at its most fiendish, whether inflicted by man or God, I am soon reminded that it is in fact illimitable and infinite.

After another moment I was able to follow the woman's directions closely enough to fit the cigarette between the base of her thumb and the index finger, which was pressed tight against it, and then to light it for her. Within seconds she was smoking away behind her fist, a savage parody of every tough guy who ever cupped a hand around a butt.

As I was about to try once more to find out who the woman was, the door to the bathroom opened and another woman rolled out from behind it and, without a word or glance, pushed herself into the hall and out of sight. "The poor soul spends half her time in there," the woman said to me. "This isn't even her room. I don't even know her name. I'm not sure she knows it herself. Thank God I still have my mind. Most of the time, at least. Now, do you have any pills for me? Dr. Slavin always brought pills."

"I'm not a doctor," I said. "I'm sorry. But I'll tell the nurses you're in pain if you want me to."

"The nurses," she scoffed. "*They* know I'm in pain. Everyone here is in pain. Did you know Papa, did you say?"

"No. No, I didn't."

"He suffered, too, toward the end. But he was a wonderful man. Who are you, anyway? I can see you're not my husband. I thought he might come one day. Are you cousin Floyd? Mary said *he* might come."

I told her I wasn't cousin Floyd. "I've come about Teresa, Teresa Blair," I explained.

"Blair? I don't know any Blair. I do have a daughter named Teresa. Teresa Goodrum's her name. Her picture's right over there, unless that old woman stole it again."

"It's there," I assured her. "I saw it."

"She's lovely, isn't she?"

"Yes."

"Poor Mary lost out all around. Looks. Brains. Her own father didn't even love her."

"Have you seen Teresa lately?" I asked.

"Why, I don't know." She frowned. "I don't think so. Have I?"

"Do you know where she might be right now?"

"Why, she'd be home, wouldn't she?"

"Where's home?"

"Why, El Gordo. We've lived in El Gordo ever since I married Mr. Goodrum. I think I was even born in El Gordo. Was I?"

"Where does Mr. Goodrum live?" I asked, trying to keep up.

"Mr. Goodrum's dead," she said brusquely. "He passed on just after his business burned. That was back in fifty-nine. He was only forty-eight. His people took his body with them, if you'd like to know."

"What street did you live on with Mr. Goodrum?"

"Winthrop Avenue. Six-forty-nine. That's where I brought Papa, after Mama died."

"Who's the woman in the other picture?"

"What picture is that?"

"The one on the table. With Teresa."

I pointed and she looked. "Why, that's Mary, isn't it? Mary and the baby."

"Mary Quilk?"

"Mary Goodrum."

"Is she Teresa's sister?"

"Well, I don't know who else she would be, do you?"

I shook my head. "Where does Mary live?"

"Home."

"Winthrop Avenue?"

"That's what I said. Mary's home with Papa, unless she's run off again. Both my girls run off a lot. I can hardly keep track."

"How old are you, Mrs. Goodrum?" I asked.

"Sixty-two. I'm the youngest one here. The prettiest, too, not counting the nurses. And even some of them!"

"How long have you lived here?"

"Since my stroke. Two years, I think. Seventy-six, it was. The Bicentennial."

"How old's Papa?"

"Papa's dead, you fool."

"Where's Teresa?"

"No one's supposed to know. Don't you even know *that*, mister? No one's supposed to know."

I didn't know that, or anything.

Chapter
10

By the time I got back to the Bay Bridge, my mind had become almost as stormy as Mrs. Goodrum's from trying to separate the real from the fantastic in what she had told me. My guess was that the woman in the other snapshot was Mary Quilk, née Goodrum, Teresa Blair's sister and the recipient of Mrs. Blair's semimonthly check for three hundred dollars. But it was too late to go prowling around down on Winthrop Avenue in an effort to learn whether any Goodrums still lived there or whether the home existed only in Charlene Goodrum's stroke-altered perspective. When I reached the city, I cheerfully abandoned my plan to endure a night in an El Gordo motel and hopped off the freeway at Clay Street, put my Buick in a lot, and walked down the alley that led to my office, feeling ancient and feeble and unable to become otherwise.

The building was dark except for the Tiffany lamp that Carson James, the owner of the building and operator of Runnymede, the antique shop on the first floor, kept burning all night above the rolltop desk that served as his office. As I climbed toward the second floor, my footsteps echoed in the narrow stairwell like picks falling in a hardrock mine. My neighbor, the tax lawyer, had gone for the day. He's always gone for the day. The door to my office rattled as I fitted the key in the lock and gave way only when I shoved it. By the time I was settled into my chair with a highball in my fist, it was after nine and dark, both outside and in. I switched on a lamp.

Peggy had left me a note. It said, "Hi!" That was it. If there had been anything else I needed to know, it would have been on there, too. That Peggy would write me a note even though there was nothing to say was why I loved her.

I picked up the telephone intending to call James Blair, but dialed Peggy instead. The phone rang twelve times before I put it down. She was out. She'd been out a lot, lately. I didn't like it, and I didn't like it that I didn't like it, but there it was. Peggy would never tell me whom she was seeing, and I would never ask. I fixed a second drink.

Loneliness entered through my defenseless pores. The familiar trappings of my office became no longer comforting but instead accusatory, symbolic of my plight. I gulped my drink, swiveled my chair, and put my feet up on the credenza that stretched along six feet of the wall behind the desk.

My eyes drifted toward the Klee hanging high on the wall above my feet, toward the airy but ominous geometry the artist had employed to reflect his view of urban life, its complexities, its immediate and insubstantial nature, its interdependent maze. The lines of Klee's abstract city all met each other, somewhere, sometime, sooner or later. Inevitably but unpredictably. For me, the painting served as a job description. That's what I did. I helped those lines meet, I linked people with each other and with their pasts. In the process I usually encountered—too often for comfort—some lines of my own. I turned away from it, picked up the phone, and called James Blair and asked if he had heard anything from his wife.

"No, I haven't," he said heavily. "I was hoping *you* had."

I told him I hadn't come up with anything helpful. "I've talked to some of her friends, and I talked to her mother, but no one has any idea where she is. At least so they say."

"Her mother? I've never heard Teresa mention her mother. Where does she live?"

I gave Blair most of what I knew about Mrs. Goodrum, which was precious little, but apparently it was all news to Blair. I kept Winthrop Avenue to myself, though, so I could be certain to be the first to check it out. James Blair seemed like the type who might try to take over the investigation himself, given half a chance, and in the process beat all the leads into scrap with his blundering.

Blair was anxious, eager. His voice uncharacteristically trilled with frustration. "I'm afraid the more time that goes by, the less chance there is of finding her. Would you agree?" he asked.

"You could be right," I said. "On the other hand, time's not always an enemy. I've still got a few more leads to check, and I'll get on them in the morning. It only takes one, remember."

"Why not check them now?"

"Because they're the kind of leads that tend to be asleep at this hour."

Blair's snort was porcine. "It just seems more should be done. I think I should bring someone else in on the case."

"That's your right," I said calmly, "just as it's *my* right to resign if I feel your decision will hamper my work. Who have you got in mind?"

"I was thinking of a large agency, one with lots of men available."

"Just where are you going to send all these men?"

"I don't know. I thought you might have a suggestion."

I kept my suggestion to myself. "Just because an agency employs a lot of men doesn't mean they'll put them all on your case, Mr. Blair. Most of the time they assign only one operative per customer, and even then he's seldom on it full time."

He thought that one over, then came with his counter. "I've also been thinking of psychics."

"What?"

"Psychics. Those people who seem to be able to divine the location of dead bodies and missing persons through some sort of telesthesia. I read about them frequently."

"So do I."

"What do you think? Their abilities seem quite credible, at least to me."

What I thought was that it was nonsense, but I didn't say so. "They couldn't hurt, I suppose, as long as they stay put and spend their time being receptive to extrasensory vibrations instead of getting in my way out in the field. Have you got a name?"

"Yes. A man named Brutus Therm."

"Where'd you dig him up?"

"A business acquaintance recommended him. He read of the man in something called *True Detective*, I believe it was. Therm lives in San Francisco, but he's been able to locate people in many different states. Apparently all he requires is a photograph of Teresa and an article of her clothing." Blair paused, as if to rerun the previous sentence. I envisioned bloodhounds. "What do you think?" he asked again.

"If it makes you feel better, then do it."

"If Mr. Therm tells me where he thinks Teresa is, will you look into it?"

"Maybe. If it's halfway credible. No promises, though. And I'd advise you to get the fee arrangement in writing."

"Of course."

"You know, Mr. Blair," I said slowly, "there's almost

no chance of my finding your wife unless you're completely candid with me about your relationship with her. I hope you realize that."

"Of course. What are you implying?"

"I'm just asking if there's anything else you care to tell me."

"Nothing."

"I'm a member of the California bar, Mr. Blair. If you're worried about the confidentiality of anything you might tell me, you can hire me as your attorney. I can get a retainer agreement to you for signature by tomorrow. The attorney-client privilege is very difficult for the authorities to break down. Virtually impossible. I could, and would, keep whatever you tell me entirely confidential. Do you understand?"

"Of course. But there is nothing more. Believe me, I wish there were." Blair paused. "You must think I'm demented, I know so little about Teresa." Blair's voice seemed suddenly childlike and distant.

"I imagine sometimes it turns out better that way," I said. "Ignorance is bliss."

"It seemed appropriate for us," Blair replied. "At least until now. Have you learned anything about Teresa that I should know?" he asked, turning my question back on me.

I thought about Tancy Verritt's description of her friend Tessa and her life-style; I thought of what I'd said to Tolson. "No," I said instead. "Nothing you need to know."

I told Blair good night and then disturbed the directory-assistance lady long enough to get the number for Kathryn Ellington Martin. She didn't pick up the phone until the ninth ring. I told her who I was and said I'd gotten a message to call her.

"Davy was throwing a tantrum," she explained, pausing between words to catch her breath. "He's not taking Wayne's departure well."

"He'll come out of it," I said, speaking from ignorance.

"I guess they all do, don't they?"

"Not all, maybe, but most," I said, thinking about the runaways I'd chased over the years. Some of them had tried to forget what was happening at home in ways that made it impossible for them ever to be the same again.

"Yes, well, I won't bore you again with my personal problems. Have you learned anything about Teresa?"

"Yes."

"Oh? You mean you know where she is?"

"No, I mean I've learned some things about her. Where she is isn't one of the things. Why? Do you have something for me?"

"No. Nothing. It's just that I've been thinking."

"Good."

"I think you should stop looking for Teresa."

"Really? Why?"

"I've been thinking it over. I mean, there's no real evidence Teresa's been harmed, is there? There isn't, is there?"

"No."

"Well, then, she must have left home on her own. And I just think she should have the right to start a new life if that's what she wants, without you or me or anyone else trying to stop her. So I think you should quit looking. That's what I wanted to tell you."

"You're not my client, Mrs. Martin."

"Ms. Ellington. I'm changing my name back." She paused, perhaps to give me a chance to compliment her. "I just wanted you to know how I felt," Ms. Ellington went on, "and to try to get you to change your mind about finding Teresa. I think you should consider her rights."

"What rights are those, Ms. Ellington?"

"Her right to make a new life for herself, the way men have been doing for decades."

"Lots of people have rights. My client has a right to get his money's worth from me. The state of California has a right to have people with knowledge of criminal acts give testimony about them. You've got a right to have a husband who doesn't treat you like a plastic statue. All kinds of rights. But it's not my job to determine priorities."

"I don't think that answer is sufficient in this day and age, Mr. Tanner," Ms. Ellington said, her voice atremble. "We *all* have to set priorities. The people who used to do it aren't doing a decent job anymore. If they ever did. The government. Business. Parents. Church. The schools. Each individual has to take up the slack."

"I'm sorry, Ms. Ellington. I've pulled out of cases before, when things weren't as they were represented to be or when the end didn't justify the means, but this doesn't seem like that kind of case. Not yet, at least."

"Just think about it, will you?"

"I think about a lot of things. I'll add that to the list."

I hung up and thought about what Kathryn Ellington Martin had said, and decided I agreed with a lot of it but not quite enough, then thought about getting some fettucini on the way home from the office. I was about to leave when the telephone rang.

"Marsh Tanner, you scum-sucking pig."

"Ruthie."

"Give the man a panatela. I'm surprised you remember."

"It's been a while, Ruthie. Too long. I'm sorry."

"Keep talking, doll."

"Dinner? Some night soon?"

"How soon, sugar bear?"

"Well, I'm on something now, but it'll be over by Tuesday, one way or another. How about Wednesday night?"

"Where?"

"Wherever."

"Gold Mirror?"

"Sure. Just like the old days. How are you, Ruthie?" I

asked, hoping she would understand I really wanted to know.

"I'm fine, Marsh. Real good."

"Busy?"

"Personally or professionally?"

"Both."

"Business is good. Oh, nothing exciting, no one taking shots at me or anything, but good steady income. The social life, well, fifty-year-old widows aren't in great demand in case you hadn't noticed, not unless they wear diamonds as big as the balls on a bear. But I get by."

"You deserve better than that."

"Oh, it's not so bad. Actually, there is one guy, we get along real well. He's as frisky as a stallion in spring, but I keep him reined in. I still think of Harry every day, but I guess that makes me better than I was. I used to think of him every time I breathed."

I knew what she meant. Not long ago I'd picked up the phone and dialed Ruthie's number, all set to talk to Harry about a case that had me hung up. I didn't remember Harry was dead until the first ring. I'd dropped the phone like it was a weasel and spent the next hour remembering Harry, the good part of his life, the bad part of his death.

"Did you ever hear from a woman named Martin, Marsh?" Ruthie asked. "Lives down in El Gordo?"

"Sure. Your niece."

"So she called you after all."

"Sort of," I said.

"What do you think of her?"

"Well, she's having a rough time, but she seems to be getting it together. A tough broad, Ruthie, just like you."

Ruthie laughed. "Did she hire you, Marsh?"

"No. We talked about it, but she finally told me she'd changed her mind."

"Really? She seemed real shook up the day she called me. Something about her neighbor, wasn't it?"

"Right."

"Did she tell you about her husband, Marsh?"

"A little."

"Never did like that little pissant. She's well rid of him. Well, if Kathy decides she wants some help after all, you give it to her. Okay, Marsh?"

"If I can, Ruthie. If I can. See you Wednesday."

Ruthie and I said good-bye. I switched off the light and stood up, then sat back down, closed my eyes, took a deep breath and let it out slowly and willed my muscles to relax. My mind drifted, untethered, a feather on the breeze. I imagined what Teresa Blair would look like, sound like, smell like, when I found her.

"Fire!"

The sound was faint, for an instant indecipherable and unimportant. I remained in hibernation. Then the word was used again, and this time defined itself.

"Fire! Anyone! Get out fast. The building is on fire. Help me! If anyone's here, come help me. Please!"

I rolled out of my chair and stumbled into the corridor and tracked a ghostly figure down the stairs and out into the alley, which was black at its ends but lit at the center by a flickering orange blot of flame. I yelled at the retreating body and it turned and stopped and then came toward me.

"Marsh. Thank God."

It was Carson James, the owner of the building; aged, infirm, homosexual, easily frightened. We had met years before, when I had removed one of the many terrors from his life. In return he gave me friendship and reduced rent. "How bad is it?" I asked him.

"Horrible. The flames. They just exploded, a gas leak or something. Look in the window. Mother of God, I could have been killed." Carson's pasty flesh puckered at the thought. The rings on his fingers twinkled brightly as he gestured, reflecting fire.

I looked. Flames sprang into the air behind the glass of

the rear window, yellow acrobats. I thought of old rock shows at the Fillmore, and of the light shows that swirled behind the performers. "Have you called the fire department?" I asked.

"No. I thought I should alert people first."

I thanked him. "Is there anything inside that's crucial?"

"*Everything* is inside, Marsh. My *life* is inside. You know that."

I did. "There's an alarm box down at the street," I said. "Go pull it. I'll go in and call. Is there a fire extinguisher?"

Carson nodded. "Somewhere." His eyes closed, gray wrinkled curtains lowered against the conflagration before and behind them. "Oh, I can't think," he mumbled desperately. "It's ancient, and I haven't the faintest idea how to use it, you see, so I kind of . . . It's by the back door! On the wall. Right inside."

What he couldn't bring himself to ask with his voice he asked with the eyes of a supplicant. "Okay," I told him. "You go on down and pull the alarm. It's not too bad, yet. You're insured, aren't you?"

"Yes, but . . ."

There are always buts with insurance, everyone knows that, and all of a sudden I started thinking about whether I should try to save anything of my own. The Klee. The desk, my grandfather's desk, except if was too big to carry. Peggy's plants. And nothing else, because the rest was mostly those things we accumulate not because we want to but because our government, our several governments, require it.

And then I started thinking not about the existence or aftermath of the fire, but about its cause. There were a number of possibilities. Carson wasn't the most stable of men. He could have been careless with the ash from one of his ubiquitous cigarettes, or with the passions of one of his ambitious young lovers. Or it could have been the wiring, or the this or the that, but one of the things it could have been had nothing to do with Carson and a lot to do with me and the case I was on.

I shoved Carson down the alley and turned to face the fire, determined to douse it after first dousing my fear. I struggled with my childhood for a time, and subdued it only by fixing full attention on exactly what I had to do inside the building and how I had to do it.

The rear door opened easily enough, but the heat behind it washed over me like a wave over a reef. I stepped into the smoky kiln of the interior with care if not with confidence, my throat already clogged with dread. I almost ran away, but couldn't.

The store was crammed with stuff, even more cluttered in the rear where I was than in the front. Sideboards, chiffoniers, wardrobes, and highboys surrounded me like the horsemen of the Apocalypse. When I knew where I was and what was around me, I turned and looked squarely at the blaze that clawed its way up the rear wall of the store.

The fire seemed confined to the back of the building, at its most intense beneath the two windows that looked out onto the alley. One of the windows was broken, and the night wind sucked black smoke out into the city. I coughed and pulled out my handkerchief to mask my nose and throat.

Carson had told me the extinguisher was on the wall by the rear door, and I began feeling my way toward where I thought it was. Unseen things tripped and nudged me. When I finally found my prize, its metal sides burned my fingertips.

It took some doing but I finally pried the extinguisher off the wall and moved on into the room, lugging the warm cylinder over my shoulder like it was a fallen comrade. The smoke thinned as I went toward the center of the store, and by the time I got to Carson's desk and the telephone on it,

I could see well enough to dial the emergency number and report the fire. Then I rubbed enough dirt away from the top of the extinguisher to read the directions for its use and headed back toward the flames. By the time I had taken four steps, I heard the eager yell of the first siren.

I got as close to the rear wall as I could, then pulled out the handle of the extinguisher and began to pump. Some milky white liquid finally spurted out. I pointed the hose at the flames and rammed the plunger home. Smoke billowed back at me, my eyes and throat closed against it. The sparks hatched by the spray floated toward the ceiling like runaway stars. I coughed and pumped some more.

The hair on my arms began to crinkle, my skin as dry as parchment beneath it despite the frantic effort of my task. My eyes burned and the tears that rushed to flush them nearly blinded me. The flames seemed alternately calmed and enraged by my labor.

I considered giving up, but I consider it so frequently that I steel myself against the impulse, often to the point of foolishness. So when the stream of chemicals began to dwindle despite my hastened pumps I threw the canister aside and cast about for another weapon. The only candidate was the rug I was standing on. I picked it up and took a breath that was filtered through my handkerchief and my shirt sleeve, got as close to the wall as I could, then rolled the rug and began beating at the flames.

I gulped for more air and moved closer. Heat and smoke swallowed me and refused to spit me out. I beat at the wall as long as I could, then backed off, drew new air into my lungs, and attacked again. The rhythm of my assault became fixed and manic; I sensed neither victory nor defeat, only effort. When I slipped to my knees on the warm effluent from the extinguisher, I continued to fight from there, senseless and ridiculous.

Some time later the rear door flew open and two firemen

charged in, black coats flapping, helmets shining with reflected combustion. They pulled me off the floor and ordered me out of the building with sign language, then trained a hose on the wall. I left them to their specialty and stumbled into the alley, feeling hurt and hot and vaguely mad.

"Is it out? What were you *doing* in there, Marsh? You could have been *killed*, for God's sake." Carson danced like a leprechaun around me.

"I think it's under control," I said between resonant gasps. "The firemen are there. It's still confined to the rear wall. You'll have smoke and water damage, but that's all."

"The rug."

Carson pointed and I looked down dumbly. I was still carrying the throw rug I'd used to beat at the flames. It was smoking in one corner, wet and tattered in another, the flag of a badly vanquished foe. Carson was on the verge of tears.

"It's a Sarouk, Marsh. Priceless."

"I'm sorry."

"It's irreplaceable."

"I grabbed the first thing I saw. I'm sorry."

Carson placed his hands on either side of his neck. "What a *heartless* thing of me to say. Forgive me, Marsh. You risked you *life* in there. For me."

"No, I didn't."

"Of *course* you did. I *saw* you. I thought of dragons. Of *purgatory*. Keep the rug, Marsh. It can be restored, I'm certain of it. I know a man. I want you to have it."

"No."

"I *insist*."

I was about to continue the dispute when one of the firemen came out of the building and walked over to us. "You the owner?" he asked me.

I pointed to Carson.

The fireman drew his hand from behind his back. In it was a can, a juice can once, grapefruit or the like, but something else more recently. "Arson," the fireman said simply. "They use these because the fire burns off the paper wrapper and any fingerprints along with it. You'll have to give a statement to the fire marshal. He'll be along shortly."

Carson nodded, speechlessly fearful. I wondered what I should say, and decided to say nothing. The fireman walked away, young, hirsute, godly. Carson's eyes stayed with him, until he left the alley.

I became conscious of a bell ringing, and looked up toward the sound. It came from my office phone. I told Carson I would be right back and trudged to the second floor for the second time that night.

My office smelled of smoke, wet wood and fabric. I hoped Peggy would know what to do about it. I picked up the phone.

"Let me talk to Tanner." The voice was flat and hard, like runways and I-beams.

"You are," I said.

"Been busy, Tanner?"

"Some."

"Cooling off a little now?"

"Some."

"Lay off Mrs. Blair."

"Who?"

"You heard me, pal."

"Why?"

"She don't want to be found."

"Says who?"

"Says someone who can drop the building you're in any night of the week. Take me about ten minutes. Kentucky Fried Shamus."

"Don't try it, friend. You'll wish you'd never learned to strike a match."

The voice laughed a real laugh. "They say you're smart, Tanner, but you don't sound smart."

"You told me that before."

"Oh, no, Tanner. You ain't heard nothing from *me* before. But if you don't quit nosing around in El Gordo you'll hear from me again. You can make book on it."

I dropped the receiver as though it were a thing long dead. At home, in bed, I dreamed of a hell with many devils.

Chapter
11

Winthrop Avenue skewered the sclerotic heart of El Gordo and constituted its oldest neighborhood. Two blocks east was the El Gordo Mission, established by Serra himself, and four blocks north was the Winthrop mansion, built by railroad profits and the land grants that accompanied them. The eucalyptus trees that lined the street were in their prime, but the neighborhood that nested beneath their peeling skin was not.

The houses were massive and dark and set well back from the street, but on closer inspection the impression of sedate tranquility gave way to one of fortified dilapidation and disrepair, of life in a state of siege. Winthrop Avenue had been abandoned by this generation, which equated newness with status, progress with quality. The old money had moved to Hillsborough or Portola Valley if it wanted to stay in the area, to Palm Springs or La Jolla if it didn't, and the new money had built its A-frames and split-levels high in the hills. The only thing left to Winthrop Avenue was its heritage.

Number 649 was a square red brick structure that was, I guessed, close to a century old. Some transplanted easterner had tried to duplicate a New York town house out of some half-baked and halfhearted Georgian motives. Now the cornices were chipped and the pilasters were missing, the once subtle symmetry had been skewed by the settling of the foundation and the disappearance of most of the frieze. An earthquake or two had doubtlessly contributed to the tilt. I pulled up next to the curb and stepped over a recumbent bicycle and walked toward what I hoped was the home of a woman named Mary Quilk, a woman who for at least a year had been receiving six hundred dollars a month from her sister Teresa Blair.

The front yard was bordered by an untamed oleander and was bare in spots and overgrown in others and littered everywhere with children's toys, most of them broken. The side yard was littered with toys as well, grown-ups' toys—workbench, grinder's wheel, trash barrel, tool chest, car jack, creeper. Three grease spots marched up the center of the dirt driveway. A pair of legs stuck out from under the pickup truck parked in front of the garage at the back of the house. The feet at the ends of the legs were gnarled and bare and black on the bottom. I decided to leave them where they were.

The front door was on the far side of a small open porch, painted white but peeling. One of the posts supporting the portico was missing entirely and the other was on its way. More toys were scattered over the porch—guns, dolls, cars—reality in miniature. I stepped on one of them without meaning to, but the little yellow truck was impervious to my bulk. Before knocking, I looked for a name by the mailbox. There wasn't one.

After my third knock the door opened onto darkness. The woman who stood like a prioress within didn't speak or otherwise inquire, but watched me with thin, unblinking eyes. She was large, a single undulation between legs and neck, her blue print dress falling over her the way sheets fall over ghosts. She was out of breath and laboring to get it back.

I asked if her name was Mary Quilk. She hesitated a minute, her body vibrating around her exhalations. "Why? What's wrong now?" Her words passed through a barrier between us that was as tangible as a screen door.

"I've come from the Silver Season," I said importantly, accurate in every sense but the ethical.

"Where? Oh. There."

The woman was middle-aged and thoroughly wearied. Grayed hair leaked down her temples like the detached webs of spiders. Her eyes seemed wary of closing, for fear of what might happen in the darkness. So far, the only link between Mary Quilk and her sister, Teresa, was a senile allegation. When she took a step backward, I stepped in to share the darkness with her.

Her weight caused the floor planking to grumble. I was close enough to see the hair that sprouted from the mole on her chin, to smell the sour musk of her breath and body. Although she was offended by my penetration of her house, she quickly abandoned any impulse to defend her rights. The surrender was clearly habitual.

"Is Mama all right? Has she had another stroke?" Her voice lacked the precise pitch of certain emotion, as though she was unsure how she wanted Mama to be.

"It's nothing like that, Mrs. Quilk. It is Mrs. Quilk, isn't it?"

She nodded and I paused for a moment and struck a pose, a bureaucrat in possession of mysterious facts, frightening powers, arbitrary and capricious potential.

"Is it the money?"

I didn't respond.

"The money was supposed to be taken care of. She promised it would be."

"Who promised, Mrs. Quilk?"

"Teresa. My sister. Isn't Teresa paying for Mama anymore? Oh, she swore and *swore* she would." Her hands clenched at her waist and she took two steps backward. I followed to keep her face from disappearing.

"Ted and me can't do it, if that's why you're here," she went on, her voice a reedy whine. "Ted's been laid off over at the plant for two months, now. He tries to make do by fixing cars, but times are bad. Teresa promised she'd pay so long as we did the other. She *promised*, mister. But I suppose it don't mean nothing, since I ain't got it in writing. Ted said I should have got it in writing." Her sigh was a bleat of betrayal.

"What was it you agreed to do in return?" I asked.

I didn't get an answer. Instead, Mrs. Quilk turned and led me deeper into the crepuscular interior, to a room only a few tints brighter than the foyer.

The furniture was sparse and featureless, the patterns scraped off by parades of days and of bodies. The rug was eroded according to the traffic pattern of the house; the velveteen divan was zebra-striped and could only have been purchased during a fit of sexual ardor. The chair behind me was draped with an antimacassar of a vintage that reminded me of the women languishing in the Silver Season. The single picture on the wall was framed in gold. I assumed it was the Son of God, but when I got closer I saw it was the king of rock 'n' roll.

Mrs. Quilk saw me notice it. "I seen Elvis once," she said simply.

"Where?"

"At the airport. He was on his way to Hawaii to do a show. He was sitting in a big red limousine and all the windows on it but the front was blacked out. I could tell it was him, though. He waved at me, too. I'm dead sure he did, no matter what Ted says. The diamond on his pinky was as big as a bean." She smiled. "I got twenty-one of his albums," she added, tabulating her devotion. "*Blue Hawaii*'s my favorite."

Mrs. Quilk took a seat on the faded zebra stripes and I sat on the chair across from them and asked again about her sister's promise to pay for her mother's care.

"She *did* promise. When Mama got sick, Teresa said she would take care of everything."

"When was that?"

"Back in 'seventy-six. The year after I seen Elvis."

"What did you agree to do in return?"

She didn't hear my question. "It just don't seem fair, somehow," the woman mused. "Not after what we done for *her*." She shook her head. The rest of her hair flew loose from its pins and fell to her shoulders, shoe-brown and gray, the length and color of old mops.

"You want some coffee?" she asked me, patently hoping that hospitality might deflect me from my mission, whatever my mission might be.

I shook my head and asked again what it was that didn't seem fair about the arrangements to care for her mother. I tried to sound neutral and curious and sympathetic. I also tried to sound as though I had the power to rearrange the world.

It didn't work. The woman simply uttered her sister's given name once again, with an antipathy so acidic it ate away my question. "What have you done for Mrs. Blair?" I asked once more, flailing her the way you flail a mule.

She heard me that time, but she shook her head quickly, casting off the irrelevance. "How much does Mama owe? A lot, I suppose," she speculated lifelessly.

"That's not precisely it," I replied

"I thought you was from the home."

"I am. But you see we're simply trying to *locate* your sister. Not for monetary reasons, let me assure you, but because there are some forms that need to be signed, formalities really, involving federal assistance programs.

Title Nineteen. Since Mrs. Blair is, ah, *funding* the resident, it's essential that we get her signature. You understand. Regulations."

"You mean she don't owe nothing?"

"Nothing at all. And your mother's doing quite well, I might add. I saw her only yesterday." I tried to sound like Mrs. Ball.

"And you're just looking for Teresa? That's all there is to it?"

"That's all." I smiled.

"Well, that's sure a load off my mind. 'Course, when Ted's unemployment runs out, the load'll go right back on, I reckon, and then Mama will get after me again."

"After you for what?"

"Oh, about how Ted ain't good enough for me, how I married beneath myself, how I could have amounted to something if I'd wanted to. Like Teresa did. Mama thinks people can get anything they want just by wanting it. They can't, can they?"

"Not in this world."

"Besides, if what Teresa did is how you get to *be* someone, I'd just as soon stay a nobody like I am." She shook her head wearily, a classic victim of poverty's cycle, a descendant of the proud but hapless occupants of Walker Evans's photos and Erskine Caldwell's books.

"Do you have any idea where Teresa is now, Mrs. Quilk?" I was trying to get her mind off her own future and onto her sister's past.

"Home, I expect."

"She's not there. Do you have any idea where she might be?"

She shook her head automatically, unused to being a source of information or of anything.

"When's the last time you saw her?"

"Let me recollect. About six weeks ago, I think. That is, she was here then. Truth is, I wasn't home. That was a

Sunday night, and they was running *Kissing Cousins* out at the drive-in. Ted was here, but I guess Teresa didn't stay more than a minute. She and Ted don't get along." The last was an aphorism, universally known, unquestioned.

"Was there anything special about the visit?"

"The usual. Teresa is always the same, seems like. She don't have no feelings, you know. Not about nothing."

"Did you and Teresa grow up in this house?"

"Yep." She looked around the room as though to confirm her worst suspicions.

"Your mother told me Mr. Goodrum was dead. Is that right?"

"Yep. Lost his business and died of it. If Ted don't find work soon, the same's going to happen to him. He's real edgy lately. Says his belly hurts him."

"Did Teresa go to college?"

She laughed, then stifled it after a glance toward the rear of the house. "I guess some might call it that," she sneered.

I asked her to explain.

"Teresa went down to Las Vegas, is where she went. She and that floozy friend of hers."

"What friend?"

"Trudy Valente was her name."

"Where is Trudy now?"

"Lord knows. In jail most likely. Or in hell."

"Why do you say that?"

"She was a wild one, that's why. Do anything on a dare. Why, she ran stark naked across the street at the Founders Day Parade one year when she wasn't but a sophomore in high school. Oh, she was wearing one of those gorilla masks, but everyone knew it was Trudy." Mrs. Quilk paused and her brow wrinkled with reflection. "Made a business out of running around naked, is what she did. Teresa, too."

"In Las Vegas?"

"Show girls, I guess is what they called themselves.

Some would call them other things." Her eyes pressed her meaning into mine.

"What club did they work in?"

She shrugged. "I forget. One of them big ones on what they call the strip. Ted and me went down there once. I like to have died in the heat. We got tickets to the big show and everything, and Ted even slipped the waiter some money so we could sit down front only he didn't put us down front after all. The curtain came up and Teresa and the rest walked out on stage and would you believe it? I didn't even recognize her. Ted had to point her out." She scoffed at the memory. "My own sister. Parading around with a bunch of bird feathers on her head. Then, when we went back after the show to try and see her, there she was, standing around in the middle of all kinds of people, mostly skinny men with hankies around their necks, and she weren't wearing nothing at all above her waist and precious little below it. Ted hauled me out of there so fast it brought on a hot flash."

"How long was Teresa in Las Vegas?"

"Oh, five years or so, I expect. We didn't talk much, back then. Don't talk much now, either. Teresa left me and Mama way behind."

"Who were her friends in those days?"

"Trudy, she's the only one I know the name of. Except for her husband."

"You mean James Blair?"

"No. The first one."

I let that percolate for a minute. The more it bubbled, the more scrumptious it got. "What was her husband's name?" I asked quickly.

"Frank something. Frankie, she called him. Like he was Sinatra or something."

"Did she marry him in Las Vegas?"

"Yep. In one of them little roadside chapels. Mama went down for it, but Ted and I couldn't go."

"Where's Frankie now?"

"Who knows? Teresa don't talk about him anymore. I met him once. He sure was handsome. Kind of reminded me of Elvis, around the mouth."

"Were there any other people Teresa was close to?"

"Not that I know of. Most of the ones from the old days, at least the ones she knew here in El Gordo, have moved on by now. The ones she might have known in Las Vegas, well, I wouldn't know what happened to them. You could probably see a whole bunch of them in one of those movies Ted takes me to whenever we go down to San Jose to play Lo-Ball." She paused to wait for her memories to catch up. "There's just me and Ted and the boy here now. We're all that's left, seems like, what with Mama so sick. God, I'm tired of this place. Nothing works, the kitchen smells like dead rats, the walls just seem to squeeze in on me. I choke on the air sometimes."

Mrs. Quilk stood up and walked to the wall and gazed at the picture of Elvis as though she expected it to counsel her. Maybe it would. Maybe it had. "Why did you and your family meet Teresa in a warehouse on Oswego Street a year or so ago?" I asked abruptly.

"Who says we did?"

"Someone who saw you."

"I ain't talking about that, mister. You can just forget it."

"Will you let me know if Teresa gets in touch with you again?"

"Oh, she'll likely be in touch, sooner or later. But I don't know if I'll tell *you* about it. Why should I, if she don't owe no money?"

I took a chance. "Because her husband's worried about her. He hasn't seen her in several days."

She froze. I'd changed my story and she'd caught me at it. "Well, now, how would you know that, Mr. Old-Age-Home Man?" The discovery of my deception made her giddy.

"He called me at my office at the Silver Season. Mr. Blair is very worried. I told him I would help if I could."

"No, sir. You ask too many questions to be who you say you are. And every time I answer questions, it costs me money."

I'd mistaken her ignorance for unintelligence and been burned. I tried once to divert her. "Do you know if Mrs. Blair's first husband is still in Las Vegas?"

Before she could answer, a loud slam reverberated at the rear of the house. Mrs. Quilk stood up and, with a fierce look in my direction, marched toward the sound and disappeared behind a swinging door at the far end of the room. "Ted best not find you here, mister," she called back to me as she left.

While I was waiting for Ted, I walked around the room, inspecting the tattered memorabilia, fingering the dusty surfaces, inhaling the moldy scents. The effort to make the room into something more than a box had been abandoned long ago. When I noticed a telephone on the little table next to the divan, I went over to it and wrote the number in my notebook. When I remembered that there hadn't been a listing for a Quilk in the El Gordo phone book, I picked up the receiver. The line was as dead as the man on the wall.

The El Gordo phone book lay beneath the telephone, pristine and unused, with a picture of a sailboat on the cover. I looked through it. There were a few scratchings, numbers and names written in ink and pencil. One of them was the letter *T* followed by a number that had been crossed out and another number written above it. I wrote both of the numbers down and replaced the book.

From behind the swinging door came a voice, male and rasping. "That woman is fucking us over. It's just like I said it would be, god damn it. Now let me by."

I went back to my chair and sat down and waited for him. In a moment the swinging door swung toward me. The man burst through the door as though it wasn't there, as though he was used to charging madly through the house and through his life. His hands were the color of graphite, his balding head as white as gypsum above his cap line and as irregular as a phrenologist's guide. Strings of muscles snaked up his arms. On the epidermis encasing them was a tattoo of the eagle, globe, and anchor of the Marines. "Who are you, friend?" he asked with excessive mildness.

There was cunning in his eyes, much like the cunning I had seen earlier on Oswego Street, and because of it I changed my story. "I'm a detective. Private. Name's Tanner."

"That ain't what you told the wife now, is it?"

I shook my head. He was holding his cap in his right hand, orange and white polyester. There were words printed above the bill: "I Snatch Kisses and Vice Versa."

"What's your game? You from her husband, or what?"

I nodded. "The police and the DA are interested, too. She's a witness for a trial that starts Monday."

"And you lied to the wife and hoped she'd rat on her own sister, is that it?"

That was close enough, but I didn't admit to it. I just sat there. Lumps came and went along the line of his jaw. "Get out. Now. We ain't got time for no more bullshit." He put his cap in his left hand and reached in his back pocket with his right and pulled out a crescent wrench and swung it, negligently but competently, at his side.

"I only want some information about Mrs. Blair," I explained calmly. "I'm willing to pay for anything I can use."

"Out." He halved the distance between us.

I stood up. "Here's my card," I said, and tossed it on the table beside the telephone.

Quilk looked at it and laughed. "We don't take money from liars," he said between the lips of an evil smile. "Now listen up. When you see Teresa, you tell her we threw you out on your ass. Then you tell her we stuck to our part of the bargain, and that she'd best stick to hers. You tell her if she don't, I'll come looking for her myself, and when I find her she'll wish to hell I hadn't. Now you tell her."

I left without a word.

Chapter
12

I left the Quilks and Winthrop Avenue and gulped a franchised burger and a no-milk shake, then rented a room in an El Gordo motel that lacked a pool and a lounge and consequently, I hoped, lodgers in the market for anything but sleep. When I asked the desk clerk about making a toll call, he looked as though I had asked him to explain the mechanics of necrophilia, but after I flashed my credit card I finally got his permission to use the instrument in my room.

My first call was to Ray Tolson. "I'd like to report a fire," I said, when he came on the line.

"You've got the wrong number," Tolson groused. "Dial nine-one-one for the fire department."

I chuckled. "This is Tanner. The fire was in my office building. Someone rubbed two sticks together under my window. I thought you'd like to know."

Tolson swore under his breath. "Was anyone hurt?"

"Only some antiques and the sensibilities of the man

who owns them. But the fire did come complete with a suggestion. Delivered by phone."

"What kind of suggestion? As if I didn't know."

"A suggestion that I come up short on the Blair case."

"Well, there it is."

"There it is," I agreed. "Except this piece of advice was supposedly unconnected with the similar piece of advice I received the day before. Assuming Fluto's people set the fire and warned me off right after, then who the hell stopped me yesterday?"

"No idea," Tolson said.

"I get the felling I'm in the middle of something a lot bigger than Tony Fluto's hit-and-run."

"If you are, I don't know what it is."

"That better be true," I said.

"Trust me, Tanner."

"I don't trust anyone with a retirement plan, Tolson. Let's just get on with it."

"Okay. Any progress?"

"Not much. How about you?"

"Fluto's still missing," Tolson said sourly. "There's no sign of him or Mrs. Blair at any of his haunts. His people don't seem particularly worried at his departure, though. Business as usual." Tolson paused, then made the noises of firing up a cigar. "The trial starts in five days," he said when he was ready.

"Any chance for a postponement?" I said.

"None. Fluto has a right to a speedy trial. You can bet he won't waive it."

"Well, it wouldn't be the first time the main witness against a man like Fluto got scared off."

"Hell, it won't be the first time I've had to ask for dismissal against Fluto himself. I did it once in an extortion case and I swore I wouldn't do it again. God damn it, I'll try the bastard if only to make him pay an attorney's fee."

Tolson's voice boiled with anger at intangible obstacles. "I got the owner of that warehouse for you," he went on.

"Who?"

"Some outfit called the Columbus Development Company."

The name was familiar. In the next instant I remembered why—the same company owned the Silver Season. "Who's behind it?" I asked.

"Still checking on that. Apparently it's buried beneath about three layers of corporate shells."

"Mob?"

"Could be."

I thought it over, then asked if he'd heard from the Vegas police about Teresa Blair.

"They called about an hour ago," he said. "It's hard to see how what they gave me can help, though."

"What is it?"

"A woman named Teresa Goodrum was married in Vegas in June of sixty-three. To a guy named Frank Zelko. Roadside Chapel of the Blessed Virgin."

"I already know all that," I said.

"Yeah? Then excuse me all to hell for wasting your time." Tolson was on edge. I didn't blame him. In five days he was going to have to watch Tony Fluto walk away scot-free from a crime everyone in town knew he'd committed, a crime that Tolson had publicly vowed to redress.

"What I need to know is where Zelko is now," I said. "Did the Vegas cops mention anything about him?"

"No, and I'd just as soon not call them back."

"Why not?"

"Vegas is like a sewer, Tanner. Sooner or later all the swill in the country ends up there, everyone from the mob chieftains to the small-time grifter out to impress a broad by throwing money around at the tables. The Vegas cops get lots of inquiries about visitors to their fair city, and they get real tired of responding to small-timers like me. I try to hold it down when I can."

"I'll get it on my own," I told him.

"Oh, hell," Tolson said. "I'll handle it. Check back tomorrow."

I was about to hang up when Tolson coughed and then spoke. "You remember what you said about this office the first day we met?"

I told him I did.

"This morning my boss, the DA himself, allowed as how it might be a good idea to drop the prosecution against Mr. Fluto. So as not to embarrass the office by coming up empty."

"And you said?"

"I said he could fuck himself."

"And he said?"

"He said I was being unprofessional."

Tolson started to laugh and I laughed with him. A second later it didn't seem funny anymore. "There's one more thing," Tolson said softly. "I got a phone call this morning."

"From whom?"

"From someone who said she was Teresa Blair."

"Really?"

"Really. She told me not to worry. That she would be in court Monday morning, ready to testify against Fluto. Nice of her, huh?"

"Very. You want me off the case?"

"What if she wasn't Teresa Blair at all? What if I stopped looking for Mrs. Blair because of what she said?"

"That'd be real nice for Tony."

"Wouldn't it?" Tolson coughed. "Keep on it, Tanner. I want the woman on ice. I want to put a subpoena in her lovely little hand and waltz into court with her on my arm, like we were on our way to the Policeman's Ball."

My next call was to an attorney I've used from time to

time, when what I need is information and not more active forms of inquiry. I wasn't going to entrust the only solid lead I had solely to Tolson and the Vegas police.

Les Anders was in law school with me, my roommate until he got married during his second year. After school he'd clerked for a justice on the Nevada Supreme Court, and after that he became assistant counsel to the Nevada Gaming Commission. Les knows exactly how the state runs, since to know gambling is to know Nevada, and he dispenses his knowledge to a few select clients who either own casinos or want to. Les knows I don't entirely approve of the beneficiaries of his expertise, and I know he scoffs at the futile insignificance of my line of work, but if we can put all that aside, we still enjoy each other when we get together, which hadn't happened in more than two years.

"You sound like you're calling from Siberia, Marsh," Les said after I told him who I was.

"Only El Gordo."

"Same difference as I remember. Hey. Did you know the first time I ever got laid was in a whorehouse in El Gordo?"

"You don't say."

"My brother took me. Cost him five bucks. Cost *me* ten times that for penicillin."

"How is your brother?"

"Dead. Heart attack. Forty-one."

"Tough."

"Makes you think."

"Still smoking?"

"Yep. You?"

"Yep."

"I run, though. Three miles a day. You?"

"Not unless the building's on fire. Which last night it was, come to think of it."

"What was that?"

"Never mind, Les. Listen. I need some information. Should be a piece of cake."

"That's what you always say, Marsh. Last time it ate up five grand in expenses, and the local chief of detectives took the time to familiarize me with the law on misprision of a felony."

"You were reimbursed, Les."

"For the expenses, yes; for the humiliation, no."

Les laughed and I laughed, too, because we both knew the times we needed help from each other were among the best times we had, and that we would do the favors for free if we had to or were asked.

"What's up?" Les asked after we'd quieted down.

"Very simple. Back in the early sixties a girl got married in Vegas to a guy named Zelko. Frank Zelko. I want Zelko's current whereabouts and anything more you can get on him. Also anything you can come up with on the girl."

"What's the girl's name?"

"Teresa Goodrum was her maiden name. She's Teresa Blair now."

"How old?"

"Forty, give or take."

"You figure she's still in Vegas?"

"No, not unless she went back there last week."

"What's the case?"

"Missing person."

"You sure that's it?"

"Sure I'm sure."

"I think I know the story on Zelko," Les said, "but let me check some details. I should be back to you in an hour."

"Good." I gave him the number at the motel.

"You coming to Vegas any time soon, Marsh?"

"Not if my luck holds. When are you and Marie going to wise up and move out of there?"

"Hell, Marsh, we love it here. Why, Marie and Wayne Newton are on a first name basis."

"Is that good or bad?"

Les's laugh was hollow. "Marie never did like you, did you know that, Marsh? Not even back at school. She said you always made her feel like she'd just cheated on an exam."

"Is that right? How does Wayne Newton make her feel?"

We talked for a while longer, and after Les hung up I dialed again. Tancy Verritt answered on the second ring. The purr fell out of her voice the minute I identified myself. I asked if I could talk with her some time that evening.

"What about?"

"About Teresa Blair."

"I already told you everything. At the club."

"It'll only take a few minutes."

She paused. "Be here at seven. I have a dinner date at eight. You can zip me up." She laughed in my ear, then told me how to get to her apartment.

I called my answering service next. The only message was from a Mr. Brutus Therm. A communication from a psychic. I took a deep breath and called the number Brutus had left, already skeptical because he'd had to use a telephone to reach me. Brutus answered the phone himself, uttering his name with the stentorian tones of melodrama.

"What can I do for you, Mr. Therm?" I asked. "I got your message to call."

"*Au contraire*, Mr. Tanner. I can, and shall, do something for you. Your client, Mr. Blair, has engaged my services. He has given me a photo of his wife, as well as one of her blouses. I have been sensitizing myself to them all day. Unfortunately, the ether is turbulent today, aswirl with cirrocumulus disturbances. I have nevertheless received certain pulsars."

"Pulsars?"

"Vibrations that meld with the beta waves in my brain to produce discernible psychic patterns," Brutus explained tolerantly, as though you should learn about pulsars the day after you learn about Bambi. I asked Brutus what patterns he had discerned.

"I sense skepticism on your part," he countered.

"You're uncanny, Mr. Therm."

"I take it you have never employed a sensitive, Mr. Tanner."

"Right again."

"I am not a charlatan, whatever you might think. I have been of assistance in many cases such as yours."

Charm oozed from his voice like jelly from a doughnut. "How much are you charging James Blair to rent your sensitivity, Therm?" I asked.

"I can't see what business that is of yours," Therm said.

"Maybe it's not my business at all. But I've got some psychic predictions of my own. I predict you're charging him five grand or more. I predict the money's not refundable, and is not contingent upon results. And I predict that nothing you tell me is going to be worth a chewed Chiclet."

Brutus was silent for a moment, breathing heavily and no doubt angrily. I felt bad about picking on him, but not bad enough to retract my slur. Failure frustrates me, and because I still didn't have the slightest idea where Teresa Blair was, I took it out on Mr. Therm.

When Therm spoke again, it was in the measured cadence of anchormen and kindergarten teachers. "I should terminate this conversation, Mr. Tanner. I've encountered your type of individual many times. Insecure. Only marginally self-sufficient in an economic sense and a psychological sense as well. Jealous of the accomplishments of others. A typical pattern. However, I shall persevere, but only because Mr. Blair wishes it. He is a man I am drawn to. He very likely possesses extrasensory abilities himself. Our conversations have been fascinating. The vibrations electric."

"Maybe it's just bad wiring."

"I hope you're a better investigator than you are a wit, Mr. Tanner."

I did, too. "Why don't we get back to those psychic patterns you mentioned. Where's Mrs. Blair?"

"I can't tell you precisely," Therm intoned. "Not yet. At this point I have only general images. I see rocks. Boulders. I see white. A broad expanse. Snow, perhaps. Or sand. I see water. Blue. Perhaps sky, but more likely water. I see an enclosure that is somehow in the air. I see globes of light. I see a word. Dodge, perhaps. Is it of any help?"

"No."

"Perhaps when your investigation is more fully fleshed out."

"Perhaps."

"When my images become more precise I'll give you a call."

"I'll be breathless until then, Mr. Therm."

"Don't flaunt your ignorance, Mr. Tanner. You may live to regret it."

I hung up, but not without the realization that there was something in what Brutus Therm had said. I didn't want extrasensory abilities to exist. I didn't want to think that by taking shortcuts others could do what I did. I'm not good at shortcuts. I stay on the road, trudging step by step until they become mile by mile, plodding and slow, but proceeding with some intelligence and perhaps even some sensitivity of my own. If you could get there with beta waves and pulsars, I was going to be out of business.

I dispatched Brutus Therm to the back of my mind and pulled the El Gordo telephone directory out from the drawer beside the bed and looked up James Blair's number. It was the same as one of the numbers I had seen written on the cover of Mary Quilk's phone book, the number that had been crossed out. The other number wasn't an El Gordo exchange.

Luckily, my source at the telephone company in San

Francisco was on duty. We had once thought we loved each other and we'd been wrong. Later on we decided we liked each other and we'd been right. We chatted for a minute, promised to have lunch in a week or so, and I gave her the second number and she left to check it out. During her absence the telephone threw Muzak at me.

"It's a Tahoe number, Marsh. South Shore. It'll take more time to find out exactly where it is."

I thanked her and gave her the number of my motel and asked her to check out the location and call me back. She said she would. I said I'd be eternally grateful. She said she doubted it, but she'd give me the chance.

I tossed the receiver back on the hook and lay back on the bed, closed my eyes, and listened to the orgasmic groan of the air conditioner. Gradually I became less conscious of noise and more conscious of images, people and places that came and went like flash cards in strobe lights. Some time later the groan became a scream and the scream became a bell and the bell became a telephone that I groped for through the thick smog of sleep.

"Marsh? Les. I got something for you on Zelko."

"Good. Where is he?"

"You want it metaphorically or you want it straight?"

"I just woke up, Les. I'm not ready for poetry, especially yours."

"I was thinking more of Dante, but here goes. Zelko's dead, Marsh."

"Since when?"

" 'Sixty-six. And that's not all. It was almost certainly a contract job. A hit. Zelko was in jail at the time on a tax beef. The word is Zelko was working his way up through the syndicate hierarchy a little too fast for some people's comfort, so they set him up for the tax fall and then decided to make sure he'd never get back in circulation. Zelko made someone nervous, someone made him dead."

"What about his wife?"

"Nothing much on her. A show girl, great legs, Zelko fell for her in a big way. Only married a couple of years when he got sent up. She visited him every Sunday for a year. Zelko got it while she was in the visitors' room, waiting to see him."

"Anything else?"

"She hung around with another show girl named Trudy. Both left town a few weeks after Zelko bought the farm. That's about it, though. You want me to dig some more?"

"I guess not. What's the best guess on who had Zelko taken out?"

"Could have been any of about ten guys, is the way I hear it. Zelko was a real dandy, played around with other men's women a lot, before and after he got married. Plus, he shot off his mouth. The cops didn't break any legs looking for the killer. One sleaze offs another sleaze, is the way they look at it."

"Thanks, Les."

"No problem. Let's get together, Marsh."

"Soon."

The phone rang again three minutes later. "The unit you asked about is in a law office, Marsh. Right on the Nevada border, the California side of Stateline. It's billed to the firm of Flowers and Lane, on Spruce Street. That's all I can give you."

I told her that was enough and thanked her. I was close, but not close enough. The lawyer was only a middleman, a delay to be avoided if possible.

There was still some time to kill before I was due at Tancy Verritt's and I didn't have anyone handy to kill it with so I went to a movie. A run-down house not far from my motel featured old films, three of them, run back-to-back, twenty-four hours a day. Admission two bucks. When I walked in, the next feature was just beginning. *Sheepman*. Glenn Ford. Great. By the time I rang Tancy Verritt's bell, there was a smile on my face and a quip on my lips.

Neither my smile nor my quip found mates on the woman who answered the door. Tancy Verritt wasn't eager to see me and she curled a lip to let me know it even before I crossed the threshold. When I made no move to enter, she waved me inside with urgent and enameled fingers.

Her living room was designed to exist without care—there were no surfaces that would absorb a stain, no plants that would thirst, no woods that would crack, no floors that would streak or cloud. Nothing visible had existed five years before. The only things on the walls besides simulated cedar paneling were an appointment calendar and a poster of Robert Redford in a cowboy hat. I thought briefly of Mary Quilk and Elvis. The only thing on Tancy Verritt besides impatience was a belted dressing gown, phosphorescent, red and long, just like her fingernails. I expected her to stop somewhere in the vicinity of the various heaps of Naugahyde in the living room, but she kept walking and I kept pace, through one door and then another.

We ended up in the bedroom. The bed was large, with tubular brass grills at head and foot. The alternating bands of orange and white that covered it were stuffed with something puffy and inviting. The ceiling wasn't exactly mirrored, but it was covered with shiny and crinkled foil that dissected my image weirdly.

Tancy Verritt walked straight to a dressing table and sat on a padded stool, picked up a silver-backed brush, and started brushing her hair. Her reflection was the hub of a wheel of naked bulbs, and it didn't seem pleased with itself. Still with her back to me, she gestured toward one of the club chairs near the foot of the bed. I had to lift some filmy fabrics off the chair before I could sit on it.

I took my seat and watched the planes of Ms. Verritt's back move beneath her gown as she stroked her hair. I watched them for quite a while, feeling absurdly domestic and content. The only sounds in the room were from quiet, silken things.

"Well?"

The crystal-thin mood shattered with a single syllable, nasal and insulting. I reluctantly adjusted to match it.

"Your friend Teresa is in serious trouble, Ms. Verritt," I began. "You're not helping by keeping quiet about her past."

"I told you at the club I didn't know anything about her past, love."

"You were lying."

"How do you know?"

"I'm a lie detector. You grew up in El Gordo and you were Teresa Goodrum's best friend, then and now."

The arm missed a brush stroke, then resumed at a faster pace. "What of it?"

"Your name isn't Tancy Verritt, is it?"

"What makes you think that?"

"Pulsars."

"What?" She stopped the brush, then put it down.

"Never mind," I said. "Your given name was Trudy Valente. You and Teresa Goodrum ran off to Las Vegas, two pretty girls on the make for cheap thrills in the city that lives off them."

For the first time since we'd entered the room, Tancy Verritt looked at me without the aid of the mirror. "Who told you all this? Teresa?"

"It's not important, but it definitely wasn't Teresa. What is important is that you tell me everything you can about the Las Vegas days. I think Teresa's disappearance could be connected with that period of her life."

"I try not to remember anything about the Las Vegas days, Tanner. I try real hard. When trying's not enough, I get help."

"What kind of help?"

"You don't want to know. Listen, love. I can't talk about Vegas. I just can't."

"Not even to help your friend?"

"Not even then."

A line of gleaming sweat had formed at the base of Tancy Verritt's neck, soaking her hair, causing strands of it to stick like lamprey's to her flesh. "Tell me about Teresa's husband," I said. "Tell me about Frankie."

Her eyes rolled wider. "You know about Frankie, too?"

I nodded.

Her eyes drifted back to the mirror, but this time what she saw was not her face. "Frankie Zelko was the most beautiful man I've ever seen," she breathed. "You could see it even in that little picture you had. He had everything. Frankie made a woman feel like she was the only woman in the world who could make him laugh or cry or come or anything in between."

"Frankie's dead," I said.

"Frankie's dead," she repeated. "You don't have to tell me that."

"Tell me how he died."

"Shot. He was shot. In jail."

"Why?"

"I don't know. And I very much don't want to know."

"Why not?"

"Do you know Vegas, love? Do you know the kind of people who run that town?"

"Only what I saw in *The Godfather*."

"Well, it's best to know *of* them and not *about* them, if you know what I mean. They don't like people to know what they do or how they do it. When people know too much, they end up dead. Or worse. I had a girl friend . . ."

She paused. A stricken look crossed her face like the shadow of a tomb. "What about your girl friend?" I prompted.

The memory had dazed her, backed her into a trance. "I had this girl friend. She knew something she shouldn't have known. Not a big thing, you know, just a thing. She saw two people together who didn't want to be seen together, and she talked about it. Not to cops, just to someone. Anyone. Now she lives in a wheelchair. Her feet don't work so good. She looks like she died and they forgot to bury her."

"Was Frankie in the mob?"

"Everyone in Vegas is in the mob. Whether they know it or not. You go down there and play the tables, you're in the mob, too."

"Was Frankie hit?"

"That's what they say."

"Who's they?"

"People. Casino creeps."

"What did Frankie know? Or do? Or say?"

"Like I said, love. I don't know and I don't want to know."

"Did Teresa Blair know whatever it was that got Frankie in trouble?"

She shrugged.

"How did Frankie end up in jail?" I continued.

"He . . . I don't want to get into that, love. I've talked too much already. Why don't you just split? Then me and my date can go drink a magnum of the bubbly and I can forget I ever saw you or Vegas either."

I stayed where I was, my mind abuzz with possibilities, all of them grotesque. "Did Teresa say anything recently about those days in Vegas?"

"Nope."

"Was she upset when Frankie died?"

"Sure. He was her husband, for Christ's sake."

"Any men in her life after that?"

"Not serious. Not in Vegas."

"When did you and she come back to El Gordo?"

"Couple of months later."

"Why?"

"It was Teresa's idea. She said we'd been around town

too long. She said we weren't fresh anymore, and Vegas didn't like stale women any more than it liked stale luck. She was right."

"What about James Blair?"

"What about him?"

"How does Teresa feel about him?"

She shrugged again. "I told you all I know about that at the club."

"Did she run on Frankie the way she does on James Blair?"

"Not once. Not even after he was sent up. Everyone in town wanted her ass, too. Some very high rollers, some very big stars."

I paused before my next question. "Where do you think Teresa is now, Tancy?"

She looked back at me with lifeless eyes, as lifeless as the thrust of her answer. "I think she's dead."

"You mean murdered?"

"I guess. I guess that's what I mean."

"Why?"

"I don't know, love. I just think it, that's all. You spend time in Vegas, it comes natural. Now leave me alone. If Teresa's alive she can take care of herself. If she's not, well, R.I.P. Hey. Who's been following me around, anyway? The cops?"

"What do you mean?"

"The day after you showed up at the Racquet Club some car started tailing me. A blue Ford. I don't like cops, Tanner. Call them off."

"I don't think it's cops."

Her lips trembled, then slowly stopped. "Somehow I was afraid you were going to say that. Christ. They promised to keep me *out* of it. I knew this would happen. God damn it to hell." Her words were wrapped in the thick wax of fear. She looked toward the door as if she expected Capone himself to walk through it.

"What do you want out of, Tancy? What are you and Teresa mixed up in? Come on, Tancy. It's important."

"Ha. My face is important. My legs are important. They're the only chips I bring to the game. I'd like to keep them looking the way they do now."

"Who are you afraid of?"

She shook her head. "Listen, love. I got to get dressed. There's a guy coming by for me in fifteen minutes. He likes me to be on time."

"Where are you going?"

Her face slacked at the relief of a new subject. "To hear Woundz. They're punk. You know them?"

"Should I?"

"They're very big."

"So are roller skating and group sex."

"You don't approve, love?"

"It's not that I don't approve, it's that I don't participate."

Tancy Verritt's lips curled like burning paper. "You're moral as hell, aren't you, Tanner? You just sit around all day and restrain yourself, I'll bet." Her words were intended as a low and crippling blow.

I smiled. "Gives me something to do till the cartoons come on."

She got up and walked to where I was sitting, her face as fixed as a fist. "Have you ever had a woman walk up and ask you to fuck?"

"No."

"Ever dream about it?"

"Not since my face cleared up."

"Well, I am."

"You are what?"

"Asking you to fuck."

Tancy Verritt was blazingly attractive, and no more morally repulsive than half the planet. In an ideal world I suppose I would have rejected her taunt, her offer of a contest, but my world is far more desperate than ideal, and more so all the time.

I reached for the rope that held her gown against her body and pulled one fringed end of it. The rope streamed softly to the floor and the gown parted, a satin sesame, to reveal a tanless breast, a queerly clipped pubis, a depthless navel. My eyes searched the red-sheathed column of flesh, its sun-browned shadings, its fuzzy and dimpled textures. When I got to the smile on her face, it was the smile of Alexander, the smile of Xerxes, the smile of conquerors. I lifted the gown away from her shoulders and spilled it to the floor and took her soft and heavy breasts in my hands.

"I want it rough," she whispered as she pressed her hand to my groin. "Rough and fast. You can hurt me if you want." She pushed me back onto the spongy bed and I took her down with me.

Because it was the way she wanted it, I didn't do it that way at all. It was a contest, after all, and in all contests the way to win is to do the unexpected. With tip of tongue and pad of finger, breaths of air and pats of palm, kiss and suck of lips, I began a conquest of my own. The ceiling crumbled our bodies and scrambled them.

"The doorbell will ring in a minute," she said at one point. "Ignore it."

The bell rang. Again, and then again. Tancy Verritt's thrashing, moaning labors were an attempt to make our coupling an achievement, an epiphany, a thing it could not be. On the fourth ring I rolled away from her and fixed my clothes.

"You bastard," she said.

"But only that," I answered.

Chip was standing outside the door, cradling posies instead of rackets. I patted him on the rump as I went by.

Chapter
13

It was half-past eight and some straggling rays of the sun were still skipping inland off the ocean when I pulled to the curb across from the Blair and Martin houses. Lights glowed golden behind Kathryn Martin's curtained window-panes. I turned off the engine and slumped in my seat and pulled out my copy of Montaigne to help me wait for something, I wasn't sure quite what.

I was in the middle of the essay on Vanity, at the point where Montaigne speaks of placing legal restraints on silly and useless writers, when I heard a noise reminiscent of street sounds of my youth. It was Davy, Kathryn Martin's son, skateboarding nonchalantly down the road toward his house. Head helmeted, hands gloved, knees and elbows padded, he crouched like a Seminole atop his board, weaving across the slanting street as though it was a flaccid, insubstantial thing instead of a skull-smashing concrete slab.

I got out of my car and watched with admiration as Davy rolled my way. When he saw me, he somehow stepped off his board, popped it into the air, and caught it as easily as an infield fly, all in one motion. I applauded and he twisted with embarrassment.

"You're pretty good at that, Davy," I said.

"I know," he replied without inflection, as comment not as boast. "The cut-back still gives me trouble," he added after a moment, eager that I not misread his skills. With his free hand he pulled his helmet off his head and cupped it under his arm. His T-shirt read Ski Incline. His hair was long and tousled. He might have just landed from one of the planets that had just begun to shine in the eastern sky.

"You remember when I visited your mom the other day, Davy?" I asked.

"Sure."

"Did she tell you what we talked about?"

He shook his head, and when I didn't say anything, he spoke, nervous for the first time. "Mom and I don't talk much," he explained. "Why? You gonna marry her or something?"

The question shocked me, and my denial was more encompassing and immediate than it should have been, and it hurt the boy. "I'm married to someone else," I added quickly, lying totally and with cowardice. He nodded silently.

Davy shifted his helmet to his other hand, which caused me to look again at his shirt, which caused me to remember what my phone friend had told me, which caused me to remember Kathryn Martin's abrupt loss of interest in Teresa Blair's whereabouts, which caused me to remember Brutus Therm and his pulsars of rocks and sky and snow and water. "New shirt?" I asked the boy.

He looked down to recall what he was wearing.

"Yeah."

"Get it up at Tahoe?"

"Yeah."

"That's right." I snapped my fingers. "Your mom went up there the other day, didn't she? Did you go with her?"

"Yeah."

"You get to skip school?"

He smiled. "Yeah."

"Did you find Mrs. Blair all right?"

"Yeah."

"She's a nice lady, isn't she?"

"She's all right."

"She staying at a pretty nice place up there?"

"It's all right."

"What was it called, now? Your mom told me but I forgot." I extrapolated from another one of Brutus Therm's pulsars. "Something 'Lodge'?"

"Lakeview."

"That's right. Mrs. Blair's in room twelve, isn't she?"

"Thirty-two."

"Did she say when she was coming home?"

He shrugged. "I was out at the horse place most of the time. Mom never lets me stay around when she and Mrs. Blair are having one of their talks. Besides, Mom told me not to tell anyone about going up there." His eyes began to shine.

"It's all right, Davy. She told me the same thing. Just to be safe, though, let's not tell her we talked about it, okay? Maybe you shouldn't even tell her you saw me."

"Okay. I wouldn't tell her, anyway."

"Why not?"

"Oh, whenever I say anything about anything, she starts crying and acting all gross and everything. She's still bummed out about my dad leaving, I guess."

His thin and puzzled voice pained me. "How about you, Davy? Are you bummed out about it?"

"No way."

That's what they all say, the kids who are left behind. The millions of them.

Davy dropped his board to the ground and put one foot on it and began to scoot off toward his house. "See you, Davy," I called.

"See ya."

When the grinding sound of his wheels had faded into the high whisper of the redwoods, I got back in my car and tossed Montaigne in the backseat and started the engine. As I began to pull away from the curb, I noticed that a car parked a hundred yards or so up the road behind me had started up as well and was headed my way. It wasn't a car I had seen before. I waited for it to pass but when it came abreast it angled to the curb just ahead of me, cutting me off. The driver hopped out without shutting off either his engine or his lights. When he began to trot toward where I was sitting, I got out to meet him. He was not anyone I expected or wanted to see.

He was large, though his bulk was soft and spillable, the result of disuse. His white loafers gleamed in the focused lights of the cars like tap shoes on a burlesque runway. The digits on his thick wrist glowed dimly in the approaching darkness. His face was beefy and square, its features loose and indistinct. The meaty hands that hung at his sides opened and closed in powerful spasms. I closed a hand of my own, just in case.

"Don't worry," he said. "I'm not going to hurt you. Not without cause. I just want to get a look at you, so I'll know when you come around."

"Why? Is it a contest?"

"Taking a man's only child from him is your idea of a joke, I guess," he said heavily. The words were stiff and agonized. I knew then who he was, and shared a bit of his agony myself.

"What are you talking about?" I asked, to get him talking.

"I know what she hired you to do, she and that baldheaded lawyer of hers. Bad enough you listened to her slander me, but then you had to go to the Blairs' as well, tell them all about it, too, as if they didn't know enough already. Probably told the whole street, didn't you? Well, it's not going to work. Believe me, mister. I'll fight you till I die." He choked on the words, as though driven to complete his threat.

"What's not going to work?" I prompted.

"You're trying to prove I'm unfit to have Davy even for the summers. You're trying to help her keep me away from him entirely. My own son," he added, as though the declaration would reestablish his paternity, perhaps even his humanity. "Did you see him just now?" he went on. "On that skateboard? He's so darned smooth. Takes after his mother in that. In everything, I guess. That's what everyone always said."

"What's your name?"

"Martin. Wayne Martin. I'm the guy she told you about when you were over here before."

"How did you know I was here before?"

"I've been watching. I watch all day every day, and most of the night."

"Why?"

"To see Davy. To make sure they're both all right. To see what she's going to do to me next."

"What about your job?"

"What job? Watching Davy is my job now." Martin's eyes widened, then suddenly rolled. His irises disappeared momentarily, giving him an otherworldly, ghoulish aspect. He staggered a few steps, caught himself, then sagged once more. "Sit down before you fall down," I told him.

Martin nodded dumbly, then tottered to the curb and lowered himself to it slowly. I went over and sat beside him, two kids ready for the parade. The rumbling car engines that rolled their owners up the hill gave the air a noxious bite.

Martin mumbled softly. "I haven't slept in weeks." He squeezed his eyes with his lids; wrinkles radiated from their corners like the grease marks of clown makeup. "My brain's on fire," he continued. "I can't put it out. I'm going nuts, I guess," he concluded, more curious than frightened at the prospect.

"Maybe you should get some help."

"You mean a shrink?"

"Why not?"

"You ever meet anyone who got anything but broke from seeing one?"

"A few. It's someone to talk to."

"Yeah. You'd think a man who lived forty years in the same town would have someone to talk to, wouldn't you? Well, you know who I got?"

"Who?"

"A bartender. Which is funny because I don't even drink anymore. I just go there to talk. Larry keeps some milk on hand just for me. See, the people I work with, in the Crusade, they aren't interested in my problems. I guess they think as a reborn Christian I shouldn't have any, you know? And if I'm not truly reborn, well, they don't want me around then, either."

"Catch twenty-two," I said.

"What?"

"Nothing."

"You know what happened to him?"

"Who?"

"The bartender. Larry."

"What?"

"Arrested. Embezzlement. Had his hand in the till for years, so they say. Took a hundred thousand, minimum. Can you believe it?"

"Happens every day. Don't go into the bar business unless you know a lot of people you can trust or have a lot of money you can lose."

"I suppose she told you about the cross," he said, a non

sequitur to everything but his life. "She told her lawyer so I suppose she told you."

I didn't say anything.

"I wouldn't have made him wear it," he went on. "Not to school. I know what the other kids would have done. Oh, yes. The fathers of those kids just got me fired down at the office. Because I *lectured* them, supposedly. Lecture. That's what they call it when I ask them not to take the Lord's name in vain." He shook his head and frowned. The world had become a stranger to him, and perhaps he was a stranger to himself. He was as alone as anyone I'd ever encountered. I decided, cruelly, to let him continue to believe I was hired to be his enemy.

"I didn't get a chance to talk to your neighbor, Mrs. Blair, the other day," I said casually. "Have you seen her around lately?"

"Why should I help you? You're trying to destroy me."

"No, I'm not. I just look for data. If she had good things to say about you, I'd report them. It's the judge's job to say who gets the boy. Not mine."

"Teresa Blair won't say anything good about me. She hates me. She convinced Katie to throw me out. No, I'm not significant enough for her to hate. Despises, is more like it."

"Why?"

"Oh, I made a pass at her once. Or, that's what she thought it was. And I guess she was right. I was drunk. I was drunk a lot then; that's why I opened my life to Christ."

"When did you see Mrs. Blair last?"

"Who remembers? Five, six days ago. I was out back there, where I could see in our kitchen, watch Katie make dinner, you know? Then a bunch of men came over to the Blairs'. Policemen, some of them. They tramped all over the place. I had to hide behind a bush to keep them from spotting me. Then they went away and a little while later

Mrs. Blair came out and drove off. Had a suitcase with her."

"Was she alone?"

"Some man picked her up. She hopped in his car and off they went."

"What kind of car?"

"They all look the same to me."

"What color? Green? Blue?"

"White."

"License?"

"Nevada, come to think of it."

"What did the man look like?"

Martin shrugged. "Davy came home about then. I quit watching Mrs. Blair and her friend. I wouldn't have made him go, you know."

"Who?"

"Davy. To that school in South Carolina. It's just that I was scared. Davy's only twelve, but already they're finding drugs in the lockers at his school. And we hear of everything from sex parties to gang fights at the junior high he'll go to next year. I guess my imagination got carried away, but really all I wanted was to make sure he didn't ruin his life before he realized that's what he was doing. Is that so wrong?"

"No."

"Is it wrong to worship the Lord?"

"No, not if you leave it at that."

"How do you mean?"

"You and your friends try to tell people how to live."

"But the Bible tells us to praise the Lord, to say unto the cities of Judah, 'Behold your God.' "

"It also tells us to forgive those who trespass against us. There's a difference between evangelism and theocracy, Mr. Martin. A lot of people are confusing them these days. What's worse, a lot of people aren't. They know exactly what they're doing."

Martin sighed. "I've grappled with this thing night after night, sitting up there on that hill behind the house. I guess what I've decided is, anything that breaks up a marriage like Katie and I had once upon a time can't be all good, can't be doing God's work."

"You don't necessarily have to blame the doctrine, Mr. Martin. Just the interpretation."

"I never said she had to accept Jesus in the same way I did," Martin protested. "I only made suggestions, though I see now that she thought they were orders. But I guess that doesn't matter. My lawyer says it doesn't, so I guess it doesn't."

Martin shook his head as if to expel his lawyer from his mind, then pushed himself off the curb and walked unsteadily toward his car, a beaten fighter trying to feel his way out of the reeling ring. "You just keep out of my way," he said to me roughly, crazily. "I've got enough problems without you sneaking around here. Just keep away, or you'll wish you had. I mean it."

Without waiting for an answer Martin shouldered his way into his car, pleased that he had accomplished his mission, unaware that his mission was needless. He backed away from the curb and, with a screech of his tires and a warning tick of his horn, drove off down the hill.

I got back in my Buick and put it in gear, then had to stop once again. The gate to the Blair house swung open, slowly, silently, and James Blair's silver Seville drove out, also slowly, also silently. The gate swung shut behind the car, and for a moment I could have convinced myself it hadn't happened. In the next moment I convinced myself, for no good reason, that I should follow him.

The last gasp of commuter traffic was all against us, so I had no trouble keeping the Seville in sight. Like metal balloons we descended through the strata of El Gordo, strata as illuminating as anything unearthed at Olduvai by Leakey or at Mycenae by Schliemann. But no one was bothering to dig in places like El Gordo. Perhaps because the discoveries would be too damning.

We reached the commercial flatlands and turned north on El Camino, our passage marked by neon come-ons and cardboard sirens. A few miles later the Seville's turn signal winked and Blair veered into a parking lot behind a restaurant. A blinking sign proclaimed its name: Wadley's. I pulled to the curb and waited in my car while James Blair got out and went inside. I pulled into the lot, parked, and went inside as well.

The foyer was lined with fuzzy wallpaper and lit by carriage lamps. The little light on top of the leather-covered lectern at the far end shone down on the pudgy hands of the little man standing behind it. The man didn't seem particularly glad to see another customer. The diamond on his pinky flashed a warning burst. The sign above his head indicated the restaurant was to the left and the lounge to the right. I smiled and pointed toward the lounge. A solitary boozer. The little man raised half a lip and nodded. I walked past him the way I walk past things afloat in formaldehyde. I was ready with an excuse in case I encountered my client.

The bar was dark and cold. In the back a layered and lacquered woman was playing a white piano—"The Shadow of Your Smile." None of the stools around the piano was occupied. The smile on the woman's face had been there since the Eisenhower administration. I took a seat at the bar and ordered a drink from a bartender who was too young to know how to do his job and who spoke with an accent, Boston. He looked like Ringo Starr. Maybe he was Ringo Starr.

The only other people in the room were a couple at the far end of the bar, where it was dark. They wore matching silk shirts in a paisley pattern and were whispering and giggling and smooching. They seemed permanently joined at the wrist and forehead. After sliding my drink at me, the bartender took a position halfway between his customers and began cleaning his fingernails with a small buck knife. I gulped and swiveled on my stool until I could see into the half of the building where people were eating.

There wasn't much of a crowd in there, either. Only two of the dozen or so tables I could see from where I was were occupied, one by a solitary diner, the other by James Blair and another man, curly-haired and florid and wearing a black tuxedo and a red cummerbund. Wadley, the restaurant's owner, I assumed. Every minute or so Wadley unleashed a booming laugh, then wiped his nose with his sleeve. He was as comfortable in a tux as a dowager in a Danskin.

I tried eavesdropping and reading lips and came up empty, with no hint of what they were talking about and certainly no hint that Teresa Blair was the subject of the conversation. Blair was in profile to me, and never once looked my way. The other man cast a proprietary glance around the room from time to time, but I was nothing he was interested in. Blair consumed his meal rapidly and seemed eager to get away, which he did about ten minutes later. When he left, I followed him. As far as I could tell, he didn't pay for his meal or notice me.

I expected him to return to his house, but instead he led me into downtown El Gordo. The evening breeze was musty, as though it had passed over too much of mankind on its way in from the sea. Blair's car was a ghost ship, Blair its cursed captain. He pulled into a small lot at the rear of a brick and glass office building.

By the time I thought it was safe enough to follow Blair into the building, there was no one in sight. I found the listing on the building directory: James Blair—Accountant. His office was on the third floor. The elevator seemed glad to have something to do.

The hall outside Blair's office was thickly carpeted in gold and the walls were lined with roughened burlap. The door to the office was closed. The letters painted on it repeated exactly the ones on the building directory. The door was wood but there were clear glass panels in it. On the other side of the panels was a woman, thin and brown-haired, sucking on a pencil as she typed feverishly on her Selectric. The plastic sign on her desk said her name was Florence Hendrickson. I decided I had gone far enough in pursuit of serendipity.

Montaigne kept me company until Blair finally emerged at midnight. He went straight home from the office. After waiting outside his house for another hour, I did the same, unsure of what I knew and didn't know.

Chapter
14

The first tendrils of spring had begun to snake up out of the valley toward the high meadows, and the opposing battlements of snow that bordered Highway 50 had begun to shrink, their foundation trickling from beneath them and crossing the road in broad, flat bands of brown. There was still plenty of packed powder on the upper slopes, of course, and the Porsches and Volvos that zipped around me in the passing lane had ski racks strapped to their tops and bragging slogans pasted to their bumpers. The road signs directed me to carry tire chains but I couldn't remember whether I had any in the trunk or not. I just rolled along, the slowest car on the road, my windows cracked to the tang of mountain air, my eyes rising regularly toward the magnet of the High Sierra, my soul more attuned to peace and perspective than to tracking down a witness to a crunching death.

Lake Tahoe had once been something special even in a state where alfalfa sprouts and pyramid shapes and hot tubs are accorded the same status. The lake and the wooded shore surrounding it were a flawless gem cradled in an antique setting, a talisman of curative and regenerative powers. In my younger days a week at the lake had, more than once, sucked the lowland poisons out of my system and transfused my urban blood with something less adulterated and more noble. But the sports faddists and the nature cultists and the casino gamblers discovered the region. Newly hewn freeways made the lake as accessible as a Burger King, and now the waters are befouled with algae and the shore is blistered with glass-and-redwood sores and the air shimmers from the fumes of high rollers and show biz groupies. The mystical magic has been squashed flat by four solid lanes of tourist traffic and condo dwellers.

I cruised all the way through Stateline once, into the Nevada side and back, confirming my memories, both good and bad, then found a gas station and asked the station attendant if he knew how to get to the Lakeview Lodge. He named some streets and some points of the compass and I set off after them. Surprisingly, I found the place within ten minutes.

The Lakeview Lodge was a four-story, rough-sided log building that hibernated quietly in the center of a stand of ponderosa pines about a hundred yards from the lakeshore in a relatively secluded area. The building was a relic from the good old days, genuinely rustic and darkly serene. The driveway was lined with lights the size of beehives. The porch that stretched along the entire front of the lodge held a row of rocking chairs, heavy and squat, constructed of thick wood and saddle leather. A consumptive old man was rocking in one of the chairs, causing it to creak like a sloop in a storm. When I walked past him, he nodded once, then spit into a coffee can. The string tie around his neck was gathered by a turquoise cinch the size of a gas cap.

The lobby was dark and pine-paneled, furnished in overstuffed and dusty comfort. A small wood fire burned in one corner of a massive fireplace that didn't draw well anymore. The rack of antlers above the mantel seemed to point at me with a felonious accusation. The magazine on the coffee table was *Guns*. There was no one in the room but me and the dead deer.

I made like a regular and followed the signs in the lobby and made my way to room 32. When I found it, I put an ear to the heavy door and listened to nothing, then knocked. The maid pushing a service cart toward the far end of the hall called out: "She's gone already. Looked like she was fixing to do some serious walking. Sometimes she don't get back till real late."

I waved my thanks to the maid and asked if anyone was with the woman when she left. The maid shook her head. "She's always alone. Too bad, too. Woman like that was made to give comfort to someone—man, woman, child, don't matter which. You the husband?"

"No," I said, then went back to my car.

At one side of the parking area was a swimming pool, deserted and empty still, a vat of pine boughs awaiting warm water, air, and bodies. At the other side of the lot was an open fire pit, scorched black from bonfires and pig roasts and other celebratory blazes. In between these hallmarks various trails led off into the woods. The trails were labeled by wooden signs nailed to the trunks of pines. One trail led to the lake, another to the horse barn, a third to something called the Grass Meadow. I thought back to the picture postcards that clung to the little wire rack in the lobby, and got out of the car and strolled down the trail to the meadow, remembering the coonskin cap I'd had when I was nine and wondering whether the world could possibly be better off with kids knowing all about the Dukes of Hazzard and nothing at all about Davy Crockett.

Pine and cottonwood and aspen lined the path. Some persistent rays of sun fought through the prickly foliage and rested in golden puddles on the forest floor. The bowed and waving branches sang like distant choirs. The air was cold and clear in my lungs, as substantial as spring water. Pine needles rolled beneath my shoes atop the springy loam. I hoped the meadow was far away.

The trail continued for half a mile. At various times I moved aside for mounted horses and human hikers and frenzied chipmunks. I really didn't expect to find Mrs. Blair at the end of the trail, and by the time the path opened onto a sun-drenched clearing, I was almost hoping I wouldn't.

The meadow was a horizontal flag of grass that rippled in the wind. The ground underfoot was soft from the spring melt. Blimps of crusted snow still dotted the edges of the field, in nooks immune to sun. In the center of the meadow some rotting stumps and fallen trunks of trees created a roofless room of black and geometric furnishings. A woman sat on one of the logs, her back bent toward me, her pale and eyeless face raised to the new spring sun. I gave one last glance to the trees and sky and snow, took one last conscious breath of pine-spiked air, then made my way through the stiff bear grass toward the woman. When I was halfway there, she heard me coming and opened her eyes and turned. I trudged the rest of the way in the black shadow of her frown.

She was appropriately dressed for the setting—stiff ankle boots, tight denim slacks, plaid flannel shirt with snaps, gray raglan sweater. Her brown hair flapped loosely about her shoulders above the white scarf knotted around her neck. Her face was a face I knew, but only in its commercially photographed state. Animate and guileless, it was even more lovely than in the photos.

She didn't know who or what I was, but she suspected I was a sexual prowler and she tried to intimidate me with her lips and her eyes. When that didn't work she spoke with a cultivated rasp. "I came out here for some peace and quiet. Please. If you want conversation, go to the bar at the lodge. The bartender's name is Rick. He hunts mountain sheep and college girls. He likes to talk about it."

I kept walking toward her scowl and her disdain. When I was five feet away she stood up, and I thought she was going to slap me. I stopped and stood silently, to see what she would do. She looked me over closely, one brow cocked. Then a link was made, and her hostility became resignation. "You found me," she said simply. "I hoped I'd have a few more days."

"You know who I am?"

"Tanner, isn't it?"

"It is."

I wasn't sure what else to say, or even what else to do now that my quarry stood like an injured doe before me. I asked if I could sit down and she nodded.

"It was Kathryn, wasn't it?" she asked. "She thinks she's doing me a favor, I suppose."

"It wasn't Kathryn Martin," I said truthfully, Davy's bemused and lovely face fresh in my mind.

"It must have been someone," she said absurdly.

"It's always someone, Mrs. Blair. That's what I do— find the someones. I'm a detective. I'm here on behalf of the El Gordo District Attorney."

"Oh, I know who you are. Kathryn raced up here to tell me all about you. Did you follow her?"

"No."

"Well, someone did. Or so she thought. She also thought I was in mortal danger." Her eyes softened, her voice warmed. "Am I in danger, Mr. Tanner?"

"I don't know," I said. "Are you?"

If there was an answer to my question, it was in the black script of her eyes, but I couldn't read them. "What do you intend to do now that you've found me?" she asked.

"Take you back to El Gordo. With maybe a stop along the way to see your mother at the Silver Season."

"My God. Kathryn didn't tell me you'd seen *her*."

"Kathryn didn't know."

"What did my mother say about me?"

"She said she wanted to see you."

"What else?"

"Nothing much that I could understand."

"Is she all right?"

"I don't know. The physical facilities seem adequate. As for the rest, well, a selective senility has its advantages, I would guess."

"Did she talk about the old days? She always talks about the old days when I go out there."

"Some," I said. "She mentioned her father, and the rest of your family. I'm afraid I couldn't keep it straight."

"Did she say anything about *my* father?"

"Only that he lost his business and died."

"Anyone else?"

"Your sister."

"Mary."

"Right."

"Anyone else?"

"No, I don't think so. Why?"

"No reason. What if I refuse to go back?" she asked after a pause.

"I'll notify the El Gordo authorities."

"And what will they do?"

"Serve you with a trial subpoena for sure. Arrest you for something or other as well, probably. Just so they can keep you on ice."

"Arrest me for what?"

"Oh, PC one-eighty-two, I imagine."

"What's that?"

"Conspiracy. In your case to obstruct justice and the due administration of the law, I'd guess. It's a real convenient statute, especially when they just want to lock someone up for a while."

"Who am I supposed to have conspired with, Mr. Tanner?" she asked sarcastically.

I matched her tight smile. "I haven't the faintest idea, Mrs. Blair. But the charge only has to hold up until Monday. Once they get you on the witness stand in the Fluto trial, the need for games is over."

"Can they do that?"

"They can do anything they want for a couple of days. Due process generally runs a little late."

"Is that what you think this is?" Mrs. Blair asked abstractly. "A game?"

There was bewilderment and perhaps wistfulness in the rhetoric. I had no answer, but she expected none. We stared at each other for a moment, each recalling what we knew about the other and what we knew about ourselves.

"Putting a man like Tony Fluto behind bars isn't a game," I said after a while. "It's serious and important business. Do you still intend to testify?"

"I called Mr. Tolson and told him I'd be at the trial on Monday. What more does he want?"

"So it really was you."

"Of course."

"I guess Tolson's a bit insecure," I said. "Any honest man in a place like El Gordo is bound to be. He wants to walk into court with you on his arm. Just like you were going to the Policeman's Ball, is the way he put it."

Teresa Blair stood up and brushed off her pants and took a couple of steps down the path toward the lodge, then turned and came back to where I was still sitting. "I won't go home," she said abruptly. "Not to James."

"Why not?"

"My reasons. And I won't go to jail, either. I've spent all the time in jails I'm going to."

"Visiting Frankie?"

Her eyes exploded to new dimensions. Her breath was louder than the wind. "What are you doing, Tanner? Who really sent you? Why are you here?" Her eyes looked wildly to the edge of the clearing, as though she feared assault and sought escape.

"I'm just here to take you back," I said calmly.

"Then what does Frankie have to do with it?"

"Nothing. Or does he? Who are you afraid of, Mrs. Blair?"

"Everybody," she said simply, then thought for a minute. "I don't want a bunch of cops playing nursemaid to me for the next three days. I don't think I could stand that."

"So what do you suggest? I could give you my bed, I suppose. And watch you myself."

She placed a slim hand on my forearm. The nails at the ends of the fingers were painted the color of tongues. "So who lives with you, Mr. Tanner?" Her voice was suddenly, oddly playful. "Wife? Lover? Cat? Mouse? Who?" Her lips were loose and generous.

"I live with a television set and some printed words, Mrs. Blair. And a lot of dust. That's about it."

"Whose words?"

"Oh, Tolstoy, Dickens, Chandler, Macdonald."

"Sounds dull."

"As opposed to shooting craps or hustling tennis bums, I suppose," I countered. Some nastiness curled the edges of the words.

"So you know about Tancy, too."

"Her and more, Mrs. Blair."

"Why am I so afraid of you, Mr. Tanner?"

"I'm not sure, but it probably has more to do with you than with me, Mrs. Blair."

She turned away from me then, toward the far more splendid sights that surrounded her. Whatever she was thinking brought the frown back to her face. Her expression washed into familiar lines and creases. There were other signs of age as well, but none as prominent as the signs of beauty.

"*Would* you consider a temporary boarder, Mr. Tanner? One more alive than Dickens?" Her eyes were bright. "I'd pay expenses, of course."

"Expenses?"

"You know. Food and drink and such."

The "and such" sounded sumptuous. I didn't think about it. "Come along, my dear," I said with mock gallantry. Teresa Blair gripped my forearm more securely. Without another word we stood and marched back through the meadow, a knight and his lady at the close of a valiant day.

When we got to the lodge, I asked if I needed to keep an eye on her while she packed. She said I didn't, that I could trust her. Without good reason, that's what I did.

I waited in the lobby sparring mental questions. Why had Teresa Blair run away in the first place? Why did she give her sister the telephone number of a law office instead of the number of the lodge? Why didn't she want to go home to her husband? Those questions and more darted at me, then soared off into space unanswered, in large part because they didn't have to be. My job was to see that Teresa Blair showed up at the Fluto trial. Three days from now I would see to it that she did just that. The rest of it was fluff. Interesting, like all fluff. But fluff.

We drove down the mountain in silence. It was only after we reached the valley floor and headed into Sacramento that Teresa Blair began to talk. "You investigated my life pretty thoroughly, didn't you?"

"A little."

"Who all did you talk to?"

I told her, everyone from her friend Tancy to her boss, Elliott, to her sister, Mary.

"You saw Mary?" she asked.

"Yes."

"Where?"

"At her house. Winthrop Avenue."

"Who else was there?"

"Just her husband."

"Ted. How is dear Ted?"

"Ted's a bit distraught. He's sick and out of work. Come to think of it, he gave me a message for you."

"What message is that?"

"He said you'd better keep up your end of the deal. He said if you didn't you'd be sorry."

"I'm already sorry," Teresa Blair mumbled to herself. "As sorry as I've ever been."

"What sort of deal do you have with Ted Quilk?"

"Nothing. It's not important."

"It is to him. And from the look of it, to you, too."

She shook her head and frowned again. I flipped a mental coin, then left it where it was. The investigation was over. At most, I was a custodian. There was more to know, but it wasn't my business to know it.

"How's Elliott and the store?" she asked a few more miles down the road. "Is he going crazy without me?"

"Professionally or personally?"

"He told you about his little crush?"

"It sounded more like something out of a bodice ripper."

She laughed. "Poor Elliott. Did he tell you that just before he met me he'd convinced himself he was homosexual? I came along just as he was about to step out of the closet. Then he got the hots for me and now he's all confused. I told him bisexuality was very in, but it didn't seem to help."

We rolled on, buffeted by traffic and by speculation. I worried about staying awake. Mrs. Blair slept, on and off, making alternate sounds of contentment and distress. "Did you sleep with Tancy?" she asked quietly, as we rolled past Davis.

"Not quite," I answered. "She was overbooked."

Teresa Blair smiled tiredly. "Poor Tancy. She values everything but herself. How is James?"

"James is fine."

"James is always fine, always in pursuit of a majestic goal. Did he admit you to his temple?"

"The house?"

She nodded. "What did you think?"

"Lovely."

"And sterile?"

"A bit. But nice."

"A nice place to visit, maybe. You wouldn't want to live there. Believe me."

"Is that what running up to Tahoe was all about? You and James are splitting?" I didn't quite manage to keep the hope out of my voice.

She gave me an enigmatic smile and dropped her head back against the car seat and closed her eyes. "Have you ever gone to court?" she asked after I thought she was asleep.

"I've been in court a lot," I said. "I used to be a lawyer."

One eye opened. "Really?"

"Really."

"I'm a little frightened. I don't know what I'm supposed to do."

"Just listen to the questions, then answer them. Don't volunteer information and don't withhold it. If you don't understand something, say so. If you don't remember, say so. If you need to explain, say so. Don't argue, don't get mad. If you need help, ask the judge."

"That's all there is?"

"That's it. Well, maybe one more thing."

"What's that?"

"Tell the truth."

I took I-80 to the Benicia cutoff, then 680 south to the Rock Valley Road exit. I stayed in my car while Mrs. Blair went inside the Silver Season. She stayed for almost an hour. When she came back out, I asked how it went.

"She thought I was Mary. She thought *you* were my father. She thinks *her* father is lost in the building somewhere, calling to her for help. The nurse told me that last night she thought someone was trying to choke her."

"Sad."

"She was a lovely woman once. My father practically gave up his whole life for her. Can we go to your place now? I'm very tired."

I put the car in gear and took her home. Or almost. I was about to turn off upper Grant onto the street where I live when I spotted the green car parked half a block down the hill from my front door. There were two dark shapes inside it. I spun the steering wheel to the left and kept going straight. "I'm taking you to a hotel," I said.

"What?"

"A hotel. I know a little place on Post. We can stay there till Monday morning. No one but the bellhop will see us."

We checked in as man and wife but we didn't act like it.

She slept until noon on Saturday, then made me go out for an omelet. While she was wolfing it down, I slipped out to a pay phone and called James Blair. Her husband. A man who had been ridiculously accused of killing her.

"I've found your wife," I told him.

"Where is she?" he demanded.

"Safe."

"But where?"

"I don't think I'll tell you that. Not just yet."

"You're working for me, Tanner. Remember?"

"Not entirely," I said. "And I wasn't hired to deliver her to you, I was hired to deliver her to court. I'll do that on Monday. What happens after that is up to you and your wife. But until then I think I'll keep her on ice."

"I take it she doesn't want to see me."

"It's not what she wants, it's what I want."

"I don't like it. Not at all."

"I don't like it much, either," I said, then hung up.

It took three more calls to track down Ray Tolson. He was at police headquarters. I went through the same routine with him that I had with James Blair. Tolson didn't like it, either. "Join the club," I told him.

"Come on, Tanner. I need to prepare her testimony before the trial. I want to put her through a complete cross-examination, just like she's going to face on Monday."

"Sorry," I said. "I'll bring her in early Monday morning. Alert the boys at the back entrance, because I'm going to sneak her in. You can talk to her then."

"What's your problem, Tanner? You in love?"

"My problem is this case. It doesn't hang together worth a shit. I can't even sort out the teams, let alone the names and numbers of the players. Your man Detective Grinder tells me not to trust anyone in the DA's office; at least two muscle-brains warn me off the case, one with a hotfoot; you lie to me about what's really at issue in the Fluto case; and now, worst of all, you tell me that one of Tony Fluto's chief competitors in the mob scene is a guy named Wadley. Well, guess who I saw having dinner at Wadley's restaurant last night?"

"Who?"

"James Blair."

"Christ. What does *that* mean?"

"I don't have the faintest idea. Which is why I'm keeping Mrs. Blair under wraps until Monday. If I were *you*, I'd give some thought to my ethical obligations in this case. If Teresa Blair's a plant by Wadley to put Fluto away, then I don't see how you can even put her on the stand."

"I don't need you to tell me what my fucking ethical obligations are, Tanner," Tolson roared. "The only thing I can't do is knowingly introduce perjured testimony at the trial. Well, as of now I don't have one single goddamned hint that Mrs. Blair's testimony against Fluto will be perjured. So you can go to hell."

"Okay," I said. "I will."

"There is one thing you ought to know," Tolson said.

"What?"

"Someone tried to kill Tony Fluto's son last night. Close but no cigar. Kid's in Mercy Hospital with a bullet hole in his thigh."

"How does that relate to Mrs. Blair?" I asked.

"Who knows?"

"Not me," I said.

"You're taking on a big responsibility, Tanner. If someone takes Mrs. Blair out, I'm going to prosecute you."

"If someone takes her out, they'll have to take me out first," I said, and hung up.

On Saturday night Mrs. Blair complained of cabin fever and persuaded me to take her out of the hotel. I allowed myself to be persuaded because by then I was more afraid of what I might try to do to her there in the hotel room than of what Tony Fluto might try to do to her outside it. We caught a movie out in the Avenues and had a burger afterward at Bill's. Sunday brunch on Union Street; Sunday afternoon at the de Young; Sunday evening a Basque dinner at the Obrero Hotel. We spent the rest of the evening in the room, with brandy and Tootsie Rolls and KQED.

"Where did you grow up?" she asked me some time around midnight. They were her first words in over an hour.

"Iowa," I said.

"Nice place?"

"It didn't seem so then. It seems so now."

"Nothing gets worse with time except women," she said, running her hands down her flanks.

"And bananas."

"Were you rich?"

"Not rich, not poor."

"I was poor. In the beginning we were rich, and then we were poor. I didn't realize it till I started school. Then the other kids made sure I knew exactly where I stood. By the time I was twelve, I knew I'd do anything not to be poor when I grew up, I'd do anything not to end up like Mary."

"Is that why you went to Vegas?"

"That was part of it."

"What was the other part?"

"I can't say."

"Sure you can."

"No. Not for a while longer."

"Why was your first husband killed?" I asked quietly.

She didn't answer for several minutes. "I don't know for sure. Frankie was in someone's way, and then he wasn't." She laughed, musically and madly, then fell silent again.

"Someone tried to kill Tony Fluto's son yesterday," I said after a while.

"Really?"

"You know anything about it?"

"Why would I?"

"I don't know," I said. "And I guess I don't *want* to know." Then I smiled.

"What are you thinking?" she asked.

"About what your sister told me about Tancy Verritt running around in a parade with nothing but a gorilla mask on."

She laughed, too. "That wasn't Tancy, that was me."

When the doors to the courtroom opened on Monday, and the Policeman's Ball began, the arm Teresa Blair was on was mine.

Chapter
15

The courtroom was a vintage chamber complete with twelve-foot ceilings, hand-carved moldings, a high-backed judge's chair, and a swinging, squeaking gate through the bar of the court. Unlike the newer civic centers, the appointments weren't pressed wood and plastic but real oak and real walnut, scratched in spots, nicked in others, maintained reluctantly but regularly by persons who spent their nights in the county jail. The public pews were yellowed by time and stain and buffed to a shine by the seats of sliding spectators. The counsel tables were worn round at the edges by the acid palms of lawyers waiting to win or lose. I remembered a friend who used to tell what happened when his clients were found guilty: "The guy usually turns to me and asks, 'What do we do now?' And I just tell him, 'Well, you go to jail, and I go to lunch.'"

Teresa Blair and I took seats near the back of the courtroom and watched people drift in and out. Tolson had told us to meet him there, but he hadn't arrived yet, nor had any other court personnel except a corpulent bailiff who lay back in his tilting chair in an unimprovable imitation of sleep.

I took Mrs. Blair's hand and gave it a squeeze. It squeezed back. The telephone on the table beside the bailiff buzzed once. Mrs. Blair's fingers jumped in mine like live bait. The deputy listened to the receiver, then stood up. "Is there a Mrs. Blair in here?" he called out asthmatically. I raised my hand and pointed to her. "The DA wants to see you, lady. Room three-oh-four. Next flight up. And make it snappy."

I started to go with her but she pushed me back. "I'm on my own now," she said flatly. "Thanks. For everything. Maybe I'll see you afterward. If you want to. If they let me."

I nodded encouragement and patted her shoulder as she slipped past me.

The second hand made a tour of the clock on the wall. More of the regulars drifted in, men and women retired and pensioned off, looking for a place to park their bodies and their time. One man wore a pair of Oshkosh bibs as soft and faded as a battle flag; he was ready to work but there was no one to work for. One woman wore a black dress and a matching pillbox hat with a ragged veil dangling from it, in mourning for something, perhaps her youth. Others filed in silently, heads bowed, shoulders hunched, braced for breeze or insult. We all, the regulars and I, sat equidistant from each other, as though to prevent our several afflictions from spreading. Each time the door opened a dozen heads and two dozen eyes turned toward it.

A minute later Conway Grinder came in, looked at me and nodded as he walked past, took a seat in the front row and stuck a match in his mouth. Then the little man with the chipped tooth who'd confronted me outside the Moran Building entered the courtroom and took a seat against the far wall. He twitched nervously and looked at nothing but the flag; I don't think he saw me. I wondered what was in the briefcase he was carrying. By ten past nine the room was full and rumbling. Suddenly the rumbling stopped.

It was Tony Fluto, no question about it, hulking but dapper, hair and flesh of pewter, eyes sweeping the room like scythes. He moved down the center aisle, wordless and resolute, more annoyed than frightened at being where he was. Two young counselors fluttered around him, eyes white, mouths desperate, foreheads bright with sweat. When you work for guys like Fluto, it's peaches and cream unless you lose or develop a conscience. Then it's dreams of chemicals in the eyes and bombs in the car and quotes on a coach ticket to Brazil, one-way. A third man, Fluto's chief counsel at a guess, trailed behind the others, lithe and luxuriously groomed, even more indomitable than his client.

Fluto had been in court before. He led his entourage to the table nearest the jury box, took a seat in the center chair, and prepared himself to wait. The glance he threw at the bailiff almost knocked him over. Briefly, Fluto swiveled so he could see the rest of us, but the rest of us didn't interest him. His lawyers arranged themselves around him like thorns around a rose, fishing briefs and motions from their satchels and Maalox and mints from their vests.

My eyes were still on Fluto when I saw him nod, grimly and silently, to someone coming in behind me. I turned and looked into the sky-blue eyes of James Blair. He frowned when he saw me, started to say something and stopped, then took a seat several rows in front of me. When I looked back at Fluto, he was facing forward once again, his back as broad and erect as a gravestone. A dozen feet away from him Conway Grinder's jaw was bulging. I was glad I couldn't see his eyes. Fluto's chief counsel walked over to the man with the chipped tooth and whispered something that caused the man to swear.

The bailiff's eyes popped open once again as Tolson and his assistant swept into the room, looking harried but confident. Tolson flashed me the thumbs up sign as he walked past, then sat at the second counsel table on which his assistant arranged papers like the china for a twelve-course meal. Tolson didn't look at Fluto, and vice versa, but each man's mind must have been on the other. This was war and they were the generals. I sat back and got ready to enjoy a good fight.

The door in back of the judge's bench opened and a little round man wearing a red bow tie and a pseudosuede sport coat and a self-important smirk strolled to the small clerk's desk in the center of the room just below the judge's bench. After shuffling some papers he turned toward the spectators. "All witnesses are excluded from the proceedings," he announced. "Witnesses please proceed immediately to room two-sixteen and wait until you are called to testify."

No one left. The little clerk sat down and tugged his tie. The court reporter came in and set up her Stenorette, then sat primly behind it. Her skirt rose well above her knees. The clerk glanced at the expanse of thigh and smiled. The bailiff left the room. Three minutes later the doors banged open and about thirty people swept in, bringing a commotion in with them. They found seats and the din gradually subsided. One by one all eyes focused on the little door behind the bench.

The gavel banged.

The clerk ordered us to rise.

The judge entered.

She was tall and sharp-chinned, with dark arched brows above steel-rimmed glasses. Her hair was black and straight and fell in folds like her robe. Her high white collar could have served a cleric or a gull. She mounted the bench and took her seat with the inevitable reluctance of a veteran jurist.

In the singsong cadence of the rote, the clerk banged the gavel again and called the court into session, named the judge and called the case: "*State of California* versus *Guiseppi A. Fluto.*" Both sides pronounced themselves ready. The Honorable Susan McMinn, Judge of the Superior Court, directed the clerk to empanel the jury.

The tallest, thinnest, and oldest man at Fluto's table stood up. "Your Honor," he began slowly, "at this time the defendant has several motions to present. Since I am confident that the disposition of these matters will obviate the trial, I ask leave to present them at this time."

The judge lifted her glasses off her nose and placed them on top of her head. "We went into this last week, Mr. Loggins. I heard your motions then, and upon due consideration I denied them. I told you I would not hear motions this morning; I told you to come prepared for trial."

"Your Honor, my client has certain rights, and as his counsel I am compelled—"

"Your client's rights have been and will continue to be scrupulously observed, as are the rights of all defendants, by this court. However, we are going to trial today, Mr. Loggins. You have had ample time to make whatever motions you deem necessary. Are you ready to proceed?"

"If it please the court, I would like the record to reflect the following seven motions which the defendant urges today, and one of which—"

"Sit down, Mr. Loggins."

"Your Honor—"

"The clerk will empanel the jury."

"May I make a statement for the record, Your Honor? Serious matters of prejudice are occurring here, and the record should reflect them. I insist—"

"You do not insist in this court, Mr. Loggins. *I* insist. The record will reflect that on Friday last you presented some twenty-one motions to this court on behalf of Mr. Fluto. All were denied. Any further record you wish to make regarding pretrial matters may be made in the Court of Appeals. The clerk will empanel the jury."

"There have been developments since last week that are significant, Your Honor. Mr. Fluto's son lies in a hospital room, the victim of an assault with a deadly weapon. This outrage clearly supports our contention that a conspiracy is afoot to persecute Mr. Fluto, to remove him from society at any cost—"

"*Enough*, Mr. Loggins. The veniremen are present. The clerk will empanel the jury."

The little clerk released his nostril and stood at his desk and began pulling slips of paper from a little container and reading the names on them, struggling with the pronunciation of every other one. The persons named stumbled toward their seats in the jury box, looking alarmed and cowed. After twelve were seated the judge spoke again.

"Ladies and gentlemen, this is a criminal trial, the *State of California* versus *Giuseppi A. Fluto*. The charges will be explained more fully at a later time. Mr. Fluto is the gentleman seated in the center of the table beside you. He is represented by Mr. Lafcadio Loggins. Mr. Loggins is assisted by Mr. Daniel Rotunda and Mr. Jacob Goldberg. All three gentlemen are with the law firm of Loggins, Swain and Rotunda. The State is represented by Mr. Raymond Tolson, Deputy District Attorney. Mr. Tolson is assisted by Ms. Roxanne Epley. Do any of you know any of the attorneys I mentioned, or the law firm, or Mr. Fluto the defendant? Fine. At this time the lawyers for both sides are given the opportunity to question you in order to determine whether you can accord both sides a fair trial in this case. Sit down, Mr. Loggins. Your turn will come. Mr. Tolson?"

"Thank you, Your Honor," Tolson said as he rose. "Ladies and gentlemen . . ."

And we were off. Tolson had doubtlessly picked a hundred or so criminal juries. He knew the kind of person he wanted and, more significantly, the kind he didn't want, and he knew how to find out which was which. Before long the spectators and I knew who was married, divorced, or single, who worked and at what, who read what magazines, who joined what clubs, who went to church, who belonged to a union, who had had trouble with the law at some time in their lives, who had previously served on a jury, and who was angry that they were losing a full day's pay in return for the measly jury fee.

Then Tolson moved into the tough stuff. Whether any of them would be repelled by photos of a dead man. Whether they would hold it against the State if such photos were offered into evidence. Whether any of them had qualms about bringing in a guilty verdict. Whether they understood and accepted the concept of circumstantial evidence. Of reasonable doubt. And on and on, rephrasings and restatements and reformulations, all to smoke out the man or woman who, on retiring to the jury room after the close of the evidence, would pop up and declare, "I don't care what anyone says, a man with a face like that just *couldn't* have done what they say he did." I went out for a cigarette and a Coke, and then came back.

I was interested to see what Loggins would do when his turn came, and it came at about eleven o'clock. Tolson had challenged one woman for cause—she was on the same bowling team with Fluto's daughter-in-law—and then Tolson passed for cause and it was Loggins's turn. As though lifted by the Lord himself, Loggins rose to his feet and stood behind the chair in which Fluto was sitting, gripping his lapels with tapered fingers, his head bowed in Lincolnesque gravity. After a few more seconds he placed his hands on his client's shoulders and offered his eyes to the jury like alms.

"I have but one question," he intoned. "Mr. Fluto sits here an innocent man, as innocent of this crime as you or me. The law *requires* you to presume that fact. And unless the State proves each element of the crime with which Mr. Fluto is charged—*each element*—beyond a reasonable doubt, Mr. Fluto must walk out of here as he came in—an innocent man—even if he does not utter a single word in his own defense. I repeat: *even if he does not say a single word during this entire trial*. Do you understand and agree to abide by that principle, Mr. Carson?

"Mrs. Robustelli?

"Mr. Lute?

"Mr. Wandrell?

"Mrs. Becker?

"Miss Abernathy?

"Mr. Nix?

"Mr. Donaldson?

"Mr. Liu?

"Mr. Mihalovich?

"Mrs. Walters?

"Mr. Jefferson?

"Thank you all. Your Honor, the defense is pleased with the panel. We pass for cause. We shall exercise no peremptories."

It was a gamble for Loggins, but it seemed one worth taking. He won points with all of them by not kicking anyone off the panel, by not asking a bunch of personal questions, by seeming to trust their integrity, by not acting like a lawyer. The ball was back in Tolson's court, and after a few seconds of whispering with his assistant he called Loggins's bluff. "The State also is confident the panel will accord both sides a fair trial."

The judge smiled for the first time since entering the courtroom, then turned to the jury and gave them the oath "to well and truly try" the issues in the case. "At this time," she went on, "each side may, if it wishes, make an opening statement. Opening statements are not evidence. They are simply statements of what each side believes the evidence it intends to present will show. Mr. Tolson?"

Ray Tolson shuffled some papers, closed his eyes for a second or two, then stood and looked, one by one, at the twelve faces in the box in front of him, the twelve faces he would have to convince by the end of the trial.

"This is a case involving a man who was run over by an automobile," he began. "The man was killed. His name was Phillip Vincent. The man driving the car that killed him was Tony Fluto, the defendant. The man sitting right there. After he ran down Mr. Vincent, the defendant kept on driving. He sped away without stopping once. This makes Mr. Fluto guilty of the charge of failing to stop and render aid. That is the least offense involved in this case. The next greater offense is manslaughter. If you believe beyond a reasonable doubt that Tony Fluto was driving the car that killed Mr. Vincent, then you must find him guilty of that charge. Finally, ladies and gentlemen, the evidence will show that the defendant, Tony Fluto, *intended* to kill Mr. Vincent, that he lured Mr. Vincent down to Oswego Street for just that purpose and that he did, in fact, carry out his intention willfully and deliberately, with malice aforethought. If you believe beyond a reasonable doubt that Mr. Fluto intended to and did kill Phillip Vincent by running him down with an automobile, then you must find him guilty of murder."

Tolson told it simply, but with a touch of raw, uncooked elegance. The jury listened carefully, and looked at Fluto from time to time, measuring him against the charges Tolson listed. They seemed interested but not repelled; curious more than anything. For his part, Fluto remained impassive and impressive, capable of anything, even innocence.

For my part, I was mad as hell. Ray Tolson had lied to me yet another time. He hadn't told me he was going for a murder conviction, and worse, he had denied that there was a connection between Fluto and the dead man. Now he was claiming Fluto had killed him intentionally, that it had been a hit. It might have made a difference, knowing that. I might have been more careful, for myself and for Teresa

Blair. As I swore under my breath, the little man with the chipped tooth got up and hurried out of the room, his features crunched into a frown. If Teresa Blair hadn't been due to begin her testimony, I would have stomped out after him and left El Gordo forever.

Tolson sat down and the judge spoke: "Mr. Loggins?"

Loggins got to his feet. "Defendant once again requests leave to present a motion to the court."

"Request denied. Proceed."

"In that event, defendant reserves his opening until the close of the State's evidence."

"Very well," the judge said. "Call your first witness, Mr. Tolson."

"The State calls Mrs. Teresa Blair."

The judge banged the gavel to wake the bailiff, and he trotted off to fetch her, his pistol flopping like a fish on his flank.

If she was nervous, she was hiding it behind the slats of a flexless, stalwart face and within clenched, bone-white hands. She marched down the center aisle of the courtroom, with the gait of the righteous and the wronged, wearing a burgundy suit and a white silk blouse and a mantle of mature and emotionless credibility. As she stood before the witness box with her right hand raised, taking the oath to tell the truth, Ray Tolson had the thin lips and languid eyes of a man holding a pat hand in a straight game.

"Please be seated and state your name and spell it," the clerk directed once the oath was taken.

"Teresa Blair. T–E–R–E–S–A B–L–A–I–R."

The judge nodded to Tolson. He stood up, checked his notes, checked the jury, checked his opponent, then gazed steadily at Teresa Blair. "Where do you live, Mrs. Blair?"

"Twenty-one-ninety Vista Grande Terrace."

"In El Gordo?"

"I'm sorry. Yes."

"How long have you lived there?"

"Ten years."

"Are you married?"

"Yes."

"What is your husband's name?"

"James. James Blair."

"What does he do for a living?"

"He's an accountant and an investment advisor."

"Self-employed?"

"Yes."

"How about you, Mrs. Blair? Do you work outside the home?"

"Yes. I work part-time at Bathsheba's, a women's store. I'm part owner of the store, and I'm the chief buyer."

Tolson glanced at the jury to make sure they were with him. "What does a chief buyer do, Mrs. Blair?"

"Objection," Loggins interjected. "The operation of a women's clothing outlet is exceedingly interesting, I'm sure, but hardly relevant, Your Honor."

"The jury is entitled to know the witness's profession, Your Honor," Tolson countered. "In aid of their assessment of her credibility."

"Overruled," the judge said. "Although to be precise, Mr. Tolson, let's ask her what *she* does for her store, not what buyers in general might do."

"Very well, Your Honor. What do *you* do at Bathsheba's, Mrs. Blair?"

She smiled. "My main function is to select the clothes to be carried in our inventory. I do this chiefly from catalogs and magazines, and twice a year I make trips to New York and Los Angeles, to the spring and fall showings."

"What size inventory does Bathsheba's carry?"

"Approximately two hundred thousand, at wholesale."

"Dollars?"

"Yes."

"And you buy all those clothes yourself?"

"Almost all. My partner, Mr. Farnsworth, makes a

buying trip to Europe each spring. He comes back with a few original gowns usually, but not many."

"Can we get on with it, Your Honor?" Loggins pleaded from his chair.

"I'm surprised you're so anxious to hear what Mrs. Blair has to say," Tolson shot back. "I doubt that your client shares your eagerness."

"No more of that, gentlemen," Judge McMinn snapped. "Continue."

"Mrs. Blair," Tolson asked, "where were you on June ninth, 1980, at approximately seven P.M.?"

"I was in my car. On my way home from a friend's house. It was a Sunday."

"Did anything unusual happen that evening?"

"It certainly did."

"Tell us about it."

"Objection," Loggins called out. "Calls for a narrative response."

"I withdraw the question," Tolson said. "Where were you that evening, Mrs. Blair? Precisely."

She shifted uneasily, glanced up at the judge, and then at the defense table, and then back to Tolson. "As I said, I was on my way home from a friend's house. I got trapped in the wrong lane of the freeway as I got near El Gordo—the traffic was very heavy—and so I got off the freeway going north on El Camino instead of south, toward my home. I didn't want to block traffic by making a left turn—I never make left turns—so I turned to the right, intending to swing around and head the other way on El Camino. But because of some road construction I had to go several blocks before I could make another right turn, and it had gotten dark and, I don't know, somehow I found myself down in the industrial area of town, in a place I had never seen before."

"What was the street?"

"Oswego, I believe."

"How many blocks off El Camino?"

"About five, I think."

"Was anyone in the car with you?"

"No."

"So you wandered off your route. Then what happened?"

"Well, I pulled to the curb to look at my map of the city, so I could figure out where I was and how I could get out of there. I was frightened, I don't mind saying. That's a pretty rough area. I wanted to get away from there as rapidly and directly as possible, without wandering into some place even worse."

"Did you have your lights on or off while you looked at the map?"

"My headlights were off."

"Why?"

"Because I was afraid. I didn't want to attract attention. I used a flashlight to read the map."

"Did you see anyone else in the area?"

"Not at first. But just as I was about to leave, a car came along. Just as it passed me, another car raced up after it, very fast, and forced the first car to the curb."

"How far were you from where all this was happening?"

"About twenty yards, maybe."

"Still parked?"

"Yes."

"What happened next?"

"Well, the drivers got out of their cars and walked toward each other, right in the middle of the street. The man from the second car said something to the first man. For some reason, I thought they knew each other."

"Why?"

"I'm not sure. They just didn't seem to be strangers. The second man had clearly been chasing the first, for some reason. It wasn't just a traffic accident."

"Did you hear what either of them said?"

"No. My windows were rolled up and my heater was on."

"Did the men see you?"

"I don't think so."

"Then what happened?"

"Well, I decided I didn't want to be there, not at all, so I fumbled around and put the map away and put the car in gear and started to drive away."

"Did you put on your lights?"

"No. I hoped neither of them would notice me. I didn't want them to know I had seen them."

"Why not?"

"I'm not sure. It just looked suspicious, like they were doing something illegal."

"Objection," Loggins said. "Speculation. Move to strike."

The judge nodded. "The jury will disregard the answer to the last question."

"What happened next?" Tolson asked.

"Well, I was looking back, ready to drive away, and I saw the man from the second car run back to his car and get in it. The first man stayed in the middle of the street for a few seconds, yelling something, it looked like. Then he started to run. And the man in the second car started it up and drove after the first man and, well, he just went faster and faster and the first man couldn't get away and he ran him down. And the car just kept going. And the first man just lay there, all bent and twisted. It was terrible."

The room lacked sound and movement. Our collective mind contemplated streets and shadows, men and cars, sounds and movements, the fatal confluence of metal and flesh and bone. Tolson let the images rage, then spoke softly. "What did you do then, Mrs. Blair?"

"I drove off, at first, because I was so frightened. But then I realized I had to do something for the man who was lying there, so I found a phone and called an ambulance. Then I went back and looked at him. He didn't move. I was sure he was dead, and when I heard the siren, I got back in my car and drove away. I, well, I didn't want to get involved."

"Did you come forward later and give a statement to the police?"

"Yes. When I saw in the paper that they'd found the man who did it but that it looked like he might get off because the case against him was weak, I knew I couldn't live with myself if I didn't tell what I'd seen."

Tolson nodded, then stepped back to a place where he could see all the stage and all the characters upon it with a single glance. "Did you get a good look at the man who drove the second car, Mrs. Blair? At the man who ran the first man down?"

"Yes, I did."

"Is that man in the courtroom this morning?"

Her eyes darted away from Tolson's face but couldn't find a place to land. "Could you be more specific, Mr. Tolson?" she asked.

Tolson smiled unnaturally. "Is the man who drove the second car the same man who is sitting in the center chair at the next table?"

She looked squarely at Fluto. He looked squarely at her. Both of them looked infinitely sad. "I've never seen that man before in my life," Teresa Blair said, her words as faint as the flight of arrows.

Chapter
16

The silence in the courtroom was of the quality that death commands. It lingered until it became a presence, a masked intruder that had forced its way among us and commandeered the room. When it was finally broken, it was by the vulgar thrust of Conway Grinder's curse, made all the more vulgar by the hush from which it rose.

The curse unloosed a murmur that threatened to become a din until the judge's gavel stemmed the sound. Everyone knew what had happened and everyone wanted to make sure the rest of us knew it as well. When I looked at James Blair, he was smiling.

From the instant of the answer, Ray Tolson had been locked in place, as though his witness had delivered a blow instead of a denial. With the sound of the gavel Tolson moved, in three giant strides, directly toward Teresa Blair, to pry the truth from her with fright. "Mrs. Blair," he roared, "are you denying that Tony Fluto was the man you saw run down Phillip Vincent on the night of June ninth?"

Her eyes were closed. "Yes. I am."

"Do you recall the statement you gave to me a few days following Mr. Fluto's indictment, Mrs. Blair? Do you recall identifying a photograph of Tony Fluto, the man sitting right here, as positively the man who was driving the car that night? Do you, Mrs. Blair?"

Loggins leaped to his feet. "Objection, Your Honor. Mr. Tolson is willfully proceeding in violation of the ethical canons, specifically Disciplinary Rule Seven-one-oh-six, in asserting his personal knowledge of facts in issue. Also, he is attempting to testify. Also, he is impeaching his own witness."

"Objection sustained. The jury will disregard the last question. You know better, Mr. Tolson."

Tolson backed away from Teresa Blair and reeled about the room, his face aflame. His assistant tried to get his attention, but she was a sparrow against the falcon of his rage. He finally staggered back to the witness stand. His nose was less than a foot from Teresa Blair's. "I ask you once again, Mrs. Blair. Is the man you saw run down Phillip Vincent in this courtroom today?"

"No. He is not."

She answered over Loggins's objection to the question, but it didn't matter. At least two of the jurors began shaking their heads, from pity or dismay. The judge's head was bowed.

Loggins rose again, a smile sliding slowly across his face. "I move for dismissal of all charges against Mr. Fluto, Your Honor. Clearly, the prosecution has attempted to manufacture a case out of whole cloth and the attempt has backfired, thanks to the courage and honesty of Mrs. Blair. There is no alternative to dismissal of the charges and the release of my client."

The judge frowned. "Mr. Tolson?"

"I request a recess, Your Honor. The testimony is a complete surprise, diametrically opposed to earlier statements from the witness. Other evidence may well be available. In the interest of justice I request a recess to explore other avenues. And to inform Mrs. Blair of the consequences of her behavior this morning." The look he gave her was one of unmasked hatred.

"In the interest of justice *I* insist that all charges be dismissed immediately," Loggins said.

The judge thought it over, her chin resting on the heel of her hand. The attorneys glared balefully at each other. Tony Fluto looked thoughtfully at Teresa Blair, perhaps to divine her motive for exonerating him. Tolson's assistant got up, went over to him, and whispered in his ear, then nodded and trotted out of the room without looking back.

The judge banged her gavel once again. "This court will be in recess until nine tomorrow morning. At that time the State will be prepared to proceed or a motion for dismissal will be entertained. Is that clear?"

"It is, Your Honor," Tolson said.

"The jury is directed to report back to the jury room at nine as well. You are discharged for the rest of the day." The jury filed out looking puzzled but relieved.

"I ask the bailiff to detain Mrs. Blair," Tolson said after the jury had gone. "Ms. Epley is on the way back with a warrant for her arrest. The charge is perjury."

Teresa Blair gasped audibly. The judge nodded and smiled with what looked like regret. "I'll be in chambers," she said, and left the bench.

The clerk trotted off after her. The court reporter folded her Stenorette with sounds of breaking bottles. Loggins and his partners whispered to each other, then gathered up their papers and prepared to leave.

For some reason Tony Fluto seemed reluctant to depart. Loggins leaned down and whispered to him but Fluto shook his head and stood up. With a shrug he pulled away from Loggins's grasp and walked over to the witness box and leaned down and said something to Teresa Blair. Tolson noticed the whisper and hurried toward them, but by the time he got there, Fluto was on his way out of the room. Tolson went back to his table and began to thumb through the file.

I stood up and looked at Teresa Blair. When she noticed me, I widened my eyes in a question. She shrugged listlessly, on the verge of collapse and tears. Her forehead gleamed with seamless sweat.

I walked toward her, memories of my own days as a trial lawyer welling up as I pushed my way through the bar of the court and walked to the witness box. "Are you all right?" I asked.

"I think so."

"You're going to be arrested, you know."

"I know."

"The charge is perjury. Can they make it stick?"

I was really asking if she had told the truth. She knew it but she evaded. "I don't know," she replied. "Can they?"

I looked at her. "Even if you were lying, they'll have trouble making a case. Perjury's tough to prove, partly because to prove you were lying when you said Fluto wasn't the guy in the car they'll first have to prove he was. But you might have made a little mistake."

"What?"

"You didn't just say that Fluto didn't do it, you said you'd never seen him before. If they can prove you have, even in the check-out line at the Safeway, they may try to convict you, as an example. And because Tolson's so mad he could eat rocks."

"I see."

"You should get a lawyer."

"Should I?"

"Do you know any?"

"No. Wait. A man named Cosgrove. He was kind of a friend, once. In high school. He might help, if he remembers."

"Where does he practice?"

"Here. El Gordo. But I haven't seen him in years."

"I'll call him. Wait here if you can. If they take you away before I get back, don't say anything at all to anyone unless Cosgrove is with you."

She nodded silently. I patted the back of her hand and got out of the courtroom without Tolson noticing. James Blair had already gone. There was a pay phone at the far end of the hall and I put a call in to Mason Cosgrove, senior partner in the firm of Cosgrove and Wilty, Attorneys and Counselors at Law.

He was in, and when I mentioned Teresa Goodrum Blair, his voice slipped out of formality and into concern. "Teresa. God. It's been years."

"How well do you remember her?" I ventured.

"I was in love with Teresa Goodrum from the time I was fourteen until the day she left town with Trudy Valente. For two years after that, even. I went to Las Vegas once to watch her dance. The most beautiful thing I've ever seen and I see it again every time I have more than two drinks. Is she all right?"

"I think so," I said. "But she's in trouble. The DA's so mad he can't see. He called her as a witness and she blew him out of the water. She's about to be booked for perjury."

"Which DA?"

"Tolson."

"She does have trouble. He's good and he's tough and he never forgets or forgives."

I told Cosgrove the story, or at least its outlines, and he promised to leave for City Hall right away. "I'll probably fall in love all over again the minute I see her," he said with a dry chuckle.

"You probably will," I said, speaking from experience. When Cosgrove hung up without asking about his fee, I knew his sentiments were real.

When I got back to the courtroom, everyone had gone except the bailiff. "Your name Tanner?" he asked as I stood at the back of the room trying to decide what to do. After I admitted it, he smiled broadly. "Tolson wants you to meet him in his office." The smile became a chuckle. "Shit really hit the propeller today, didn't it?"

"Something like that. Where's Mrs. Blair?"

"Being booked."

"Where's that?"

"Basement." The bailiff raised his gunbelt off his belly, then let it flop back into place. "A man like Tony Fluto," he said reflectively, "they ain't never gonna put *him* away."

"I guess not."

"Just as well. Hell, those guys, the mob, they just give folks what they want. Women and booze and a roll of the dice."

I decided Mason Cosgrove could find Teresa Blair quicker than I could so I took the stairs to Tolson's office. He and Conway Grinder were there. Each looked as though he had been blaming the other for what had happened, but when they saw me they both got ready to toss the blame my way.

"What the hell, Tanner?" Tolson exclaimed as I walked in. "You brought her in. Did you know she was going to pull that shit?"

"No."

"Well, what the hell?" he repeated. "What's going on?"

"Fluto got to her," Grinder growled. "He bought her or he scared her. Either way, Fluto walks."

"Maybe that's what happened," I said. "But maybe not. She doesn't need money and she doesn't scare easily from what I can see. Could she be protecting someone else?"

"I don't know who," Tolson said.

"By the way," I went on, "you didn't happen to mention that this was a murder case. Who the hell was the dead man? Why did Fluto take him out?"

"Never mind that," Tolson said. "I don't want you involved in that at all. Syndicate operations in El Gordo are my problem, not yours. What you know could get you killed."

"What I don't know could, too."

"Leave it, Tanner. It doesn't matter now, anyway."

"You know, Tanner," Grinder said, "you don't seem all that upset. It occurs to me that maybe you told the Blair broad to back off. Maybe you wanted to make sure Tony didn't mess up that body of hers. Maybe you wanted to keep it just the way it was this last weekend. While you were shacked up with it."

"I didn't tell her anything, Grinder, except to steer clear of you. Which is the same advice I'd give anything above an amoeba."

"You know what this is, don't you?" Tolson interrupted.

"I know," I said. "The perfect crime."

Tolson nodded as though the phrase had dazed him. "Fluto and that woman set me up. Suckered me into going to trial, into thinking I had a case, and like a fool I fell for it. The minute that fucking jury was sworn, jeopardy attached; now if he's acquitted or if I have to dismiss the case he can take an ad in the *Chronicle* and confess he killed Vincent and there's not a damned thing I can do about it. Well, the Blair woman's going to pay, I'll tell you that. Her tits will have sagged to her knees by the time she gets out." Tolson rubbed the back of his neck as though his bruised and battered ego was housed somewhere deep within it.

"What's this new evidence you told the judge you're going to turn up by morning?" I asked.

Tolson shrugged listlessly. "Hell, I just wanted to make Fluto sweat one more night."

"What about the other witness? The lush?"

Tolson flipped his hand in a gesture of dismissal. "Across the hall. He's okay for corroboration, at least if we can keep him away from the sauce for another day. But I can't go with him alone. I'd be laughed out of the profession."

"How about the kid?" I asked.

"What kid?" Tolson said wearily, then answered his own question. "You mean the one who supposedly saw the whole thing? The one we never found?"

I nodded.

Grinder sat up straight. "What the hell do you know about the kid?" he asked suspiciously.

"Nothing," I said.

"You sure?"

"As sure as I am that you need a new blade in your razor."

Grinder started to frame a retort but turned to Tolson instead. "I'll go down to Oswego Street and try to come up with something on the kid. Maybe after all this time someone will have forgotten there was a reason not to talk about what happened that night."

Tolson nodded. "It's the only chance we've got, I guess. You got any ideas on the subject, Tanner?"

"Maybe one or two."

"You willing to spend another day on this?"

I thought it over. I didn't really care whether they got Fluto or not. He was a minor hood in a world that's full of hoods, so the sun wouldn't shine more brightly on my block if he went to jail. And if I helped put him there, and he knew it, my apartment might get real warm all of a sudden, the way my office had. Plus, Tolson hadn't played straight with me, even at the beginning. Plus, I wasn't comfortable working with cops like Grinder, cops with their backs to the wall, desperate for a conviction. That's when the rules get bent, when the conscience gets calloused, and the vision blurred. All of a sudden things are overlooked that were spotted easily when they first joined the force. But there was one thing they had that I could use, something I decided to shoot for. "How about a trade?" I asked.

"For what?" Tolson replied. "The only thing I got to trade is justice, Tanner. The only ones who want to trade for that are scum. You weren't supposed to fall in that category."

Grinder mumbled something that I ignored. "I'll spend the next twenty-four hours trying to come up with that kid," I said. "But if I find him, will you drop the perjury charge against Teresa Blair?"

Grinder laughed evily. "She must throw a mean fuck."

I took a step toward Grinder but Tolson held me back. "Shut up, Grinder," he said, then looked at me. "I'll drop the charge," he went on. "What kid you got in mind?"

"I'll tell you when and if I know more than I do now. I'd like to talk to your other witness. The lush."

Tolson shrugged. "Help yourself. Room across the way. We cleaned him up some, but he still smells like a wet rug."

I crossed the hall to a storeroom filled with piles of tattered law books and mounds of broken furniture and stacks of unused copy paper and file folders and adding-machine tapes. And one other thing. A man. Slumped almost prone in an upholstered chair that tilted oddly on its three functioning legs. His eyes were closed, his lips quivering with his breaths. His wrists and ankles extended well beyond his clothes, which I suspected had been worn by at least one man before him. His skin was jaundiced and dull, as though he'd been gathering dust for years. He was brown-haired and younger than he should have been to be in that condition. He was my age.

When the door banged shut behind me, he opened his eyes and blinked. "Time?" he asked. The words were formed with cracked and thickened lips.

I shook my head. "There's been a complication. You won't have to testify until tomorrow. If at all."

"Then I can get out of here." He curled his legs under him and started to roll out of the chair. His socks flopped down below his knobby ankles.

I held up a hand. "I can't let you leave yet," I told him. "That's not my decision to make. Tolson will be in later to talk to you. I just want some information."

"About what?"

"About what you saw the night Phillip Vincent was killed."

He sighed and rubbed his lips. "I've told it all a hundred times. It just makes me thirsty." His eyes narrowed. "You don't happen to have a pint on you, do you? A pint of anything?"

I shook my head. "My name's Tanner," I said cheerily. "What's yours?"

"The name is Lufkin. Colin Lufkin. Known to the denizens of Rutland Avenue as Scabs."

"Why 'Scabs'?"

"This."

He raised the left leg of his slacks. The white skin over his shin was broken by a score of red-brown sores, some still festering, the rest crusted over in flaking mounds of dried blood and pus. Scabs smiled as he watched me view the leg, smiled with the smile of a man who knows exactly what will happen next in the world. But I didn't say anything. "Aren't you going to ask me how I could let myself get this way?" he prompted. "Everyone does."

I shrugged. "Everyone's got scabs," I said. "Some just show more than others." I returned his smile. He looked at me more closely.

"I think you know," he said finally.

"Know what?"

"That the difference between what I am and what you are is only a matter of adaptability."

"Adaptability to what?"

"To doing less than we were put here to do."

"Which is?"

"To fight the bastards."

"What bastards?"

"The bastards who want the rest of us to be just like them."

Lufkin looked at me intently, with faded black eyes that floated like smoke signals over his scraggly beard. What he saw must have convinced him that I agreed with him, and maybe what he saw was right. "What do you want to know, Tanner?" he asked expansively, leaning back in the chair and clasping his hands behind his head.

"Start with what you were doing down on Oswego Street that night. Is that your usual turf?"

"Naw. I hang out around Rutland Avenue, at the relief mission there, you know? I was on Oswego because of a woman."

Lufkin suddenly became a degenerate pixie. Because booze usually rots the capacity for lust, I had one more bit of proof that Colin Lufkin wasn't quite what the world assumed him to be. "Explain," I said.

"It was a Sunday, right? Well, I know this woman. This lady. She's married to a trucker, name of Rex. He's on the road all during the week, so there's no problem, but when he's home, weekends, he drinks. And when he drinks, he beats her. He beats her bad. One night when she ran out of the house to get away from him she ended up running into me. We talked. We liked each other. We made love in a boxcar and then she went home. I told her I'd be there on Oswego every night on every weekend. I told her if it ever got bad again she could come find me."

"Did she come that night?"

"No."

"When's the last time you saw her?"

"Only that once. Nine months ago."

"And you're still waiting?"

He shrugged. "Gives me something to do."

"What's her name?" I asked.

"Fuck you, my good sir," he said, gallant and proud of it.

"Why doesn't she leave the guy if he's such a bastard?"

"What would she do, Tanner? Live with me in a boxcar? I'm not part of the landed gentry, in case you hadn't noticed. And she can't support herself."

"Why not?"

"She's only got one arm."

I couldn't resist. "What were you before you hit the street, Lufkin?"

He nodded, content that I was finally predictable. "Car salesman. Fords. I've sold a thousand Fords in my life. Every one of them a bigger piece of junk than the last. The early Mustang was the only one worth driving. And Ford was better than anything else Detroit put out."

I could have asked him why he quit, and why he turned to liquor instead of merely changing jobs, and why he lived the way he lived, but I didn't. I'd listen if he started to tell me, but I wouldn't ask. "What's the first thing you saw that related to the killing?" I asked instead.

"Well, I didn't see the Blair woman drive up or anything, if that's what you mean. I got there about six, and there wasn't anyone around. I had my Ripple, and a relatively sanitary doorway, and I was probably nodding off, as usual, when things started to happen. The first thing I heard was the bang of a car door."

"Just one?"

"I don't know. There were a whole bunch of cars down there. I looked to see what was making all the racket—I was afraid it might be a cop, you know—and I saw these two guys standing out in the middle of the street talking to each other."

"You hear what they were saying?"

"Nope. I didn't pay that much attention, but then one of them hopped in his car and started it up and just plain ran down the other guy. Made a sound like a beached boat when he hit him." Lufkin chuckled. "Another night of fun and excitement down on Oswego Street."

"Why didn't the guy in the street run away?"

"He tried to."

"Was he on the sidewalk when he got hit?"

"Nope. Come to think of it, he started to run toward one of the buildings but it was like there was something over there in the dark that he was afraid of."

"Or someone."

"Right."

"You ever see either of the men before?"

"I don't think so, but who knows? I don't see so good anymore."

"Were you drunk?"

Lufkin laughed hoarsely. "I been drunk since 'sixty-two, so that's not the right question. The question is, were the spiders out."

"What does that mean?"

"It means that when I've been into the sauce real bad, two or three quarts a day, then it's like there's these spiders crawling on my eyeballs. Big, hairy spiders that scratch me and tickle me at the same time, and they won't get off, not even when I shut my eyes or rub them or claw them or anything. They just stay right there, crawling up and down, the fuzzy little bastards. Man, it's something." Lufkin wrenched his head to the side fiercely, as though the spiders had arrived again.

"Was it like that that night?" I asked.

"No, but then it wasn't exactly normal, either."

"Why not?"

"Because after things died down, and I looked at the woman in the car stopped way down at the end of the block, I began seeing double."

"What about the kid you saw? Where was he?"

"Down there, too. Screwing around on the sidewalk, tossing rocks, kicking cans. Probably looking for a drunk to roll."

"What did the kid look like?"

"A kid. Long hair. T-shirt. Levi's. A kid. A punk. Used to be one myself."

"Do you think he lives down there?"

"He might live there, he might live on the moon. If he's lucky, it's the moon."

"How about Fluto? He do anything after he ran the man down?"

"Just sped away, man. Like he'd run down a skunk."

"Anything else you can remember?"

"Nope. Well, one thing. Just before he hopped in his car, Fluto told the other guy that he'd broken the law. 'You broke the law,' that's what he said."

"What do you think it meant?"

"Who knows? Maybe the guy was double-parked."

Chapter 17

He trudged up the hill along with four of his buddies, pushing his bike with one hand, slinging a book bag over his shoulder with the other. They were five cookies made from the same cutter, boys dressed as men who dressed as boys. One of them was shoving or being shoved, taunting or being taunted, each step of the way. The energy expended could have lit El Gordo for a week.

I had been sitting on the front bumper of my Buick for half an hour, wishing I'd worn a sweater under my sport coat, waiting for him. When he saw me, he peeled off from the group and walked over toward me, his eyes dodging with uncertainty. The rest of the boys eyed us like guests at a second wedding.

"Hi," he said.

"Hi, Davy."

"You waiting for Mom? She won't be home till five."

"What will you do till she gets here?"

"You know. Hack around."

"You like being on your own?"

"Sure." His smile was less positive than his word.

"I was waiting for *you*, actually, Davy."

"Yeah? Me?"

I nodded.

He frowned and thought a minute. It made his pug nose wrinkle. "I'm not supposed to talk to strangers," he said. "Are you a stranger?"

"I don't know. What do you think?"

He thought about what he thought, kicking at the street dirt all the while with a shoe that had a score of black rubber nipples on the bottom and a two-inch slit in the side. The sock that puffed through the slit was black with dirt. "I guess you're not," he concluded finally. "You know Mom, and everything."

"Right."

"What did you want to talk about?"

"Mrs. Blair."

"Oh."

"Hey, Martin." The kid who shouted was freckled and red-haired and half a foot smaller than the others. "That your old man?"

Before Davy could answer, another boy said, loud enough for Davy to hear: "Naw. His old man's *fat*. Besides, his mom told his old man if he ever came back here again she'd *shoot* him."

"How do *you* know?" the redhead asked.

"My *mom* told me."

"Maybe that's Martin's *new* dad," the redhead said. The sneer on his face contorted everything below his cowlick.

Davy dropped his eyes and stuffed his hands in his pockets and shuffled from foot to foot. "He's already married," he called out to his friends, republishing my earlier lie.

"So what?" the redhead answered. "He can get unmarried and married again any time. If he *wants* to."

I groped for something to say, then stood up and turned

toward the gang. "I'm with the government," I called loudly. "Davy here has some information we need. I can't tell you much about it, because it involves the national security. Now, we can't be disturbed for a few minutes, but I'd like you all to do something for me while we're talking. I'd like you to fan out and make sure no one tries to get close enough to hear what we're saying. If you see someone coming, someone on foot, you yell and let me know. Got it?"

They didn't all buy all of it—it's been tough to shuck a kid ever since they started getting shucked for four hours every Saturday in between the cartoons—and I wouldn't have even tried it down in the flats, but up on the hill enough of them bought enough of it so that they nodded collectively and divided into two groups and started up and down the street, walking more on their toes than their heels, speaking in the whispered tones of worshipers and adulterers.

Davy looked up at me and grinned. "You aren't really with the government, are you?"

"Not really. But sort of. Temporarily."

"Is it dangerous? What you do?"

"Sometimes, but mostly not."

"Do you shoot people?"

"No. I . . . no."

"Is Mrs. Blair in trouble with the government? Is that what you want to talk about?"

"That's not exactly it. But if I can get certain information from you, she won't be, for sure. How about it?"

Davy shrugged. "Okay. Mrs. Blair's neat. She took me to a football game once. I don't think she's a criminal or anything." He frowned. "She knows a lot about football," he added with awe. "More than me, even."

"She's not a criminal, Davy," I said with more hope than truth. "Now, I want you to think back about five months ago. Back to June."

"June."

"Just after school let out."

"Sure. June. What about it? My mom's birthday's in June."

"Something happened last June ninth. On a Sunday night. Down on Oswego Street. That's over on the other side of the freeway, down in the industrial area."

"What happened?"

"Well, I was hoping you could tell me. I thought maybe you went down there with Mrs. Blair that night and saw something."

Davy thought for a few seconds, crinkling his nose again, but nothing came, even though he clearly wanted it to. "What was it, can't you give me a hint? Maybe I just forgot."

"You wouldn't forget this, Davy."

"I don't know," he said dubiously. "I forget all kinds of stuff. Mom says I'll forget my name some day."

"I'll bet you don't forget all that much."

"I forget to eat my liver every time we have it."

His grin was elfin and endearing. I wanted to put him in my pocket and take him home. I put my hand on his shoulder instead. "Just think once more, Davy. Were you and Mrs. Blair down on the other side of the freeway one night? When it was getting dark? With a bunch of old warehouse-type buildings around? You were running up and down the street, kicking a rock or a can or something? Do you remember anything like that?"

"Naw. The only place I been with Mrs. Blair are the ball game and a *Smokey and the Bandit* movie and some toy stores. She always wants to know what kind of things I like to play with. I think she tells my mom, and then I get it for my birthday."

I patted him again. "Okay, Davy. That's all I wanted to know. Thanks for talking to me."

"Sure. Hey. Is Mrs. Blair going to be in trouble because I didn't know what you wanted me to know?"

"Nope. You did just fine. She'd only be in trouble if you didn't tell the truth."

"I did. I guess."

"No doubt about it," I said. "You can tell your friends it's all clear."

"Okay. Mr. Tanner?"

"Yes?"

"You aren't going to be my new dad, are you."

"No, Davy."

"Do you think I'll ever have a new dad?"

"I don't know. I think you should talk to your mom about it."

"Mom never tells me anything. Not anything important."

"I'm sure she tells you all she can."

He scowled, his face as warped as a week-old jack-o'-lantern. "I'm going inside," he said. "Don't tell them, okay?"

"The kids give you a rough time?"

"Some. Not too much. Their dads all left, too, most of them. You know that red-haired kid? Scott? His *mom* left. Went to Hawaii to paint pictures. She sent him a coconut in the mail." The enormity of the betrayal silenced Davy for a minute, and silenced me as well.

"It's been tough on your mom, too," I said. "You two have got to stick together."

"I guess."

"I saw your dad the other day. He talked about you a lot. He said he'd be by to see you real soon."

"Yeah? I thought I saw him the other day, too. He was hiding behind a bush up there on the hill." His eyes grew perfectly round. "But it couldn't have been him, *could* it?"

I didn't know what to say; I said I didn't think so. "See you later, Davy."

"See ya."

He started away and then turned back. "Do you think my mom would really shoot my dad?"

"No chance," I said. "No chance at all."

He nodded once and walked away again, pushing his fragile bike toward his fragile home. As I watched his reflector twinkle in the street light, I got an idea and climbed into my Buick and drove back down the hill.

Winthrop Avenue was where and how I'd left it. I cruised past the Quilk house and looked it over. The toys were gone from the front yard and the feet were gone from under the pickup, but the joyless aura was as persistent as camphor. I turned around and pulled to the curb at the far end of the block and checked my watch. It was a little after four. I leaned back and waited for the child that I guessed and hoped was in that house to come out and play.

Time curled up and napped on the front seat beside me. A garbage truck roared past but didn't stop, its vapors as unapparent as longing. I filled the car with smoke. Somewhere a chain saw ate through a log, and somewhere else a baby cried.

I wondered about the people on this sad street, wondered how they would fare under a government headed by a puppet-president and guided by men with neither political nor philosophical or emotional fealty to them. In a step out of history, we had just given a man a mandate to terminate fifty years of national concern for the people on Winthrop Avenue. I'd thought a lot about why it had happened, thought too much about it, truthfully, and still the only reason I could come up with was that in America, for the first time anywhere, more people consider themselves nobles than serfs. Sadly, most of them are wrong.

The sound of a siren jolted me out of my reverie and I looked around. The house I was parked in front of was a five-room bungalow that probably rested on the remains of a much grander structure, which had long ago succumbed to

the fate that awaited the rest of the block. Two of the front
windows were broken and patched with brown plastic. A
long slat of siding was missing from the length of the house.
The tar paper that showed through the gap created a
toothless grin, moronic and perpetual.

As I was looking the place over, the front door opened
and two boys came out, each carrying a brick in each hand.
The taller boy had a pine board tucked under one arm. He
was slim and wore a thin red T-shirt with a faded picture of
Suzanne Somers on the front. A cigarette dangled from the
corner of his mouth. He couldn't have been more than
twelve.

The other boy was thin as well, but small. His jeans
were worn almost white, the sleeves of his shirt were rolled
to his shoulders. A sheath knife hung from his belt. Both
boys had rags wrapped around their knees and elbows and
the smaller one had a thin strip of the same rag tied around
his head in the fashion of Indians and jocks.

With a religious solemnity the boys strolled into the
street and stacked the bricks on the pavement near the
gutter, then placed one end of the board on the bricks and
the other on the ground, making a ramp about eight inches
high. After testing the ramp for stability, the boys went back
to the yard and pulled a couple of small, knobby-tired
bicycles off the ground and mounted them. The shorter boy
reached into his rear pocket and pulled out a round tin can.
The thick pinch of leaf went into his left cheek, making a
bulge as attractive as a goiter. They both adjusted their knee
pads and their belts and pulled gloves from their back
pockets and donned them.

The taller boy flicked his cigarette into the grass, the
smaller one spit, and they both rode off, their hips bobbing
high above the bike seats, their legs churning like the rods
of steam engines. They circled to a point some twenty yards
behind the ramp and stopped and talked it over for a minute;
then the smaller boy took off, popping a wheelie for several

yards then pumping madly until just before he reached the ramp. The bike and rider sailed into space, evoking memories of cowboys and thrill shows.

They kept at it for almost an hour, increasing their speed and their nonchalance with each approach. They never once crashed and they never once laughed; they were afraid only of fear and they were as silent as snails. Twice they disappeared briefly, then returned with more bricks. When they finally gave it up, it was because the stunt was mastered.

The taller boy grunted something, then swung off his bike and went into the house I was parked beside. The smaller boy yelled a fraternal curse and rode slowly down the street, coasting with the wind. I started the car and followed him. When he dropped his bike to the ground in front of the Quilk house, I stopped the car and honked my horn.

He gave me a convict's look. I got out of the car and walked to the curb side and leaned against the fender. "My name's Tanner," I said. "I'm from San Francisco. I'd like to talk to you for a minute."

The boy spit, the brown, pulsing glob landing a foot from my shoe. "About what?"

"About your aunt."

"What aunt?"

"Teresa. Mrs. Blair."

The boy spit again. "So I've got an aunt. So what? Do I win a prize?" He'd worked real hard on his sarcasm. Hard enough to make it real.

"No prizes for that," I said, "but it might be worth some money if you talk to me. What's your name, first of all."

"Maybe that's for me to know and you to find out."

"Oh, I'd find out, son. That's my business, finding out."

"You a cop?"

"Nope."

"You from the school?"

"Nope."

"You going to talk to Ted and Mary after you talk to me?"

"Not if you tell me what I want to know. Then it stays with us."

"What kind of money?"

"Twenty bucks."

"For what, exactly?"

"The truth."

"Yeah, well, I know all kinds of truth. The truth is, I been hassled by guys like you ever since I could walk."

"No hassle, son. Just tell me about the night of June ninth."

His grimy brow wrinkled. He stripped off his gloves and stuffed them into his back pocket to give himself some time. The rag around his head, his slight build, his oily, yellowed flesh, his active eyes, all recalled pictures of Viet Cong sappers taken captive inside the perimeter, expecting to be tortured to a distant death. When he looked at me again, his head was tilted and a scheme was brewing behind his eyes. "What's the big deal about June ninth?"

"If you were where I think you were, you know that already."

The kid had played the angles every day of his life and he was playing them now. "My memory ain't worth shit, you know? I think it's going to take more than twenty to fix it."

"How much?"

"Fifty?" It wasn't a demand and it wasn't nonnegotiable. The kid had a lot to learn.

"No chance for fifty, son. And you won't get a nickel unless you tell me your name."

"Gus. The name's Gus."

"Short for what?"

"Augustus."

"Nice name."

"For a fag, maybe," he sneered. His eyes swept the block and something down the street caught his eye. I turned and saw a girl, his age or a little older, riding a ten-speed down the middle of the street. When she saw Gus, she pedaled faster. "Hey, Grace," Gus yelled. "Come here a minute."

The girl kept riding, head down, clearly fleeing. "Blow me, bitch," Gus called after her, then turned back to me. "What about the bread?"

I put my hand in my pocket to keep from slapping him.

"Thirty," I said. "And you tell me exactly what you saw that night."

"Hand it over." The paw he thrust at me was as filthy as his vocabulary.

"First you talk."

He gave it some thought. I took out my wallet and pulled out three tens. Gus was doing so much thinking I knew whatever I got from him wasn't going to be exact, but I decided to go ahead. Gus looked at me with false candor. "I saw a guy get run over," he said flippantly. "What's the big deal? Happens every night on the tube."

"This wasn't the tube, Gus. This was for real."

He shrugged. "What's the difference? Real life, the tube—down here it's all fucking unbelievable, man."

"Tell me what else you saw that night," I prompted.

"Just two old guys. They were pissed at each other."

"Did you get a good look at them?"

"I guess. Sort of."

"Would you recognize them if you saw them again?"

He gave me a twisted smile. "I might. Then again, I might not."

"You ever see either of the men before?"

He paused. "Nope."

"You ever see the man who drove the car since that day?"

"Nope."

"What were you doing down there?"

"I was with Aunt Teresa, Einstein. I thought you knew all about it."

"Why were you there?"

He frowned. "We were riding around. Me and Aunt Teresa ride around lots."

"Where had you been before you got to Oswego Street?"

"I forget."

"Was there anyone else there?"

"Maybe. I forget." His smile became a laugh. He enjoyed what he thought was happening. I was just going through the motions.

"You ever hear the name Tony Fluto?"

His face darkened. "That's all I got to say. I don't know nothing else, so hand over the bread."

"Why didn't you talk to the police about what you saw?" I asked.

"I didn't talk to them because they didn't talk to me."

"Why didn't Mrs. Blair tell the police you were with her that night?"

"Hey. Am I a fucking mind reader? I'm just a kid. Maybe she wanted to protect my innocence."

His grin was as innocent as Manson's. I could have taken it further, and I probably should have since Gus knew more about the incident than he let on, but I'd had more than enough of Gus. I stuck the tens in my pocket. "Ever been to the Cash Country shopping mall, Gus?" I asked.

"Sure."

"Know the bookstore there? The Book Bag, I think it is."

"Yeah. So?"

"So you go down there tomorrow and tell the woman behind the counter who you are. She'll point to some racks of books. You can pick any one you want, up to thirty bucks' worth."

"Hey, you shit. Cash is what I want."

"Books is what you'll get."

"You son of a bitch."

"Someone's going to teach you the art of conversation some day, Gus. I hope I'm around to see the lesson."

"Yeah?" he snarled. "Why don't *you* try to teach me something, old man?"

"Someone might charge me with child abuse," I said, "although I can't imagine who."

Just then the door to the house slammed and I looked to see who it was. Ted Quilk was standing on the front porch, his arms folded across his chest, his tattoo rippling as he clenched his fists. "You the guy was here the other day?" he called to me.

I nodded.

"You give Teresa my message?"

I nodded again.

"Hey, Ted," Gus broke in. "This fucker took money off me. Thirty bucks. Come on down and let's take it back."

"If he took money off you, it's because you stole it off him in the first place. Now get your bony ass in the house and wash for dinner."

"Aw, get fucked," Gus muttered.

"What'd you say, boy?" Ted Quilk screamed. "You get in here right now, before I get the horse whip, you goddamned punk. Now move."

Gus scowled at me then trudged toward the house, head down, momentarily subdued by a cruelty greater than his own. I looked at Ted Quilk. He seemed to be considering whether to come down to where I was. I decided not to give him the chance.

Chapter
18

The woman at the Book Bag thought I was nuts. And Ray Tolson thought I was lying when I called and told him I'd found his child witness, and thought I was subversive when I told him I'd driven off and left the kid unattended by anyone but his brutal father. I ignored all this, reminded Tolson of our deal and asked if he knew where Teresa Blair might be. He claimed he didn't. Then he claimed I'd jeopardized his case by not bringing in Gus Quilk on my own. Then he claimed I'd hear from him real soon if the Quilk boy wasn't where I said he was. I hung up and unplugged the phone. I wanted to paint the windows black and sleep for a week. Instead, I woke up at five.

The world is not at its best at five. Neither are scrambled eggs, nor milk, nor burnt toast. Coffee, however, is at that hour as essential to life as oxygen and a forced-air furnace. After scraping the sleep and stubble off my face I tuned my radio to a station in Modesto and listened to the farm market reports while I waited for the *Chronicle* to arrive. When it bounced off the door downstairs I retrieved it. What with

Herb Caen and the radio and the crusty paraphernalia in the sink I managed to find something to do until almost eight. For the next five minutes I watched Jane Pauley. I try to glimpse Jane Pauley every day. She makes me feel better. At eight I got in my car and drove south, toward the vaulted chambers of the El Gordo City Hall.

The regulars must have predicted Ray Tolson's ultimate defeat, because none of them had shown up for the second day of the trial. Another attraction had doubtless captured them, another melodrama of anguish, treachery, and debauch.

I was still the only person in the courtroom when Ray Tolson poked his head in the door and looked around, his once-ruddy face now twisted in the clutch of anxiety. When he saw me he came over and sat beside me. "What brings you back here?" he asked wearily.

"Thought I'd catch the last act," I said. "Also, I thought you might need reminding of the deal we made."

"My word's good, Tanner," he said. "The charges against Mrs. Blair will be dropped by noon."

"Have you seen her?" I asked. "I can't reach her at home. Nor her husband, either."

"I haven't seen her," Tolson answered, "and I haven't seen Grinder, either. He hasn't been in here, has he?"

I shook my head. "You going to have a case to put on this morning?"

Tolson sighed. "The kid'll get us to the jury, I think. If he decides to talk. And if I decide to let him live. He spent all night playing games, trying to cut a deal. Christ. Only fourteen and already he's as savvy as a three-time loser. Which is what he'll be by the time he's twenty-two. And then the old man got into the act."

"Ted?"

Tolson nodded. "Real sweetheart. Between him and his kid this office will have to expand."

"What did Ted want?" I asked.

"Seems he got busted in a gambling sweep last month. A Lo-Ball parlor that didn't stick to Lo-Ball. Ted wants the case dismissed and his stake money back."

"How much money?"

"A grand and a half, so he claims."

"Quilk hasn't worked in weeks. Where'd he get that kind of money?"

Tolson shrugged. "Maybe he hit the Exacta. Maybe somebody paid him to move out of the neighborhood. Maybe he got a part in a Coors commercial. Anyway, that's not my problem. My problem is, where the hell is Grinder? He was supposed to have the kid here at eight."

"Maybe young Gus took off."

"We had someone in the room with him all night. No chance."

"That's what you thought about Teresa Blair."

"Fuck you, Tanner."

I laughed. "He probably mugged Grinder and stole the squad car."

"With anyone but Grinder I'd say it was a definite possibility. But Grinder would just as soon shoot him as look at him. How'd you find the kid, anyway?"

"Just a guess. He wasn't the first one I tried, either, just so you'll know I wasn't holding out on you. How'd you get him to talk?"

"Oh, I let him think he was conning me, telling me bits and pieces but not enough to be of any use. Then when I was sure he'd really been down there that night, I scared him a little. He's tough but he's young. You can scare them till they're sixteen or so. After that, you can send them to jail or turn them loose. Anything in between is a waste of time."

"He may change his mind about testifying when he gets here and sees Fluto staring at him with those musket balls he uses for eyes."

Tolson smiled. "I think I got that covered. The kid's

worried, who wouldn't be, but he's also looking forward to being a big shot for once in his life. I alerted some newspaper people to be here when he arrives."

"You're a bastard, Tolson," I said.

"That's what it takes, so that's what I am. I figure Gus won't have the guts to clam up when he sees all the attention he's getting and what it'll imply if he chickens out. You've got to be a lot older than Gus before you're brave enough to tell the media types to get fucked."

"Lots of people never get that old," I said.

"You got that right." Tolson looked back at the door once again and shook his head. "Christ. To think my career depends on convincing a jury to believe a wino and a delinquent. They didn't tell me it was going to be like this in law school, I'll tell you that."

I nodded. "In law school they pretend every judge is Learned Hand and every client is Mahatma Gandhi and every lawyer is Daniel Webster."

"I think I'll invite some of those profs down here some time." Tolson's laugh curled around the words. "They'd go into the aluminum siding business in a week. You know," he went on, "your friend Mrs. Blair neglected to mention that her nephew Gus was with her down on Oswego Street that night. I'm not sure that little omission is covered by our deal, Tanner."

"The hell it isn't," I said. "I've been in El Gordo for a week and I haven't heard anyone tell the truth yet. Including you, Tolson. You pull out and I'll go to the papers with how your key witness got found and who found him."

"Relax," Tolson said, then rolled his eyes and went out in the hall. A few seconds later Fluto and his retinue rolled in, the same boiling, roiling menace. Then Tolson's assistant entered, towing behind her the pickled, listing form of Colin Lufkin. She deposited Lufkin in the front row, gave him what looked like a temperance lecture, then took her seat at the prosecution table. No one paid any attention to her and she seemed relieved.

A few minutes later Tolson came back, looking glum and wretched. He seemed to have shrunk even further since I saw him moments before, the sinew and muscle somehow missing from his physique. If Grinder and Gus Quilk had arrived, they were somewhere in the wings, awaiting their cue. Neither Teresa Blair nor her husband was visible. The regulars were still in another theater.

The gavel banged and the judge took her seat. "Shall I bring up the jury, Mr. Tolson?" she asked brightly, indicating she was prepared to begin afresh, to ignore the previous day's fiasco.

Tolson whispered to his assistant and she got up and hurried out of the room. Then Tolson stood. "We have been able to locate an important additional witness, Your Honor. An eyewitness to the murder of Phillip Vincent. He is now on his way to the courtroom. I'm therefore happy to say that the State is ready to proceed."

Loggins stood up, feigning exhausted patience, a frown slicing like a scar across his forehead. "If the prosecution has a surprise witness to trot out, a witness not listed in response to our previous discovery requests, we would, of course, raise strenuous objection, Your Honor. Apparently the farce continues."

The judge copied Loggins's frown. "What is the name of your witness, Mr. Tolson?"

"Augustus Quilk."

"And has his name been previously given to the defense?"

Tolson nodded. "My assistant called Mr. Loggins's office last night, Your Honor, only minutes after we first located Mr. Quilk ourselves."

"Last night?" The expression of the judge's face was rueful.

"This is preposterous, Your Honor," Loggins pronounced. "Defense moves for dismissal."

The judge smiled wearily. "Is this Mr. Quilk essential to your case, Mr. Tolson?"

"Yes, Your Honor."

"Where is he?"

"On his way."

"I don't want a song and dance, Mr. Tolson. My calendar is full. Is your witness in the building?"

"I'm not sure. My assistant is looking for him now. Detective Grinder of the El Gordo police is bringing in the young man."

The judge's eyebrow rose. "Oh? A child?"

"I . . . not quite a child, not quite a man, Your Honor." Tolson dredged up a smile. "If you know what I mean."

The judge smiled back. "I believe I do, Mr. Tolson. I have one of those at home myself."

"Your Honor," Loggins intoned. "The production staged by the prosecution grows more absurd by the minute. There are constitutional rights being trammeled here. I insist upon dismissal."

"Relax, Mr. Loggins," the judge snapped. "Your client's rights are uppermost in my mind."

And suddenly there was silence in the room, as thick and tangible as a drape. The principals eyed each other brazenly, the bailiff closed his eyes, the clerk tugged his tie, the judge hummed what sounded like a lullaby. What Tolson had planned as his coup was fast approaching his funeral, and he was as jangled and disarrayed as the alcoholic witness who fidgeted quietly in the front row. But Loggins wasn't as confident as he made out, either. He had doubtless assured Fluto that the State would have to dismiss, and it was still too early to tell, so Loggins was examining everything in the room except the frozen countenance of his client. It was a script from Beckett, a set from

Fellini. No one wanted to be where they were except me. I was working to keep from laughing.

The silence vanished with the sound of the rear door opening. All eyes but the bailiff's turned toward it. Tolson's assistant hurried to her boss and whispered in his ear. Fluto and Loggins watched with leery interest. Then Tolson's curse displaced everything else in the room.

"Your Honor," he began, getting to his feet with mammoth effort. "Detective Grinder's squad car has just been located. Mr. Grinder is dead. A gunshot to the head. The witness he was bringing in is missing."

Voices made the sound of motors. The judge closed her eyes and leaned back in her chair and shook her head from side to side, to evade thoughts that were trying to nest there. Loggins leaned over and whispered to Fluto and Fluto nodded. Loggins stood up. "We are, of course, chagrined to hear of the events of the morning, Your Honor. However, I must again insist that all charges against my client be dismissed without further delay."

Tolson and the judge started to speak, and then both stopped, lacking for the moment the focus that words require. Tolson's assistant looked at him, and whispered a question, and stood after Tolson shrugged absently. "A detective will be here in a minute, Your Honor," she said. "To question Mr. Fluto about the murder of Detective Grinder. I ask that you order Mr. Fluto held by the bailiff. Also, we request a further continuance, until tomorrow, so that we may inform the court more, ah, more in detail about the, ah, apparent criminal abduction of the key witness in this case and the assault upon Detective Grinder."

Loggins exploded. "The suggestion that Mr. Fluto has knowledge concerning the alleged murder of the officer and the supposed kidnap of the witness is outrageous and slanderous, Your Honor. For my part I doubt that any such witness ever existed. In any event, the motion is renewed."

"Sit down, Mr. Loggins," the judge ordered sharply.

"The State's motion for a brief continuance is granted, given the circumstances. You may do what you wish concerning the imminent arrival of a detective, however, Mr. Loggins. I have no power to hold Mr. Fluto." The gavel banged. "The bailiff will proceed to the jury room and once again excuse the jury for the day, with instructions to report back at nine tomorrow. Court is adjourned." When she left the bench, she was talking to her clerk about scheduling a hearing in another matter for later in the morning. Loggins and his assistants hurried Fluto out of the room as though it were ablaze.

I guessed that Tolson was exerting every ounce of his will to keep from taking a swing at someone, anyone, as Fluto and his people swept past him. The growing realization that I had been a major cause in the events of the morning was working on me as well. A drop of sweat trickled down my side. I loosened my tie.

Tolson seemed to make a decision of some sort. He scooped up his papers and marched out of the courtroom, his assistant in his wake. Although he didn't look or speak to me, I followed him anyway. As I was about to push my way through the door a hand gripped my arm and stopped me. The hand was trembling. It belonged to Colin Lufkin. "What do I do now?" he asked. The question seemed to encompass more than hours or days.

"I don't know," I told him.

"Is the case over?"

"Not quite."

"It isn't going well, is it?"

"No."

Lufkin's bleary eyes found mine. "I'm not stupid, Mr. Tanner. A witness, a boy, has been kidnapped, hasn't he?"

"Looks that way."

"To prevent him from testifying in this case."

"So it seems."

"I'm leaving," Lufkin said firmly.

"Where will you be?"

"Inside the nearest bottle."

"Tolson may need you tomorrow," I said.

"What Mr. Tolson needs I no longer have," Lufkin answered. His face drooped with apology. I patted him on the back and we walked in opposite directions, each of us something less than the world thought we should be.

Tolson was pacing his office when I arrived, a beast in a cage of circumstance. His assistant sat on the chair in a corner, the same one James Blair had been sitting on when I first entered the office a very long week before. The poor woman was waiting, like all acolytes, for the least sign from her master.

I coughed and Tolson looked at me. The sight didn't ebb his fury. "Well? What do you want, Tanner? To gloat?"

"I want to know exactly what happened to the kid I touted you onto yesterday, Tolson. I want to know what the fuck went wrong."

My own anger served to neutralize some of Tolson's, to make us allies once again. "Grinder was bringing in the kid," he said stiffly. "Along the way Grinder got his brain blown out. It was a hit, and it was Fluto's boys who hit him. Ten to one we never prove it."

"Anything at all on the kid?"

Tolson shook his head. "We'll find him in a culvert somewhere. He'll be nice and ripe."

"If they wanted to kill the kid, why didn't they just leave him there with Grinder?" I asked.

"How the hell should I know? Maybe they wanted to bugger him first." Tolson shook his head. "You know, ten years ago the mob would never have hit a cop, even an El Gordo cop. Now they don't give a damn about anything."

I stood up. "I'm going to be in the middle of this one, Tolson. I don't like remembering how Gus Quilk came to be in Grinder's car."

Tolson slammed his hand on the desk. "You're out of it

completely, Tanner. As of now. I never should have brought you in in the first place."

"I'm in, Tolson, whether you like it or not. I've gotten used to sleeping nights; I want to keep the habit. If Gus Quilk dies, it's going to be hard to do."

We exchanged glares. Then because I knew Tolson was feeling the same things I was I started to grin and Tolson matched me and we stood there a minute, amazed at our raging impotence. "One thing that occurred to me is that they're holding the kid in order to make a trade of some kind," I said when we got calmed down.

"Trade for what?" Tolson asked.

"Who knows? But I'm telling you that if they do make an offer, whatever it is they want you're going to give it to them."

"The hell I am."

"The hell you're not."

We drew our glares again, but this time the phone rang before damage was done. Tolson looked at the receiver and then at his assistant. She hurried over and picked it up and listened. "Just a minute," she said, and held the phone out to Tolson. "Loggins."

"That pimp," Tolson grumbled, and took the phone. "Loggins? Whatever you've got to say can wait till morning. I don't want to talk to you without a judge present."

Loggins's answer made Tolson frown, then look at me, then hang up without another word. "Loggins just gave me a message, Tanner," Tolson said grimly. "His client, Mr. Fluto, would like to speak with Mr. John Marshall Tanner. At Mr. Loggins's law office. As soon as it would be convenient for Mr. Tanner to be there."

"Well, well," I said.

"Well, well," Tolson mocked. "I didn't realize you and Fluto were intimate, Tanner."

I just smiled.

"You'd better get going, hadn't you?" Tolson sneered.
"Tony won't want to be kept waiting."

"I guess I had," I said, and walked to the door.

"Tanner?"

"Yeah?"

"You willing to wear a wire?"

"Nope."

"You sure?"

"Yep."

Tolson swore. The last thing I saw before I left his office
were the eyes of Ms. Epley. They were as big as buoys and
they bobbed on tears.

Chapter 19

I was eager to talk with Fluto, but there was one thing I had to do first. I got to Winthrop Avenue in ten minutes, by driving recklessly beneath a cloudless sky.

Ted Quilk had his head buried beneath the raised hood of the pickup. His feet were still bare and black. I watched him work for a moment, impressed by both his epithets and his knowledge of what went on in there. When he finally heard me walking up the drive, he lifted his head and squinted, then directed a curse at me instead of at the engine. We glowered at each other like professionals. When his left hand emerged, it was brandishing the wrench I'd seen inside his house. The chrome cast the morning sunlight at me in quick, darting sparks.

"You again?" His mouth ejected the words like rancid food. "Ain't you done enough already, siccing the law on the boy?"

"You didn't seem so worried about the boy yesterday, when you were threatening to beat him to a pulp."

"Yeah, well, that's the way I handle him."

"How are you going to handle him when he learns he's tougher than you are?"

Quilk grinned thinly. "When he learns that, he'll be gone."

Quilk placed the wrench on the fender of the truck and reached into his hip pocket for a rag and started to blow his nose on it. When he saw the rag was soaked with oil, he replaced it and pressed a thumb to a nostril and blew a plug of snot into the dirt. I asked him if his wife was home.

"What business is that of yours? You got no truck with her."

"I came to apologize for what happened to your son. I wanted her to hear it."

"She's in church, praying to some statues. Tossin' good money into the basket as well, 'less I miss my guess. The woman still figures the Lord will smile on us if we stay poor. I never seen that to be true, myself. Not in this life. And I wouldn't take bets about the next." Quilk snorted again, then swallowed. "They find any trace of him yet?"

"Not that I know of."

"I'm gonna start a lawsuit against you if he turns up dead. I swear I am. You and the city, both. I been talking to people. Them cops should have looked after the boy better."

I laughed. "You do that, Mr. Quilk, but when you talk to a lawyer about it, keep your hand on your wallet. An attorney who'd take a case like that needs money worse than you do, and he'll know a hell of a lot of ways to get it out of your pocket and into his."

"We'll see about that."

"I guess we will."

Quilk scowled and slapped his hand against his thigh, loosing a cloud of brown dust. I wondered what the man had been like before he realized nothing in his life would ever be better than it had been the day before.

"Get the fuck out of here," Quilk ordered suddenly. "I

got to get the timing set on this clunker by five." Quilk snarled, showing frosted teeth.

"Tell Mrs. Quilk I'm sorry about what happened to Gus," I said. "Tell her I'm looking for him now. Tell her I'll call if I find out anything."

"I'll tell her what I please," Quilk muttered. "You just be sure if you do find him alive you bring him straight back here, where he belongs. No matter what the cops or his mother or anyone else says." He could have been talking about the return of a borrowed lawn mower.

"One more thing," I said. "Did you see anyone suspicious around here last night? Anyone looking the house over, or parked for a long time in the neighborhood? Anything at all?"

"If I saw anything, why would I tell you?"

"Because it might help get your boy back."

Quilk frowned with the effort of thought. "Between the time you left and the time the cops came there's only one thing that happened, that I recollect, except for the usual racket I put up with."

"What racket is that?"

"Elvis the Pelvis."

"What happened?"

"The wife got a call from her sister."

"Mrs. Blair?"

"That's the only one she's got."

"But you don't have a phone."

"She calls the neighbor lady and she comes to fetch the wife." Quilk smiled crookedly. "Pisses the hell out of her, too. I wouldn't get a phone put in now even if I had the money."

"What did Mrs. Blair want?"

"Said she was coming for the boy. Said she wanted to take him to a movie show. Said she'd be here in an hour."

"Did she show up?"

"Yeah, but the law beat her to it."

"When the police came, did they drive a black-and-white?"

"The first ones did, the ones in the little blue suits. One was that bastard Doolittle. He busted up a game on me down on Rutland Avenue last month."

"The Lo-Ball parlor?"

"Yep. You play?"

"I don't like to waste my luck on cards."

"Hell, I don't see luck any other time," Quilk said. "Now move. I got to make a living. If that's what you call this."

I left, careful to avoid the snot and the grease on the way out of the yard.

The Yellow Pages that dangled from a chain at a pay phone two blocks down told me Lafcadio Loggins's law office was on Mission Boulevard, in the center of the city. The ad for his firm said Loggins specialized in divorces, criminal defense, civil rights, bankruptcy, personal injuries, and evictions. It might as well have said he specialized in the law of the misguided and the desperate.

When I got there, I thought for a minute I'd looked at the wrong street number in the book, but after a couple of laps around the block I finally figured out that Loggins's office was on the top floor of the Hotel El Gordo, which preserved a rather musty version of gold rush opulence in its lobby and adjoining bar. The elevator took me to the top without stopping, further confirmation of my impression that there weren't many, if any, guests in the place. The only reason I could think of for Loggins to be there was that he owned it. The hotel had probably been taken in lieu of a fee from someone who'd spent his years subsequent to Loggins's services in an institution.

There were eight names painted on the office door, and the remains of two more that had been scraped off not long ago. Behind the door was a windowless waiting room with a parquet floor, a soundproofed ceiling, a pink plastic couch, and a Wyeth reproduction curling behind its matting. At the far end of the room a buxom woman sat behind a sliding glass partition with the doubtful expression of a quiz show contestant who had been asked the wrong question. When I tapped on the window, she slid back the panel. "Yes?" She was as regal as the Queen Mother.

"My name's Tanner. I'm here to see Mr. Loggins and his friend Fluto. We're starting a new chapter of the Sons of Garibaldi."

She had been inoculated at birth against mirth. "Have you an appointment?"

"I do."

She wrinkled her lips and inflated her thickly swathed chest. "I don't have you in my book."

"And I don't have you in mine."

"I see. I'm afraid Mr. Loggins is occupied for the remainder of the day, Mr., ah, Tanner. Perhaps you will call ahead next time."

I put some fingerprints on the glass. "I came down here because Loggins asked me to. Now you're asking me to leave. You two should rehearse before you perform in public." I made a quarter turn.

The woman inhaled half the room and edged reluctantly off her chair. "I shall try to locate Mr. Loggins."

"Try to locate some civility, as long as you're up," I said, my sarcasm only a little warranted. I was still upset about what had happened to Gus Quilk.

The receptionist was gone long enough for me to smoke half a Camel. Her reappearance was preceded by the groans of floorboards. I wondered how long the Hotel El Gordo had been with us, and whether it would last an hour more. "Mr. Loggins is in the library. The third door on the right."

She was about to give directions when the outer door opened and a man hopped through it on his one good leg. The other was stiff and temporarily useless, wrapped from groin to calf in a thick, white bandage. He stood there, one hand on the doorknob, the other around a pair of aluminum crutches, while he estimated his chances of making it to the couch without falling over. His face was round, molded from thick and florid flesh. He needed a shave and a diet. His lips were far too red.

"Good morning, Mr. Fluto," the receptionist cooed. "Do you need some help?"

"Naw. I got this thing figured out." Simultaneously with the utterance of the final word, the crutches dropped to the floor. He swore bitterly. The receptionist hurried over and picked them up and handed them back. Since I knew who he was I stayed put.

"The old man still here, Gladys?" the man asked.

"Yes he is. He'll be a while, though. This gentleman has an appointment to see him."

"Yeah?" He looked at me for the first time. "Who are you?"

"Tanner. The guy you called on the phone the other night. The guy you decided needed a little extra heat and a bit of advice to go with it."

"Yeah?" His eyes widened with ridiculous innocence. "What makes you think that?"

"Your voice and your ancestry."

"You gonna try to make something of it with the cops?"

"Not yet."

"You gonna tell my old man about it?"

"I hadn't thought about it. I assumed he knew."

Young Fluto shook his head. "Sometimes I help him out on my own. Sometimes he don't like the way I help him. So you keep quiet."

"I'll think about it."

Fluto stuck the crutches beneath his arm and hopped to the couch and eased himself down onto it, careful that his bad leg remained well away from the cushions. The movement caused him pain, which caused me pleasure. I had an impulse to kick the exact center of his bandage.

He saw me looking. "You know, Tanner," he said, his voice thick with artificial menace. "I been giving some thought to who it was had the nerve to take a shot at me. I couldn't figure anyone in this town had the guts, knowing who I am. But you're from the big city. Maybe you don't know exactly what it means to be a Fluto. Maybe you didn't get the point the other night, maybe you decided to act tough. So I'm telling you, pal. I find out it was you who shot me, I'm gonna come looking. And when I look, I find. And when I find, I leave them begging me to stop, you get what I mean?"

I put his threat in the quiver of threats I carry on my back. "Oh, I get it, Little Tony. Now you get this. You better not come after me unless you've developed a real strong attachment to those crutches."

I turned back toward the receptionist. Her eyes were popping wide and helpless. She opened a side door and guided me into a dark hallway and watched as I walked down it.

All the doors I passed were thick and closed. The covering on the walls resembled woven weeds. The muffled buzz of an automatic typewriter ground out inhumanly perfect copy somewhere behind me. I tapped on the designated door and opened it.

Loggins and Fluto were sitting face-to-face on opposite sides of a long walnut table that was surrounded by chairs and topped with a thick coat of polish and a crystal ashtray in the shape of a pentagon and the large, clasped hands of Tony Fluto. As I strolled into the book-lined room, Loggins's thin lips pursed. "Come in, Mr. Tanner," he invited cheerily. "I'm Lafcadio Loggins. Thank you for coming down on such short notice." He stood up and shook my hand.

"My pleasure," I said, then glanced at Fluto.

Loggins trotted out his courtroom smile. "Do you know Mr. Fluto?"

"Only by reputation."

"Then I'm afraid you have acquired much misinformation."

"There's a lot of it going around."

"Won't you sit down?"

"Sure."

Loggins and I spent some time getting comfortable; Fluto was already there. "I believe I have seen you in court the past two mornings," Loggins observed after a minute.

"Right."

"A shameful burlesque, was it not?"

"I guess I missed the funny part."

Loggins inclined his head and shrugged. "I'm told you were once an attorney yourself."

"Right."

"Then you know what a travesty has occurred."

"Right."

There was more to be said, to that question and the one before it, but there didn't seem to be any point in going into it right then. Loggins nodded several times, still not certain of my stance. I wasn't certain of it myself. "I believe you are also the man who drove Mrs. Blair down from the lake, are you not?"

I changed tactics. I shrugged.

"And directed the estimable Mr. Tolson to young Augustus Quilk as well, am I right?"

That time I didn't even shrug. Loggins seemed resigned to my reticence. I was wondering what papers he read to get the information he had. "Tell me, Mr. Tanner," he went on, "do you have a principal in this matter?" The cheer had left his voice.

"What matter is that?" I asked.

"The matter of Mr. Fluto's prosecution for the crime of murder."

At the mention of the evil deed Loggins and I both glanced at the accused. The only visible reaction came from behind the narrowed slots that guarded his eyes. "I have no client, if that's what you mean," I said.

"Then you no longer have an interest in the case. Good."

I held up a hand. "I didn't say that. Yesterday I made a lucky guess and came up with a witness and handed him over to the DA A child. An obnoxious little brat, but nevertheless a child. Because of what I did, the boy is missing. Maybe dead, maybe not. Well, wherever or whatever he is, I'm going to find him. That's my interest in the case. Not in convicting Mr. Fluto here, or exonerating him, either. Just in finding young Gus Quilk. And I'm as interested in that as I've ever been in anything."

Loggins glanced at Fluto, then nodded. For some reason both of them seemed pleased with my answer.

"I'll warn you now," I went on, "that means I'm going to be seeing a lot of your client." I nodded toward Fluto.

"You think he knows something about the events of the morning?" Loggins asked.

"It's as good an assumption as any, better than most."

Fluto shifted position but I kept myself from looking at him. Loggins turned toward his client. "Shall I proceed?"

Fluto shook his head. "Just him and me." His voice was a growl of something wild.

"I don't think that's wise," Loggins protested. "The criminal charge is still pending. Tanner is or has been an agent of the district attorney. I should be present."

Fluto's face reddened. "In court I do what you say. Out here you do what I say. Is the room clean?"

Loggins nodded.

"What does that mean?" I asked.

Loggins's smile was extravagantly paternal. "Because of the nature of my clientele, certain branches of the federal government have, from time to time, concealed electronic listening devices on the premises. Not only in this office but in my home as well. Mr. Fluto is similarly plagued. These invasions are, of course, as illegal as they are fiendish.

Nevertheless, they persist. I bring a gentleman in to sweep the building at least twice a month. The last time he did so was approximately forty minutes ago."

"Okay," Fluto grunted. "Leave."

Loggins left quietly on loafers as soft as paws. Fluto looked at me with the vibrant eyes of visionaries and madmen. "I talked to some people about you," he began bluntly.

"What people?"

"Some business associates up there in San Francisco. They told me you went up against Duckie Bollo a few years back."

"Sort of. Fortunately the collision wasn't head-on."

"You took out one of his boys."

"Right."

"And now you're trying to take me out. I'd like to know why." He seemed genuinely puzzled.

"That's not the way it started," I said. "No offense, but I'd never even heard of you before last week. And even then I wasn't told the kind of, ah, business you were in. All I agreed to do was find a witness to a hit-and-run. Which I did. And then the witness didn't turn out to be a witness, and the hit-and-run wasn't a hit-and-run, and things got complicated."

"Is that straight?"

"It's straight."

"So why did you give them the kid?" The question carried an implication, and the implication seemed to originate in the basement, to carry dust and dung, to threaten death.

I thought it over. "Partly I did it because I think crimes ought to be prosecuted and witnesses to crimes ought to tell juries what they saw."

"And that's it?" Fluto bellowed. "A do-gooder, is what you are? You thought sending me to Tolson would mean a better world? Would mean justice?" Fluto seemed enraged at the prospect of my naïveté.

Strangely, I found myself wanting to explain more fully. "It didn't have anything to do with you personally," I began. "Like I said, I didn't even know who you were. To tell the truth, I gave up the kid because Ray Tolson said if I found the boy, then he'd drop the perjury charge against Mrs. Blair."

"An honest man. A man of passion. You gave up the kid for a lady. I like that." He paused. "She stayed with you a couple days, huh?"

"No comment."

"Hey. I like that, too. Teresa's a nice girl."

"Hardly a girl."

"It's good you wanted her out of trouble."

Fluto's eyes had glazed, freeing his brain for recollection. I looked at him until he looked back. "Why did Teresa Blair do what she did in court yesterday?" I asked.

"Hey," Fluto demanded. "She didn't do nothing but tell the truth."

I didn't respond to the lie. Fluto squirmed to a new position and rubbed his lips as if to erase the words.

"You seen her today?" Fluto asked suddenly.

I shook my head. "Have you?"

He shook his. That seemed to take care of the woman whose spirit floated somewhere between us.

Fluto began to drum his fingers on the table. I looked at the spectral dance of the sunlight as it worked its way through the crystal ashtray, wondering whether I really wanted to know any more about Teresa Blair than I already did. "I guess this Tolson's pretty mad about the way his case is going," Fluto said finally.

"That's putting it mildly."

"I guess he figures my people killed Grinder and snatched the kid. So he wouldn't help Tolson send me up."

"That's about it."

"I guess he's got every cop in the city trailing my boys, staking out my house and my business, searching for the kid."

"I guess so."

"That's what I figured," Fluto said needlessly, then fell silent again, his smile lazy and satisfied, as though he'd just solved a quadratic equation. I had nothing to do but look at him and wonder where all this was going.

Fluto was, or had been, a handsome man. His head was triangular and inverted, wide and rather flat on top, capped with strips of thin, white hair combed straight back over a bare, rumpled crown. His chin was sharp, lightly scarred just off its tip and deeply clefted. His aquiline nose seemed slung from the black spikes of his eyes. Thick pouches of flesh had collected beneath his jaw and they rolled as he spoke. Like the rest of him, the face exuded strength and the doggedness of a pit bull. He had not been able to pass on that trait to his flabby-featured son in the outer office.

Fluto caught me inspecting him. "I guess you figure I'm some kind of louse, huh, Tanner?"

"I've heard rumors."

"Rumors. Wars start on rumors. Guys go to jail on rumors. Guys get killed on rumors, too. Well, the rumors about me ain't true. I just run a business. I help people who need it. My kind of people. People who worked hard all their lives and whose luck ran out. People who been pushed and got a right to push back."

"Pushed by whom?"

His shrug encompassed the world. "People who got the government pushing them to do this for safety and that for the ecology, people who got the unions pushing pay scales higher and higher while the workers turn out less product every year, people who got their big suppliers pushing costs out of sight and their big competitors dumping goods on the docks for next to nothing so they can grab the market. Them's the guys I'm helping, Tanner. The guys do-gooders like you never think about. The guys who made America great."

"So you help them out by burning down their businesses?"

Fluto's lips thinned. "Hey. I don't know nothing about no fires." He paused. "But if I did, I'd tell you that no one's ever been hurt in any of them fires. Not ever."

"How about the insurance companies? How about all the people who pay higher premiums because of the losses you cause? How about Phillip Vincent?"

Fluto's cheeks glowed red, then blanched. "Those insurance guys are crooks. Whatever they lose because of a few fires, they already made up turning down claims they should have paid. Vincent, he was different. But I ain't here to discuss old business."

I started to say something, then stopped. Fluto had built a life out of that warped rationalization of benevolence and it would take a better sophist than I to knock it out of him. That's why people like Fluto are both dangerous and ineradicable. They become criminals not out of need or desperation but out of conviction, out of a premeditated, preterlogical, almost genetic determination that crime is the only honorable mode of existence, the only way to retaliate against a government and a society they assume to be alien and oppressive. The mob rises out of that psychology, but Christianity and Nazism have their roots in alienation, too. Doctrine and ritual are the sanctuaries of the outcast, and I had encountered a lot of proof of that in this case.

"Hey. Tanner. I got you down here for a reason."

"What reason?"

"I want you to tell this Tolson that I didn't kill Grinder and take the kid. I want you to tell him he'll be wasting time trying to prove I did. He should be looking at someone else, see, at the guys who maybe decided to go up against me, who want me out of the way."

"Like who?"

"There's plenty of them around the Bay. A couple of the locals I'm checking out myself, but I can't be sure. The business I'm in, people get jealous. They think they know more than an old man. That's why I'm calling you in and the cops, too. I want the kid back, and it won't happen unless we look in the right place."

"Can't you be more specific?"

"Hey. The cops, the feds especially, they know who's interested in taking over my business even better than I do. They got men inside all the operations, mine included, probably. So ask them. Someone's on the move, that's sure. First they try to take out my son Tony, and now this. You tell Tolson he finds out who decided to move against me, he finds the kid."

"But why would one of your enemies want to kill Gus Quilk? He was going to testify against you. To put you in jail, possibly for good."

"Yeah, well even assuming the kid said what they thought he was going to say in court, and I went up for a while, things would go on as usual. Plenty of guys like me run their business from a cell. You see, they had one real good reason for snatching the kid."

"What?"

"The kid. Gus. He's my . . . I'm his grandpapa. His *nonno*."

Chapter
20

The word dropped into the center of my brain, sending ripples toward its edge. "You're Mary's father?"

"Yeah. Right."

"And so you're Teresa's father, too."

"Sure."

"And Mrs. Goodrum? She's your wife?"

"My first one. Yeah. Goodrum was her second husband. A real loser. Hey, You know Charlene?"

I nodded. "I saw her at the Silver Season. She thought I was you, I guess."

"Yeah? How's she doing?"

"Physically she looks fine except for the arthritis. Mentally, I'm not sure. Her whole life seems to have been compressed into a single day, about a week ago Thursday. I'm no doctor, but on the whole I'd say she's as happy as any of us. Maybe more so."

Fluto's eyes were closed. "She could have been somebody, you know? But she didn't want it. I treated her like a queen but she just walked away. I still don't get it. I moved back to El Gordo to be near her. Every year I called her on her birthday and told her she could come back. She never did. She just laughed and hung up on me."

"You should go see her," I said.

It was something he didn't want to hear. He opened his eyes and rubbed them. "I should do a lot of things," he muttered, then clenched his hands. His knuckles creaked and he rubbed them. "But it's too late."

"You pay Teresa to keep her mother out there, don't you? Twelve hundred a month?"

"Twelve hundred. Yeah. Teresa won't let me pay it all. Says I don't deserve the honor. Whatever that means. You think it's a nice enough place, this Silver Season?"

"As nice as they come, I guess. Haven't you ever seen it?"

"Not since it was bare ground. I own the place. Me and some business associates. I was out there when we bought the land. I didn't like it. I'm allergic to horse shit. My mama's out there, too. She's ninety-two. Just lays there all day, I hear, yelling for help. Maybe you heard her."

"I probably did."

"Teresa says I shouldn't worry, that she don't know what she's doing or what they're doing to her. You think that's right?"

The forlorn cry still echoed in my head. I thought the voice knew exactly what its world was like, but I didn't tell that to Fluto. "I don't know," I said instead.

Fluto unclenched his fingers and seemed ready to leave. "How about your son?" I asked quickly. "They guy who got shot? Is he Teresa's brother?"

He shook his head. "He's family number two. See, I married Teresa's mother when she was real young. Too young. She couldn't understand the business."

"Where were you married?"

"Here. El Gordo. We were locals. My old man ran a bar, hers was a shipbuilder. She was a Swede. Blond all over. We married up and had kids right away. Things were real good till I had to move to Vegas. On business. Charlene wouldn't go, so we split. Some people owed me favors, we got a dispensation. In Vegas I married the wife I got now. A sister to an associate of mine. A decent woman, a good mother, but not Charlene." Fluto's eyes clouded. "Then we had young Tony. He was trouble from the start. No respect for nothing. Vegas ain't good for kids. I got tired of the town, tired of the people, tired of the business we did out there. I came back to El Gordo. I like it here. Good place for business."

The Chamber of Commerce would have been thrilled with the testimonial. "Mrs. Goodrum must have married again," I said.

"Yeah. To a loser, like I knew she would. They ended up poor as niggers."

"Her husband lost his business, I hear. A fire."

"Yeah. A fire. Real sad."

I couldn't read him but I didn't think I had to. "I offered her money," Fluto went on. "Lots of it. She could have had anything she wanted."

"Except a clear conscience," I said.

"What's that mean? Huh?" His hands made fists. Then he sighed and his fingers uncoiled.

"How did Teresa find out you were her father?" I asked.

"I told her. How else do you think? I drove back here from Vegas and checked out the house and watched her go to school and waited for her after and told her who I was and how she could reach me if she wanted. She was sixteen. I gave her some money. We had a nice talk. Mary, she wouldn't even get in the car with me."

"What did Teresa say when you told her who you were?"

"Not much. She just got this big smile on her face and asked me if the car was really mine. A Continental, it was. Real leather interior. Sharp."

"And later on she went down to Vegas."

"Right. Teresa and her friend. I set her up in business but then things went bad and she came back here."

"You mean Frankie." I tossed the snapshot on the table.

Fluto's eyes narrowed as he looked at it. "Who told you about Frankie?"

"No one told me much about him. Why was he killed?"

"That's all over now. Old business."

"Did Mary ever go to Vegas?"

"Naw. Charlene turned her against me, made sure she stayed home. And look how she ended up. I should have that husband of hers put out of his misery. Always with the hand out for a loan. Loan. Hah. He says he spends it on the boy but I know different. As soon as Gus comes in the business, this Quilk will get his. Believe it." Fluto picked up the ashtray and banged it on the table. "But enough of this crap. What I just told you is confidential, Tanner. You know what I mean? My boy, Tony, he don't know about my other family. Plus, some people around the Bay, they'd be real interested to learn that Teresa's my kid. You said you gave up Gus to keep her out of trouble. Well, you want Teresa out of trouble, you keep quiet about what you know about my family. You might know some but you don't know all. Just give this Tolson my message. The feds, too, while you're at it."

"Which feds?"

"That cockamamy Strike Force they got up there in Frisco. They been buzzing around here like bees, know more about my business than I do. You tell them I don't got Gus, so they should keep their eyes out for him. Also, if you're the first one finds Gus, you tell me where he is and I handle it from there. Me and no one else. You got that?"

"I can't promise."

"You don't got to promise, you just got to do."

"It would help if I knew who would have a reason to take Gus. Who might want to shake you down?"

"I got some ideas, like I said, but for now I keep them to myself. That's business, and I don't talk about business. If it's not business, or if I guess wrong, then you and the cops, maybe you'll find him."

I tried to catch him off guard. "What happened down there on Oswego Street?" I asked.

"You don't need to know," he said.

"Who was the guy you hit? What was Phillip Vincent to you?"

"Old business. It ain't got nothing to do with this."

"I think it might."

"Forget it. Just find Gus. Bust your ass." It was an order, the last one he intended to give me, at least right there. Fluto stood up.

"Hold it," I said. "If you want me to hunt for your grandson and carry messages to the DA and the feds, then you have to do something, too."

"What?"

"Buy me a rug."

"What the hell you talking about? You making a joke? What kind of rug?"

"A Sarouk. It's Persian. Three feet by five. Write it down. I want exactly that kind."

"What do you need a rug for? You a goddamned Arab or something?"

"A friend of mine lost one. In a fire. It was my fault and I want to pay him back."

"I don't know nothing about no fire."

"I didn't say you did."

"A rug. A lousy rug."

"When you see what it costs, you won't call it lousy," I told him.

"Hey. If they got one in this town, it won't cost me nothing. Now you go find Gus." His eyes shoved me toward the door, then through it.

I left Fluto in the library and found my way out without

passing through the waiting room. I stopped at a pay phone in the lobby and tried to reach Teresa Blair, but there was no answer at the house. James Blair wasn't in his office. So I put in a call to Tolson. He came on the line with a grumble.

"Any luck finding Gus Quilk?" I asked.

"No. You?"

"No, but I'm looking in the right place and you're not."

"What's that supposed to mean?"

"Fluto doesn't have him."

"Oh? What'd he do, cross his heart and hope to die? And you believed him? Well, if you think Tony Fluto would hesitate to kill a cop or a kid either one, *you're* the guy who's driving down the wrong fucking street."

"Fluto wouldn't kill *this* kid."

"Why not?"

"Take my word for it," I said. "Which mean Gus was most likely snatched by someone who's moving against Fluto."

"Like who?"

"It's your town, you tell me. When we talked about this before, the only name that I recognized was this guy Wadley, owns a restaurant. Any other names come to mind?"

"No, but I'll check around."

"With the Strike Force?"

"How do you know about them?"

"Fluto told me. He said the feds have been paying a lot of attention to El Gordo lately. Somehow I don't think they're down here for the cuisine. In fact, I think the two guys who warned me off the case last week were Strike Force people. I told you about them, remember? One with a head like a peach; his partner with a petrified tongue? You got any ideas about that?"

"They're feds," Tolson said simply.

"Why didn't you tell me this before?"

"What good would it have done? I was trying to keep you out of all that."

"I'm in it now," I said.

"Yeah, well, I'll pull some men off Fluto and have them look elsewhere. Like down the nearest sewer. By the way. The guy behind this Columbus Development Company? That you had us check? It's Fluto."

"I know that already," I said.

My next call was to Tancy Verritt. When there was no answer at her apartment, I called the Racquet Club. The receptionist acknowledged that Ms. Verritt was on the premises. I was on the premises, too, in about fifteen minutes.

The security guard came out of his little house still wearing his pith helmet and his consternation. I warded him off with a day-old version of the truth: "I'm working on an official police investigation," I said. "If you need confirmation you can call Ray Tolson, chief trial deputy of the El Gordo district attorney. If you try to stop me you'll be up on obstruction charges by the end of the day." I smiled. "At least that's what you can tell your boss."

He didn't have anything in his job description or his world view to incline him to go up against me, so he waved me on with one hand and reached for the phone with the other. Then he dropped them both. "Fuck it," he muttered. "Which one of 'em you gonna bust?"

"Which one do you think?"

He shrugged. "All of 'em could use a night in jail," he said happily, then repositioned his helmet and went back inside his lair.

Tancy Verritt was sitting with the same people, wearing the same clothes, wasting the same time. She tried very hard to ignore me, but since curiosity was the only organic emotion left within her, she looked my way within three minutes.

I beckoned for her to join me. She said something to her

friends and stood up. Chip put a hand on her forearm but she shrugged him off and walked to where I was. "What's the matter?" she asked frostily. "Didn't you dish out enough humiliation the other night?"

"That wasn't humiliation, that was salvation."

"I don't need saving, thank you."

"It wasn't you I was talking about."

"Oh." She frowned. "What do you want?"

"Let's sit down," I said. "This could take a while."

She hesitated but finally we crossed to a table off by itself and sat. A waiter was there in a flash. "When I saw you last, I was looking for Teresa Blair," I said after the waiter had ambled off without a smile or an order.

"So?"

"So I found her."

"Good for you."

"Now I'm looking for someone else."

"Who?"

"A boy named Gus Quilk. You know him?"

"No."

"I think you do."

"I could care less what you think."

"Unfortunately for you, not everyone in town feels that way," I said. "One person who doesn't is the El Gordo DA. He's going to care a whole lot when I tell him that it wasn't only Teresa Blair and Gus Quilk who saw Tony Fluto run down Phillip Vincent, that there was one other person down on Oswego Street that night."

"Who? As if I cared."

"You."

Her eyes danced, a whirling reel that told me my hunch was right. "What makes you think I was there?" she asked when she got her nerves in check.

"Something you said about a promise to keep you out of it, and something a man named Lufkin said about double-vision."

"Who's Lufkin?"

"No one you'd know; he does his drinking in public."

Tancy Verritt rubbed her mouth with her palm, smearing red off her lips and onto her cheek, making her mouth seem bruised and bloodied. "I didn't see any killing," she said softly.

"DAs hear that a lot. They get real good at deciding who's telling it straight and who isn't."

She sniffed. "What are you here for? Who sent you?" Her voice rose like the call of a night bird.

"No one sent me," I said. "I just need some information. Like I said, I'm looking for a boy."

"And if I talk to you?"

"I let the DA find his own witnesses."

"How do I know I can trust you?"

"I'm not a member of this club."

She squirmed in her chair, her face slack and overworked. Fear coursed through her like poison. "This scares me, you know," she said. "I don't *need* this. I left Vegas to get away from all of it, but now it's back. Worse than before. Why don't they ever stop? That's what I can't understand. They say they'll stop, but they don't. It's in their blood. I swear it. Congenital mayhem."

"What exactly are you talking about? And who?"

Her voice was shrill. "I'm talking about this . . . hatred. This *war*. This fighting and killing and pushing to get more or to keep someone else from getting more. I'm talking about madness. No one wins, and it'll kill them all, sooner or later, and they know it, but they still keep on. Death junkies." Tears streaked her cheeks and her words.

"Who's behind it?" I asked softly.

"I'm not going to tell. I can't. I'm no more than a roach to them. I'd be dead in a day."

Her face was closed to me, locked, and it would take a tool far more powerful than any I could use to pry it open.

I decided to level with her. "I just came from a meeting with Tony Fluto," I said.

"Great."

I shook my head. "I know Fluto is Teresa's father. And Mary's father. And Gus Quilk's grandfather."

The knowledge made me fearsome to her. She looked desperately around the deck for help. "What do you want to know?" she asked at last. "Just tell me, then get out of here and leave me alone." She shuddered and not from cold.

I leaned toward her, capturing her eyes. "What were you doing down on Oswégo Street that night? What was going on? What brought all of you together? If I knew that, I might get a lead on the boy."

"I don't know anything about the killing," she repeated. "You've got to believe that."

"Then start at the beginning. Why were you down there?"

"I was just along for the ride. With Teresa. She takes Gus down there every Sunday, almost."

"Why?"

"Because Tony, Mr. Fluto, can't stand the Quilks. Ted, especially, but Mary, too. I guess because she could have come over to him any time and didn't, even though she's had it about as bad as a woman can. The only way Tony could see the boy was for Teresa to pick him up and take him to the warehouse Tony owns down on Oswego Street. They would meet there."

"Was he alone that night?"

"Always. He had a real thing about keeping it secret that Gus was his grandchild. He was afraid they'd do something to Gus to get at him, if they found out."

"Who's 'they'?"

She shrugged. "It could be anyone. Even a complete stranger. You live like they live you have enemies you don't even know about. Tony's paranoid. All of them are. Especially James."

"James who?"

"Shit."

"James Blair?" I repeated.

"Yes," she said softly.

"What does he have to do with this?"

"He's Tony's son." She took a deep breath and forced it out. "James and Teresa are brother and sister. They, I don't know, they work for Tony somehow or other. Now get out of here. I don't care *who* you call, I'm not saying anything else about that."

Tancy Verritt saw the streak of shock on my face. "That's a new one, huh, Mr. Detective? Your new pal Tony didn't happen to mention that one, huh? People always think guys like Tony are playing straight with them, but guys like Tony never play straight. They don't know how. Their kids don't, either. Like I said. It's in the blood." Her laugh was meant to inflict pain and did.

"Why did they pretend to be husband and wife?" I asked, still struggling with the ramifications of the Blairs' true relationship.

"I don't know, exactly," Tancy Verritt said. "I just know that ever since she came back from Vegas and started living with James, Teresa's been a different woman. It's like *The Three Faces of Eve*, remember that? Joanne Woodward, I think. Well, that's the way Teresa is now. Nice one minute, cold as a clam the next. She doesn't even *like* James—who does?—but still she stays out there in that, that *doll* house with him, doing something or other, who knows what. It's weird."

"What do you think they do?"

"I don't know and I don't want to know. If you're smart, you'll stay just like me. Dumb and happy."

"I think that only applies to animals." I was having trouble focusing on what I had just learned and she took advantage of my silence.

"I'm going now," Tancy Verritt said. I held up a hand to stop her.

"Why was the little man on Oswego Street killed? What was going on down there that night?"

"I don't know, I told you. I didn't see anything."

"You were there."

"No, I wasn't. Not exactly. We were all down there, and Tony and Gus were messing around like always, and then Tony said we'd better go because he was supposed to meet a guy in a little while. We started to leave but Teresa couldn't get her car started. Tony got real nervous as time went past, and finally he told me to take Gus for a walk and not come back till someone came for us. So I did. I was real scared of the neighborhood but even more scared of Tony and what he might be doing, so me and Gus wandered around for about half an hour and then Teresa drove down and picked us up and we dropped Gus off on Winthrop Avenue and Teresa took me home and that was it."

"So Fluto was expecting someone."

"Right."

"Someone he knew."

"Right. That's right."

"But you didn't see what happened. Did Teresa say anything about it?"

"No. Nothing."

"How about Gus?"

"No."

"Could he have seen the killing?"

"I don't think so. He was running around all over the place, but we were pretty far away from the warehouse most of the time."

"So he probably bluffed the cops, doing the same thing his Aunt Teresa did."

"What's that?"

"Saving the godfather's ass."

Tancy Verritt took two steps and stopped. "I'm leaving.

If you turn me in to the police, I won't tell them anything. But I guess that's up to you."

"I guess it is," I said. "Do you know where Teresa is now?"

"No."

"James?"

"No."

"Do you have any idea who might have snatched Gus?"

"Anyone who knew the little prick. Hey. What do you mean, 'snatched'?"

"The cops were bringing Gus to court to testify against Tony this morning. He didn't make it. The cop is dead and Gus is missing."

"Oh, my God."

"Who could have done it?"

"I don't know. Anyone I ever *met* in this town could have done it. They're all crazy, those people." Her last word was a scream that attracted other eyes.

Tancy Verritt wiped the tears from her cheeks and hurried back to her friends. When she got to their table, she stood stock still, looking down at them, one by one. Then she turned and ran through a door marked "Dressing Room." A moment later I heard her muffled sobs. I went off to find a phone.

Once again I couldn't track down the Blairs, sister or brother. I thought about calling Tolson and telling him that Gus was probably a red herring, just like his Aunt Teresa, but I decided against it. I wanted Tolson to keep looking, to get me off the hook.

Chapter
21

I couldn't get where I wanted to. A burly cop directed me to take a left turn away from the roadblock he was standing by, then urged me to keep moving. I did what he told me to for only a block, then parked the car and set out on foot, back the way I'd come. They were keeping pedestrians back as well, but when the cop was giving directions to a girl in a Fiat, I ducked under the sawhorse and walked down the middle of the street toward the restaurant, trying to look like I belonged there.

The neon sign above the building was still blinking out its name, but the word was barely visible through the black geyser that engulfed it. I made my way through red pumpers and long ladder trucks and the reptilian swirl of fire hoses until I had a good view of the burning building. Black-slickered men rushed past me, lugging salvation and the equipment that produced it toward the flames. I looked for something or someone that would tell me what had happened.

Smoke poured out of the rear of the restaurant in

columns, then mingled with the breeze and followed it everywhere. I was increasingly conscious of the heat of the blaze and of the terrible memories it evoked, memories too recently rekindled in the alley behind my office. I grabbed the arm of a fireman who seemed momentarily to lack a mission and asked him what had happened.

"Grease fire, probably," he said. "Usually is, with these joints." His face was gaunt and smeared with soot; he might have just emerged from internment. "Started back by the kitchen, looks like," he went on. "Going pretty good by the time we got here." He sniffed, then rubbed his nose. "All these food joints are firetraps. Every one of them. Their safety record ain't worth shit."

"Anyone inside?"

"Nope. They're closed between two and five, is the way I hear it. Real lucky."

"Maybe too lucky."

"You saying something here, buddy?"

"I don't know," I said. "Someone should check it pretty carefully."

"And why is that?"

"Have the fire marshal call Deputy DA Tolson. He can tell him."

The fireman put a finger on my chest. "Who are you, mac?"

"Tanner."

"What are you doing here?"

"I was going to try to talk to the owner. Looks like I picked a bad time."

I tried a smile but the fireman wasn't in the mood. "You better stick around," he ordered. "The fire marshal will want a statement. I'll tell him how to find you."

Someone called out a name from behind one of the trucks and the fireman gave me a narrow look and trotted off. When he was out of sight, I nosed around a bit longer, tense as always in the presence of fire. I didn't see anyone

I knew except Wadley. He was standing in a group of fire officials. I waited till he moved away from them and then went up beside him. "Mr. Wadley?"

"Yeah? I'm busy. Who the hell are you?"

His face was well tended, determinedly young; his attire casual but expensive. His curly locks were scrambled and speckled with ash. "I'd like to talk to you a minute," I said.

"About this?" He gestured toward the pyre, which chose that moment to make the sounds of steam.

"No. About a boy," I said.

"A kid? My kid? What about him? He swipe something again?"

"Not your boy. A boy named Quilk. Gus Quilk."

"Don't know him," Wadley said, shaking his head. I didn't see the flash of awareness I'd been looking for.

"I think I might have some information of use to you," I lied. "I'd give it up in trade for information about the boy."

Wadley shook his head impatiently. "I got all the information I need, pal. What I don't got is full coverage on my fire and casualty plan. Now excuse me."

"I just came from a meeting with Tony Fluto."

The name got me his full attention for the first time. "Tony, huh. My old pal Tony. What's on his mind?"

"The boy."

"This Quilk?"

I nodded.

"Tell him I'm real sorry, but I don't know anything about it. Now I got to talk to these guys about the fire." He started to walk away and then turned back. "Tony. That gets me thinking. And what I'm thinking is that Tony might know a lot about this fire himself. A whole lot. What do you think about that?"

"I don't know," I said.

"Tony and me, we haven't been getting along. Maybe he mentioned it to you."

I didn't say anything.

"It occurs to me," Wadley went on, "that Tony might have done this as some sort of warning. Of what, I don't know. But these people here, if they tell me it was a torch job, well, the first name I think of will be Tony's. You tell him that, at your next meeting. You tell him if I find out my place was torched I'll be talking to him. And it won't be about kid stuff."

Wadley swung abruptly away from me and stomped back to the group of firemen. I decided I'd better leave before someone told me I couldn't. I also decided that Wadley didn't have Gus, because even in these circumstances he would have toyed with me longer if he had. I thought of someplace else to go and headed back toward my car.

They were walking side by side, speaking in low tones, the large one tilted slightly to his left so he could hear the small one's words. They almost stepped on me before they saw me. "You," the big one blurted when he looked up and saw my face instead of the sun.

"Welcome," I said. "Always glad to see a federal presence at a disaster site."

The little one smiled and bowed. "What happened up there?" he asked stiffly.

"Fire. Wadley's Restaurant. Everything on the menu tonight comes well done."

"Anyone injured?"

I shook my head. "The place was closed between meals. The fire people think it was a grease fire."

"And you?"

"Me, I think it was anything but."

"Specifically?"

I smiled. "I never like to be more specific than the occasion requires."

"We should talk," the little one said simply. His eyes

never quite met mine. He seemed to read his words off a cue card held somewhere behind me.

"I agree," I said.

He frowned. "Not here. We've got to go up there and investigate on a level two basis, then we've got to get back to the city by seventeen hundred hours. We could meet you in our office then. Would that be acceptable?"

I checked my watch and thought about it. "Do you know about the Quilk boy?" I asked.

"We know."

"Has he been found, by any chance?"

"Not that I am aware."

"Are you looking for him?"

"Incidentally, yes. Specifically, no."

"Why not?"

"No jurisdiction. Our mission doesn't cover nonspecific criminality."

"It's a kidnapping. That's federal, right?"

"The victim must be held twenty-four hours, first of all. Second of all, we're not FBI."

"Then who?"

"Justice. Organized Crime and Racketeering Section. Strike Force Twenty-two."

"How many are there, for God's sake?" I asked.

"Twenty-six. One short of the number of LCN families in the country."

"LCN?"

"La Cosa Nostra," the big one blurted, tripling my collection of his words.

"And here you are in El Gordo," I said. "Hard to believe this town is that big a deal."

"Let's not go into that just now. See you at strike base?" the little one pronounced.

"Where is it?"

"Federal Building. Turk and Larkin. Room sixteen-twenty-four. The door is not designated. Just walk in."

"See you then."

"Roger."

They marched away like toys. I drove to a filling station and tried to call the Blairs and then Ray Tolson and I didn't reach any of them. I tried to think of what else I could do to turn up Gus Quilk but I couldn't come up with anything, so I got some lunch and drove back to the city I live in.

The office was empty and cold, without light or sound or things that needed doing or even a note from Peggy. I fixed a drink and turned on the radio and tried to put together a mental map to Gus Quilk's whereabouts. Somewhere in the middle of my musing something occurred to me and I looked up a phone number and dialed it. "I'd like to speak to Mr. Therm," I said to the woman who answered.

"I'm sorry, Mr. Therm is not in," she replied.

"When do you expect him?"

"Not for several days. He's been called away to consult on a non-obvious occupation. May I take a message?"

I guessed she meant a haunted house. "Tell him Mr. Tanner called. Tell him he said thanks."

"Will he know what it's in reference to?"

"I think he will," I said, then left the office and took my Buick out to Turk Street and put it in a lot that charged five bucks for the first hour. It was ten minutes before five when I walked through the door of the Federal Building, smiled at the guard checking bags and briefcases for bombs and took the express elevator to the sixteen floor.

Room 1624 was the only one in the corridor that didn't have a sign beside it identifying the department it was charged to. The office on the near side was the NLRB and on the far side was the Securities and Exchange Commission, which put the Mafia right in the middle of labor problems and the stock market. Which was about where they were anyway.

The door opened onto a two-room suite, bureaucratically barren, a jar of daisies on the desk the only pleasant thing in the room. There was a chart on the wall with words like *caporegima* and *soldato* written on it, and a map of California with some red pins sticking in it. There were a lot of pins in San Francisco and San Jose, and even a few in El Gordo. A picture of Jimmy Carter still hung on the wall, as though it had refused to be removed.

The young woman standing in the middle of the office was either coming or going, and when she took her rabbit fur jacket off and hung it on the coat rack, I decided it was the former. After a quick glance and a nod at me, she took the seat behind the gray metal desk, put her purse in a bottom drawer, and looked up at me with the almond eyes and kneaded features of a Ming princess. The plastic sign on the desk in front of her said her name was Arlene Wong. A small curved scar beside her left eye looked like it had been made with a spoon.

"My name's Tanner," I said. "Are either of the, ah, agents in? I have an appointment."

"Agent Lucas has just returned," she said brightly. "He's down the hall a moment. Please have a seat."

I collected dust and my thoughts for the next five minutes. The girl busied herself with typing from a tape cassette, head phones wedged in her ears, her foot pedal squeaking merrily as she moved through the dictation. When she stopped to change tapes, I asked her a question. "Which one is Lucas?"

"I beg your pardon?"

"Which one of them is Lucas? The big one or the little one?"

"The little one."

"Who's the other guy?"

"Armbruster. Agent Armbruster."

"Is he around by any chance?"

"No. He's . . . no."

"You know where he is?"

"Yes, but I can't tell you."

"Why not?"

"Because I don't know who you are."

"I'm Marsh Tanner."

"I know, but who *are* you?"

"I'm helping the Strike Force with the Fluto investigation."

"I see."

"So where's Armbruster?"

She shook her head reluctantly, embarrassed at her continued opposition. "I still can't say. Reginald doesn't like me to talk about our work. He says anyone in the building could be a double agent. He says the LCN has penetrated every department of government. Even ours."

"Reginald?"

"Agent Lucas."

"Just tell me this," I said. "Has either of them come up with anything on Gus Quilk?"

"I wouldn't know."

"Okay," I said. "How long do you think it will be before Reginald shows up?"

She said what they always say: "He should be here any minute."

I took out a cigarette. When I couldn't find a match, I asked her for one. She dug a book out of her desk and told me I could keep it. I said thanks. She put her headset on again and typed. Twenty minutes later the door opened and Agent Lucas hurried in. "Sorry I'm late," he said. "Washington on the line." He motioned me toward the inner office. "Anything?" he asked the girl.

She shook her head. The look on her face indicated that Agent Lucas was more than an agent to her.

"Midnight okay?" Lucas asked her.

"Sure," she said. Her smile was beautiful and as real as the daisies. Lucas nodded, told her she could leave, and guided me into his office.

Sets of the *United States Code Annotated* and the *Federal Supplement* climbed the walls. Behind a glass-fronted bookcase were row upon row of spiral notebooks with the names of cities on their spines—New York, Buffalo, Miami, Las Vegas, and San Jose were the ones I could see. On the corner of the desk nearest me was a stack of file folders. The nearest label had a man's name on it: Angelo Bruno. He was dead, I knew that. He'd supposedly been a big-time Philadelphia hood. If each of the files on the desk was for a different Mafia boss the Strike Force wouldn't run out of work for a century.

Lucas saw me looking at the files. "Know what I'm doing here?" he asked, a queer smile on his face.

"What?"

"Answering a request under the Freedom of Information Act. Know who made the request?"

"Who?"

"Tony Fluto. Or, more precisely, his lawyer."

I laughed. "You mean Fluto has filed an official request to see what you have on him in your records?"

"That's a roger."

"And you have to give it to him?"

"Some of it. Lots of it, in fact. You know what kind of problem that causes?"

"I'd say it plays hell with keeping an undercover agent in place inside his operation."

"Right. Once Fluto knows what raw data we've collected on him, he can easily calculate its parameters and determine its locus."

"Presto," I said. "One dead agent."

"That's a roger," Lucas said. "Sometimes I wonder whose team Congress is on. Under our earlier configuration we were able to employ the tax laws and IRS data to prosecute almost any LCN member we wanted. But the Tax Reform Act made that tactic inoperative. Now the IRS can't interface with us at all. Same problem with the Right to Financial Privacy Act."

"But they gave you RICO," I said.

"Ah, yes. The Racketeer Influenced and Corrupt Organization statute. It's not inutile, but it's not nearly pervasive enough, either. Now with Fluto, we're proceeding under the Continuing Criminal Enterprise law, particularly its forfeiture provisions. That contracting business of his. A negotiated casualty is what it amounts to. In a couple of months we'll have a prima facie case to present to the U.S. attorney for transmission to the special grand jury."

Lucas's jargon was attacking my brain like a Mixmaster, but I had to hang in there. He was the only source I had left. "Who else you after down in El Gordo?" I asked.

"Well, there's a branch of La Nuestra Familia down there, and a pretty tough group of Hell's Angels, but compared to Fluto they're subordinate considerations. Fluto's the chief of the conventional LCN operation in El Gordo, and the main feeder into the Bollo family in San Francisco, and that's what we're trying to functionally decapitate."

"You sound real happy in your work, Agent Lucas."

He didn't even fake a smile. "Organized crime earns a hundred and fifty billion in untaxed income each year, Tanner. I'd like to see some of that go to Uncle Sam. The benefits would impact across a wide spectrum, socioeconomically."

"From what I read, you've been having some luck lately around the country."

"Some. Jersey. Miami. L.A. But hell, it's still just a few vectors out of many. If you look at the big picture you still see the LCN operating at full capacity, expanding its base. The last statistical bulletin I saw said the LCN had moved into more than seven hundred legitimate businesses in the country. Movies. Records. Insurance. Banking. The increase is geometric."

"So why am I here?"

Lucas clasped his hands in front of him in prayerful solemnity. He was as humorless as anyone I'd ever seen. "Our first encounter was counterproductive, Tanner," he said. "I was overly sensitive to a possible compromise of our mission. I apologize for my unwarranted remarks."

"Forget it."

"I was concerned that you would become congruent with an impact area without realizing it, and thereby ruin months of field work. This time I simply want a favor."

"What?"

"Stay away from all phases of the Fluto investigation."

"I think I heard that one before."

"But now you've accomplished the mission Tolson engaged you to do."

"True enough," I said. "Tell me. Did you make the same suggestion to Tolson? That he lay off Fluto?"

"In a slightly different conformation, yes."

"He go along?"

"That's not your problem."

"You're right. My problem is a fourteen-year-old kid. I can't get out of the Fluto case till he turns up."

"I recognize that tangent," Lucas said. "Believe me. But we'll locate him. Leave it to the Bureau."

"I can't."

"Sure you can. Here's the format I suggest. Give us a week. If the subject hasn't surfaced by then, give me a call. We'll bring you down and brief you on the four corners of the investigation, including the input of the FBI, El Gordo police, Strike Force, everything. Then you can do as you please. With our full cooperation. But for now, we're asking you to cool it."

In the middle of the buzz words the vernacular was jarring. "You won't ever find the kid if you think Tony Fluto's the one who has him," I said.

"Why not?"

"Fluto doesn't know where he is."

"You sure of that?"

"Reasonably."

"Okay. I'll plug that into the circuit. It'll advance the momentum of the investigation."

"And pass it along to the FBI?"

"And lateralize it."

"Tell me something," I said. "Who's Fluto's main opposition in El Gordo? Who wants him out of the way?"

Lucas smiled. "You mean who besides his kid?"

"Young Tony?"

Lucas nodded. "They all have this family component, you know. The way we hear it, Fluto is ill. His son's the presumed successor, that is if Tony can dictate the succession, which he will unless he goes down first."

"Who besides young Tony is in the running?"

"Well, Fluto's main competition has had a way of being prematurely disengaged over the years. We're talking maybe six, seven corpses since Tony returned to El Gordo from Vegas. The last one, a guy named Moskowitz, jumped from a building in Seattle last October. Halloween. Local law ruled suicide, decided Moskowitz didn't have a thing to live for. Well, the asset he had was the biggest hot car operation in the West Bay, and enough troops in his organization to threaten Fluto or anyone else, even Duckie Bollo, the head of the San Francisco family."

"How about right now, though? Who's the main contender?"

"Well, there's Wadley. He's smart, and has a great laundry for his cash, but he still charts out a step below Fluto. Then there's Theopholis Buck, a black who runs narcotics and street numbers. The blacks don't like to subserve anyone. Then there's a guy named Abrams, he inherited the Moskowitz car operation. They're all the secondary units. Of course there's three times that many tertiary units who want to vertical their way into a higher rank. That's why the LCN are always looking over their shoulder. They never know where it's going to come from."

"You got undercover men around those three guys?"

"You mean would we know if they had the Quilk boy? Negative. We haven't tried to penetrate them as yet."

"Why not?"

"Because it's contraindicated. If Tony drops off the chart, at least two of the second tier will foreclose each other from trying to vertical into his slot. If you want to know how the scenario will play out, read the papers about the Bruno family in Philly. They just blew Chicken Man Testa all over the block. When the thing sorts itself out, then we can mount a mission. We don't have unlimited resources, you know."

I was starting to think it was a good thing they didn't. "Fluto told me if he went to jail he'd just run things from his cell," I said.

"Some LCN units could do it and have. But not Fluto. You have to have someone on the outside to execute the directives. The only one Tony's got is his kid, and young Tony's not equipped for the mission. He'd go on the same vacation Hoffa went on about two weeks after Tony was incarcerated. But to get back to the point, Tanner. Take a week off. Drive to the mountains. Pretty up there this time of year."

"I just got back."

Lucas nodded. "So you did. I must admit, her testimony was unexpected. Though not unwelcome."

"If I leave it for a week, and Gus Quilk isn't found, the judge in El Gordo will dismiss Tolson's murder case against Fluto."

"She probably will," Lucas agreed. "But that's not your problem, is it?"

"I guess not," I said. "There's one more thing."

"What?"

"Who the hell was it that Fluto squashed down there on Oswego Street?"

Lucas shook his head. "You come back in a week. If the Quilk boy hasn't surfaced by then, I'll brief you on full background. Believe me." Lucas looked at his watch and pulled a file toward him and thumbed through it.

I smiled. I stood up. I left. I didn't believe Lucas for a minute, but I pretended otherwise in order to match all the other pretending that had been going on in the case.

When I got back to the first floor, I went inside a phone booth, pulling the door shut behind me. I listened to the hum of the little fan at the top of the booth as I stared at the telephone that was a foot from my face and thought about using it. I finally decided I didn't have to make the call right then, so I didn't. Instead I drove back to El Gordo, for what I hoped was the last time.

Chapter 22

The lights across the bay were vague and timid, shrouded in evening fumes and mist. I parked the car and turned my back on the lights and the view and walked toward the fence and the low, dark house which lay beyond it. I tried the two front gates, careful not to make a sound, and confirmed that they were locked, then started around to the back, moving with the stealth of felons.

There were lights coming from the Martin house to my left, and the indistinct drone of television words. Periodically I could see Kathryn Martin's head pop in and out of the small window above her sink, a frown of concentration on her face as she prepared the evening meal. I walked beside the fence between the Blair and Martin houses, hoping the Martins didn't have a dog or an alarm system, wondering if I'd made the right assumptions.

The night air shouldered past the redwoods that spread their boughs above me, making sounds of silks and satins. The stars peeked in and out of clouds. As far as I could tell, the Blair house was dark and vacant, which was all right with me. And then nothing was all right, because a human sound crawled toward me from somewhere behind the house. It was the sound of pain, of the end of consciousness. I hurried in the direction I was going.

The only light came from the Martin windows and from the chip of moon above them. The hill that rose behind the terraced lots was a high hull of impenetrable blackness. I still wasn't sure what had happened, only that something had. I couldn't see well enough to run.

When I rounded the back corner of the fence, I saw the slats of an open gate. I moved into a jog and trotted toward it, wary, alert for the movements of someone besides myself. I couldn't see anything but the thick splash of shadows when I tripped and fell.

Dirt and rocks scraped flesh from my hands and knees. A fat, wet worm of blood inched down my leg. I rolled to my feet as quickly as I could, then bent back down to feel for the thing I had stumbled over. My hand felt bulk and warmth and the slick ribs of polyester; my fingers slid over enough textures to confirm my guess, then I struck a match.

It was Wayne Martin. I guessed he was dead. The match went out.

His head was oddly bent toward the point of his shoulder, his neck necessarily broken. One of his eyes was a ball-less socket. I felt for pulse and breath. Nothing bulged, nothing tickled. I struck another match and saw only the white face of a black Bible that lay open just beyond Martin's four dead but grasping fingers, its pages fluttering in the wind like broken wings. I heard a sound behind me. When I looked up, I saw James Blair.

He wore the same simple robe and slippers as the first time I had been at the house and he was carrying some kind of blanket draped over one arm and a rope looped over his wrist. When he saw me, he started, but only briefly, and dropped them both. I couldn't see what was in his other hand but I thought it was a knife.

"Good evening," Blair said, immediately and totally composed. I could have been pulling weeds from the petunias.

"Is this your doing?" I asked, gesturing toward the body behind me.

"Unfortunately, yes."

"Unfortunately," I repeated. I saw Davy's face for an instant, a new star, the brightest of the night. Then it vanished, perhaps to make room for the soul of its father.

"He wasn't who I thought he was," Blair said softly. "He shouldn't have been back here."

"You stupid bastard," I said. "He was just trying to see his son. He hung around back here so he could catch a glimpse of the life he used to live." My voice sounded hollow in the open air, the shell of a blown egg. I was suddenly exhausted, and I knew I couldn't afford to be.

"I realize all that now," Blair said. "I thought someone had sent him."

"Who?"

"Never mind. I think you'd better come inside."

It was more than a suggestion. The thing in his hand caught light for an instant. "And leave him here?" I asked.

"For now."

"Could he be alive?"

"Not possibly. His neck is broken. At the fifth or sixth cervical vertebra, I believe."

"His eye popped out when you hit him."

"Yes."

"Karate?"

"A similar art, though more deadly. Come."

I patted my coat pocket, pressing it flat, feeling no comfort of a lump—my gun was back in the car. I had shot too many people with it, and now it seemed I always found an excuse to leave it behind. Blair stood to the side and pressed his eyes on me as I walked into the enclosed and foreign compound in which he lived. The gate closed behind us with the sound of an ax on wood.

I crossed the gravel garden and went through the open glass door into the darkened living room, then turned and waited for Blair to join me. He was still in the shadows when the room was suddenly lit by a dim and bluish light. When he entered I saw that the broad blade of a cleaver still dangled at his side, its edge buried in the folds of his robe. I gestured to the knife. "You're not planning to do anything with that, are you?"

Blair lifted his brows.

"It'll be hell getting my blood out of all these mats. A real tough laundry problem."

"Indeed," Blair said simply, then carefully placed the cleaver on the table beside him. I shuddered. The stainless blade was made for dismemberment and nothing else.

"Who did you think Wayne Martin was when you were breaking his neck?" I asked.

"It doesn't matter now."

"Someone sent to retaliate?"

"Something like that," he observed absently.

"Sent by whom? Young Tony? Your half brother?"

Blair smiled. "You do get around, Mr. Tanner. My compliments for unearthing our little secret."

"Where's Teresa?"

"I don't know. I haven't seen her since she took the witness stand in court."

"How about the Quilk boy? Did you grab him?"

"Why would I do that?" Blair asked.

"I'm not exactly sure. I haven't got all this straightened out yet. Maybe you can help," I added. If he had time to think, he would think about me. I was trying to prevent it.

"Why would I want to help you?" Blair asked artfully, and laughed for the time it takes to wink.

"To square yourself with the Buddha, maybe."

"Oh, I did that long ago, Mr. Tanner. The Buddha is

infinitely accommodating. It's his most attractive quality."

"I doubt that he can accommodate what you just did out in the backyard."

"Perhaps not. It's really not important. I no longer need the Buddha. I no longer need anyone." The words were apocalyptic.

"I remember you told me earlier that in this day and age a man could only choose to withdraw from the world or to become twice mad," I said. "I assumed you had chosen the former. I was wrong, wasn't I?"

"Some would say so." Blair's serenity was so complete I began to wonder if he was drugged.

Blair watched me silently, as interested as I was in what he would do in the next minute. "I am going to kill you now," he said after time had passed. "I am not happy about it, but I have no choice, because of what you have learned and seen. I want you to know I bear you no ill will. Circumstances compel me to save myself and my destiny."

"So it's destiny, is it? A heritage of crime and death?"

Blair smiled. "I don't expect you to understand."

"The police know I'm here," I blurted.

"Oh, I doubt that very much. Truly I do." Blair nodded to confirm his words. "You came here to learn. Sadly, you will die in ignorance. But then, perhaps, you will know all there is to know. In a sense I envy you."

"Bullshit. Have you killed your sister, too?"

"Teresa? Why would I kill her?"

"I don't know. I don't know which side you're on. Did you shoot young Tony Fluto? Did you fire-bomb Wadley's Restaurant?"

Blair just rubbed his palms and fingers against each other and breathed, regularly and deeply, in some sort of exercise.

"Are you trying to succeed to Old Tony's arson empire? Is that what this is all about? Is that the swamp I wandered into when I drove into this fucking town?"

"Swamp is a good word," Blair said. "Your speculation is reasonably accurate as well. I have worked for my father for many years, since I learned what he was and what I was. Doing his bidding, doing my duty, risking much and receiving little but a dream in return. Now I claim full benefit. Now I actualize my heritage."

"Tell me one thing," I said. "Was Teresa working with you? Is that why you pretended to be man and wife? Were you some kind of secret commando team Tony had behind him, keeping the opposition in line, eliminating the pretenders to the throne?" I saw Teresa's face as I said the words, and heard her voice, and the coupling of the image with my guess was horrible.

Blair held up a hand to block my words. "I have no more trivial answers, Mr. Tanner. Only the ultimate one." He raised his other hand as well, and straightened both of them, turning their edges toward me, wielding them like the cleaver he had just abandoned. His body turned as well, his stance becoming martial, threatening and confident. I knew I didn't have a prayer if the fight was fair.

Blair advanced toward me in that silly sliding motion of Kung Fu movies and playground antics, but I had no doubt that for him the moves were practiced, as effective as ordnance. He was a walking truncheon and I had nothing that would fend him off. It wouldn't take more than one blow to kill me, if it was the right one. The one he had used on Wayne Martin. The expression on Blair's face was mixed, but a part of it was regret. "Good-bye, Mr. Tanner. I feel that you are a man who need not fear death. If you allow me to proceed unimpeded I can guarantee the end will be quick and painless."

I laughed. "Oh, I'm not going to allow you to do a damned thing, Blair. You're going to have to do more than talk like a dentist to roll me up in the same blanket with Wayne Martin."

Blair had expected my response. Without another word

he slid toward me a step. I took a step backward. My leg bumped a table and I glanced quickly down. What I saw gave me an idea, faint and desperate, like my chances of survival.

Blair's eyes had brightened into azure jewels. He advanced on me relentlessly, left leg and arm cocked and forward, right side in reserve. His slippers scraping across the floor mats made the only sounds in the room except for the interior sounds of my heart and lungs.

When I sensed he was about to advance another step, I reached down behind me and, without taking my eyes off him, groped for and finally grasped the deep green and delicate vase that rested on the table to my rear. When he saw what I had in my hand, Blair's eyes flickered once. His right hand rose to shield his face and he lunged toward me, ready to slash my throat.

I dove to the side. At the same time I threw the vase, not at Blair, not where he anticipated it would go, but at the wall across the room. The sound it made as its form and history shattered caused Blair to halt for an instant, then glance momentarily toward the wall that had destroyed his prize. The momentum of his initial move was as broken as the vase. I retreated to a sliding door that was a thin and flimsy ally at my back.

Blair came on again, his face no longer casually engaged but grim and deadly. I felt silly, a grown-up playing at kid games, until I met his eyes. Then I felt cold and as old as I would ever be.

As he came toward me again, I shifted from side to side, reminded absurdly and distinctly of dodge-ball games, my back to a red brick schoolhouse, my only threat a deflated volleyball. Blair grunted and launched a flying kick to my chest.

I leaped to the side again, so slowly that my trailing arm was nicked by the hurtling pad of Blair's slipper. His momentum carried him into the thin door screen, shattering it. It took him several seconds to escape the shredded bamboo and rice paper. By the time he found me again, I had ripped his favorite scroll off the wall, the one that recommended the killing of the Buddha. I held the long strip of paper in front of my body like a towel.

Blair again assumed his assault position. I waited for him to meet my eyes, and when he did I took the brittle strip of paper in both hands and ripped it down the middle. From the look on Blair's face I had torn his heart as well.

I threw the tattered scroll at him and turned back to the wall and swiped at the print of the tranquil fishing scene and sent it tumbling off its hook and to the floor. The glass over the print shattered, the mat bent awkwardly. "You bastard," Blair muttered.

He grunted once and bent his knees and I was in retreat again, my diversions gaining me only time, not advantage. Blair was enraged, but not so much that he abandoned the discipline of his technique. I wanted him to come at me like a street fighter. Instead, he advanced like a warrior god.

I backed away again, then jumped toward the wall and pulled one of the kendo swords off its pegs and brandished it awkwardly in front of me. But I sensed immediately that it was the wrong thing to do, that I should not have armed myself, that it would be my undoing. "I shall now kill you with your own weapon, Mr. Tanner," Blair said. "It is always the preferred result."

He was back in control now, because I was again predictable. I thought for an instant, then waved the sword in front of me, forcing him back a step. Then I whirled it about my head like a bolo and threw it at the paper carp that hung, gay and colorful, on the far wall. When the sword miraculously impaled the carp, the symbolic thrust seized Blair more powerfully than I could ever have. He was suddenly confused and doubtful, and I hurried to pull my one last trick. By the time Blair had turned back toward me, I had the little bonsai tree and its heavy lacquered pot in my hands, my right fist wrapped around the undulant trunk of the tiny evergreen that emerged from the thick, damp dirt.

"It has lived two hundred years," Blair whispered. With a mad cry I yanked the tree out of its bed of soil and threw it to the floor and crushed its needles and branches, its bark and roots, its centuries of life, beneath the thick hard soles of my shoes. The blasphemous sounds of destruction were displaced by Blair's scream, which was as pointed as the sword still sticking in the wall behind him. But it was his chest, not mine, that felt the wound.

Blair leaped at me in sprawling, flailing fury. I stepped inside his punch and smashed him just above the ear with the heavy ceramic pot that had once held the ageless tree. Blair went down with the groan I had heard Wayne Martin utter, the groan of fallen men. I sank to my knees beside him.

He wasn't dead, but he'd be unconscious for a long while. I breathed deeply and slowly, until my adrenaline had subsided. After several minutes I rose and went to the back fence and Wayne Martin. I draped the blanket over his body and returned to the house with the rope and tied Blair's hands and feet. When I looked up from the last knot, I looked into the eyes of Teresa Blair.

"How did you get in here?" I asked stupidly.

"Through the front door. This is my house, remember?" She gestured toward her brother's body. "Is he dead?"

"No."

She looked at the shambles around us. "What happened?"

"He was trying to kill me. I was trying to stop him."

"Why did he want to kill you?"

"Because he just killed your neighbor, Wayne Martin, and I just learned about it. Neither Martin nor I were in his plans, and it shook him."

Her eyes widened, revealing the red rims of strain.

"Wayne Martin? Why would James do that? It doesn't make any sense."

"I know. Blair thought Martin was someone else. Someone sent to kill him."

"Poor Katie," she said.

"Poor Davy," I said.

"I wish someone would kill me," Teresa Blair said then, so softly I didn't think I'd heard her, a prayer of sorts. She sighed deeply and sank to the couch. She was still wearing the clothes she had worn to court. She seemed not to have slept. I stayed on the floor across from her, not knowing where to look or what to think. "Why are you here?" I asked finally.

"I'm trying to find Gus."

"So am I."

She nodded as though she understood, that and everything else about me. Maybe she did. It wasn't going to make any difference. "Do you think your brother knows where Gus is?" I asked her.

"No," she said. "I mean, I'm sure he didn't take Gus. But so much has been happening because of James I thought he might know who most likely had done it." She paused. "You said 'brother.' "

"I talked to your father," I said. "I know you and Mary and James are Tony's children. I know you and James work for Tony, somehow or other, but I don't know exactly what you do. Do you kill people, Teresa? Is that what you do for dear old dad?"

She closed her eyes for a long moment. "You don't need to know that, you know."

"Don't I?"

We looked at each other atop the question. Then I didn't want to look at her anymore.

"Not to find Gus you don't need to know that," she said finally.

"Is that all that's left?" I asked.

"That's all."

"I think I need the whole story," I began after a silent sigh. "First, someone just fire-bombed Wadley's Restaurant. The feds tell me Wadley is your father's chief rival for the top mob slot in El Gordo. True?"

"True."

"So who tossed the bomb?"

"James, probably."

"Why?"

"To start something. A war between my father and Wadley. And maybe incidentally to warn Wadley that he'd better give up Gus if he was the one who took him."

"Why would James want to start a war between Tony and Wadley?"

"So James could finish it," she said sadly. "So he could show Tony that only he was fit to take over the business."

"That would also give him a good motive to shoot little Tony," I said.

"Yes. It would."

We both looked at the body on the floor. Strung up like a roped calf, it hardly seemed capable of the crimes we were speaking of. "James wants to inherit the business," I said. "He's been doing the shit work and now he wants to be top dog. Is that why you left home? Because he was out of control?"

Teresa Blair nodded. "Tony knows James is the better man, but it might not look right to the rest of the family to pass young Tony over without giving him a chance. James and I, we're like the idiots in the attic. No one really wants to acknowledge we exist. No one except Tony. But Tony still hasn't made up his mind, so James decided to force the issue. I was afraid he might even decide to go after father, or try to keep me from saving him from the murder charge."

"Is Tony dying?"

"He thinks so, but he won't go to a doctor. So no one knows. I guess if he wants to die he will."

"Are you sure James wouldn't have grabbed Gus? To make sure of starting a fight between Wadley and your father?"

She shook her head. "He'd think about it but he wouldn't do it."

"Why not?"

"He just wouldn't. Tony would kill him."

"Which leaves us one other possibility."

"What?"

"That night on Oswego Street. The guy who Tony ran down. Phillip Vincent. Who was he? Why did Tony kill him?"

She sighed and shook her head. "I shouldn't tell you this. It will hurt Tony, maybe Gus, too. But I don't care anymore. Not about anything, anything but Gus." She walked to the sedan opposite me and sat on it and crossed her hands over her breasts, as though the gesture would protect her.

"Phillip Vincent used to live in Vegas," she said. "He was a pit boss at the casino where my husband worked. He was called Johnny McCall then, and he was the main witness against Frankie at his tax evasion trial. Vincent helped them send Frankie to jail. He helped them *kill* him."

"Who's them?"

"It doesn't matter."

"Why?"

"They're all dead. Dead like Frankie."

She began to cry, making sounds as anguished as the other sounds that had been uttered in that house that night. "I think I know who has Gus," I said, over the noise of tears.

Chapter 23

"Hello? Anyone here? Teresa?"

The voice came from behind us, the queries floating in innocent musicality down the long hallway that separated her from where we were. In another moment footsteps followed her questions.

"She shouldn't see her husband the way he is," I told Teresa Blair. "Why don't you go over to her place with her? I have to call the cops and let them do their thing in here. Then I'll come get you. If we want to find Gus, we should be out of here by eleven."

"Should I tell her about Wayne?"

I shook my head. "Leave it to the cops. In fact, it might be best if you were out of sight when they came over to her place. Explain to her that you don't want to deal with the police tonight. You're afraid they'll arrest you for what you did in court."

"Okay."

"And tell Davy I'll be by to see him later. You know. After he learns about his dad."

Teresa Blair nodded, then turned to watch Kathryn Martin enter the living room with a tentative but expectant smile on her face. "I *thought* it was you," she said. "How *are* you, Teresa?" She was still pert, wearing sandals and slacks and a pencil behind her ear.

Teresa Blair smiled only briefly, her thoughts necessarily on the dead man lying out beyond the fence. "I'm fine, Kathryn. How are you?"

Kathryn Martin shrugged and frowned. "We're okay, I guess. Coping. Glad you're back. You are *back*, aren't you?"

Teresa Blair looked at me before she answered. "I don't know," she said. "Not for long, probably. It depends."

"On what?"

"Things. Mr. Tanner, here, for one."

I wasn't quite sure what she meant by that, and perhaps she wasn't, either. Mostly I wanted them out of the house. I also hoped Mrs. Martin wouldn't notice James Blair on the floor behind me, but in the next instant she did.

"Who's that?" Her eyes ballooned, and looked at Teresa and then at me.

"James Blair," I said. "He and I had a little fight. I tied him up for safe keeping."

"I *thought* I heard noises over here. It sounded like someone was being murdered." Her laugh was uneasy. "Say. You haven't seen Wayne, have you?" She looked at both of us again, and we both shook our heads, afraid of speech more than anything. "He was supposed to come see Davy tonight," Kathryn Martin went on. "He hasn't shown up. Davy's kind of upset." She paused, still waiting for us to say something. "I suppose I should have expected something like this," she concluded lamely.

"No, you shouldn't," I said, then wished I hadn't."

"What? What do you mean?"

"Nothing. Just that I met your husband the other day. He didn't seem like such a bad guy."

Kathryn Martin's face softened and her eyes skipped over the mess in the room. "He didn't used to be a bad guy," she said in dream words. "In fact, I suppose that's why I married him. He was such a nice guy. I wonder what happened?"

"It's hard to be a nice guy sometimes," I said.

Teresa Blair walked over and put her arm on Kathryn Martin's shoulder. "You got any coffee over at your place, Katie?"

"Sure."

"Am I invited?"

"You know you are."

"Let me get my cup. We'll leave James and Mr. Tanner to their little spat."

Teresa Blair trotted back to the kitchen and returned with a large brown mug with orange flowers on the sides and linked arms with Mrs. Martin and left by the front door. James Blair remained a silent package of flesh. I made sure he was breathing, then found a telephone and sat in the chair beside it, thinking first of calling Tolson but then of making another call, the one I had thought about making when I was up in the Federal Building, the one I didn't have to make then but had to make now that I had seen Teresa Blair again.

I looked at my watch. It was after seven. Probably too late. Probably too tricky to work. But then if I learned what I was afraid I *would* learn, why then that would be a sign of some kind. Wouldn't it? Sure. I glanced at the body on the floor, and at the ghost of the woman who had just left, then picked up the phone and dialed.

"Mr. Blair's office."

"Is Mr. Blair in?"

"No. He isn't expected till morning. May I take a message?"

"Perhaps you can help me. Are you Ms. Hendrickson?"

"*Mrs*. Hendrickson. Yes."

"Good. Mr. Blair has listed you as the person who

would have the information I need in the event he wasn't available himself."

"Just who are you, please?"

"My name is Wickersham. I'm executive secretary of the San Francisco regional office of the International Air Line Pilots Association. We are running a survey of the various complaints lodged by air travelers in this region over the past year, to see if the follow-up service initiated by the carrier subsequent to the complaint adequately met the problem." I paused. Listening to Agent Lucas an hour earlier had trained me superbly in bureaucratese. "You are Mr. Blair's secretary, am I right?"

"That's correct."

"I wonder, Mrs. Hendrickson, would you have records of his air travel available to you at this time?"

"Why, yes. Some of them, at least."

"Then perhaps you could check to see if Mr. Blair made a flight to Seattle this past October. Halloween, it was. Do you have that information?"

"I believe I do. One moment."

During the time she checked the only sound in the room came from the reflexive inhalations of James Blair. In a minute Mrs. Hendrickson came back on the line and cleared her throat in my ear. "Mr. Blair did fly at the end of October. But not to Seattle."

"Oh? Where?"

"Portland."

"Ah. Just a moment. Yes. On the form it lists where the *luggage* deplaned, you see, and unfortunately that didn't occur until Seattle. Now, it appears that the luggage in question might have belonged to a woman. Was Mr. Blair accompanied on that flight, by any chance?"

"Yes, he was."

"By whom?"

"By his wife."

"Yes. Thank you. It was her luggage that was missing,

I believe. That confirms our initial data. Now, do you know if Mrs. Blair's luggage was ever recovered?"

"I wouldn't know that."

"Very well. Mr. Blair will receive a form from us shortly, so he can describe fully his complaint and his reaction to the follow-up. Thank you for your time, Mrs. Hendrickson."

"You're welcome."

"You're certainly working late this evening."

"Well, it's tax season, you know. Mr. Blair is an accountant."

And an assassin.

My head ached fearfully, so badly I could hardly see. I tried to put the pain and the rest of it out of my mind, then took some deep breaths and called Ray Tolson. His first question was about Gus Quilk. When I told him I hadn't found him yet, the only scrap of interest fell out of his voice.

"I turned in my resignation today," Tolson said before I could tell him about either Martin or Blair. "Effective tomorrow."

"So you aren't looking for Gus Quilk anymore?"

"Oh, we're looking. But even if we find him alive, I won't use him against Fluto. I can't put a kid through that, even a kid as lost as Gus."

"I don't think he'd have helped much anyway," I said. "From what I can learn, he was shucking you."

"Probably. In any event, as my last official act I'm going to court tomorrow to ask Judge McMinn to dismiss the case against Fluto. If Tony takes a fall, it'll be someone else who brings him down." Tolson's voice was as exhausted as his patience.

"So what now?" I asked.

"Private practice, I guess. Hell, the next time you're in town I'll probably be defending Fluto myself. That's usually the way it shakes out."

"Usually," I agreed, "but not this time."

"No. I hope not, anyway."

"Good luck."

"Yeah. So why'd you call?"

"To report a crime."

"What kind?"

"Murder."

"Who?"

"Man named Wayne Martin."

"Who killed him?"

"James Blair."

"Our James Blair?"

"Our James Blair."

"Where's the body?"

"Blair's house."

"Where are you?"

"Same place."

"Where's Blair?"

"He's here, too. Unconscious at present."

"You okay?"

"Yep."

"This have anything to do with Fluto?" Tolson asked, the culmination of his increasingly strident interrogation.

"A little."

"Enough so I can use it to make a case against Fluto in court tomorrow?"

I thought about it. "No," I said.

Tolson paused. When he spoke, the animation was again missing from his words. "Then it's not my problem, I guess. I'll make some calls, get the lab boys moving and all the rest. Stay where you are. Don't touch anything."

"Okay," I said. "You sure you're out of it."

"Yes. I . . . yes."

"Then I guess this is it."

"I guess so. Drop in when you're in town the next time."

"It may be a while," I said.

"Yeah. I understand. Thanks for your help. If I didn't play square with you, I'm sorry. I did what I thought I had to do."

"Don't worry about it," I said.

When the cops came, I played dumb, said it had all been an accident, my stumbling onto Blair and the dead man. I knew enough to keep both the uniforms and the detectives off my back, and for most of the time I just watched the lab men do their thing with flashbulbs and tape measures and evidence bags and the like. When James Blair came to, they read him his rights. He didn't say anything to them or to me, but when the cops started to take his ropes off, I suggested they leave them on. They looked at me, then they looked at Blair, then they looked at the mess in the room and left them where they were. Then Wayne Martin was taken to the morgue and a cop went over to tell Kathryn Martin about her husband. They finished up at ten and they let me go at ten thirty. After the last car had disappeared around a bend, I got out of mine and went over to the Martin house and rang the bell. Teresa Blair answered the door.

"How are they holding up?" I asked.

"Okay," she said. "Kathryn had pretty much ended her attachment to Wayne already, you know. And Davy, well, he seems to be waiting for *you*, oddly enough. He says he has a question he wants to ask."

"Where is he?"

"In his room."

"Show me."

She led me down a hall past two doors and stopped in front of the third. I tapped on the door and said who I was. Davy's small voice told me I could come in.

He was lying on his bed, which was rumpled like his hair. The comforter was decorated with the logos of professional football teams. On the floor were a thousand cars, the size of mice. The books on the shelf were about sports and war. The globe on the stand had a light bulb inside it, and blue mountains. "How's it going, Davy?" I asked.

"Okay."

"Can I sit on the floor, here?"

"Sure."

I tried to think what I could possibly say to him, how I could explain death and violence and murder and what caused them and what came after and how to survive it all and how to keep believing in anything. But I hadn't even begun to speak when he interrupted my thoughts. "Can I ask you a question, Mr. Tanner?"

"Sure."

He looked at me carefully. I was certain he would detect it if I lied, but I wasn't certain I would. "Did my mom shoot my dad?" he asked.

"Why do you think that?"

"Remember? Scott said she told him she would, if he ever came back here."

"No, Davy. She didn't shoot him."

"For real?"

"For real."

"Okay."

"Okay," I repeated. "Anything else?"

"Nope."

"Want to go back to the kitchen?"

"Sure. I think Mom probably needs me."

"I think she probably does."

I followed him down the hall, hoping he was as strong as he seemed, wondering how you could tell. We all made small talk for a few minutes, dancing around death the way death is always danced around. Then I looked at my watch and told Teresa Blair we'd better go. Kathryn Martin asked her where we were going. Since she didn't know, she didn't say anything.

"San Francisco," I said. "We have to be at the Jack Tar Hotel by midnight."

Chapter
24

It seemed crowded in the car, I guess because of the answered questions and abandoned responsibilities that lay on the seat between us. We stopped only once along the way. For Tootsie Rolls and a phone call.

I didn't bother wondering whether Charley Sleet was on duty—Charley was always on duty. I found him in the Central Station. We made some small talk and then we quit. "What's up, Marsh?" he asked.

"I need to stage a bogus raid, Charley."

"Where?"

"Jack Tar."

"Who's in the room?"

"Not sure. A woman. A kid. And one, maybe two, guys."

"Armed?"

"Yep."

"Likely to shoot first?"

"I don't think so." For a brief instant I envisioned

Conway Grinder's head with a hole blown through it. "But no guarantees."

"You want them to know I'm a cop?"

"I think that's the only way we'll get inside."

"Backup?"

"I don't think so."

"Vice?"

"Not exactly."

"Snatch?"

"Close."

"When?"

"Twelve thirty."

"Okay," Charley said, and hung up.

When I got back to the car, I resolved to end it quickly, to get Gus Quilk back and then be done with it, with no regrets. The only responsibility that mattered anymore was to myself. Or so I made myself believe.

Traffic was still heavy. Teresa Blair said nothing, even though I glanced at her from time to time, trying to read her thoughts. The lights from the opposing cars swabbed her cheeks like yellow tissues. It was a quarter to twelve when I pulled into the little parking area in front of the Jack Tar and hid my car behind the red double-decker bus the hotel used for promotional jaunts.

"I can't go inside," I said to her. "Not yet. You go in and sit in the lobby where you can see the elevators. In a few minutes an attractive Oriental girl should come in. She'll probably be wearing a short fur jacket. She has a curved scar just to the left of the corner of her eye. Follow her into the elevator and see what room she goes in, then come back here. I'll take it from there. She may be alert for trouble, so play it cool."

"How do you know all this?" Teresa Blair asked.

I fingered the book of matches embossed with the name of the hotel that Ms. Wong had given me at the Federal Building earlier in the day. "I just do," I said.

"Is Gus in that room?"

"Maybe. If he is, I'll get him out. Don't try anything yourself. Remember what happened to Grinder."

She nodded and got out of the car and started to walk away, then turned back and tapped on the window. I rolled it down. "What you're thinking about me," she said. "It's probably true."

"I know."

"Then you aren't doing this for me."

"No. For Gus. And me."

"Good," she said, and walked away again.

I didn't intend to but I fell asleep. When she came back, she had to shake me to wake me up. "Did she show?" I asked thickly.

"Room nine-fourteen."

"She suspect you were following her?"

"I don't think so."

"Okay," I said.

"What do we do now?"

"Wait."

She opened the door and got out of the car again. "Don't try anything stupid," I said.

She smiled and walked to the red bus and climbed inside it. A few seconds later I saw the faint glow of a cigarette high atop the English bus, in the middle of the second deck. I got out of my car and climbed inside the deserted vehicle and trotted up the steps and sat on the seat across from her. "Are you sure Gus is in there?" she asked me.

"Reasonably."

"Are the men who have him the same ones who killed the policeman in El Gordo?"

"Yes. But they didn't plan it that way. Grinder must have forced their hand. The men are Justice Department lawyers. Feds. Part of the Organized Crime Strike Force."

I couldn't see her face but I guessed it was amazed. "And *they* took Gus?"

"Right."

"For God's sake, why?"

"Because they don't want Tony Fluto to be tried for the murder of Phillip Vincent. The same reason they tried to keep me from finding you."

"But why don't they want Tony to be tried? I'd think they'd want just the opposite."

"Because Phillip Vincent, or Johnny McCall, was a witness against your husband Frankie in Las Vegas. Because after he testified, he disappeared. With the help of the government. They call it the Witness Security Program now. Key witnesses against organized crime figures are given new identities and new jobs and all the rest in exchange for their testimony."

"I've heard about that. But what does it have to do with Gus?"

"Tolson was trying Fluto for murder, because he wanted him out of El Gordo for good. To prove his case, he was going to have to prove exactly who Vincent was, in order to establish premeditation on Tony's part. When it came out that Tony had penetrated the feds' security system and found out where Vincent was, and then killed him, the Witness Security Program wouldn't have been worth a damn. Word would get around fast. The next time the feds promised a witness a new ID, the witness would laugh in their face and refuse to testify. These federal guys are real gung ho. Tolson's case was expendable. It was screwing up the big picture."

She didn't say anything for a while. I made myself think of things other than her. "Will there be shooting?" she asked softly.

"I don't think so. They aren't killers. They just underestimated Grinder's pride. I'm sure they only intended to keep Gus until the case against Fluto is dismissed. Which is going to happen tomorrow morning. I think I can cut a deal. If I can get through the door."

"Maybe we should wait."

"No. I want it over with. Tonight."

"How are you going to get in the room?"

"With him."

I pointed to the lot below and to the gray Ford that had just pulled in it. Charley Sleet got his bulk out of the car and walked to my Buick and looked inside. When he saw it was empty he just leaned back against the door and waited. If necessary he would have waited for a day. I went down to see him, and Teresa Blair came after me.

"Charley."

"Marsh."

We shook hands. Mine fit like a pebble inside his. "How's crime?" I asked him.

"Way up."

"How's punishment?"

"Way down."

Teresa Blair coughed with nervous impatience. I introduced her to Charley. She asked us both to be careful. I told her we would. Then I turned to Charley. "They're in room nine-fourteen. The boy is her nephew. The men, if they're there, are feds. Justice Department. Lucas and Armbruster. Know them?"

Charley laughed. "As it happens, yes. Nice of you to tell me this earlier."

I ignored his complaint. "Do they know you?"

"By name maybe. They know you?"

I nodded. "I think the only way to do it is knock and tell them we're cops and get inside. I'm pretty sure they'll want to know the situation before they make any kind of move against us. If I can get in there I think I can cut a deal that will keep things calm. Okay by you?"

"Okay."

"They're pretty big wheels, Charley. They could bring some heat down on you."

"No they couldn't," Charley said.

I nodded and told Teresa Blair to stay where she was and got my gun out of the glove compartment and followed Charley Sleet into the hotel, more secure behind him than behind anyone I knew.

Business was still brisk enough with revelers from out of town that no one paid any attention as we strolled through the lobby. We had the elevator to ourselves and the corridor outside room 914 as well. "Got any suggestions if it starts to foul up?" Charley asked as we got to the room.

"Just don't shoot the kid."

"I was thinking of something more positive."

"Just don't shoot me."

"As usual."

"As usual," I repeated.

Charley laughed and knocked on the door. There was a long pause, almost a minute. Charley looked at me; I looked at him. Then someone inside grunted. "Yeah?"

"Police," Charley said. "Open up."

"Why?"

"Routine check."

"Check for what?"

"Suspected PC two-eighty-eight—lewd and lascivious acts with a child under fourteen; suspected PC two-eighty-eight subparagraph A—oral copulation with a person under eighteen. Open up." Charley sounded like Jehovah.

The buzz of an epithet edged around the door. A few seconds later it opened part way. The eye in the crack looked directly at Charley's barrel chest. I was far enough to the side that it couldn't see me. Charley flashed his shield. "What's the problem, officer?" It was Lucas, sounding half-asleep.

"A young male was seen entering the room," Charley said, "in the presence of an older man believed not to be his father. Gives me probable cause to inspect the premises."

"For Christ's sake," Lucas swore. "I guess you better

come in. You're going to feel like an ass in about three seconds, officer."

Lucas opened the door and Charley went through it and, just before he shut it, so did I. "Tanner," Lucas said when he turned and saw me.

"Reginald."

"What's going on? Who's this?" He gestured toward Charley.

"Sergeant Charles Sleet," I said. "SFPD. Know him?"

"I think I've heard the name. Do you know what the hell you're doing, Tanner?"

"I think so."

"Does *this* man know what you're doing? Does he know who I am?"

"He does." I looked at Charley. "Maybe you better check the next room," I told him.

Charley disappeared through the door into the sleeping room of the suite. I looked around the sitting room. A couch, two chairs, a table, and a television. The TV was tuned to a black-and-white movie. Virginia Mayo was on the screen. An open bottle of Scotch was on the table. The elastic end of a black brassiere was sticking out from under the couch. Charley returned a minute later. "A boy, asleep or playing like it. A girl, scared and half-undressed. Looks real incriminating." Charley was enjoying himself and so was I.

I looked back at Lucas. As usual he didn't meet my eyes. "Sergeant Sleet here doesn't know about El Gordo, or the boy, or any of the rest of it," I said. "Now, I can fill him in, or we can just be nice and excuse him right now. Which will it be?"

Lucas frowned. "What is it you want, Tanner?"

"I want to leave here in about five minutes. With the Quilk boy. I want to get him home."

"And after that?"

"Nothing. I'm out of it."

"What about Tolson and his murder case?"

"Tolson's going to dismiss first thing in the morning. Then he's going to resign his office."

"Straight?"

"Straight."

Lucas paced the length of the little sitting room, thinking it over. "Okay. The cop can go," he said at last.

"Thanks, Charley," I said.

"Any time." Charley left and the room seemed to double in size.

Lucas went over to the bedroom door and went through it. I could hear him whispering something to the girl and then he came back and sat on a chair and gestured for me to do the same. "It wasn't supposed to go down the way it did, you know," he said.

"Grinder wasn't a man who could be taken without a fight."

"We discovered that only too late."

"Is the boy all right?"

"Physically. Mentally he's as antisocial as I've ever seen. He shouldn't be on the streets."

"Maybe not, but that's not for you or me to decide. His aunt's downstairs. She'll take him home. She's not a fool and she's very concerned about him. If he can be salvaged, she'll see that it's done."

"He'll be in jail in a year," Lucas muttered.

"Maybe. Is he coming out?"

"Arlene's getting him up."

"I don't want to hear you've messed with the kid after tonight, Lucas," I said. "I'm going to check. If I learn you've picked him up again, I'll go public with what I know. Otherwise, I'll keep quiet. I guess you'll just have to trust Gus to keep quiet on his end."

"Oh, I think we've taken care of Gus. He won't compromise the operation."

"Why not?"

"We made him a deal."

"What deal?" I asked.

"We found out what Gus is most afraid of in the world, and then we told him how we could arrange for just exactly that to happen to him."

"You must have read Koestler," I said. "So what's Gus afraid of?"

The bedroom door opened before Lucas could answer and Miss Wong came into the room. She bowed slightly to me then looked at Lucas. Her attire and her composure were awry. "He'll be out in a minute," she said hesitantly. Her nipples poked the threads of her blouse. Her eyes searched the room and found what she was looking for.

"You can go home, Arlene," Lucas told her. "The boy's going with Tanner."

Arlene grabbed her rabbit fur and her brassier and left. I pointed to the bottle of Scotch on the table and Lucas nodded so I poured some into a glass and drank it. Lucas went into the sleeping room. I poured another Scotch. A minute later Lucas came back, dragging Gus Quilk behind him.

The boy was dressed in jeans and a red T-shirt. A round tin of chewing tobacco was rolled into his right sleeve. His belt was a chrome-linked chain. He looked at me above a surly lip. "Hey. You're the prick that stiffed me for thirty bucks. I ain't going *nowhere* with *you*."

He looked at Lucas. Lucas looked at me and smiled for the first time ever. "Enjoy yourself," he said.

I sighed and reached in my pocket and pulled out my gun and laid it on my thigh, then finished off the Scotch. "I'm tired of you, Gus. Now put on your jacket and come along. Your Aunt Teresa is down in my car. You'll be going with her, not me."

"One thing, Tanner," Lucas said.

"What?"

"You can't take the boy back to El Gordo for two more days. Or at least until the case against Fluto's dismissed."

"Okay," I said.

Lucas turned his back on Gus and headed into the bedroom. Before he got there, he stopped and looked back at me. "There's no way we can take a fall for what happened to Grinder," he said. "No way at all. There's a new team in Washington. They won't moan and groan about petty details."

"I suppose not," I said.

Lucas left the room.

"Move," I said to Gus. He didn't have any leverage and he was wise enough to know it.

When we got to the car Teresa Blair got out and hugged the boy and asked if he was all right.

"No sweat," he said. "Them guys didn't dare lay a hand on me."

I took a deep breath and guided the two of them into my Buick and drove off. "I'm going to take you to my place," I said. "You have to stay there for two days. Then you can take Gus home."

"Why the two days?" Teresa Blair asked.

"That's the deal."

"How many people were killed in this fucking wreck?" Gus said.

No one said anything else the rest of the way. The city that could at times seem so threatening seemed suddenly to be a pat on my back, a shake of the hand, a refuge. I double-parked outside my apartment and everyone got out of the car. I pulled out my house keys and handed them to Teresa Blair. "Aren't you coming in?" she asked.

"No."

"Where will you be?"

"I don't know."

"Will I see you again?"

"I don't think so. If you need a ride back to El Gordo on

Friday, call my office. My secretary's name is Peggy. She'll take you down. Everything in the apartment works, and there's nothing so complicated you can't figure it out. There's a grocery store two blocks down. Have a nice time. The girl across the street sells drugs."

"You didn't have to say that," Teresa Blair said.

"Yes, I did."

She nodded as though she understood. "Maybe this is for the best," she went on. "I need to have a talk with Gus. I need to tell him things."

"Someone sure as hell does."

"That someone should be his mother."

"Yeah. Let's leave it to her, why don't we."

"We have."

"What?"

"Gus is my son. Frankie was his father. I was afraid to have him with me before, for fear they'd try to get to Tony through him. But it was a terrible mistake. I want Gus with me now. If I get out of all this I want to try and save him."

"Hey," Gus yelled suddenly. "I'm freezing my balls off over here. Move your ass, huh?"

"Good luck," I said.

"Thanks," she said. "You, too." I touched her cheek then turned away.

I drove a long time before I stopped. El Gordo was always at my back.